OATHBREAKER
ASSASSIN'S APPRENTICE

OATHBREAKER
ASSASSIN'S APPRENTICE

S R VAUGHT and J B REDMOND

BLOOMSBURY

NEW YORK BERLIN LONDON

To my friends and family, who believed
in me when I could not believe in myself.

—JBR

To my son J B,
who has the power to inspire.

—SRV

Text copyright © 2009 by S R Vaught and J B Redmond
Maps copyright © 2009 by Laura Hartman Maestro

Published by Bloomsbury U.S.A. Children's Books
175 Fifth Avenue, New York, New York 10010

Library of Congress Cataloging-in-Publication Data
Vaught, Susan.
Assassin's apprentice / by Susan Vaught and JB Redmond. — 1st U.S. ed.
p.   cm. — (Oathbreaker)
Summary: Follows the intertwining adventures of Leyr Mab, high prince
and heir to the throne, Aron Brailing, a farm boy with a destiny greater
than he can imagine, and Dari Ross, a mysterious halfling with ties
to a powerful race of shapeshifters long believed to be extinct.
ISBN-13: 978-1-59990-162-6 • ISBN-10: 1-59990-162-5
[1. Fantasy.] I. Redmond, JB. II. Title.
PZ7.V4673Asg 2009   [Fic]—dc22   2008043272

First U.S. Edition 2009
Book design by Donna Mark
Typeset by Westchester Book Composition
Printed in the U.S.A. by Quebecor World Fairfield
2 4 6 8 10 9 7 5 3

You broke the boy in me, but you won't break the man.

—John Parr

"St. Elmo's Fire (Man in Motion)"

CODE OF EYRIE

I. **Fael i'ha.**
The Circle in all hearts. To disobey the Circle is Unforgivable.

II. **Fae i'Fae.**
Fae keep to Fae. Cross-mixing is Unforgivable.

III. **Graal i'cheville.**
Graal to the banded. An unfettered legacy is Unforgivable.

IV. **Massacre i'massacres.**
Murder to murderers. Unsanctioned killing is Unforgivable.

V. **Chevillya i'ha.**
Oaths to the heart. To break an oath is Unforgivable.

VI. **Guilda i'Guild.**
Guild dues to Guild. To dishonor Stone or Thorn is Unforgivable.

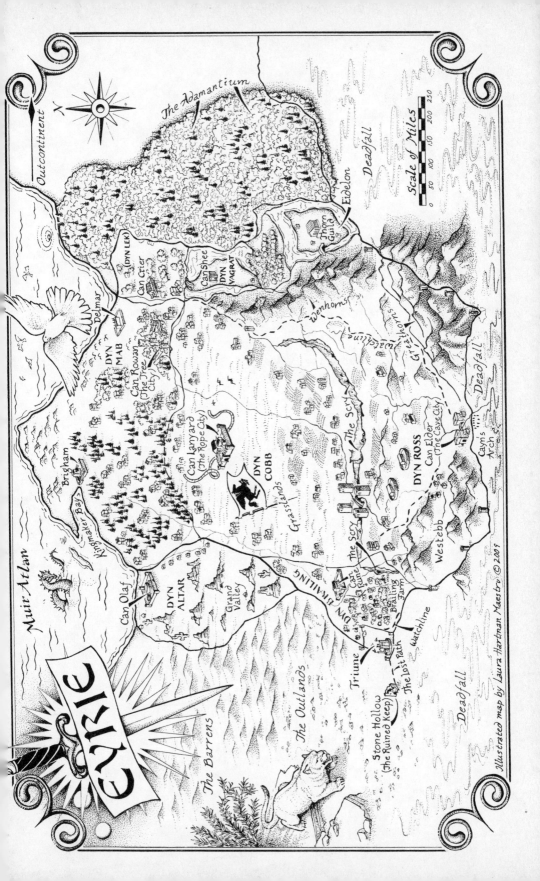

PART I

Elhalla

FATE TURNS

CHAPTER ONE

ARON

Hot winds blew across the Watchline, twisting rusted wires against rotted fence posts. Grit swirled through the flatlands, coating hardwoods and evergreens alike. Toiling in the shadows of the tree-break to mend panels in the barn wall, Aron Brailing felt the dusty warmth on his cheeks and knew it for a lie. Autumn was coming with its chill and drizzle, with its death and decay, no matter what the hot breeze tried to tell him.

Harvest was upon them.

Everything turned. The years, the seasons, the cycles of the moons—fate itself. It was the way of the land, of the world. That's what his father taught him, and that's why he shouldn't be worrying about tomorrow. Harvest would come in its own time, its own way, and the likes of Aron Brailing could do little to stop it.

Aron tried to center his plank, caught a splinter in his thumb, and bit it out. He ignored the sting and tried centering the plank again, this time with more success. Their small barn faced the Watchline, the sparse stretch of dirt and tumbledown huts and fences that separated inhabited lands from the uninhabitable territory beyond.

It was once tradition to build all barns in such a fashion, so people could shelter inside and keep a lookout for predators slinking across the boundaries of the Outlands, or worse yet, up from the misty southern

Deadfall. Aron had never known a time of great activity along the Watchline, though. Neither had his father, or his father's father, and the old Guard houses on Eyrie's western and southern borders had long since been abandoned. It had been many years since any large incursion of manes—bloodthirsty spirits from the Deadfall—or the vile part-animals called mockers that congregated in the Outlands. Still, barns were built facing danger, just in case.

Beyond the barn, their meager house stood on its poles, shuttered windows staring stubbornly toward the Watchline and byway as if to remind Aron and his family that travelers could be predators, too, in their own ways.

He shouldn't think about tomorrow.

He shouldn't, but he did.

And the thoughts made the air squeeze out of his chest.

The sweet-copper taste of his thumb's blood permeated Aron's senses as he lined up the next board. He glanced to his left, where Wolf Brailing hammered a thick peg through a hole to steady one of the last planks. Wolf didn't even blink in the dusty breeze scraping his scarred cheek and close-cut brown hair. His intense black eyes seemed to order the smoothed wood into place, and well-marked muscles bulged in his upper arms as he swung the mallet.

Not for the first time, Aron turned his gaze to his own puny wrists, then to the thin fingers gripping his smaller mallet. His arms and legs were no bigger than sticks tipped with twigs, dwarfed by the overlarge sleeve of his threadbare brown tunic and breeches. His hair was still a light copper-brown, and his skin smooth.

Would he ever gain his father's coloring and toughness and build, as his older brothers had done? Could he, too, be a hero in the Dynast Guard when it came his time to serve? More than anything, Aron wanted his chance to earn his own rows of tiny rune tattoos like the ones that marked Wolf Brailing's arms, *dav'ha* marks from sacred cer-emonies of loyalty following great trials.

"We have no time for woolgathering or soft daydreams," Aron's father said in his low, steady voice, without ever taking his eyes from the wood he worked. "We still live along the Watchline, even if it's peaceful for now. Fate can turn fast for men in Dyn Brailing—and rarely for the better, if they're not paying attention."

Aron dipped his head and hurried to drive the last few pegs into his board. He struggled to keep time with his father's strokes, and his heart beat harder with each slam of mallet against wood. Blood from his thumb dotted the white-gold hue of the rough plank. He managed to get the last stubborn bolt into place, but the lay of it didn't suit him, so he kept at it until he felt the pressure of his father's heavy hand on his shoulder.

"Enough. That will do."

Aron looked into his father's dark eyes, searching for a hint of happiness as his father surveyed the boards Aron had hammered. His father studied each peg, running his fingers over the craftwork as if assessing every decision, every blow struck by Aron's mallet. As seconds ticked longer and longer, Aron's breath came shorter and shorter.

Then his father gave him a wink. "You've improved. No splitting this time."

Pride tightened Aron's muscles and pushed up the corners of his mouth. He drew a deep, satisfying breath of the peppery simmer of podbean stew drifting from the house. His stomach also gave a loud rumble, as if to protest the length of time since midday meal.

Wolf Brailing's appraising eyes moved from Aron to the house, to the meager vegetable patch. His gaze moved on to the hayfields where Aron's mother, brothers, and sisters still worked, temporarily out of sight. "Come," he said, "here, to the barn's corner."

Aron followed his father and sat when he gestured toward the packed dirt. Wolf sat between Aron and the fields, sending up a tiny puff of dust that smelled faintly of hay and manure. He reached into his battered waist-pack and produced a small lump wrapped in a wide green *dantha* leaf. After a glance over his shoulder, Wolf presented the lump to Aron.

The soft leaf tickled Aron's fingers as he peeled back the filmy layers, careful to preserve the green fibers. This *dantha* leaf wasn't old yet. It could be used again as a wrap or light cloth, and in Dyn Brailing, nothing, not even aging *dantha* leaves, was wasted.

Aron's eyes went wide as he reached the center of the tiny package. A leftover bit of spiced bread from this morning's breakfast—made in celebration of his youngest sister's birthday. He touched the sweet, crumbly crust, not quite able to believe his good fortune.

From inside the barn, Tek, Aron's young talon, let out a whistle as if she could smell the sweetness of the bread. She stomped her big clawed feet and rattled her scales, and Aron knew she was probably pawing at the air with her shriveled forelegs, maybe bobbing her over-large head like a chicken, too. Even though she stood at twice Aron's height, close to the size she would achieve when she matured, she still behaved more like an excitable baby lizard.

Wolf glanced over his shoulder again. "Eat it before your mother springs from some shadowy hiding place. She'll shape-shift like a mocker and spit poison at both of us for ruining your dinner."

Aron laughed at the image of his mother as a crazed, venomous beast—and which would she be? A false bird perhaps? No, no. A rock cat, straight out of the Scry. She'd crawl out of that long set of stone trenches and caves that pocked part of Dyn Brailing, rear up on her big back legs, shift from a fairly normal-looking feline into some twisted, scary human form, and—

"Eat, Aron." Wolf sounded mildly amused.

Once more coming back to himself, Aron managed, "Thank you, Father," before he grabbed half the slice and crammed it into his mouth. The tang of cinnamon, which his family rarely had the fortune to possess, made his eyes water. And the bread itself, even hours after baking, still so soft and warmed from the sun on his father's waist-pack. The taste and texture flowed over Aron's tongue. He was sure the bread was sweeter than any exotic treat in Dyn Brailing, maybe in all the wide lands of Eyrie.

Aron swallowed and took the next bite, trying to hurry and slow down and enjoy his boon all at the same time. When his father glanced toward the fields again, Aron looked with him, but saw no sign of his mother or siblings.

"You have your brother Seth's talent for building, I think," Wolf said, once more turning his attention to Aron. "That will serve you if you take up livestock for a trade. What would you think of that?"

Aron gulped his mouthful and blinked at his father. "Livestock is . . . it's too . . ."

"Expensive to begin. Yes." Wolf nodded toward the barn beside them. "But you have a great advantage, since you already possess one talon. And a female, Aron. If you apprentice at Grommond's farm, you could save your payment, and in two years, perhaps three, you would have enough to purchase a male for our barn."

Wolf clasped his big hands, then released them. "Another year and you could add a pair of goats, perhaps a pair of oxen, before you ever complete your time in the Dynast Guard. I would help you until you were ready to establish a parcel of your own, and until you build your own barns."

The last bite of spiced bread stuck in Aron's throat. His mind spun slowly around his father's words, like a spider trying to thread together something with meaning and substance. To be offered such an opportunity, it was almost more than he could comprehend. If he could manage to breed livestock for a living—even just a few hatched talons, to be sold to reasonable buyers—he could change the fortunes of his entire family. His heart flooded at the thought of his mother and sisters in nice dresses, his brothers with fine tools, perhaps even small parcels to farm and carve a living for their families.

And his father.

Aron would buy his father wagons and tools and real leather clothing.

He would buy his father everything, especially after he enjoyed the good pay of a guardsman for two years.

"Grommond rarely takes apprentices," Aron said, his voice breaking because he couldn't let himself accept that such an amazement might be possible. He was the youngest son of a farmer, a nothing, a nobody— to apprentice with Grommond?

His father's smile broke Aron's disbelief like nothing else could. "Grommond has seen you work with Tek, and he's already spoken to me. He told me he thought you have a good touch with animals. Next year on your fifteenth birthday, he'll take you—if that's what you want. I would never force you to make such a decision."

Then Wolf Brailing repeated something Aron had heard many times. "My children will have choices. Always."

Aron choked down the last of the spiced bread, already battling excitement and daydreams of what it would be like to learn from Grommond, to have access to horses and cattle and fowl and poultry, to full-sized talons and oxen and goats—he couldn't even imagine. He would learn so much, so fast. And all the while, he'd be earning a *wage* for such delight.

"I would be honored, Father. I would be—yes. Of course I'll accept Grommond's kindness."

"The day you saved Tek from death in the trenches of the Scry and earned her as a boon from our Lord Brailing, you did a great service for yourself. Perhaps for all of us." His father reached out and squeezed Aron's forearm. "Kindness, honest labor, honor, and truth. You know these are the things that matter—what I value and what I've tried to teach you. You set a good example on all counts. I'm very proud of you."

Aron had to fight not to burst into tears. He was grinning and sniffing at the same moment, awhirl inside, unable to speak.

An apprenticeship with Grommond.

An apprenticeship in *livestock*.

Not carpentry like his eldest brother, Seth, who had already returned from his Guard service without ever seeing a war or battle— not that Seth's betrothed cared much about that. Seth would marry next year, after his twenty-first birthday, as was custom, but Aron couldn't imagine being married, or being a carpenter. His seventeen-year-old twin brothers, not yet old enough for their Guard service, were planning on an apprenticeship in grain farming after they served, as were his sixteen-year-old brothers. Aron's nearest-age brother was more interested in leatherwork, which bored Aron mindless. But livestock . . . and Grommond had already assured it. With Aron's acceptance, the deed was as good as done, except—

Aron felt his smile falter.

Except for Harvest.

The joy blazing through his essence snuffed to darkness in mere seconds.

Harvest is tomorrow.

Harvest could change everything.

Aron began to wish he hadn't eaten the spiced bread at all. It churned unpleasantly as his father studied his face.

Wolf Brailing seemed to understand Aron's deepest concerns and fears, as he so often did. He reached to the dirt between them and began to trace a shape Aron knew very well.

The image of a great bird emerged in the dust, wings outstretched, divided into uneven sections that represented the dynasts—large provinces ruled by lords or ladies with strong Fae heritage. History told that after the Great Migration into Eyrie from the original world of the Fae, dynasts formed, each with its own language, customs, talents, and traditions. Dyn Mab was the head of the great bird, and Dyn Cobb and Dyn Ross comprised the body of the bird, with most of the land and population.

The lesser dynasts of Altar, Brailing, and Vagrat formed the bird's wings, two on the left and one on the right. They had fewer citizens, and fewer miles within their borders. Stone and Thorn, the two guilds established long ago to see to justice, mercy, and healing for goodfolk no matter which dynast had struggled its way into power, sat like feet on either side of the bird. So small, yet so strong and important.

"Rock and leaf, stone and thorn," his father murmured as he added circles around the main guild location—Stone in Dyn Brailing, and Thorn in Dyn Vagrat. "Both guilds were once essential to the life and growth of Eyrie. Stone and Thorn stood against dynast royalty on behalf of goodfolk. They balanced the power of the dynasts just as feet balance the largest bird on a branch."

The rest of his meaning—that things were different now—went unsaid, but Aron understood. His father was trying to tell him that no matter how frightening Harvest might seem, Eyrie's guilds didn't wield the power they had once enjoyed. Even dynast lords and ladies weren't as powerful as those of legend, because Fae blood and Fae mind-talents had become so rare.

Aron watched his father draw and knew that his family, as Brailings of Brailing, had a touch of Fae blood, but none of the special mind-talents of the ancient kings and queens who once ruled Eyrie's dynasts. Aron's family didn't even have the meager mental abilities common to the provosts who controlled Stone and Thorn, or the children they chose to apprentice at the guilds. Wolf Brailing had taught his family how to go through the Veil—the Fae term for achieving a state of meditation useful for calming emotions and controlling the workings of the body. Wolf had also taught them about skin and vessels and blood, and how to speed the healing of cuts and bruises, which he had learned in his time as a member of the Dynast Guard. Minor healing was the extent of Wolf's abilities on the other side of the Veil, though, and Aron's too.

More important than any meditation skills, Wolf Brailing had made sure all of his children knew Eyrie's geography, as well as the styles of worship, the main trades, and some of the customs and words used by the other dynasts. *Those in other dynasts might be different from us,* Wolf often said, *perhaps more educated, more privileged or even less— but we will meet our fellows heads high, as equals.*

"Recite the dynasts," Aron's father said as he completed his sketch, and Aron did so. His father went on to make him name and show the general location of each dynast capital, beginning with Can Rune, their own. Then he pointed to the small corner of Dyn Brailing, far from Can Rune, to that spot near the Watchline, where their small farm lay. "Do you see how distant we are from the main cities, the main roads?"

Aron nodded.

His father let out a soft breath and tapped the map to indicate the small but dense mountains to the east of their farm, the forests and Scry to their north, the Watchline area to the east, then the misty Dead-fall rising up from the south. He connected his tap marks as if he might be drawing a fortress around their tiny farm. "We are closer to the Stone Guild stronghold at Triune than I would like, thirty-five to forty days on horseback—about one cycle of the moons—but why try to reach us when so many villages, towns, and great cities offer easier pickings? My father's father did not choose this spot by happenstance or chance."

Aron realized his father's tone was confident, soothing—but there was also an edge of something else. Something like anger, or maybe worry. When he gazed into his father's eyes once again, he saw an unfamiliar glint in those dark depths, and he didn't know what to say.

"Our forebears selected this distant corner of Dyn Brailing because the demands of greater society rarely reach so far into noth-ing." Wolf smiled, but Aron noted that his father's scarred face didn't brighten like it usually did. "Harvest will come and go. Of that, we can be certain. I doubt it will be much more to us than another pass-ing day."

The chaos inside Aron began to settle. He studied the *dav'ha* tattoos along his father's arms, picking out symbols for friendship, sacrifice, and courage. Then symbols of places and battles. Wolf Brailing had explained many of his obligations to his son, but no one had ever appeared at their farm demanding that Aron's father honor a *dav'ha*.

For the first time, it occurred to Aron that this might be unusual. That if they lived in Can Rune or one of the other great cities, people might show up from all quarters, calling on their sworn allegiances like merchants demanding coin for cloth or spices. Kindness, honest labor, honor, and truth—of course his father would have answered every call.

"The demands of greater society rarely reach so far into nothing," Aron murmured, and his father nodded.

"The sun still shines in the sky, yet I have two men lazy from afternoon's business," Aron's mother said from the corner of the barn. "Where is this honest labor you're always discussing, Wolf Brailing?"

Aron flinched at the sound of her voice and tried to collect the *dantha* leaf along with all of its incriminating crumbs, but his mother's eye was far too sharp for sleight of hand. She approached them, her reddish brown hair escaping from the tie that bound it at the nape of her neck. The blue-green flecks in her brown eyes seemed to flash as she scowled.

"I suppose you'll need less portion at supper, boy." Her expression seemed fierce as Aron sheepishly offered the folded *dantha* leaf to his father, but her tone was light, almost teasing. She seemed to be directing her words more to Aron's father than Aron himself. "May the Brother of Many Faces keep your belly full until morning. *Both* of you."

Wolf got to his feet along with Aron. His expression remained placid, but Aron saw no severity when he said, "There, woman. I chose you for your kindness, didn't I? You'd never deny a man nourishment on his youngest daughter's birthday."

When Wolf reached for his wife, she didn't smack him or pull away, but leaned in to him and kissed his craggy cheek. From behind his mother came the calls of Aron's eight siblings, returning from the hayfields and vegetable patch.

"Go," his mother instructed with a point to her left. "Tend to your talon, then fetch the little birthday girl and see that she and her sister scrub themselves clean while I finish preparing our meal."

Aron's eldest brother, Seth, came closer, adjusting his long hair in its looped leather tie, then wiping sweat off his tanned face. Not for the first time, Aron marveled at how Seth had come to resemble their father, so much so they could have passed for brothers.

"I'll gather the girls," Seth said. "Meet me by the well when you've finished with Tek."

Aron nodded his thanks to Seth, who went to sweep up the dark-headed girls spatting with each other near the front door. The older boys headed for the house, obviously grateful that they didn't have to manage their little sisters, who could be as fierce as rock cat cubs fighting over a meat scrap.

As Aron slipped into the barn, he saw his father gazing at the sky with that strange look on his face again. The odd sensations inside Aron's belly started up anew, and he paused just inside the shadow of the door, curious to know if his mother would reveal what Wolf Brailing was thinking.

After a long moment, his father said, "They'll pass us by tomorrow. They stay away from dynast lines to avoid hard feelings from the ruling seats."

"We are far down the line of succession from the dynast seat." Aron's mother spoke gently, but from the divide between barn door and barn wall, Aron saw his father frown at her. Behind them, between barn and house, Seth had one little sister over his shoulder and the other pinned against the well, doing his best to wash her face.

"True, we're nothing but root farmers scratching a living from the dirt," Wolf said in a strained voice, oblivious to the chaos behind him. "But we're Brailings of Brailing. That bears some consideration."

Aron's mother answered with a shrug. "Can Rune's rectors said our children were Quiet—they have no Fae legacy of mind-talents. So even if the Stone Guild comes to our farm, our blood might not speak."

"Stone's testing methods are more refined," his father said, the edge in his tone growing. "They prefer children with a touch of legacy even if they don't use the legacies in their hunts and killing—because legacies go hand in hand with intelligence and learning ability."

"Well, if the blood does speak," his mother countered, "at least one of our children would have a chance to get a proper education."

"From *Stone?*" Wolf growled the words so angrily Aron faded backward into the barn's cool depths. "What does the Stone Guild teach beyond murder and death? One of ours, an assassin. Cayn's teeth!"

"I'll thank you not to call the name of the horned god in my presence," Aron's mother said with a distinct chill in her voice. She was a devoted follower of the Brother, and such women didn't brook mention of the horned god of death. "Even outside, I'd prefer not to call ill fortune."

Aron's father showed no remorse. In fact, his voice grew loud enough to drown out the sounds of arguing at the well. "If it's guild training you want for our children, slay a dynast heir and steal his purse so we can pay to place our offspring with the Thorn Guild. Better our children turn out to be healers or scholars than trained killers."

"Thorn . . . doesn't take as many children as it once did, or so I hear at market, whenever the girls and I take thread to sell to the cloth-makers." Aron's mother kept her tone more casual, but he heard the undertone of worry. Maybe even hopelessness. "The Thorn Guild has forgotten Eyrie's orphans. I know you've always admired Thorn and its work, but Thorn's Lady Provost—she's a different sort of leader, I think, than Thorn has ever seen."

"I don't want to hear gossip about the Lady Provost of Thorn." Aron's father seemed to turn a deeper shade of red as each second passed. "The Thorn Guild has always been the keeper of honor and truth in our land, and I don't see that changing. You don't hear of Thorn stealing children to thicken their own ranks, do you?"

Aron's mother remained silent for a moment, then finished the conversation simply and directly. "You can't save us from Harvest, Wolf Brailing, no matter how much you rage and bluster. Fae or goodfolk, castle or hut, to Stone go the Stones."

She walked away then, and Aron stepped back again, until he could barely see his father. He put both hands atop his belly and pressed, hoping to silence the loud rumbling, maybe ease the twisting and turning.

To Stone went the Stones. Meaning, those chosen by Stone had no choice but to become Stone Guild members themselves.

That was the way of things, just like the turning of fate.

To the Stone Guild went the poor, the simple—those with nothing to protect them. To the Thorn Guild went the rich and privileged. The two guilds had once balanced the needs of Eyrie's goodfolk, but one had become filled with darkness, judgment, death, and the children of paupers. The other had filled itself with light, learning, healing, and the children of wealthy families. Families with less coin could send their children to trade lodges like the Carpenters' Union or the Blacksmiths' League, lower in status, but still a way to learn, and ultimately to earn. Farming families like Aron's, they occasionally managed to arrange apprentice training for one or two of their children, and they had no choice but to take their chances on Harvest.

To Stone go the Stones.

But I am no Stone. Next year, I'll be with Grommond, learning the ways of livestock and preparing to change my family's lot in this land.

Aron told himself this, and he did it more than once, but he didn't feel it. He didn't feel anything but a strange misery in his muscles and a growing catch in his breath.

Some seconds later, Wolf glanced into the barn, directly at Aron, as if he knew the exact spot where Aron stood. He gave a wink and a smile. *Don't fear, little one. My children are a wealth I won't surrender. You will always be my son.*

Aron's shoulders chilled.

He was almost certain he was simply reading the meaning of his father's expression, or imagining what he might say. The sensation made his insides lurch, but he dismissed it as nerves and folly. If Wolf Brailing had any of the Brailing legacy, any of those old Fae mind-talents, they would all be wealthy and spoiled, living in Can Rune and working in service to their dynast lord.

Behind him in the barn, Tek let out a trumpet. No doubt she was irate over Aron's failure to bring her a prompt dinner.

Aron moved to a space in the barn wall and watched his father walk toward the house. He saw how Wolf Brailing worked to keep his step light, his manner calm and comforting.

"Tomorrow is nothing," his father said to Seth as he passed the well and his wailing, wet daughters.

But at almost fifteen years of age, Aron knew tomorrow would bring long hours of wait and worry.

From sunup to sundown, children would be Harvested from all over Eyrie—including Dyn Brailing—for this was their one year in six to pay tribute to the Stone Guild like the other five dynasts.

To Stone go the Stones.

Seth went back to scrubbing his little sisters, and Wolf Brailing kept walking, but all Aron could do was stand and watch and listen to Tek's bleating, and hope that Eyrie's blue-white sun forgot to rise and bring the morning.

CHAPTER TWO

NIC

Cured wooden walls and turrets creaked above Can Rowan, the Tree City, the glorious capital of Dyn Mab. Rope bridges swung and groaned in predawn breezes, and windows both high and low remained lightless and curtained.

Nicandro Mab heard each sound and studied each darkened window in turn, and tried not to lose his mind.

Trapped in his sister's vast and sweltering bedchamber, Nic imagined lurking dangers on the black ground far below, almost wishing one of those dangers might find him, claim him, and put an end to his hours of pain. Sane people remained safely inside during Eyrie's nights, even in Dyn Mab. He knew that all through the six dynasts, fires burned against the menacing darkness, because light was the best protection. Light and fire, and of course, silver daggers.

Sweat stung Nic's eyes as he pushed away from his sister's windowsill. He had known no rest for two miserable nights. His overlarge body ached to rest, and on this, the third and longest night of his vigil, he was so hot and tired that he feared he might fall to the board floors. His lungs didn't want to draw from the bedchamber's stifling air as he once more settled himself at his sister's bedside. His soft muscles cramped to protest sitting again, but he couldn't imagine standing another minute, or how he would move from his watch once the time came.

He took Kestrel's fingers and held them tightly, even though he could see death slinking down the slack lines of her open mouth, feel it burning through her papery skin. Kestrel, who had always loved him despite his clumsy hands and clumsier wits, would leave him soon.

Her face looked so perfect, but so pale beneath tangled mats of golden hair. Dark rings underscored her eyes, which had once been wide, bright, and blue, like his eyes, like the eyes of his two brothers who had been murdered in the year past. Like their father, who had succumbed to a hunting accident three years ago.

The accident meant to kill me. Nic closed his eyes then opened them, unable to shut out the bitter truth. *I should have been first to die, since I was youngest and easiest. My tragedy would have aroused no suspicion—or sorrow.*

It was just a hunting trip, a lark, a recreation day—but a mocker had attacked the hunting party not even a full league from Can Rowan's walled edge. Nic's father had seen the misshapen eagle before the beast could snag Nic with its claws. His father battled the creature even after it shifted to its twisted man-form and spit poison and slashed him with daggerlike nails. Nic had escaped through a grove of heartwoods and found the honor guard, but even the dynast's finest guardsmen couldn't save Lord Mab. Nic had watched his father, Eyrie's king consort, die much as Nic's sister was dying—holding Nic's hand and gasping for one more draft of cool air.

Why do I keep living when everyone I love dies?

Nic shifted his weight, drawing a groan from his overburdened chair. The moments between Kestrel's breaths stretched longer, and he marked them by counting, by begging death to keep its distance for another minute. Maybe one more hour, to give him a last sunrise with her.

Perhaps she would wake, or say something to ease his guilt. She had offered to let him taste his first mead on her birthday a week ago, but he had refused. If he hadn't, he might already be dead. If he had knocked her cup and horn to the floor with some ham-fisted gesture as he so often did, she wouldn't have swallowed the treacherous drink, and she wouldn't be dying at all.

Torn between wanting peace for his sister and wishing to keep her forever, Nic continued to count seconds between Kestrel's breaths and whisper prayers to the horned god of death, even though most citizens of Eyrie worshipped the Brother of Many Faces and, in the Brother's honor, shunned direct pleas to Cayn. Most goodfolk were so superstitious, they wouldn't even say the horned god's name indoors, especially not in a bedchamber.

Nic didn't think it mattered, or made any difference at all. He knew that shunned or welcomed, Cayn would come as he chose to the house of Mab, just as he had three times before. The horned god had been wicked to Nic's brothers, who were large and strong. They had lingered for weeks before they died, fighting the mysterious creeping death the rectors later declared a deep-acting poison.

The sight of her sons dying so terribly had finally driven his mother into madness—though she had walked close to that abyss since Nic could remember. The women in the Mab bloodline were prone to fragility. There was nothing to be done. Nic was glad Lady Mab had thus far chosen not to attend Kestrel's passing. He didn't know if he could bear her frenetic presence, or watch her agony as the poison claimed yet another of her children.

"It must have been tasteless," the rectors had told Lady Mab. "Perhaps mixed with sugar and laced on the tarts . . ."

This time, Nic was sure the poison had been in the mead. Kestrel became ill only hours after the meal, and the mead was the only thing he hadn't shared with her. No one would believe him, of course. Nic wasn't known for his observant nature—only his impressive girth and the number of jokes goodfolk made at his expense.

These he put from his mind.

At least his sister was dying quickly. Maybe if Nic welcomed and respected Cayn, the horned god would show Kestrel some small mercy the Brother had forgotten.

Nic wanted to cry, but he was sixteen, and he knew he could no longer afford to behave like a child. It was bad enough that his body was soft, that he couldn't learn his letters and lessons, or keep his attention on the tasks his tutors set before him. He could not, on top of that, be spineless. Dynast lords had to be courageous. Dynast lords had to think of others and not their own selfish desires. Nic knew that if Kestrel died—*when* she died—he had to be a proper heir to Dyn Mab, the most powerful of dynasts, with its bounty of heartwood, salt, fish, and other blessings from the sea. In time, he would have to be a good and true high king to all of Eyrie's six dynasts.

"I hope I die fast if they poison me before I take the throne," he whispered to Kestrel.

From his right he heard sniffs and grumbles, which reminded him he wasn't alone in his sister's bedchamber. Three black-robed rectors stood in attendance, sweating in the heat of the roaring hearth fire. Their shadows danced on the wooden castle walls, fell across the chairs and benches, and stained the whites and yellows of the bed's canopy and linens.

One of them whispered a word Nic knew all too well.

Hobbledehoy.

They weren't being unkind, not really. Only calling him by gentlest of the nicknames Eyrie's goodfolk preferred. Most people in Eyrie thought Nic was dim. They believed he would be an awkward, clumsy child forever, both in body and in mind, not fit to inherit the mantle of his proud bloodline.

Nic Mab, Eyrie's hob-prince.

He shoved such thoughts out of his mind again and fast went back to ignoring the rectors, shadows and whispers and all. They hadn't been able to halt the poison's progress despite their vaunted training with the Thorn Guild, and more from their own elders once they took vows at the Temple of the Brother. Nic judged the rectors useless except to stoke the flames and keep his sister calm with nightshade wine. Thorn itself seemed to be growing more useless by the day, too. Where were the Thorn Guild High Masters that usually attended the death of a numbered heir to the throne? Where was the Lady Provost of Thorn, herself?

Nic didn't much like the woman, but she had come when his father died, and when his brothers lay sick and fading.

Was Kestrel any less important?

As if hearing his thoughts, Kestrel drew a labored breath. Nic pressed her long fingers tighter in his palm as the air rattled out from her open mouth.

One, two, three, four . . . He ticked off seconds between her breaths as the rectors stirred and muttered amongst themselves.

"Sister," Nic said in his steadiest voice.

Her eyes flew open, suddenly wide and horribly, painfully alive. Nic startled, almost pulled away, but kept his head—and stayed by her side. She opened her cracked lips, but no sound issued forth.

Despite the protests of his chair, Nic leaned forward, heart clenching and pounding all at once. "What is it? Do you want to tell me something?"

Yes! screamed her eyes. *Everything. My life, from beginning to end. My secrets. My truths!*

Yet she said nothing. Nic had none of the Mab legacy, none of the special talents of thought and mind, none of the unusual abilities that sometimes blessed members of the ruling Fae families. The rectors had declared him Quiet in the mind many years ago, so he could only guess at his sister's purpose.

"Do you know who did this to you?" He moved closer, until he was nearly touching her small nose with his larger one. Determinedly, he kept her gaze and ignored the clucking of the rectors.

Kestrel blinked once, then twice. She seemed to be measuring him with her stare, judging him for eternity. Nic found himself shaking with despair and eagerness.

"Tell me, sister. Speak."

A fusty puff of breath brushed Nic's cheeks. Then Kestrel looked past him. As he stared desperately into those feverish depths, the light inside his sister faded away.

"Wait!" Nic grabbed for her other hand, kissed her cheek—still warm, still warm. "The sun isn't up yet. Don't you want to see the light? The rectors will open your shutters and pull back your sheets so you might feel it. One more morning, sister. See the start of day with me."

She made no response.

One, two, three, four . . .

An impossible chill laced through the hot chamber. Nic gripped her fingers harder and harder, as if to squeeze some of his own life into her motionless body.

Eight, nine, ten . . .

A gnarled hand closed over his shoulder. "Be easy, Lord Mab. This watch has ended."

Nic eased back from Kestrel's face but shook off the rector's grip.

Fifteen, sixteen, seventeen . . .

His gut twisted. His jaw throbbed from clenching, and his eyes ached to cry. Still, he didn't let himself unravel. He counted even though no breath came to start the numbers over again.

Nic refused to surrender his hold on Kestrel's hands until he reached one hundred, and another hundred beyond that. Even then, he had difficulty releasing her, despite the fact that her skin had chilled beneath his beseeching touch.

"So sad," one of the rectors said in a voice like the crackle of parchment. "To die in the small hours, only minutes before seeing the sun's splendor one more time."

A rush of heat blurred Nic's vision. He let go of his sister and wheeled on the three healers. "Get out! Out, you Brotherless idiots!"

They ignored him, of course. Even in his crazed state, he knew they had no real choice, no matter his barbs and slaps. They had to stay. Deathwatch was deathwatch, and after that, deathguard until Kestrel's essence could be properly dispatched so it wouldn't transform into a mane and kill everyone in the castle.

Sometime later, minutes, maybe longer, Nic writhed in the grip of the eldest rector as the other two methodically closed Kestrel's unseeing eyes. On the darkened lids they placed silver pieces, then lodged a third piece of silver in her lips. Without speaking, they folded her hands around a silver scepter to further ward against her spirit rising as a mane. This was more custom than necessity, since this was a dynast castle. Unlike goodfolk in outlying villages, Eyrie's ruling Fae always employed those who could immediately dispatch the essence of the dead.

No sooner had Nic finished that thought than the door to the bed-chamber opened. A blue-skinned Sabor, a creature human and yet not human, bound by a promise of loyalty to the line of Mab, entered as the two rectors stepped away from his sister's body. The two displaced men came over to stand next to Nic and his captor at the fire. He had stopped struggling, at least for the moment.

The Sabor spoke ritual words to free the spirit, then tapped the ruby-studded Mab *cheville* on Kestrel's left ankle. The jeweled stone band sprang open and broke into two pieces, disrupting the subtle energy field emitted by all precious stones. At the same moment, the chill in the room swept upward in a breath-snatching rush.

The Sabor waited a few more moments, then collected the broken *cheville*. "Kestrel Mab's essence has departed," he said in that mad-deningly calm voice used by all servants of the horned god. His unset-tling golden eyes contracted at the center until he was studying Nic with a lionlike gaze that made Nic want to shout and beat the blue man, demand that he restore his sister's spirit, fasten back the *cheville*, and let the powers of the stone hold her essence close to him.

Instead he hung his head and stared at his own *cheville*. The ruby band, created by masons who still had enough mind-talent to imbue the stone with the ability to grow with the leg it adorned, seemed unnaturally bright in the light of the fire. Nic imagined that it was glaring at him, chastising him for his unreasonable wishes. Sabor worshipped the horned god of death, Cayn, and they carried so much of Eyrie's old blood. They could command the spirits of the dead, but they could not raise the departed. No one could raise the dead, except maybe the Stregans, the strongest of the shape-shifting races that had once existed—but the mixing disasters had killed the Stregans and all the shape-shifters except the Sabor, just as surely as poison was killing the line of Mab.

Nic squeezed his eyes shut against the truth for another long moment. *The murderers have ceased to care who sees their dark design. They know we cannot stop them. The line of Mab is doomed, and me with it.*

With Kestrel dead, with no other heir remaining to Mab, Nic knew he would have only duty henceforth, the endless labor of a dynast lord, for as long as he managed to live. And his sister wouldn't be there with him, no matter how strongly he willed it. Nic might have many powers when he became Eyrie's high king, but even kings couldn't command the relentless turn of fate.

Elhalla.

In the Language of Kings, spoken by Fae and those trained by the Thorn Guild.

Elhalla.

"Fate turns," Nic said aloud, calling the meaning of that bitter, bitter word. Half in a dream, he opened his eyes and realized the Sabor had approached him. Cayn's servant knelt and extended one bony blue hand, offering Nic the two pieces of his sister's broken *cheville*. His dark golden pupils had become pinpoints against a field of lighter yellow, and Nic knew the Sabor was ready for anything, even an attack.

Nic blinked as the rector restraining him finally let go of his arms.

He's bringing her cheville *to me because I'm the last remaining heir to the ruling line of Mab, through my mother. I am Lord Mab now, and I will be King of Eyrie.*

The thought numbed Nic yet more.

He almost reached for the dull red relics of his sister, but thought better of it at the last moment and shook his head.

"Take them to my mother," he instructed, doing his best to muster some authority in his voice. "She will need them."

To go with all the other bits of cheville *she carries. To endlessly handle and stroke, to rattle in the bag of doom she keeps bound to her waist.*

The servant of Cayn lowered his head in a formal bow, then obeyed without comment or question.

After a cold, quiet length of time, long enough for the blue man to descend with his sad offerings, the queen's wails pierced the heavy wooden walls.

Nic grimaced.

The rending and crying drew closer.

With a dull lurch, Nic realized that his mother was headed toward Kestrel's chambers. She would come to shriek and cradle her only daughter. Her weak, broken mind would trick her into insane suspicions, and she would curse Lord Ross, the dynast leader she believed to be conspiring against the throne and bribing murderers to poison Mab's heirs.

Given long enough, she might end up cursing Lord Brailing, Lord Cobb, and Lord Altar. She might even extend her venom to the Lady Provost of Thorn, the Lord Provost of Stone, even Lady Vagrat, and Nic didn't think he could stand the battering of his mother's invectives. As for Nic—to Lady Mab, high queen of Eyrie's six dynasts and holder of the Circle's seventh vote—she scarcely knew he existed. She, like everyone else, had dismissed Nic as unimportant in the workings of Eyrie's highest royal family, and she would little notice his absence.

So, wordless and overcome with private grief, Nic Mab escaped his mother's agony and his sister's corpse by following the black-cloaked rectors out of the bedchamber, down the long castle hallway leading away from private quarters, through the massive reception room, and up a twisting, turning staircase to the castle's highest tower. The rectors were deep in conversation and did not look back to see him, which was fortunate. He certainly could not have hidden himself from view. Nic kept his footfalls as quiet as he could, and did his best to breathe without gasping, even when he lost his wind on the narrow tower steps. Outside smaller and smaller windows, he could see the branches cradling the castle growing thinner.

The rectors moved out onto the open turret, which rose far atop the trees supporting the castle. Pinks and oranges painted the dawn sky. Soft blue-white light broke over the horizon as Nic crept behind the rectors, savoring a first view from the tower he had never been allowed to climb, where no Fae usually visited for obvious reasons of risk and safety. The top of the tower held only three square huts full of birds, joined by fencing and circled by a scant wooden platform.

It wasn't until the healers reached the first of the three huts in the rookery that they glanced back and noticed Nic. Their duties were clear and urgent, and they couldn't stop now to scold him and force him back down to the castle proper. The rectors were charged with releasing the tidings of tragedy to goodfolk and Fae in cities far and near, and delays went against customs much older than Nic.

"Have care, Lord Mab," said the eldest rector, who had restrained Nic in his sister's bedchamber. "You should not have come here, but be still and cautious, and we will escort you down from the tower as soon as we have finished."

Nic ignored the man and his worrisome scowl and made his way around the platform of the open turret as the rectors worked. He positioned himself where he could look up to the sky to see the birds, then watch them soar across the city below. He wanted to see them fly. He had to. It would be like watching his sister's spirit hurtle into the sun.

Metal creaked. Wood shifted. The roof of the third building opened.

Nic heard the excited chittering of birds. Then one, then two, then all of the passerines exploded from their nests, a whirring cloud of wings and feathers that made his aching heart pound.

Light from the rising sun gleamed off the birds, turning them to swirling jewels in the sunrise. Jewels that would be seen for leagues. At other watch towers and rookeries, lesser flocks would be released. Like flash signals of old, the message would travel all through Eyrie in just hours, a day at the most to the far reaches of Dyn Brailing and Dyn Ross.

White passerines. Tears in the sky! A Mab of Mab has joined the clouds.

"The heir to the throne didn't make it to morning," Nic whispered into the rushing wind, feeling the chafe of tears on his cheeks. "My sister is gone."

Were it his mother who had died, the rectors would have set free the black flock to summon dynast lords and ladies to the Circle of Eyrie for a thronemaking. Brown birds would have summoned the nobles to Circle, but with less urgency, for a regular meeting of government.

I'm alone, and soon I'll be made king, and all of Eyrie will laugh—or wail—at such a misfortune.

A gust buffeted Nic, and he leaned back fast against a bit of rookery fence. Above him, the white birds circled, making wider and wider patterns. Nic watched them, nearly oblivious to the risk that the rector had warned him to avoid. The castle at Can Rowan, suspended in massive, ancient heartwoods above the city it commanded, had been rendered ages ago, when the Mabs of Mab would have been winged like the birds they kept. For many long centuries after the Migration, and before the mixing disasters that destroyed the shape-shifters, the Fae could fly and speak with their minds across infinite distances. No rails had to keep hobbledehoy princes from falling from the trees.

Better days in better times, Nic had heard his mother say in lucid moments. *Freedom of body, of mind.*

The winds eased. Nic stepped forward again and gazed down at the beauty of Can Rowan to give himself comfort. Houses sat snug in welcoming trees. Towers rose off the ground like fists reaching toward the trees. Shops and barrows and homes, some landbound, some branch-cradled—the Tree City seemed to stretch forever in all directions.

Cutwinds stung his cheeks and blew his hair into his face. As he reached to swipe the golden curls from his eyes, shadows fell across his view, and cold, firm fingers closed on Nic's shoulders. Nic caught his breath, then realized it must be one of the rectors, worried that he might fall.

"Leave me. I'm fine." Nic started to turn—but whoever had his shoulder began to shove him forward.

"Stop!" he yelled.

The wind turned his cries into whispers. Nic's heart squeezed into a tiny, pounding fist.

He tried to struggle, tried to throw his weight backward or turn around, but he could only stumble forward. Toward the edge. On the edge!

Swaying high above Can Rowan, Nic screamed for help.

He thought about the rectors. Just a moment, but long enough to realize that the rectors in the rookery might be the murderers who poisoned his sister and his brothers, too.

Then Nic was screaming again, this time without words—and flying with no wings to bear him into the sky.

CHAPTER THREE

ARON

Aron knew the rest of his family was hard at task in the vegetable patch and hayfields, so he worked his muck rake, keeping his eyes fixed on the hogs just a body's length away from him, as his father taught him to do. A body's length, and no closer. Hogs were dangerous. Aron knew he shouldn't let his attention wander even for a moment. Even on Harvest.

The barn cast shadows on his work, and today no scent of stew seeped from the house. They would dine on bread and fresh picks from the garden, and hope no flash of brightness, no tempting smell, no hint or whisper of anything good or unusual escaped their farm to attract attention.

Aron didn't mind the work. Hard labor suited him, spent his energy and calmed his nerves. There was no shame in labor, he had learned from his father. Working men were brave, strong, and prepared for what came. Callused hands were honest hands, after all.

Harvest will end, and I will still be here, where I belong. I will go to Grommonds. I will learn and prosper, and live and die with callused hands.

As if in answer, a sow rooted and grunted. Mud splashed on Aron's caked breeches and leather boots. His tunic, handed down through three of his six brothers, reached past his knees to gather its own filth. Still he shoveled, moving with rhythm and purpose, but no matter how hard he tried, he couldn't go through the Veil. He couldn't reach the quiet place inside his mind where light turned bright and even the smallest sounds grew loud. That place his father had taught him to seek, where his nerves calmed and his temper eased, where his troubles faded and his awareness focused sharper and sharper, until he saw only the task at hand.

For a time, Aron tried reciting the Code of Eyrie, to which all citizens of Eyrie gave an oath at the moment they grew old enough to sort right from wrong. He even managed it in the Language of Kings, taught by the Thorn Guild. His father had learned the old words from Thorn initiates and adepts during his guardsman days, and Aron had little trouble speaking the six laws that brought the dynasts out of the mixing disasters that destroyed the shape-shifters.

So what if his father had no store of wealth, no inheritance of godslight—gold that never lost its value—or treasures like those Brailings farther up the line of succession. Aron accepted that with no grudge. He was content to work the farm beside his father, his mother, his sisters, and his brothers. One day, he would have his own large, healthy family, a livestock farm to feed them—and he would teach his many children about the Code, about going through the Veil, and about Wolf Brailing.

If Eyrie's blue-white sun would move across the sky and set.

If Harvest indeed came to an end with Aron safe in his hog pen, mucking and mucking and mucking.

The entire land felt . . . wrong to him today, even beyond Harvest, beyond anything rational. He almost expected to see shadows forming above each tree and hill, or darkness breaking through the bright sky to swallow him and the hogs, too.

Tears formed and waned in Aron's eyes as he felt the pull of the farm like a tether in his gut, connecting him to the ground he worked. He sensed the mud deep in his blood. He breathed the dust, tasted the dirt, and took in the greens and browns of the nearby tufts of grass. The farm yielded only sparsely, but Aron helped in the planting and tending. They had one ancient ox and nothing else but a few hogs and chickens, but he had raised the pigs and birds almost by himself while the rest of his family saw to other chores.

Aron glanced at the fence around the hog pen and hated himself for his spineless urges to run away and hide from Harvest. Yet if he crawled through those slats, if he dashed behind the barn and slipped into the trees, he could disappear better than most. No one would find him. He knew the southern reaches of Dyn Brailing better than anyone, from the Watchline to the deep, dangerous Scry.

Except my father and my brothers. But would they search for me? Guilda i'Guild. To disrespect Stone or Thorn is Unforgivable. Every citizen of Eyrie is sworn to the Code from birth. My family wouldn't shelter an oathbreaker, or they would become as guilty as me.

He frowned and forced himself to stare more deeply into the muck. He needed to find his courage, establish his peace. The day was waning, after all. Harvest was half over, at least, and he needed to concentrate. His arms moved. His legs moved. The muck rake started to work again. Aron tried to let his mind sink into the pen's deep browns and blacks, into the hogs' contented snuffles, into the breeze and the smack of the rake and the rocking, rocking of his back and elbows as he turned the mud and turned it again, again, again to pull under old slops and make ready for tomorrow's feeding. Hard work. Good work. Honest work.

A rustle of wings made him jump.

Aron jerked his gaze upward, following the sound. A small flock of white birds streaked past the farm, circled back, then flew onward. Passerines. They must have been set loose from a nearby rectory.

For a moment, Aron imagined the message of the flock moving down from the north, as flock after flock took flight across all the dynasts, all of Eyrie. This flock would have been signaled from Can

Rune, town to town, village to village, until even goodfolk who lived in nowhere and nothing could see the sad truth.

"A Mab of Mab has joined the clouds," he murmured. "Again!" This would be Kestrel, the princess. Now only the hob-prince remained. He made a sign against ill fortune, touching his cheek to ask for the blessings of the Brother.

Wings. It was just wings in the sky. Not travelers on the road, as he feared.

Callused hands . . . callused hands . . .

Aron's breathing gradually slowed to normal again, and he closed his fingers tighter on the muck rake. "Hobbledehoy," he repeated, silly with relief as he once more turned his attention back to the hog pen. "Hobbledehoy."

A loud creak answered him—from the road leading up to the farm.

Aron's joints slackened like broken harness straps.

That creak sounded like a wagon.

Like a wagon moving up the byway.

Aron almost dropped the rake. "Tree branch. Falling rock. Don't be foolish."

The creak came again, followed by a clack. Soon he recognized the rhythm of clawfeet, hooves, and wagon wheels laboring up the aged dirt byway. Aron dug his fingers into the rake handle as he made himself look up to see who was coming. Shadowy figures approached the farm through a cloud of dust on the road, as if emerging from some hazy dream.

They were moving at some speed, these travelers.

Aron started to shake. His thoughts raced back to the afternoon before, to the fortress his father drew in the dirt by the barn.

Breached.

And then his father's voice whispered in his mind. *Don't fear, little one. My children are a wealth I won't surrender. You will always be my son.*

A mule's bray brought Aron back to the present, to the sight of the sun, still blazing blue and hanging stubbornly high in the sky. He closed his eyes. Opened them. Tried to breathe. Tried to hold himself still. No amount of denial could shade the truth at hand.

The Stone Guild had come to nowhere, ridden far into nothing, to collect their due.

Two Brothers in telltale gray robes, armed with broadswords crossed behind their backs with hilts showing over their shoulders, rode leather-skinned talons with eyes like orange-red flame. Behind the winged lizards rattled two mule-drawn carts hooked together back to front. A boy of perhaps twelve years with the yellow-haired, haughty look of a northern dynast sat astride the front wagon's driving board, guiding four pulling mules. He had no broadsword, but wore a long dagger belted at his waist. His garb was simpler, too, gray breeches and a gray tunic, and he steered the mules with a deft touch. His wagon protested and swayed under its weight of hides, barrels, and crates, while the one tethered behind it looked empty. Behind the empty wagon, a breeding pair of goats struggled against a stout chain.

Mouth dry, breath scraping painfully against his throat, Aron squinted into the light of the blue-white sun. He gripped his rake, desperately trying to go through the Veil even though he knew he'd never reach that calmness now. The Stone Guild would Harvest him.

He was the youngest male, and the Brothers preferred young boys for training. He was also the fairest of feature, with the light brown hair, thin build, and sapphire eyes the color of Eyrie's sun, said to come from the old blood, the first mixings, before the Fae had tried to join their legacies with the shape-shifting races. His *cheville*, the band of lodestone fastened about the left ankle of every citizen of Eyrie with a trace of the old Fae bloodlines, was the same rare, glittering sapphire as the sun and Aron's eyes. He glanced down at his ankle, which was so coated with mud that he might as well have been wearing a *cheville* made of rock glass. No matter. The Brailing *cheville* would not save him now.

By law and right, the guild could select one of his elder brothers or even his baby sisters. Stone Sisters were rare, but rumored to be the most deadly of all the trained assassins. As long as a child was too old for mother's milk and too young to start Guard service or be pledged to trade or marriage, he—or she—could be taken from any family, Fae or goodfolk, blessed with more than five healthy heirs. Only one child could be chosen, so no family paid more than any other, but Aron's father always said the price was steep indeed.

Harvest was Eyrie's oldest tradition.

To Stone go the Stones.

Aron knew he should leave the pen and call out to his parents, but his voice deserted him. The hogs, crazed by the approach of the long-clawed, heavy-jawed talons, began to grunt and squeal. In response, one of the talons let loose a skin-flaying shriek.

From the small barn behind Aron, his own small talon, Tek, gave an answering squeak.

One of the big talons screeched again, the sharp note of male noting female.

Aron threw down the muck rake and scrambled out of the hog pen just as his mother and sisters came running into the yard from the back field. A few seconds later, his brothers spilled into view from all directions. Some carried harriers and hoes. Seth wielded a scythe, though Aron couldn't imagine what he would be doing with a clearing blade. It was too early to take down the stalks and vines.

The hogs screamed and screamed. Aron's skin crawled at the sound, and at the sight of his brother and the blade.

Does Seth mean to fight them?

Guilda i'Guild. By the Code, the guild could take its due. To lay hands on a Harvesting Stone Brother would bring down the wrath of the assassins, not to mention the force of the dynast Fae.

"Seth." Aron's father arrived from the fields and hurried to his eldest son. "Be still!"

His command hammered through the noise of the rampaging hogs. Wolf still carried the harness straps he had been oiling, and for a moment, Aron feared his father would strike Seth across the back of his head.

Instead, Seth wheeled to face his father, blade raised. His hands shook as he stood for a second, then two, then three. His shoulders twitched as his father glowered at him.

"This family follows the law," Wolf said in firm tones. "We're Brailings of Brailing, and there will be no oathbreakers under my roof. Hold up your head and put aside that weapon."

Seth seemed to struggle against unseen hands, then dropped the scythe to the ground. He swore, leaped to pick up the blade, swore again, and abandoned it where it lay. When he turned back to Aron, Seth's dark eyes had gone cold.

The other five boys lined up beside Seth, leaving space for Aron between the last and the two small girls. Beside the girls, Aron's mother buried her face in her field apron. The dirt on her hands turned slowly dark with her tears. Wolf dropped his straps and joined his wife, looking anguished and furious all at once.

Unable to swallow, Aron took his place in line. The hogs railed, and their terror knifed into his belly.

The Stone Brothers came to a halt in the yard. Both men dismounted, leaving the talon leads, mules, and wagons in the care of the boy.

Foolish. Aron frowned. If the talons took a mind to fight or fly, they would slaughter the boy and likely the mules, too. Then the beasts would be at his hogs before anyone could stop them.

One Brother walked to the hog pen, quieting the stricken animals with clucks and soft words. The other Brother strode straight toward Wolf. The hilts of his broadswords jutted up from behind the man's shoulders. Aron could imagine the sharp, jagged blades crossed over the man's back, though he hadn't yet seen them. He also couldn't see any daggers, but if he had learned correctly from his father, the man would have knives concealed all over his person.

A Stone Brother fights like a porcupine in close combat. The Judged often try to win their way free, but it's damnable hard to account for all those slashing quills.

The approaching Stone Brother carried a simple hammered leather bag, bleached as gray as his *cheville* and his finely woven garments. Aron eyed the ankle band and the robes. His father said many goodfolk believed the gray cloth and *cheville* changed colors to allow the wearer to fade into the background, but Aron saw no indication of this. Perhaps it took a bit of legacy to notice the change, but even the great houses had weak legacies now, and Brailing the weakest of all. Each of Aron's cousins were Quiet, even those closest to the dynast seat. Perhaps his mother was correct. Their blood wouldn't speak, and they would all be spared from Harvest.

The Stone Brother reached Wolf, and when he pushed back his cowl to greet the family properly, Aron sucked in a sharp breath. The man had the unnaturally white hair and skin common only to Dyn Vagrat—a Stone Brother colored as if he came from Thorn—and eyes as green as wet summer grass!

Aron had no idea that such a thing was possible. He couldn't imagine the Stone Brothers Harvesting from Dyn Vagrat, from the dynast that housed the Thorn Guild. Did Thorn even allow such a thing?

And those eyes . . .

Loud eyes, the rectors would have called them. Colored eyes suggested a strong dose of Fae blood. People with colored eyes—shades other than black or brown—especially those closer to the recognized ruling lines, often had legacies, or traces of the old talents once coveted and cultivated by dynast lords. Aron's own loud blue eyes had proved no true indicator of mind-talent, but that green . . . no doubt this Stone Brother had a legacy, maybe even a strong dose of the

Vagrat ability to heal the wounded. Why was he not in the service of some dynast lord?

Centered on the Brother's pale forehead was a three-sided black spiral. The same marks had been carved under both of his eyes. Aron knew from his father's teachings that those three tattoos signified very high rank in the Stone Guild.

Aron's father blinked several times. The Stone Brother's rank in society was far higher than Wolf Brailing of Brailing, even though his family carried a dynast name. After a few seconds, Wolf gave a grudging, shallow bow, acting first since he was of lesser status.

"Greetings." The Stone Brother gave a polite bow in return. "Forgive the lateness of our arrival, but we have been long on the road and one of our wagons was beset with troublesome spokes and a broken bolt."

Silence was Wolf's only answer.

Aron puzzled at this. The proper thing would have been to offer drink, food, aid, even lodging for a traveler—especially one claiming distress in his journey. In Brailing, traveler courtesies were strictly observed upon penalty of dishonor, disfavor of the dynast lord, even retribution from a traveler's kin.

The Stone Brother, however, offered no expression of surprise or anger at the slight. Instead he smiled and took his gray leather bag off of his shoulder. "It would be best if we made haste to get back on our way. I am Dunstan, called Dunstan Stormbreaker by my Brothers, and I have come to Harvest. Male or female, it makes no matter to me so long as the blood speaks."

Wolf grabbed his wife's hand before she could slap the Stone Brother. Aron saw her blazing red cheeks and figured her to be angry at the thought of surrendering a daughter to three males. Though Brailing folk were less obsessed with honor and virtue than many of the dynasts, safety was safety, and women tended to keep the company of women for that reason if no other.

"Dunstan," Wolf said. "I once met a boy called Dunstan, during my Guard days. He and his sister were in some need—and his hair was the same straw white as your own."

"Dunstan is a common name," Stormbreaker said as if to dismiss the possibility that he had been that boy, and turned his attention to the children.

Aron looked away before the Stone Brother could meet his eyes.

"You would Harvest a child from a family carrying the dynast name?" Aron's father asked with the same grudging courtesy he had demonstrated with his earlier bow.

"With leave from Lord Helmet, Brailing of Brailing, I would," Stormbreaker replied with no trace of tension or annoyance, though his tone seemed pressed. "Since the Brailing bloodline was kind enough to donate the land where our stronghold was constructed, we Harvest from this dynast only one year in every six, and we never take from dynast lines without the dynast leader's permission, and usually special circumstance, like needing to select a child who will enjoy privilege of rank. In this case, the child I claim will be my first apprentice, and thus one day will share my status in the guild, and in Eyrie." He smiled as he glanced around the farm. "Perhaps a status greater than he or she already enjoys."

Wolf's face flushed a dark, dangerous red. "Do your business, Stormbreaker," he said through clenched teeth.

The second Stone Brother arrived from his calming work at the hog pen. He introduced himself as Osfred, called Osfred Windblown.

Hardly a fearsome name despite the broadswords and his other hidden quills, Aron realized. The man seemed slightly unfit, with paunch and soft arms, and he bore no marks of rank. Were it not for the sword hilts showing behind his shoulders and the gray robes and *cheville* of his killer's trade, Aron might have taken him for a gentle shepherd or a village baker.

Wasting no time, Osfred Windblown and Dunstan Stormbreaker

took carved-bone chalices from their gray bags. They emptied a small vial of amber liquid into the chalices, then removed slender daggers from their sleeves. Windblown approached Seth, who scowled and thrust out his arm as the Brother's cutting blade flashed in the meager sunlight. Aron's youngest sister Helga cried out as Stormbreaker's blade bit into her flesh on the soft side of her wrist. Then, in typical Brailing fashion, Helga tried to kick the man who hurt her.

"Be easy, easy there." Stormbreaker's voice made a chant as he held her firm and let her wrist bleed into the chalice. "The pain will pass. All pain passes in the end."

"Rock cat," Helga hissed. "Mocker piss!"

"Hush," Wolf whispered, and that fast, the first two were tested. The bone cups both gave off thin gray smoke.

Aron felt his stomach sink. The Brailing blood was speaking, at least a bit.

"Hardly impressive," Windblown noted, passing a finger through the feeble mist rising from his chalice. The broadswords on his back gave a rattle as he dumped his cup and wiped it with a cloth.

The rank-marked Stone Brother didn't respond. He simply dumped his own cup, extracted a cloth, wiped his chalice clean, and emptied another vial of the amber liquid into the bowl. Windblown moved to the next brother as Stormbreaker moved to Aron's other sister, Freda.

She grabbed for Aron's hand and he let her grip his fingers. Stormbreaker reached out for Freda just in time to meet Aron eye to eye.

A stillness overtook the man.

Aron's cool fear mingled with a fierce wish to protect his sister from Harvest. He would not be spineless. He would honor his father by doing his duty as an older brother, and by following the law without flinching. He released Freda's hand and stood fast as the Stone Brother appraised him.

Fine.

Let them test him first, and perhaps spare her the pain.

"Another weak response," Windblown muttered about one of Aron's brothers, then fell as silent as Stormbreaker.

Aron's jaw clenched. He would not be cowed by this mocker piss and his pale skin and his branded face. Aron was a Brailing of Brailing with a sapphire *cheville* and distant claims to the dynast seat. He was an animal-handler and already a competent worker of the land, with a promised apprenticeship in livestock, by the Brother's grace. Strong mind, strong stock. The Stone Guild could eat dirt and die, for all he cared.

Dunstan Stormbreaker let go of Freda without cutting her. He did not open the lock of his gaze as he extended his hand. His sleeve fell back, revealing rows of *dav'ha* marks to rival those on Wolf Brailing's arms.

So be it. Aron wanted to snarl the words aloud, but he held his peace. Heat built in his gut and flowed up through his neck and cheeks. He felt himself turning red, felt his life catching fire and burning away to nothing, and Aron Brailing thrust out his wrist for cutting.

CHAPTER FOUR

ARON

Stormbreaker grabbed Aron's wrist and held it.

Aron felt an odd pressure on his mind, but he kept his face as flat and smooth as his father's.

"Are you Quiet?" Stormbreaker asked in that low, hypnotic voice. "You are most certainly composed. You give me neither fear nor anger. Do you think that means you're strong?"

No power in Eyrie could have compelled Aron to answer.

From the barn, Tek mewled with concern. The little talon always seemed to know when Aron felt unsettled.

The sound brought Stormbreaker's head around. He glanced at the barn, then back to Aron. "I thought I heard a talon when we approached. Tell me, how did a family such as yours come to possess such a costly animal—and a female at that?"

"She escaped the dynast herd," Wolf said. "My sons and I were hunting in the Scry, and Aron found her injured and dying. He made a pulley to lift her free. She would take food from none other after that, and our Lord Brailing made her a gift to Aron."

"She's but a runt," Aron's mother cut in. "Her claws are too small for battle and her wings too weak to lift her for a fighting jump."

Stormbreaker kept Aron's wrist tight in his fingers. "Any female may breed."

"And any male may break an egg," Aron's mother fired back. "The talon is weak. So is this boy. Aron weighs less than my daughters and he has no man's bulk to his frame. He hardly eats. He—"

"I like the name Aron." Stormbreaker smiled at Aron. "It's powerful. Honest. Aron with eyes like the sapphire sun, and you're the one who found Lord Brailing's talon. You're a quick thinker with a talent for animal-handling. Good. Weight, height—such things matter little to Stone. We have room for many sizes and shapes."

Without further comment, he raised the small blade in his chalice hand and sliced open Aron's wrist.

Aron focused on the glimmering hilts of Stormbreaker's broadswords and held his iron expression despite the burning pain. His blood spurted into the bone cup, a red line, then a red pool. He made himself keep looking even though the sight made his insides roll.

Stormbreaker pressed a thumb over the flow, then let go of Aron altogether. The cut throbbed, but Aron still refused a reaction. His gut churned as the Stone Brother stood.

The chalice gave a loud sizzle and belched a geyser of gray steam.

Aron stared at the powerful blast of mist, stunned at such a strong response caused by his blood. His mother's expression mirrored his own feelings, then shifted to one of abjection. None of Aron's brothers had tested near that well. Like someone with Fae blood. Like someone with a legacy.

But how was that possible?

Aron knew he had been declared Quiet at birth.

Aron's mother started shaking her head, as if to deny what her senses told her.

Seth's eyes closed, and Wolf Brailing's face betrayed nothing at all.

"Well." Windblown smiled. "I'd say his blood speaks loudly enough to suit our purposes—and he *is* the one who found the talon. Let's take him and go." Almost as an afterthought, he added, "The sun sinks lower and we've miles before we reach a shelter. The land feels restless today. I shouldn't like to linger."

For a moment Aron wondered why the Stone Brothers didn't shelter at the farm. His thoughts wouldn't cooperate enough to make sense of it, but he finally realized they wouldn't stay here because they were taking him. The Stone Brothers didn't want to antagonize his family with their presence, or endure a long night of sobbing and possibly futile attempts at rescue or battle.

Because they're taking me.

They're taking me.

"This boy will meet our needs." Stormbreaker poured the chalice contents on the ground, wiped the bowl, and stowed his cup in his hammered leather bag. To Windblown he said, "Get the talon from the barn."

Rage and awe went to war with the fear blossoming in Aron's chest.

Just then, his father raised a hand. "Hold," he demanded, his face near the color of fall berries on the vine.

He's going to bargain for me! Aron's spirits leaped. He had never heard of a successful bargain with a Stone Brother, but surely such had happened. Perhaps his father would offer one of Aron's elder brothers, since Aron was good with the beasts and already had his apprenticeship with Grommond assured. Or maybe one of his brothers wanted to volunteer.

Windblown did not take a step toward the barn, and he did not speak. His hands twitched, as if he was considering drawing a weapon.

"Do you challenge my right to Harvest?" Stormbreaker asked lightly, though Aron heard the deadly intent behind the words.

"I am no oathbreaker." Wolf responded slowly, speaking too clearly, as if the Stone Brother might have some mental impairment. He cleared his throat and gestured to the barn. "I respect the guilds and pay tribute as demanded, but mounts are not part of the Harvest price. If you take the talon, you owe payment for her as well."

Stormbreaker hesitated, then laughed. "How could I forget that I was dealing with Brailings?" He laughed again. "Will the sum of thirty godslight bring us to balance?"

Aron's father frowned. "She's a female, worth fifty at least. And there's the cost of the riding tack as well."

The Stone Brother whistled. "Fifty. I see." He extracted a gray pouch from his hammered leather bag and counted some slender godslight into Wolf's palm. "This is what I can spare. Forty pieces. You may expect a courier from our guild stronghold at Triune before season's end with forty pieces more, in addition to the goods we leave now for the price of the boy. You have my promise."

Wolf hesitated, glanced desperately at Aron, then stepped back into line, as tradition and respect demanded.

"Get the talon and have Zed unload the Harvest payment," Stormbreaker told Windblown again, and this time no one challenged him.

Aron's heart went still, and not from calm thought or the meditation of toil. Was it that simple, then? Would his father hand him over with no protest?

A wealth I won't surrender . . .

Had his father said that to him mind to mind, in truth? Aron thought he had.

You will always be my son. . . .

Stormbreaker turned around to assist the boy Zed as he carried goods from the laden wagon, giving Aron a full view of the blades crossed over his back. Each sword was as long as Aron himself, hilt to tip, and the grooved edges of polished metal looked ready to bite and chew and tear. Aron kept his eyes on those terrifying blades as the Stone Brothers worked. Minute after minute passed, and with each trip to the laden wagon, the pile of treasures stacking up beside Wolf grew. Blankets. Clothing. Barrels, probably full of grain or wine, maybe even cured meat. This would be the best winter his family had ever known, and Aron wouldn't be here to share it with them.

The thought almost made him cry out with rage.

At last, Stormbreaker helped Zed to lead the breeding pair of goats forward, and they tethered the animals to one of the barrels.

Aron watched, wordless and sweating, as the fair-haired boy returned to the tandem wagons, the ground-tied talons, and the mules. Wind-blown met him there with Tek, already saddled and ready for travel. At that sight, Aron felt like his life was sliding into hog muck by the second. How could he go with these men and train to be a killer? He was no Stone Brother. He couldn't be an assassin.

A wealth I won't surrender . . .

But his father *was* surrendering him!

What of Grommond, and learning livestock, of serving in the Guard and bettering his family's lot in Dyn Brailing?

This could not be happening.

He would not let it happen—but how could he stop it, especially if his father did nothing on his behalf?

Stormbreaker bowed to Wolf, showing the hilts of his swords more clearly. "The Harvest is finished. We have made payment, and we ask our due."

Aron looked up to find his father gazing at him in that way people did when they weren't really looking, when they weren't really seeing.

No! His cry was wordless, but surely Wolf Brailing saw the plea in his eyes. *Look at me!*

His mother sobbed into her hands. His brothers stared at the ground. His sisters eyed the Stone Brothers as if searching for weak spots to bite or kick—but his father—his father . . .

Aron found only emptiness when he searched his father's eyes.

The hero of the Dynast Guard. The master of his house and fields. The man who had preached to him for hours on hours about kindness, honest labor, honor, and truth. And he would say nothing when professional murderers came to take his son?

Aron kept looking at Wolf, willing him to wake, to see.

Had Aron become invisible to his father for the price of hides and goats and winter stores, and forty pieces of godslight?

"We ask our due," Stormbreaker repeated, this time with less patience.

Wolf slowly turned his face toward the Stone Brother—and the emptiness was gone.

Aron flinched from his father's expression.

The men in gray might make killing their trade, but it was Wolf Brailing who had murder in his eyes. Through clenched teeth, looking at Stormbreaker instead of Aron, he said, "Flesh of my flesh, you are my son no longer."

It took Aron a moment to realize his father's words were meant for him. It took another moment for the meaning to sink from his mind to his heart.

No!

Aron's teeth slammed together. His fists clenched so hard he felt his ragged nails dig into his palms.

Wolf strode out of line and walked until he stood in front of Aron. This time, when Aron met his gaze, he knew his father saw him only too well. The pain and rage in Wolf's eyes mirrored Aron's own feelings.

"You are dead to me, to your mother, to your brothers and sisters," Wolf said, his tenor denying the meaning of his words. "I disinherit you before these witnesses and lay foul any claim you might have to my lands or my name."

Aron wanted to weep, but couldn't, not with his father staring at him. He couldn't help the shaking in his legs, but he wouldn't disgrace his name or his heritage by bawling.

"Go from this place and never return." Wolf's voice broke. In a sparse whisper, he finished with, "You will find no welcome at this farm."

Wolf bent forward, rubbed his hands in the dirt at Aron's feet, then rose and smeared his cheeks with the crumbly brown earth. Next, he dirtied his wife's cheeks and those of his two daughters. His five remaining sons completed the gesture on their own. With a last long look of misery and helpless fury, Aron's father—the man who had just cast him out—returned to his place in line, again showing respect for tradition. No argument, no resistance. Harvest was to proceed unimpeded.

On his order, the family that had been Aron's moved away from him, linked arms, bowed their heads in ritual grief, and turned their backs.

Aron looked first at them, then at Dunstan Stormbreaker. The Stone Brother held out his hand.

Hating the man, despising his tattoos, his smug expression, and his maddening gray robes, Aron considered rejecting the offer even though he knew he had no choice. In a moment's negotiation, the painted monster had divested him of all he understood, all he valued, save for Tek. What if the guild took Tek, too, and he never saw her again?

Grinding his teeth until his head ached, Aron took the offered hand. Suddenly, Stormbreaker's grip was firm and commanding on his wrist. A soldier's grasp.

"We have three score and seven boys by the name of Aron at Stone, my new apprentice. For now, you shall be Aron Frosteye, until your actions win you some other distinction."

Aron refused his captor the courtesy of a response.

Stormbreaker pressed ahead. "Aron Frosteye, as your guild master, and by rights of Harvest, I will speak your vows for you. You have no family save for Stone. You have no name and no title beyond what Stone provides. All claims, rights, and inheritance are forfeit. From now until your spirit is released, your blood is Stone, your life is Stone, and you serve only Stone. Welcome."

With that, he pulled Aron into a brief embrace to seal the contract. Aron shoved the man away from him.

Dunstan Stormbreaker chuckled as he lifted his cowl with one hand. Then he doubled the force of his grip on Aron's wrist and dragged him from the yard, down the dirt path, straight toward where Windblown waited with Tek.

Aron stumbled and fought even though he knew the penalties. If he fled the service of the guild before or after his formal oaths, if he broke the Code of Eyrie, he would be hunted by Stone Brothers and Stone Sisters and lords alike, until he was captured, thrown into a wagon of the accused, and sent back to Stone to be judged.

But Aron didn't care.

He wanted to stay on his farm. He wanted to follow the plan of his life, just laid out only the day before. He wanted to run back to his family. By the dark face of the horned god, he wanted to see them, just see them, one more time!

Stormbreaker moved him like a relentless force, no matter how hard Aron kicked at him.

"You have no choice, boy," was all he said.

Aron wondered if he could kill these three in their sleep. He could steal their swords easily enough, for surely they unstrapped the blades before they slept. But what of the daggers?

Damnable hard to account for all those quills . . .

Still, if he could succeed, it might be weeks before the Stone Guild realized that this Harvest party wasn't returning. Aron could be gone far to the east by then, maybe even safe behind the walls of the Thorn Guild, the one place no Stone Brother or Stone Sister had authority.

But would the Thorn Guild shelter a murderer? By the Code of Eyrie, surely not. They would hand him back to Stone, too.

Aron swore to himself as Stormbreaker forced him toward Tek.

"May the Brother save us from Brailings and their stubborn, evil tempers." Windblown twisted around in his saddle, as if expecting bandits to burst from the woods. "You're daft for doing this much, Dun. Let's put this farm at our backs, and now."

Stormbreaker hefted Aron and jammed him onto Tek's back just above her small, folded wings, drawing a chirp and squeak of distress from the little talon. She stood to her full height, barely taller than the Stone Brothers—and only a third the size of the two bulls. With another squeak, she stretched her withered foreclaws in an attempt to look menacing, but when she stomped her clawfeet, they barely stirred the dust.

Stormbreaker ignored Tek's posturing. With expert hands and help from Zed, he lashed Aron's legs to Tek's sides, securing them with a loop around Tek's useless foreclaws. He then used softer straps to bind Aron's hands to Tek's lead rope.

Aron struggled against the bindings, but found them firm and tight. The more he struggled, the tighter they became. He could not move more than a few inches. He couldn't even turn toward his home one last time, to see if his parents or his brothers or sisters stood vigil for him.

Not my brothers and sisters anymore. Not my home. I've been disowned. The vows have been spoken by the guild master who Harvested me. I'm of Stone now, by the letter of the Code.

But the heat of his father's gaze yet lingered in Aron's memory.

Wolf had followed the law in deed, but certainly not in his heart. Even as he had spoken against Aron, his expression gainsaid the words.

Aron felt that odd pressure against his mind again. *You will always be my son, Aron Brailing of Brailing. You will always be my son.*

Aron's stomach lurched, and once more, he tried to look back toward his home. This time, he managed to catch a glimpse of his father, who was now standing alone near the hog pen, glaring at the Stone Brothers. The sight made Aron's heart thunder with joy. Such a small thing, to ignore custom and watch the departure of those sent—or damned—to Stone. But his father ignored it nonetheless, and Aron knew Wolf

Brailing wanted him to know he still mattered, that he was still the son of his father, his mother, still brother to his brothers and sisters.

The boy Zed snickered as Stormbreaker fastened Tek's lead rope to the lead rope of his own talon. "He doesn't give up, that one. Do you see him standing there? We may have to fight our way off this land."

I will kill that northern brat first, Aron thought. *Arrogant stream of mocker piss.*

Stormbreaker's hands stilled on Aron's wrists as he glanced toward the farm.

"Leave the man to his grief and tell him no more," said Wind-blown. "The risk is too great. He could attack you for taking the boy— or worse yet, others might come before we leave, and we'll be hauled back to face Lord Brailing."

A second passed, but only one. Then Stormbreaker turned Aron loose and gave Windblown a look Aron couldn't read. "When Stone forgets truth and decency, all of us are lost."

Windblown started to argue with him, but Stormbreaker strode away from him and the talons, back toward the hog pen.

"Dunstan!" Windblown's bellow might have lifted dust off the road.

Stormbreaker didn't turn around.

Aron's heart pounded harder.

Would the Stone Brother draw weapons? Would he force Wolf Brailing to turn his back on his son again? Would his father decide to fight for him after all?

Stormbreaker made no move, however. He simply stopped in front of Wolf, extended his right arm, and pushed up his sleeve.

Aron couldn't make out the details of his father's face, but he knew the magnitude of that frown. Wolf studied Stormbreaker's *dav'ha*, then shoved his own sleeve up, held out his right arm, and dropped it to his side.

Stormbreaker raised his hands as he spoke, as if measuring time or distance—and a very small amount. Then he pointed to the house and back to the wagon.

"No!" Wolf Brailing bellowed. Aron's eyes widened as his father stepped back, beat his hand against his chest once, and shouted curses. Without so much as another glance in Aron's direction, Wolf spun toward his house and ran for the door.

What in the name of . . . ? Aron shifted his weight to keep his eyes on his father, but Tek stomped, and Zed gave her lead a tug and turned her away as Stormbreaker hurriedly returned. Stormbreaker mounted with abrupt movements. He didn't look at Aron. He made no comment, but Windblown couldn't seem to keep his own counsel.

"Brother protect us," he murmured, sounding both horrified and angry. "I cannot believe you did that."

Stormbreaker's glare was swift as he raised his arm and once more bared some of his impressive *dav'ha* marks. "What choice did I have?"

"Think on that," Windblown snapped. "The Lord Provost may ask you the answer before he sends you to judgment for interfering in a dynast's affairs."

Aron leaned away from Stormbreaker even though the brutal stare wasn't meant for him. Windblown looked about to lose his temper completely, but he didn't say anything else. Wise, Aron thought.

For a brief but notable moment, Stormbreaker, Windblown, and Zed looked north and east up the road, in the direction from which they had come.

Aron had the disquieting impression that they expected to see something—and not something desirable. The day now seemed oddly still and silent, but for the blowing of the talons and the snorts and grunts of the mules.

Stormbreaker spoke quietly, yet with urgency. "Move out."

That fast, Aron found himself using his knees, elbows, and bound hands to cling to Tek as they thundered away from the Brailing farm.

CHAPTER FIVE

ARON

Aron had no time to consider what had passed between Stormbreaker and his father. Most of his strength and focus went to keeping his seat on Tek and trying to determine his options.

As he expected, they headed north and west, toward Triune, the ancient castle of the Stone Guild, rumored to be the worst place in all of Eyrie. It sat on the boundary of Dyn Brailing at the top of the Watchline, in the cursed spot where Barrens joined Outlands and the mists of the Deadfall pressed upward from the farthest reaches of Dyn Ross. The land around Triune was filled with mockers and manes and other abominations from the mixing disasters. Once they got him to that forsaken stronghold, he would have no way to escape.

When will they take my Brailing cheville *and chain my essence to my body with one of dead gray?*

Aron clenched his fists around his bindings. He had to get free and take Tek with him, no matter how fast they were moving. No matter the consequences. He couldn't, he *wouldn't* join with these murderers. So his task was simple enough. Aron, once of Brailing and temporarily of Stone, needed to escape before their traveling party got too far from the Watchline.

He slowed his breathing and tried to relax into Tek's herky-jerk lurches. After a few minutes, he found he could rock himself slightly without damaging his wrists, flow with the little talon's movements. Good. All the better for meditation. All the better for focus.

Just as he found the edges of peace and began to slip through the Veil, something in the wagon farthest from him set up a fierce kicking and high-pitched ranting. The sound startled him so badly he cut his wrists on his bonds as he jumped.

Windblown let out a breath, beating Stormbreaker by the barest second.

"Joy from the Brother himself," Zed said in a dreary voice. "She's awake."

The shrieks in the back wagon grew louder and angrier.

Stormbreaker withdrew a pouch from his leather bag. "Hurry. We've got no time to lose."

He tossed the bag to Zed without looking. The boy caught it easily as Stormbreaker and Windblown slowed their talons, then stopped the big beasts. Stormbreaker turned his mount toward the back wagon, pulling Tek's lead until Aron faced it as well.

The buckboard tethered behind the front wagon, the one Aron had thought to be empty, actually contained several bundles that looked like supplies and a large blanket with a thrashing lump beneath it. From the lump came sharp shouts that had to be curses. Aron still didn't recognize the accent or the words, but the intent was clear enough.

Zed and Windblown dismounted, removed their visible weapons, and climbed into the back wagon.

"On my count," Windblown said, and gave a hand signal Aron couldn't interpret.

Zed nodded, but he looked nervous.

"Sun," Windblown muttered. "Stars. Moons."

At "moons," Zed yanked off the blanket and Windblown reached forward and grabbed the girl, Aron assumed by the head. He couldn't see much for the big man's girth.

Windblown's curses joined with the girl's, and Zed's too.

Aron saw a flash of ebony hair. Then he saw bound hands strike out, nails first. Tethered feet swung like a club.

Yes! Aron leaned forward on Tek as much as his own ropes allowed. *Beat them. Hurt them!*

Zed managed to upend the pouch.

A few seconds later, the girl stopped fighting. Windblown and Zed covered her again before Aron could catch a glimpse of her face, then climbed out of the back wagon and collected their weapons. Windblown was bleeding from his cheek and hand. Zed had a burgeoning bruise on his jaw.

"Are you sure she doesn't belong with one of those Watchline families?" Windblown grumbled as he mounted his talon. "She acts like a Brailing."

Stormbreaker shook his head. "That hair—and her skin. Dark as middle-night on the new moons. She's a Ross pigeon, or I'm a mocker."

"Yeah, well, I've long had my suspicions about you." Windblown rubbed his bloody cheek. "Next time you put the rock cat back to sleep."

Aron tried to keep looking in the back wagon, but Tek turned away from it.

They started on their way again, moving up the Dyn Brailing byway faster than he thought possible. Yet onward they went. Hour by hour, they left the settled countryside behind—and the land Aron had roamed most of his life. Farther and farther he plunged with Tek, into unfamiliar territory, and he could do nothing to stop their relentless progress.

The Stone Brothers seemed to be intent on covering league after league, even at the expense of bumps and jostles. As trees grew more dense, Stormbreaker checked over his shoulder more and more frequently. Heartwoods and pines alike crowded the edges of the road. Smells changed from loam and manure to the tang of evergreen needles, moss, and sweetly rotting wood. Aron glanced into the thick depths now and again, checking for mockers even though he knew he was helpless to fight. Did these fools know what lurked in the woods so near the Watchline? Why did they look behind them, as if danger came only from the road? Didn't they know what could leap out at them from the trees?

If so, they didn't seem to care.

He ground his teeth together over and over, then tried once more to catch a glimpse of the blanket or the girl beneath it. Who was she? Why were these dirt-eaters keeping her prisoner? Had she been Harvested like him?

She couldn't be a child-criminal or an incorrigible, could she?

Perhaps she ran away from Harvest and Stone caught her already.

If she were a Ross, what was she doing so far from home? Could she have run that far, or escaped from a Stone Brother after traveling some distance?

Except for their representatives in Dyn Mab, members of the Ross dynast weren't known to venture into other dynasts. When they married out of dynast, it was usually with Dyn Vagrat to the east, where the Thorn Guild sheltered.

"Don't fear for our guest, Aron Frosteye," Stormbreaker said as if tracking Aron's thoughts. "We don't judge children. We have our own laws, or tenets, from the Canon of Stone, as you will learn."

Aron made a last effort to look into the back wagon. Dust from the bull talon's stomping clawfeet obscured his view. He sniffed and coughed as his eyes watered.

If only he could communicate with the girl, form some plan with her, his odds of escaping might increase. Hope flared deep in his chest, and the tension in his muscles eased again. The rhythm of Tek's strides settled in his bones, along with the four-footed beat of the mules' hooves and the creaking of wagon wheels.

Perhaps he could make his mind still. Concentrate. Perhaps Aron could reach for what his father taught him, and find some answers on the other side of the Veil—but as it had all day, the calm state of mind, the meditative place where thought flowed easily—eluded him.

League after league, he grew only more exhausted as the Stone Brothers led them forward. In desperation, he eased his mind with thoughts of making a clean escape, perhaps all the way to the Thorn Guild. He imagined how the Lady Provost there might look, young and beautiful, with his mother's kindness and the fierceness of his little sisters. She might help him. Surely she would.

Darkness fell in increments, first taking the brighter light of the sun, then coloring the byways and ever-thicker stands of trees an unwelcoming gray. Stormbreaker pushed the party even harder, noting the distance they had to make before full night, and Aron began to shiver with worry. He had never been caught out at night. His father was far too good a teacher to allow that mistake. Back at home—it *was* his home, it *was*—Wolf would be penning and protecting the stock and making certain all of his children were finishing their tasks with time to spare.

Hours turned into more hours. As the day's light waned, Aron's captors drove their party north and east into even thicker forest, where the byway narrowed to not much more than a packed dirt path, barely wide enough to accommodate the wagons.

Aron's nostrils flared against the rising dust. His wrists grew bloody from struggling against his bonds. His legs ached. His eyes burned, and he was so thirsty his tongue stuck against his teeth. Beneath him, Tek trudged ever forward, flanked by the bull talons carrying the Stone Brothers. Behind them, Zed whistled to himself as he steered the wagons around ruts and mudfalls.

The Brothers spoke for a time about supplies and best routes back to the Stone Guild stronghold, but Aron noted a semblance of tension between them. He watched first Stormbreaker on his left, then Windblown on his right. Every time Stormbreaker glanced away, Windblown turned his attention to Aron.

He follows his master, but he doesn't want me here. Aron resisted glaring at the man. He tried to act like he didn't notice the looks, or the lesser Brother's obvious discomfort. After a time, conversation grew louder and more relaxed, and Stormbreaker and Windblown discussed the flight of the passerines, the misfortune of the line of Mab, and what might happen to Eyrie if the hob-prince took the throne and the Circle's seventh vote.

"Better a Mab of Mab than the chaos of arguing succession rights," Windblown observed. "I wouldn't want to see a thronemaking with no Mab to take the chair."

Stormbreaker agreed, and they fell to debating which dynast lord might attack Dyn Mab if the last heir died. Windblown had his money on Lord Brailing, who had always wished to restore Brailing to the power of its bygone years—not to mention reclaim land lost to its neighbors Dyn Cobb and Dyn Altar during the mixing disasters. Stormbreaker disagreed, and reminded Windblown of the line of Lek, yet to recover from Mab swallowing their dynast whole, even though that was centuries ago.

"You're both mad," Zed announced, urging his mule to keep the pace. "I've met Lord Ross, and if ever a man was destined to be high king, it's him."

"Dyn Ross is too far away to send its guardsmen against Mab," Windblown said, and Aron didn't like his dismissive tone. "Even pushing an army at full run, it would take Ross the better part of a year to mass a force on Mab's border."

Zed leaned forward to make himself heard. "Not the lower border, the eastern line they share with Dyn Vagrat."

At this, Windblown actually laughed. "The Thorn Guild would never give free passage to war-makers. The Lady Provost would shed her hair if they even dared to seek permission, and you know Lady Vagrat won't fight anyone over anything."

At the mention of Lady Vagrat, Stormbreaker grimaced and looked away.

What if the armies don't seek permission? Aron wanted to ask the question so badly he almost spoke. *What if Ross simply marches and dares Thorn to stop them? What can a bunch of healers and scholars do against legions of armed men?*

"The Sabor might join Ross," Zed said, louder now. "The Sabor used to fight, in older days."

"Never happen," Windblown insisted. "The Sabor value their own blue hides too much to take up arms in a common conflict."

"But if they did, what a conflict!" Stormbreaker sounded fascinated by the thought. "The outcome would be anyone's guess."

Windblown made no reply for a few paces, then laughed as Zed whistled and agreed with Stormbreaker. The conversation turned to sword tactics on the battlefield.

Aron kept his teeth firmly clamped to hold back a stream of cursing. He would not speak. He would not cry. His gaze drifted toward the dense trees, then to the wagon carrying the girl. He also couldn't afford to be drugged senseless like that Ross pigeon.

As for the men, how could they chatter so? And Zed—how could he be so full of his own wisdom? The arrogant boy probably blabbered about fighting and battles to hide his misery.

What right did killers have to converse so freely?

Silence born of shame would be more fitting. Even though the Code of Eyrie permitted sanctioned killings, common decency raged against such atrocities.

"Would you like a drink, boy?" Windblown asked, cutting into Aron's silent rage. The Stone Brother sounded so cheerful Aron despised him for it.

No matter his hot, sticky tongue, Aron gave no answer. His fisted fingers dug into his palms and he doubled his efforts to tear free of the bonds that lashed him to Tek. She trilled in response to his unrest, causing the bull talons to sidestep and snort. Windblown muttered something to his beast when the brute stretched its murderous foreclaws. The big talon calmed slowly, returning to his typical rhythmic stride.

"Keep your female calm. If you cannot manage her I'll sell her or turn her free." Stormbreaker's manner was maddeningly like that of Aron's father, as was his matter-of-fact law-speaking. Aron realized the man was accustomed to being obeyed without question. Such was the discipline of Stone, if the legends and tales could be believed.

Aron turned his attention to Tek. He whistled to her to soothe her, then hummed and did his best to stroke the leathery scales covering her withers.

Easy, he thought to her, as if she might hear him. *Do you wish for these fools to take you from me and leave you to fend for yourself in the Watchline forests?*

Tek gave a snotty, noisy blow, then settled in again, jerking along beside the big talons, taking two steps for every one footfall of the massive males.

At twilight, in a spot where heartwoods crushed against the byway's thin dirt borders, they came to a small divide in the road. Stormbreaker stopped them, dismounted from his talon, and set about checking their position using the sliver of sky above the road to view the emerging stars. In his hands were a map and a dirty piece of twine.

Aron took a deep breath and coughed at the sharp tang of pine. He had heard of maps from his father, but he had never seen one. He leaned over Tek's back to squint at the parchment, which had marks and lines and shapes, some of which looked like they might actually rise up for his fingers to brush. His throbbing hands ached to take the paper, to explore it for himself and see if he could match it to the stars.

Windblown chatted affably with Zed, who held the lead for Stormbreaker's riderless talon. Stormbreaker's fingers moved around the map, stretching the string. He paused, and Aron realized the man had caught him watching. He straightened himself and looked away.

"Curiosity is a virtue," Stormbreaker said in low, encouraging tones.

Aron heard the echo of his father's voice in his mind. *Curiosity is for mockers and magpies. Labor is the truest virtue.*

When Aron didn't respond or look at him, Stormbreaker continued anyway. "Stone has cartographers who trained in the trade lodges."

Aron couldn't stop himself from whipping around and giving the Stone Brother an incredulous glance.

Stormbreaker's green eyes seemed alight in the gloaming, and his smile was gentle. "Stone Brothers and Sisters move freely in Eyrie, even in Dyn Vagrat, as you can tell by my appearance. We Harvest in all six dynasts. We abstain only from the island of Eidolon, where the Thorn Guild makes its home—and their guildhouses in other cities, of course."

Aron wasn't certain, but he thought some sort of darkness had passed across Stormbreaker's face at the mention of Thorn, but Aron's attention wouldn't linger on that point. New questions were forming too quickly in his mind. He had never been to a Can—a great city—to know if Stone, too, had guildhouses in other places. Had his father mentioned them? But then, his father rarely spoke of Stone—only of Thorn, and the kind, brilliant, old Lady Provost he had met on his travels during his Guard service.

So perhaps Stone didn't hide only at Triune, scurrying out to assassinate the Judged or steal children during Harvest. Did they keep a larger presence in dynast Cans? What about smaller towns and villages? Even out on the farm, his father had taught Aron it was polite to avert his gaze if a wagon passed by on the road loaded with accused bound for the judgment of Stone, or the ailing and dying off to seek Stone's cruel mercies. It would make sense that the monsters had guildhouses so such people need not travel great distances, but if Stone was everywhere, how would Aron ever escape them?

Faster than Aron thought possible, Dunstan Stormbreaker strode forward and seemed to tower over Aron even though Aron was still mounted and tied to Tek. Stormbreaker's eyes glowed brilliant green, and Aron thought he could see streaks of yellow fire dancing in the frightening depths.

"I will give you another hour of tolerance, but after that, no more disrespect. You'll speak to me when I speak to you. Is that understood?"

Aron glowered right back at him, loud eyes and all. What could the monster do to make him talk?

Light from Eyrie's twinned silvery-blue moons flowed across the byway like splashes of molten ore.

"You may begin slowly, with simple yeas or nays, using my proper title, which is High Master."

It took force of will for Aron to bite back his gasp. So this man Dunstan Stormbreaker was one of the seven high masters of Stone, the equivalent in rank of a true dynast heir. One day, he might become Lord Provost of the Stone Guild—and he had chosen Aron as his apprentice?

Why?

The question tried to force its way out, but Windblown interrupted.

"Darkness presses too close—not to mention these woods, Dun. Should we take the right fork or the left—or should we stay here and climb trees for the night?"

Stormbreaker held Aron's stare for another few seconds, then shifted his attention to his companion and Zed. "Left fork. According to my map, there's a shelter less than a league ahead, and we can sleep with the talons and mules protected. When we top the small hill before us, we should see it in the valley."

Aron could have answered the Stone Brother and Zed, but he didn't. If a mane attacked and rendered all of them bloodless husks, it would serve the Stone Brothers right.

They crested the hill, still hugged tightly by trees on either side of the byway, and a high, shrill cry knifed out of the unseen forest depths. Gooseflesh flared along Aron's shoulders and arms.

That was no mane, but almost as bad. A rock cat on the hunt.

Aron's heart began a frantic pound. He cast about desperately, judging his surroundings as Tek bounced beneath him and clucked her distress. Down the hill on his right, maybe a quarter-league, firelight blazed from what could only be a travelers' shelter, so large and so close to the road, and well mounted on sturdy, thick poles the height of three men standing foot to shoulder. It had what looked to be a stone and wood barn, landbound, probably cornered with pyres for the safety of the beasts at night. Between Aron's party and the shelter walked another group, larger, maybe ten travelers in all, most of them children. In places, trees hung so close branches seemed to touch their shoulders.

At the sound of the rock cat's howl, the adults began herding the smaller ones toward the widening of the byway and the safety of the shelter.

"Stop!" Aron cried before he thought better of it. The sound tore at his dry throat, and had no force behind it.

Tek lurched forward against her tether to Stormbreaker's talon. "Be still!" Aron croaked. "Give them no movement to sense!"

But it was far too late for such warnings.

Moonslight or no, mockers and manes—and in this area of Eyrie, rock cats—ruled the night.

CHAPTER SIX

ARON

Tek shrilled as a massive rock cat slunk out of the absolute darkness of the trees on Aron's left. And another. And another. More. Aron couldn't see their tawny coloring, but he knew them well from many near encounters. Even in the dark, he could make out the heavily muscled, wickedly clawed forepaws, and his mind supplied the thick fangs hanging over bearded chins flecked with blood and drool.

"Brother of Many Faces, have mercy," Zed murmured. "A pack." He started to climb down from his mule, but Stormbreaker stopped him with a gesture.

Many yards below them on the byway, the children started to scream and scatter. The lead cat bounded forward, snatched the smallest and slowest of the little ones, and shook it like a helpless cloth doll. A woman, presumably the child's mother, wailed.

Aron's stomach twisted at the sound. If he had taken any water or food, he would have lost it. As it was, bitter fluid surged up his throat.

"Zed, stay with the wagons and see to the girl and Aron." Stormbreaker drew a toothy broadsword and hacked through the lead tethering Tek with one stroke. "Keep his talon safe if you can; cut him loose and cover him in the wagon if you can't."

Before Aron could say a word, Zed had Tek's lead and Stormbreaker and Windblown had swords at the ready. They let out an undulating cry that frightened Aron almost as much as the rock cats, but he had heard of such. He knew what they were doing—goading the bull talons into a frenzy.

The big males needed little prompting. Hungry and no doubt fierce of temper from their long travels, they bellowed in response, and the long, sharp scales at their necks lifted to form battle rings around their massive heads.

The rock cats halted their charge toward the remaining travelers and wheeled to defend themselves. Aron counted twelve—no, wait. Fifteen! Even with talons, the Stone Brothers had no chance against such numbers.

His breath caught hard, a weight in his chest. If the rock cats slaughtered the men, Aron would be free . . . but the rock cats would eat the travelers, too, and likely Zed, Aron, Tek, the girl, and the mules as well.

How could Aron escape?

Even if he found a tall enough tree to climb, one of the smaller cats might be able to leap high enough to snag him.

Stormbreaker and Windblown thundered toward the ruthless predators, shouting even as their bull talons bellowed. Dust rose and scattered in the moonlight. Windblown's beast unfolded powerful wings and flapped, lifting off the ground just high enough to escape the lead cat's leap. Talons couldn't fly high, but they could stay aloft for a few seconds, about double a normal man's height, and the ability gave them an advantage in most battles. Windblown shouted with triumph as his talon landed on another rock cat, crushing it in its tracks.

The pungent smell of blood and excrement flooded up the hill. Aron choked against the stench, but kept his gaze firmly on the battle.

Stormbreaker's talon stayed landbound as he roared around the pack, cutting off access to the travelers who had fallen down screaming with fear.

"Go!" he commanded to the distraught woman, who was futilely tugging at the dead child. Stormbreaker cut down a leaping cat only a hand's width from his leg. "Get inside now. You there, in the shelter—help them!"

His snarling talon reached down and snatched up a rock cat with his powerful jaws. Aron's heart hammered as the beast broke the cat like a thin stick, then threw it aside to eat later.

Four down, but still so many up and attacking, snarling, digging into the ground and launching themselves at the Stone Brothers and the furious winged lizards.

Aron's thoughts whirled with the growing cloud of dust that shifted and glittered in the moonlight. One moment, he was praying for the Stone Brothers, and the next, hoping they died horribly. He thought about goading Tek. She could rip her lead from Zed's hands without much difficulty—but there Aron would be, bound and helpless, fleeing into the woods and likely straight into the paws and jaws of more rock cats and the Brother only knew what else.

Down the byway, Windblown rode out of the swirling dust and skewered a cat with each sword, then used his heels to kick the corpses off the blades. He barely got his feet stirrupped before his talon took flight again, just in time to avoid the murderous claws of a third cat. Zed hooted his appreciation. Aron was too afraid to scream, hoot, or curse.

Stormbreaker emerged from the cloud and attempted to drive the pack remnants back toward Aron and Zed and the wagons, away from the helpless travelers, but he was having little fortune in that respect. At least the frightened people were moving now, running toward the shelter—and other travelers already safe inside were lowering the steps for them to enter.

Tek's neck scales flipped up in a battle ring and she trumpeted as one of the rock cats barreled toward them. Her weak foreclaws slashed out, and her pitiful wings stretched as if to lift her little body skyward, but Aron knew she didn't have a hope of success.

The sound of his own shouts filled his ears. The world seemed to move too slowly as that cat got closer, closer. Aron could see its gleaming eyes, feel the rip of its teeth. His shouts turned into screams of rage and frustration as he yanked against his tethers.

Windblown saw the attack coming, shouted to Zed, but Zed had already mounted the front wagon. As the cat approached, before it got close enough to Tek to draw blood, Zed hacked through the bonds on Aron's hands and stuffed a slim dagger into Aron's numb, blood-covered fingers.

"Keep the girl alive or answer to me," Zed shouted, and flung himself at the charging rock cat.

The cat roared.

Zed roared louder, and Aron gaped as the boy tackled the cat and rolled with it back down the hill. He shook his head to clear his senses, then cursed and fumbled to release the ties on his feet. His jaw clenched. The knot was too tight. His fingers felt clumsy and useless and he almost dropped the dagger as he sawed it back and forth. If one of those cats attacked, he was finished, and Tek along with him.

He had to get loose. Now. *Now!* Drifting dust made him cough, and the awful stench of gore kept his eyes tearing. Still he worked, and worked fast, sawing, pushing, cutting through the rope.

Farther down the road, the bull talons shrieked as rock cats slashed at their tender flanks. Aron heard the bloody sounds of sword work. At last he managed to cut the remaining tie on his foot. When he jerked upward, he had to push up on Tek's neck to see over her battle ring.

Only two rock cats remained standing. Zed picked himself up from the carcass of the cat he battled. In the swelling moonlight, Aron saw dark stains all over the boy.

Zed's blood? The cat's?

No matter. Aron knew he could make a run for it now, but Tek's agitation had to be calmed. He tried to whistle to her, soothe her—and then he saw what troubled her. Fear and exhilaration flowed into abject terror, and Aron froze in place, not daring to move.

More rock cats circled the bull talons.

Only, too big. More like small oxen than anything feline, and not right in proportion. The heads were overlarge, and the paws seemed misshapen, almost clublike.

Zed raised his long dagger in victory, then, at a hand signal from Windblown, raced back up the hill toward Aron and the wagons. Aron was vaguely aware of something slipping away—his best opportunity for escape—but he couldn't take his eyes off the unnatural rock cats.

Dust settled slowly back to the ground, revealing more and more of their tense, muscled frames.

The talons treated them with great wariness.

Beneath Aron's legs and hands, Tek trembled. Aron trembled with her.

Zed reached the wagons, saw Aron's face and Tek's posture, and whirled, long dagger raised.

"Mockers," Aron managed to whisper. "Two of them."

"Brother of Many Faces, have mercy." Zed lowered his dagger, ran the rest of the way to the wagons, climbed aboard, and put his hand on Aron's shoulder.

On the byway, the rock cats began to change.

Aron huddled on Tek's back as Zed shrank into the wagon.

The largest mocker cat took on the shape of a man with hooked nails as long as a talon's neck scales. His screech of rage made Aron's teeth slam together. The smaller rock cat took on a man-shape as well, more feminine—and this one had wings.

"Wings," Zed babbled. "It flies."

"Hush." Aron elbowed him. "They might sound-hunt as well as using their eyes and noses."

"But it has wings," Zed whispered. "They don't have wings, the ones around Triune. I've never seen a mocker with wings."

Aron had.

He had seen winged mockers before, and *all* of them had been able to spit. Their venom could flay a man, or blind him, or eat the scales off a talon. The last mocker he had encountered at home was a little one, just a crow—but its man-form had wings, and it had killed one of his hogs with a single jet from its fetid mouth.

Tek flinched as if in response to the image.

Aron sucked in a breath.

Did the Stone Brothers know about winged mockers? If they didn't . . .

If they didn't, this could all be finished in seconds. The Stone Brothers and their talons would be dead, and Aron could take on Zed and free himself, Tek, and the girl.

The winged mocker circled Windblown.

Part of Aron's mind screamed for the mocker to attack, to dissolve the Stone Brother and his talon, too. The other part of Aron's mind rebelled against that viciousness. Windblown was a living being, and his talon—did the brave, powerful animal deserve such a death?

Windblown stabbed at the mocker. With a flap of its wings, it shot backward out of his reach.

Aron saw its neck arch, and he knew what was coming.

"It can spit!" he managed to yell. "Winged mockers can spit venom!"

Windblown's head snapped upward. He jerked his talon sideways, and the beast leaped away from the winged mocker just as it—she— spat.

The venom landed on the dead child and sizzled.

Aron's stomach wrenched. After seeing what happened to his hog, he knew there would be nothing left of that little one for the mother to burn and scatter.

Windblown charged forward on his talon before the winged mocker could spit again, and he slashed at her.

She evaded. Spat again. This time the venom struck the dirt road, and once more Aron saw steam rise from the spot.

"Hit her in the wings!" he yelled, slicing the air with his fist as if Windblown could see him. "Bring her down!"

Windblown's talon danced and lunged. The winged mocker spat twice more, almost landing both streams on the beast's clawfeet. The talon trumpeted. Aron nudged Tek's sides with his heels, and she answered the bull with a high-pitched whistle.

The winged mocker turned to track the new sound.

With a thrust and hack, Windblown sheered off one of the distracted monster's wings. It shrilled and spat toward the stars, searing nothing but air and grass and dirt. It tried to turn, but Windblown leaned forward and took the mocker's head with a clean stroke.

Next to the carnage, the clawed mocker swiped at Stormbreaker and leaped. Stormbreaker yanked his mount out of harm's way. Windblown shouted and stabbed at the mocker's back. It whirled on him, and Stormbreaker jerked upward on his talon's reins. The big bull leaped into the air with a powerful flap of its wings.

Without a cloud in the bright night sky, lightning blazed directly over the talon. Thunder rattled the night and seemed to pound against Aron's head.

Stormbreaker bellowed with the talon when it landed, and together, man and beast crushed the clawed mocker into bones and blood.

Aron turned his head away from that sight, and kept it turned as the Stone Brothers allowed their talons the noisy reward of feeding on their kills. His skin felt clammy. So many rock cats—and led by mockers? He had never heard of mockers hunting with pure animals. His mind whirled like that flock of passerines he had seen earlier in the day. Dead heirs. The throne destined for the hob-prince. Mockers consorting with animals. And a Brailing of Brailing Harvested by the Stone Guild.

Elhalla.

Curse fate and its turning, too.

What was happening in Eyrie?

Zed gave a little yelp, and Aron jerked his eyes upward to see Stormbreaker and Windblown charging back up the hill. Wild energy roiled from Stormbreaker, almost as if the man towed a thunderstorm in his wake—and there *was* lightning, real lightning, from a cloudless sky!

For a moment, the lightning struck in all directions. Then it drew toward Stormbreaker, blasting holes in the ground and burning the bark off of nearby trees.

Aron felt his hair lift off his head. He leaned back in spite of himself, and Tek took a nervous step backward as well. From the back wagon, the unconscious girl let out a low moan of terror.

"Don't worry," said Zed in a quiet, almost friendly voice. "He's just provoked from the battle and worry over us. Stormbreaker would never use his legacy to harm another living creature."

When Aron turned to look at the boy, who was stripping off his garments, Zed shrugged and added, "Just the sight of it scares everyone so badly, I've never known him to have to."

Aron closed his eyes and set his jaw.

With his hands and feet unbound, he could turn Tek around and run for the trees—but if he fled now, Stormbreaker could cut him down with a single bolt of that unnatural lightning.

A legacy that allows him to tamper with natural elements? What is he?

None of the six dynasts boasted that power as part of a legacy. It must be a bastard talent, some freak occurrence reaching back to the mixing disasters.

But it's dangerous. More than dangerous! Why was he allowed to live?

Because he had never used it to harm another living creature, as Zed said. The question answered itself. Stormbreaker contained his talent and never used it, even when it would give him great advantage. Too great was the danger it might escape his control.

Yet there is always a first time. . . .

Aron opened his eyes as Stormbreaker and Windblown reached the wagons. The lightning was nothing but sparks now, fading into Stormbreaker's lean, muscled frame. With his cowl lying about his shoulders, his wild hair seemed more yellow than white, and his eerie green eyes blazing, Stormbreaker looked as feral and dangerous as the rock cats he had killed.

"Are you injured?" Stormbreaker asked Aron immediately, even as Windblown, sweat-soaked and still breathing hard, guided his talon toward the back wagon.

"No, High Master," Aron murmured.

The words simply came out, with no thought to hold them back. Spots still danced before Aron's eyes, crystalline and unnerving, in the shape of lightning bolts. He could never overpower such a man. Tears pressed against his eyes, but Aron held them back even as he forced himself to meet Stormbreaker's gaze. How could he escape a villain who could set the very clouds and thunder to track him, and rain and lightning to pound him into the mud until captors could reach him?

Stormbreaker remained silent for a moment, as if hearing every hopeless thought in Aron's troubled mind. When the High Master spoke, his tone was genuine. "Thank you for your warning, Frosteye, and for using Tek to help us in battle. You have a gallant heart as well as a quick mind."

Aron wanted to vomit. He lowered his head and sat in silence, throat closing against the reek of battle blood and talon oil. The big winged lizards excreted a slick, odorous film on their scales when roused to frenzy. He had no doubt Tek was covered in the slime, too, and it smelled no better than a rabbit dead two days and left in the sun. The two males would clean themselves, but Tek— Aron sighed. He usually had to lead her into a stream and wipe her down.

"Intact," Windblown announced, pounding Zed on the back. "Just a scratch or two. You had me worried, boy."

Zed had finished removing his battle-soiled clothes. He stood naked in the back wagon beside the sleeping girl while Windblown bent down, reached over the wagon's side, and retrieved a gray tunic and some breeches from the supply bundles. He handed them to Zed like a prize for a task well done.

Zed dressed with haste, stopping only to ask, "Will we be sheltering, or will the travelers close us out?"

"We'll shelter," Windblown said. "They'll put down the steps, or we'll climb up. I've no mind to spend the night with mockers and manes." He tossed a glance at Aron. "Or wild Brailings."

Stormbreaker's snort sounded like that of a talon. He grabbed Tek's lead and turned them all toward the shelter and the barn. "Take Zed and the girl and go inside, Osfred. Tell them she's ill, or exhausted. Tell them whatever you like. That mother who lost a child will need soothing, maybe even a sleeping draft. Aron and I will tend to the beasts and keep watch, and we'll manage whatever comes."

Aron looked up sharply.

Was Stormbreaker suggesting they would spend the night outside the shelter? If so, the Stone Brother was two leagues beyond mad.

Even Windblown seemed put off by such crazy talk. "Are you sure, Dun? The boy's newly taken."

Stormbreaker's jewel-bright eyes fixed on Aron as he spoke. "Did he not help us in battle?"

"But—" Windblown protested as Aron squirmed on Tek's back, all too aware of the High Master's stern gaze.

"He might hate us, yes." Stormbreaker's interruption completely silenced Windblown and stilled Zed, who held his fingers against the laces of his tunic.

"But Aron Frosteye has shown us two important things," Stormbreaker continued. "First, he possesses courage. Second and more important, life—even ours—has meaning to him. Those virtues will see us through tonight's task, I think."

CHAPTER SEVEN

ARON

On the talon side of the landbound barn, the floor was littered with chunks of goat jerky Stormbreaker had used to feed Tek. Aron stood on a stool inside the smallest talon stall, washing the smelly secretions from Tek's neck scales. Reflections of lamplight flickered in the basin of water Stormbreaker had brought him. Sweat coated Aron's face and arms, but he wasn't hot or winded. It felt so unnatural to be outside safe quarters in the darkness that his own heart seemed to be trying to climb out of his body.

Each time the barn creaked, Tek squeaked and Aron almost jumped out of his skin. The bull talons snorted and rattled against the chains securing their stone stalls, but overall, the big males were peaceful.

Aron was not.

A few minutes before, after tending the bulls, Stormbreaker had gone through the large wooden gates in the wall separating horse-side from talon-side, to put up the mules beside the few packhorses in for the night. Now, though the Stone Brother was only on the other side of the structure, behind gates and a wooden wall erected to keep talons and horses separate, Aron felt absolutely alone. His muscles ached. His knees trembled. His fingers and wrists tingled from cuts and bruises earned fighting his bindings on the ride, and blood still streaked his filthy arms. Worse still, his stomach fairly ached from hunger.

"Make haste," came Stormbreaker's muffled command through the wall. "We have much to do before middle-night. Come horse-side when you've secured your beast."

Aron ground his teeth.

The man was completely mad, no question.

Would he take them outside to dance naked in front of a horde of manes? Better yet, perhaps he had some extra jerky to attract rock cats and mockers.

Aron scooted the stool around, washed Tek's face, and gazed into the fiery red of her lidless eyes. A membrane slipped up, then down, up, then down, clearing the little talon's eyes. It was almost like blinking, but faster. Aron kissed her wide, leathery nose and wished, not for the first time, that he had a trace of the Cobb legacy so he could truly talk to Tek, not just sense her needs. Animal-speaking would be a gift to him now, with Tek his only true companion. Even plant-speaking would have been a relief. Aron would have gladly conversed with the roots under the barn or the trees outside instead of climbing down from his stool and fastening the heavy chains to keep Tek in her stone stall. Only the memory of Stormbreaker's control of lightning kept him moving.

Tek let out a wet snort as Aron eased out of the small door beside the wide wooden gates Stormbreaker had already closed and bolted. Aron fastened the smaller door immediately, and tested it to be certain it was firmly shut. In a barn, talon-side and horse-side should never mix without handlers present, or the horses might get eaten.

"Excellent," Stormbreaker said from just outside the barn's open main gates. "You already have good habits. I had hoped by taking a farmer's son, I could avoid having to cover some of the basics."

Aron stood inside the dark barn, glaring at the man's back. Moonslight illuminated Stormbreaker, along with the fires burning around the shelter and the tallow lines and pyres burning on either side of the barn. In the dancing light, with his cowl raised, the tall Stone Brother looked less than real, less than formed, and ready to combust into sparks and swirl into the night sky.

Thinking of sparks brought Aron back to images of lightning, and he shivered.

"You'll find another basin and clean clothing near the horse stalls," Stormbreaker said. "Wash yourself, Aron, and dress. Do not waste time."

Aron complied, though the water chilled him as he scrubbed blood, mud, and dust off of his bare skin. When he finished, he emptied the basin in a waste trench, stared into the impassive faces of the stabled mules and packhorses, then forced himself to don the gray tunic and breeches of a Stone apprentice. The fabric felt soft, soothing, even pleasant—but Aron would have chosen nakedness or robes of flame instead, if he had been presented with those options. He balled up his soiled garments, intending to keep them. His mother had spun the tunic herself, and his sisters had helped. His father and brothers had tooled the breeches and leather lacings. They were relics of his true family and true home, like his sapphire *cheville*.

He clutched the soiled clothing to his chest and made himself walk toward the barn gates. Did that fool of a Stone Brother really intend for them to go outside, to stay outside after dark—almost to middle-night?

"Join me," Stormbreaker ordered without turning his head. "Do not fear. I will keep you safe—and you will keep me safe. We have work to do, Frosteye."

Because he didn't dare refuse, Aron put out the lanterns in the barn, walked outside into the dangerous night, and took his place at Stormbreaker's side.

Stormbreaker turned to Aron and gestured for Aron's dirty clothes.

Startled, Aron held the filthy rags tighter.

Stormbreaker's eyes narrowed. He gestured again.

Swallowing curse upon curse, hating himself for being so spine-less, Aron thrust the tunic and breeches forward and let the Stone Brother take them. Then he watched in absolute horror and disbelief as Stormbreaker strode to the side of the barn and casually tossed Aron's clothes—Aron's clothes from *home*—into the burning trench of tallow.

The flames blazed and spit as they consumed the discarded cloth and leather. Aron opened his mouth to protest, to yell his rage and dismay, but tears clogged his eyes and grief sealed his voice tight.

Without slowing down, Stormbreaker returned to Aron's side and gestured to the barn gates.

Mute with shock and sadness, Aron stared, uncomprehending.

Stormbreaker waited patiently.

Slowly, old habits elbowed forward in Aron's thoughts, and he per-ceived the risk of open barn gates.

Tek.

He had to make Tek safe, no matter that Stormbreaker wanted him to do it. He would do it for Tek and the bulls, for the mules and the horses, and for no other reason.

Aron felt wooden when he moved, but he did move, and with Stormbreaker's help, he closed the animals safely inside the barn. Stormbreaker slid the heavy bolt into place, took a long silver dagger from his robes, gripped the tip of the blade, and presented the hilt to Aron.

"Take this," he instructed.

Aron stared once more, his thoughts still slow.

"Take the dagger," Stormbreaker said more firmly. "Now. You will need it shortly."

Aron reached up and wrapped his fingers around the hilt. He was still cold from his washing and now doubly cold from night air, fear, the loss of his precious clothes—and total shock.

"Yes, you could use that blade against me," Stormbreaker said as he returned to his position in front of the barn gates, facing out toward the shelter and the road. "I've robbed you of all you've known since birth. I wouldn't blame you if you did find my ribs and try to gut me."

Aron clenched the hilt of the knife and stared up at the Stone Brother. He had kidnapped Aron, cost him his family, stolen his birthright, his dreams, even his clothes—and now he handed him a dagger and as much as dared him to use it to avenge himself? Aron's chilled muscles quivered.

Could freedom possibly come so easily? And with the man's permission?

Stormbreaker lowered his cowl, setting free the tangles of his white hair. He took a slow breath, spread his feet slightly, clasped his hands palms up at the level of his stomach, and assumed a standing meditation pose. Aron blinked. He had seen his father do the same thing many times. Aron had gone through the Veil in such a pose, just as he had done it sitting in a quiet place, floating in a peaceful pond, dangling his feet in a stream, and even mucking the hog pen.

His hands began to tremble. He willed himself to use the dagger, to plunge it into Stormbreaker's side, or, yes, gut him like a hog hung for dressing. The dagger shook in his fingers. He almost dropped it.

"It's a simple thing to kill in a moment of passion or rage." Stormbreaker kept his eyes closed and his hands clasped. "Such killing is almost always wrong, except in defense of self or family. It's much harder to kill with calculation and planning."

Aron snarled and threw down the dagger. "I'm no oathbreaker. You can't make me a murderer."

"I cannot," Stormbreaker agreed. "Killing is always a choice—a choice only you can make. Pick up the dagger. It's pure silver, and you'll need it."

Once more, Aron blinked at the man who stood so still, so calm, ordering an enemy to retrieve his weapon.

He knows I'm not a murderer, that I won't hurt him. Aron faced the meditating Stone Brother, raised his dagger—and still he hesitated. Images of stabbing the man filled his mind. Stormbreaker's belly would be soft like a hog's gut, and blood would color his gray robes forever.

And stain my hands. And stain my essence. And make me an oathbreaker forever and always. Massacre i'massacres. *The Code of Eyrie's fourth law. Unsanctioned killing is Unforgivable.*

"Cayn's teeth." Aron whirled and faced the road. The silver dagger felt heavy, and he gripped the hilt tighter as he lowered the knife.

"Do you know the legacies of the greater dynasts, Frosteye?"

Aron stared at the empty road, at the darkened spots where the rock cats and mockers had bled out their lives, and said nothing. The man couldn't expect to hold lessons now, could he?

"Mab speaks for the future," Stormbreaker began.

"Mab speaks for the future, Cobb speaks for animals, and Ross speaks for the dead." The words galloped out so fast Aron felt like he had lost the rein on his tongue. Before Stormbreaker could ask another question, Aron added the lesser dynasts as well. "Altar tracks, Vagrat heals, and Brailing finds the truth."

Stormbreaker muttered surprised approval, then had Aron recite the Code of Eyrie, all six laws in the Language of Kings. Each time Aron wanted to hesitate, he thought about the lightning and wondered if Stormbreaker could call such terrible energy at will.

"Impressive." Stormbreaker's voice was so quiet it seemed as unreal as his body. "Your pronunciation of *Sidhe* words is flawless."

Aron glanced up at him. Stormbreaker's face had gone slack, and Aron wondered if he was somehow speaking even though the essence of his being seemed to be on the other side of the Veil.

"*Fae i'ha*," Stormbreaker said in *Sidhe*, the Language of Kings, and spread his arms outward, then folded them over his chest. "All Fae, close to the heart. To fail to protect the weak is Unforgivable." Once more, he lowered his hands and clasped them in meditation. "Repeat that, Aron, and know it from this day forward. *Fae i'ha*. It's the first tenet in the Canon of Stone, and speaking it will be your oath to follow that tenet, no matter the cost to you."

"*Fae i'ha*." Aron said the words without hesitation, because nothing in that oath violated his father's teachings. Kindness, honest labor, honor, and truth. Yes. Protecting the weak was something his father would approve of, without question. At the same moment, Aron decided that even if the penalty came to death, he wouldn't give his oath to follow a principle he found evil or heartless, or anything that went against the four principles his father taught him to live by—no matter what Stormbreaker demanded of him.

He turned his eyes back toward the road, feeling weak and innocent and stupid, all at once. He still didn't want to anger Stormbreaker, but his new oath demanded that he ask a question. "Couldn't we protect the travelers better if we sheltered with them?"

"Windblown and Zed will see to them. Our responsibility is to the dead child."

Aron once more glanced up at the motionless Stormbreaker, this time with eyes wide. He barely comprehended the fact that questions were permissible before more tumbled from his mouth. "Didn't the mocker's venom destroy her remains? What can we do for her?"

Stormbreaker's even breathing continued for a moment before he answered. "Her *cheville* was broken with no dispatching. If she had a trace of any legacy, you know what she will become."

"But her people are goodfolk, not Fae. Just common travelers, moving on foot, with no guardsmen, like us." Aron's attention shifted back to the road as unpleasant chills racked his spine. "How could she have a legacy?"

Stormbreaker sighed without moving. "The mixing of Fae and

Fury legacies left many remnants—and you never know when a child might be some Fae's pigeon."

Aron chewed his bottom lip. "Fury" used as Stormbreaker had just used the word was an old term. Furies were the shape-shifting races—human in form, with the ability to shift to winged creatures—that had been wiped out by the mixing disasters. Only the Sabor survived, and they lived mostly in Dyn Ross. The Sabor could command the spirits of the dead, as could people with some level of the Ross legacy, and they could shift into fearsome gryphons. Aron was no Sabor, and he had no touch of the Ross mind-talents. Best he could tell, the same was true for Stormbreaker.

So what could they do to dispatch a mane?

"Use your dagger, and I will use one of mine," Stormbreaker said smoothly, anticipating Aron's questions. "If the child makes a mane, we'll dispatch her ourselves, in the simplest, kindest way. Have you ever seen a mane, Frosteye?"

"Of course I have." Aron stared harder at the road, muscles tensing. His hands started to shake anew, even though he held them tight against his sides. He had seen the writhing, smoky shapes flow across the Watchline and creep out of the tree-break like carnivorous fog, and in the morning, he had found the wasted remains of animals sucked dry of all their life's fluid. The thought made his teeth chatter. He couldn't believe he was standing outside at night, with no close fire for protection, only a stone's throw from a raised shelter.

"I don't mean have you seen a mane with your eyes," Stormbreaker said. "I mean have you seen a mane with your mind, as they truly appear?"

"No. I—no." Aron's jumbled thoughts spun in wide circles. His teeth chattered harder, and he felt like he'd never be warm again. Gods. The shaking. He had to stop shaking. A low hum started in his ears, competing with the rush of blood from his pounding heart.

Stormbreaker was speaking again, but Aron couldn't make out the words. Panting, almost gasping, he tucked his dagger into the waist of his breeches, spread his feet, folded his hands palm up over his belly, and closed his eyes.

Driven by panic, Aron leaped rather than drifted, hurling his consciousness through the Veil, demanding entrance rather than seeking peace in the normal, careful ways.

Black nothingness rushed to meet him, a void he had never before seen when he meditated. He swayed in the all-encompassing blackness, but managed to keep his feet anchored firmly on the ground—though the ground seemed less firm than it had before. His heart pounded, pounded, then abruptly slowed, squeezing painfully in his chest. He heard his own ragged breathing in his ears, tried to slow it down, made himself slow it down.

For a moment, Aron saw nothing at all but that awful darkness.

Then light blazed so brilliantly he thought his consciousness might shatter from the force of it.

His head ached, or the essence of his head, since bodies didn't accompany minds through the Veil.

Almost immediately, Aron saw far too much laid out before him, more than he had ever seen when he was on the other side of the Veil, from a completely different perspective. He was too high, actually above where his body waited, and he seemed to be able to view leagues and leagues all at the same time. At some level, he realized he had accidentally gone farther through the Veil than he thought possible, that his panic had driven him beyond the meditative state he knew how to achieve—but he had no idea how to rein himself back.

The night continued to explode around him, from the luminous stars and moons to the thunder of wind in the trees. Aron's thoughts soared skyward toward all those sights and sounds, expanding over more distance, and more, until he saw what looked like all of Eyrie, splendid in moonslight, yet filled with shadows. In some spots, the shadows seemed darker, and they slithered back and forth, unpleasant and menacing. Aron felt a danger he couldn't identify, sensed chaos about to froth over the edge of all the dynasts but Ross to the south. The lands of Dyn Ross seemed quiet and still, brooding—almost worried, or worrisome.

He turned away from the dark mass of Dyn Ross's Greathorn Mountains, moving his senses north and west, toward Dyn Brailing. There, instead of shadows, he found fire. The Watchline, which stretched the length of the dynast north to south, seemed to be burning.

Aron fought to pull his mind back into itself, bring his thoughts down to a lower level. He wanted to see only the barn and the shelter and the road. Only the area immediately around him.

Images wavered. Aron closed his eyes to clear his mind, opened them again, and let his muddy vision clear. This time, he saw dozens of Stone Brothers securing their Harvest prizes and bedding for the night. He saw boys and a few girls struggling against bonds or bindings, even chains and manacles. He saw one group of Stone Brothers lighting tallow in a circular trench and returning to their wagon, which glowed a deep, startling red, almost like flames through a wall of rubies.

Drawn to the color, Aron wanted to see what was in the wagon—so he saw it.

Inside the buckboard, two boys fought against ankle ropes and wrist ties while a third, a big one, lay utterly still, head on a straw-stuffed pillow and a blanket tucked tight around his large, broken body. His hair was stained with blood, but it looked like golden frost in the moonslight, and his skin was whiter than unmarked snow. Fluids soaked the blanket, and the boy's breath came in jerks and wheezes. But it was this boy, this broken boy, who gave off the ruby glow.

Too broken to fix, too close to death for healing.

Stone had taken this boy because he was near death, Aron realized. He must have suffered a wicked beating or some terrible fall.

The wounded boy's spirit sat up suddenly and its deep blue eyes blazed straight at Aron, even as its body remained slack below. Aron's heart thumped and skittered. He had to bite his lip hard to keep from yelling.

Where am I? The spirit asked through split lips, jaw slack with broken bones. Aron could tell the boy still clung to his essence, still struggled to hold to his last bit of life. *Are you a rector?*

No! Lie down! Mastering his revulsion, Aron tried to tell the spirit to give itself back to its body before the Stone Brothers took pity on the half-dead boy and used their poisons to end his pain, but all he could do was shout, *Heal. Heal yourself!*

Other syllables eluded him, clashing and dropping through his mind.

Desperate to convey his meaning, Aron let his own essence flow forward and join with that of the waiting spirit. He had heard of this being possible on the other side of the Veil, but he had never done it, had no real idea how he was doing it now.

Yet he was.

Unformed thoughts and words flowed between them until the boy's spirit seemed to hear Aron's simple commands to return to its body, and to find a way to make itself whole again. The spirit nodded. Then it eased down, down into its injured shell, surrendering itself back to the boy's body, giving the boy a definite spark of life, and leaving Aron whole and alone once more.

Aron made himself close his eyes, slow his breathing, and concentrate until his heartbeat stilled to a perfect, rhythmic whisper. The image of the wounded boy and the wagon inside the circle of flames faded away from his mind.

He opened his eyes once again, and piece by piece, the actual slice of the world Aron occupied shifted into view, blazing with detail that could only be seen on the other side of the Veil. Fire roared from nearby pyres and sizzled along tallow lines on the far side of the barn. Aron focused on the pillars holding up the shelter. He could see them sharper than he could in daylight, and closer than if he stood right over them. He could see into them, to the channeled grooves and the insects making pulp out of the aged wood.

It'll fall in a few years, he mused, forgetting that all focused thoughts were audible on the other side of the Veil.

By the gods, boomed an unnatural voice from beside Aron. *You are not Quiet!*

Aron yanked his awareness from the shelter's pillars, spun toward the sound—and screamed.

A monster towered beside him, three times the height of a normal man, made of swirling lightning, rain, and wind.

It reached for him.

Aron shouted again and staggered back. The monster paced him.

It raised both arms.

It would catch him. Embrace him. Draw him into that terrible storm.

Get away from me! With the full force of his will, Aron struck the lightning-coated hands with his fists and kicked at the monster's knees.

A shock jolted through Aron's fingers and foot, traveled up his arm and leg, and burst behind his eyes like a spray of stars.

The horrible being stumbled backward.

Before Aron's vision cleared, the creature vanished, sucked back through the Veil by forces Aron didn't even care to understand.

At the same moment, Aron felt a weight sag against his body, then fall away. He looked down to find Stormbreaker sprawled on the ground beside him.

With his senses so heightened on the other side of the Veil, Aron saw little sparks dancing like mad candles along the man's snow-white skin. Stormbreaker's robes smoked, and his gray *cheville* flashed as if battling to hold tight to the Stone Brother's spirit. Blood—gods, so dark, dark red under the moonslight—trickled from his nose and mouth.

I killed him. I hit him with my mind and murdered him!

Before Aron could fully grasp what he saw, or think of what he should do next, a loud wailing jerked his attention back to the road.

Again, he saw the scene as if it were bathed in daylight, yet the images were off-color from the actual darkness and the white-blue glow of the moons.

From a burned patch of grass near the road's edge, a shadow drifted upward, stretched, and assumed the form and substance of a hairless Fae child.

Aron saw the child's blue eyes sparkle as it gazed down at its limbs. Clothes took shape and color, a simple spun shift, like so many goodfolk women made for their girl-children. As if to confirm her gender, brown hair sprouted from the bald head and grew past the child's shoulders.

The little girl looked toward the shelter and took a few halting, stumbling steps toward the structure.

"Mama?"

The sound had struck Aron's mind like a fist, almost clubbing him senseless. He pressed one hand against his head and gripped the silver dagger tight in the other. He knew on some level that he was, as Stormbreaker had asked him so many long minutes ago, seeing a mane as it truly existed. Things always showed their true nature on the other side of the Veil.

He braced himself for the child's next shout.

"Mama!"

A wall of pressure slammed against Aron's dagger hand, but the silver seemed to split it, cut through it, and keep the pressure from crushing him.

Silver. Silver. Thank the Brother for silver!

The child staggered toward the shelter, toward Aron and Stormbreaker, but she was fast changing shape.

Her features shifted and flowed, a girl but not a girl. She looked to be made of mud, then clouds, then mud again. Several times, she got her full features back, but just as fast she lost them.

Aron gaped.

Yes. His father had said something about this. How the newly dead and undispatched didn't understand their situation. How their essence sought what it knew or wanted the most, how that first night was the most dangerous for everyone near it if the spirit wasn't contained.

The girl—now more mud-thing than child—stopped shy of the shelter and sniffed the air.

Slowly, she turned to face Aron, and for a moment, she pulled together her Fae shape. A sweet-looking, pretty girl, not unlike his own sisters, with a saggy, dirty shift and braided hair, strands escaping in every direction. Aron felt a pang deep in his chest, and more than anything, he wanted to hug the poor creature, comfort her, and try to explain the terrible tragedy of the rock cat attack.

The girl gazed at him.

Then her gaze became a glare.

She sniffed the air again.

The blue of her eyes faded, replaced by a dull yellow glow. Only a skull now, with candles where the eyes ought to be. A collection of bones, rattling toward him. Aron watched, transfixed, as the skeleton became a slobbering, wheezing beast with no definite shape.

It gained speed, and it grew a hideous set of fangs.

Moonslight gleamed off the shadowy curve of those fangs.

Aron's mind absorbed the reality of his situation. He was standing alone in the night, facing a new, hungry mane. In seconds, the thing would attack him and bleed him dry unless he could pierce it with the silver dagger in his hand.

He turned and leaped over Stormbreaker, back toward the tallow line burning at the side of the barn. If he could get to it, get to the flames, the mane wouldn't approach him.

It would feed on Stormbreaker instead, if Stormbreaker still had breath in his body. It would feed on the man Aron struck down and left helpless for the kill. And the barn. Without a ring of fire, the mane could enter. All the horses and mules would die, and the talons, too.

Aron swore and jumped back to his previous position. Holding his dagger in front of him with both hands, he stepped between the charging mane and Stormbreaker's motionless body.

Like a wild boar, he told himself as his teeth clattered together. *A wolf or a rock cat. Wait until it leaps. Cut it midjump, when it's helpless.*

But it was a girl. A child. He would be killing a child!

No! It's a mane. Already dead. Pierce it with silver. Send the spirit on its journey.

He heard his thoughts aloud, and the sound distracted him.

By the time Aron found his focus again, the mane had taken flight. Fangs gnashed. Shadowy claws of fog stretched toward him like a rock cat's deadly paws.

He swung his dagger out and upward, slashing with no more conscious thought. The silver blade disappeared into the mane. A jarring coldness struck Aron's shoulders, his outstretched arm, and his dagger hand all at once. It spilled like oil, covering his head, his face, his shoulders, chest, and legs in an icy blanket of death. He tasted blood, felt his essence move out of his body, as if sucked into the coldness. His vision swam and dimmed. His stomach flipped so fast and hard it made him heave.

A shriek ripped the night and almost sundered Aron's mind. His bladder and guts emptied as the cold oil tore away from his skin. He fell to his knees, arm still outstretched.

A shadow rose before him in the moonslight.

It took the form of the dead girl, faint but definite. A winged girl, made of something like dark, gleaming sand.

Aron thought of the winged mockers. He opened his bile-filled mouth to yell, but no sound came forth. He had no energy. No breath. All he could do was spit on the ground and heave.

The winged apparition flapped once, twice, then shot upward and became one with the black sky.

Gone. Dispatched.

The essence of a life on its journey.

He had killed it.

No. I killed nothing. That thing was already dead.

Aron's silver dagger slipped from his numb fingers.

What have we done to ourselves? His mother's voice echoed through his mind, from somewhere in his distant past, as they stood beside a neighbor's funeral pyre. *We destroyed the Furies and lost our own wings. Our spirits are trapped and turned to monsters unless we're pierced with silver or dispatched by a servant of the horned god. Half our animals have been bred into mockers, and our legacies have been strangled to nothing but intuition. Brother of Many Faces, how could sane and rational beings bring themselves to such a pitiful existence?*

If Aron could have answered the mother in his memory, he would have said much about Fae sanity, about Stone Brothers and mockers and manes—and none of it kind—but he never got the chance.

More shrieks ripped into his mind, more bellows and howls from manes.

Shaking, hugging himself on his knees, Aron lifted his head.

The manes were coming.

Two, then three snuffled and moaned and slid and staggered over the hill, flowing down the road, sweeping toward him.

Three more. And four. And five. More. More than should be in these forests. More manes than should be anywhere, even south of Dyn Ross, down in the mists of the Deadfall.

How could there be so many?

What could send so many manes flowing across the northern reaches of Dyn Brailing?

Ten more manes crested the hill, then twenty, then too many to count. They tracked Aron's heat, smelled his blood, the one food that would sustain them for weeks if they could drink it from him.

Aron could feel how cold and empty they were . . . and how very, very hungry.

CHAPTER EIGHT

DARI

Darielle Ross woke to the cold intuition that all the dead in Eyrie were descending on the shelter where she huddled beneath a rough travelers' blanket.

Dari had been north enough times to know about travelers' blankets and travelers' shelters, but she had never been north as a captive before. A prisoner. Her cousin Platt would kill her for this foolishness, for even being so far north, so far away from home, and putting everyone at risk. But no. Her grandfather would kill her before Platt ever had the chance.

Dari opened her eyes without fighting her bonds or swearing or calling attention to herself in any fashion. It was difficult remaining so still, so silent, but she had come north to rescue the most important person in her life. When she found who she was looking for, she would go home where she belonged, no matter what these Stone Brothers planned—and no matter what sanctions she might face at the hands of her family.

At least her hands and feet were no longer bound. She still had on the brown peasant-shirt she had fashioned for herself, long modest sleeves and hem to the midcalf, as most lower dynasts preferred. It was ripped and shredded in places from her ordeal, but it still gave her cover. The Stone Brothers must have brought her in sleeping, and they must not have wanted to alert the other travelers to the fact that she was a prisoner and, as far as the Stone Brothers knew, a Harvest prize. Many children resisted Harvest, but no doubt it was better not to pour salt in that wound on the day itself, when some of these people might have lost their own kin to the foul Fae tradition.

Her eyes rapidly adapted to the low firelight, and she took in the rough-hewn walls and beams of the shelter. By turning her head slowly to the left, she could see the ashy stone hearth and the embers of the night's fire.

Fools!

How could they let the light burn so low? Distance from the ground did not always mean protection. Dari's anger grew by the moment at the absurdity of her situation, and her captors, too. The Fae had fallen so far from their time of glory, they were almost pitiful. Mixed almost completely with the human followers who had migrated to Eyrie with them centuries ago, the Fae had let their bloodlines and great talents die away—the ones that hadn't been destroyed in the mixing disasters. And now, it seemed, they were turning loose their common sense as well.

Dari let pride in her own race surge through her bones and muscles, powering her, driving her own abilities to a higher level. Her people were survivors. Her people knew what had importance in life—and her people always, always took precautions against Eyrie's dangers, both natural and unnatural. She sent a blast of focused energy to the unburned wood, and it blazed bright enough to chase back some of the shadows in the wooden tree-building. She knew the shelter was in the forest, because she could smell the trees and dirt. She also caught the tang of recent kills, blood—probably rock cat and small game. That wasn't ideal. Blood-scent always drew the manes.

Dari's stomach rumbled. Her head throbbed, and her thoughts still felt fuzzy from the sleeping powders the Stone Brothers had given her after they trapped her in the woods along the Watchline, just south of Can Rune. Cayn's teeth, she couldn't believe she had let

herself get snagged in adder vines. She had been poisoned, unconscious and bleeding, and though she didn't want to admit it, Stone
had rescued her. Then, with her unbanded ankle and crazed appearance, no doubt they took her for mad or feral or orphaned, and fair
game for Harvest.

No matter.

She had her senses back now, and she had rested. No human, Stone
Guild or not, Fae blood or not, could hope to contain her.

Dari listened to each sleeping traveler until she had the rhythm
of their breathing. Then she eased into a sitting position and let her
thoughts slide through the Veil, to that mystical world written over the
tangible world—not a change in place at all. Just a shift in level of
awareness, and in the freedom to expand or contract her senses until
she saw and heard the distinct essence of every person in the shelter.
Most of the travelers gave off dull browns and grays, though the family in the corner nearest the door had a tinge of silver in their essence.
A trace of the Vagrat legacy, mind-talents that her people called *graal*
in the older Language of Kings.

One by one, Dari touched the minds of the travelers, suggesting
deeper, longer-lasting sleep. The people in the shelter breathed more
easily and more slowly, in and out, in and out, as their minds sank
into the nether reaches of consciousness, where even dreams did not
tread. They would feel more tired when they woke, but otherwise be
no worse for their prolonged rest.

Dari rested for a few moments, then turned her attention to the
two captors present in the shelter. The boy had a touch of copper
color to his essence, a remnant of the old tracking *graal* from the Altar
bloodline, but Dari used no more energy on him than she had used
with the family by the door.

The large Stone Brother, however, the one who called himself
Windblown, had a strong, pulsing red essence. Mab *graal*, and a fair
dose at that. No one could have guessed that by looking at the man,

but then, Fae bloodlines had become so blended and jumbled that appearances were no longer reliable markers of family ties.

Dari kept her thoughts inaudible, but wondered if he had sensed or seen danger coming toward him this night. Most with Mab blood had instincts about their future, though few could see the true shape of it. Fewer still could see aspects of the futures of others.

Was Windblown so strong?

The image of his essence crouched, fully formed, above his prone figure like a trap-lizard guarding its lair.

This man had training.

He would cost her.

Dari centered herself and closed her eyes, moving her senses farther into the other side of the Veil even as she regulated what her own essence would project—what Windblown would "see" if he perceived her presence at all.

Just a dark girl, with dark eyes and dark hair. Nothing unusual. She made certain she gave off a shade of peridot green, mimicking a weak Ross *graal*. Given the color of her skin, Windblown would expect that—if he had enough talent to see the essence of legacies.

With great caution, Dari eased her essence forward, toward Windblown's essence. It noticed her with a flick of its gaze, but paid her little heed. Instead, Windblown's awareness seemed drawn to the door, toward the world outside the travelers' shelter.

Dari resisted the temptation to explore what had distracted the Stone Brother. She moved her thoughts forward until her essence almost mingled with that of her adversary.

Still, Windblown's essence kept its attention on the shelter's wooden door.

For a moment, Dari hesitated.

What she was about to do was distasteful, even to her. Attacking another living being from the other side of the Veil felt cowardly, given the level of her talents, but in this case, she knew the action was justified. She also knew she had to be gentle—more gentle than she wanted to be. There was something about Windblown that she didn't like, something other than the fact he had Fae blood, though she couldn't name the sensation beyond an unpleasant stirring in her gut. She also had to acknowledge that she hated the fact he had captured her and drugged her. Twice.

So much the worse for this pinioned son of a dirt-eater.

Windblown's essence slowly turned toward her, as if alerted by her displeasure.

No time to debate or hesitate.

Dari spread her essence and enveloped Windblown's.

His essence struggled, but mounted no real resistance against her abilities.

Being so close to Windblown, so intimate, made her stomach roil. She kept her inner defenses high so his awareness could not mingle with hers in any real way—but still. Something *was* off about the man.

He wasn't to be trusted, or treated lightly.

As Dari grimly dragged the Stone Brother's awareness back through the Veil, she sensed levels of deception so deep that Windblown had to be deluding everyone, most importantly himself.

As if it sensed her judgment, Windblown's essence pushed hard against her. His body thrashed as he tried to wake, but Dari held him with increasing force until he exhausted his resources.

His collapse felt both sweet and startling to her, as all sense of Windblown's unpleasantness faded back into his sleeping body.

Steadying herself, she drew back all of her energy but the bit she needed to urge him onward, into ever-deeper slumber.

His breathing slowed. Then he opened his mouth and let out a loud snore.

Dari sagged back against her rough pillow and drew the blanket over her arms to calm her shivers. Her chill was a natural consequence of expending so much energy on the other side of the Veil, but knowing that truth didn't make it easier to tolerate. Her teeth chattered, and she had to force herself to perform rudimentary checks of her own body, from the rate of her heartbeat to the race of blood through her vessels. In time, she settled her breathing and warmed her arms and fingers, and brought the rhythm of her blood back to a slow, relaxed tempo.

What she had done to the travelers in the shelter should last a few hours, at least. That was plenty of time for her to get away. She had no reason to fear manes and mockers like these pitiful beings. Let them cower here and lose the moonslight.

Quietly, Dari stood and tested her limbs. She stretched a few times to be certain she was prepared for a climb down from the tree, then let her awareness return to the other side of the Veil, and walked quietly toward the door.

The moment she touched the handle, she knew something was terribly wrong outside the shelter. She should have gone farther through the Veil for a better understanding, but her patience ran short. She could take any human in a struggle of minds, and most in a struggle with weapons. She could even take a full-blooded Fae, though there were none left, so far as anyone knew. So let them come, then. Whoever waited, let them fear *her*. She adjusted her essence on the other side of the Veil to create the image of a massive, snarling rock cat that would warn off any fool who might be looking, and she opened the door.

Dark, starving energy struck her like huge fists, driving the air straight out of her body.

Dari strangled with her shout of surprise and pain.

The restless dead.

Dozens of manes. Tens of dozens. They rattled and moaned and screamed, and the sound seemed to shake the foundations of the world.

Dari's mind whirled farther into the Veil, stretching out her sight and senses to touch the hundreds of wandering spirits. Newly killed, most of them. Burned. Cut with blades—no, run through. Some guardsmen. Most goodfolk, and from Dyn Brailing.

Instantly, Dari lowered the temperature of her body so she would not be noticed by the hungry manes. She eased out the shelter door and closed it tight behind her to protect the living creatures inside and made her climb down the ladder to the ground, still searching through the spirits of the dead for answers.

Words and images came to her slowly as she moved toward the ground.

War . . .

Betrayal . . .

Houses burning. Farms razed to the ground. Dynast Guard turning on their own people.

By the time she reached the ground, Dari knew the stunning truth.

Lord Brailing had moved against his own. He was slaughtering his own people.

Why? By the gods, what kind of ruler commits such an atrocity?

In the madness of the mixing disasters, Fae lords and Fury kings had done such insane things, but now? Under the Code of Eyrie? She had no love for humans, especially those with Fae blood, no, of course not, but even she wouldn't have wished this on so many living creatures. It was unthinkable. It was horrible.

Just then, two active, pulsing bits of essence caught her attention, over by the barn—human. Human with strong traces of Fae heritage and strong legacies.

Out in this sea of death?

Dari turned away from the shelter's tree. Manes brushed past her without distinguishing her from a rock or a plant.

A boy was standing in front of the barn, ringed by a partial circle of tallow fire—fire that was dying away to nothing. He seemed to be guarding the fire circle's opening. Inside the circle lay the unconscious body of a gray-robed man. Stormbreaker, the Stone Brother bearing the marks of a High Master, whose faint but steady essence suggested he was in a healing trance. And the boy, she remembered him from when she woke so briefly in the wagon. The boy with the old eyes, sapphire eyes she rarely saw except in her own people.

What was he doing?

But even as Dari asked the question, she saw. His blade flashed again and again as he dispatched mane after mane.

And that amazingly bright essence . . .

"Gods. The old strength is in him."

The sight of the boy's powerful potential drove Dari into action. Her hatred and suspicions surrounding the Fae—none of that mattered, not in the face of a legacy of such worth. Whoever this boy was, he couldn't be lost, at least until she found out where he came from, and how any Fae-human mix came to have such a formidable—and dangerous—set of mind-talents.

She pushed her way toward him, using her own *graal* to dispatch each mane she touched with a shove and a blessing.

Killed by the Brailing Guard.

Killed by fire.

Killed by panic.

Killed by a fall . . . a blow to the head . . . Watchline . . . Watchline.

Lord Brailing had marched against the families who made their homes on the edge of the civilized world, who worked the hardscrabble and, in older days, protected the rest of the dynast—the entire lower lands of Eyrie—from the rock cats and mockers from the sandy, wasted Outlands and manes slipping up from the mists of the Deadfall.

Such senseless cruelty made her physically ill. The lord of a dynast, committing outright murder of his own people. To Dari, it was proof that most of what was left of Fae bloodlines should be left to rot in the cesspool of their own civilization.

Yet there stood a boy more Fae than human, who could have fled to save himself, defending the life of a fallen man. A man he probably hated and wished dead.

The boy never saw her coming toward the circle of tallow fire.

His essence radiated brilliant sapphire, and his image on the other side of the Veil was his own normal body. Only people with the greatest of inner strength saw themselves as just what they were. And this boy knew he was small and exhausted and overmatched, yet he kept fighting, cutting one mane after another, sending them to dust, sending them onward to whatever afterlife Cayn, the great horned god, had planned for the sad lot of Fae-human mixes that now ruled most of Eyrie.

His teeth chattered. His hands shook. He looked half-dead himself—he *was* half-dead, and yet he stabbed, and stabbed again, taking on all comers, no matter what frightening form the manes chose.

The boy didn't even seem to notice Dari when she took up a position beside him and used her hands to do what he needed silver blades to accomplish.

She eased her mind toward his, to draw out his name. If she had his name, perhaps she could communicate with him, guide him, or at least pull him back from the other side of the Veil before he dropped dead from such an exertion. Just a brief contact, to get what she could from thoughts that would probably be panicked and jumbled.

Her thoughts made contact with his, and—

I am Aron, son of Wolf Brailing of Brailing, and I will be Aron Brailing when I die.

Agony tore through Dari's mind as the boy shoved away her contact. Her eyes filled with tears as she pressed the sides of her head with both hands. The sound of his words rang through her being, so loud, so forceful that it drove her to her knees. She coughed, gasped for air. Her nose started to bleed, and she had to use all of her own considerable power to keep her bodily functions from shutting down completely.

Her awareness flickered, and she lost control of her inner temperature. It was rising. She could feel it. And when it reached a level to attract the manes, they would drain her blood and her essence, and leave her a dead black husk on the ground.

How foolish was she, to have risked herself for a part-Fae, to have ended her own life to save one obviously untrained boy who didn't even know she was alive? Her thoughts rushed desperately toward her lost sister, toward Kate, wherever she might be, and Dari let her sorrow and anguish flow to her twin.

I'm so sorry I failed you. Find your way home to the mists, please, please Kate. I love you. I love—

Fabric brushed her arms. The shock of physical contact. Hands, shoving her backward.

The boy.

Aron.

That was his name. She felt it in his rough, detached touch.

He moved away from her, straight back to the opening of the circle of tallow fire, preventing any mane from entering.

Aron had struck her down, but now he was defending her, just as he had defended the collapsed Stone Brother.

The angry moans of the dead rose in frustration, and the fizzling, sizzling sounds of the tallow fire seemed pitifully small in comparison.

Dari ground her teeth and forced her body to respond to her commands. She would pay for such brazen disregard of natural patterns later, but with a bit of will and luck, she might survive this horrid mistake.

First, she calmed her internal systems, made sure blood and fluids moved as they should. She sank her awareness into the tissues of her nose, burning closed the small vessels the boy's attack had opened. Then she lowered her internal temperature once more, below the threshold noticed by manes and wild animals.

She tried to stand, but she was too dizzy from using her energy in such a blind rush. Cursing, she did the only thing that made sense, the only thing that might increase their odds of survival.

She crawled through the opening in the tallow circle, toward the Stone Brother called Stormbreaker and found the frequency and rhythm of his healing trance, raised her hands—and hesitated.

That bright silvery wisp of *graal* was undeniable. He had some of the Vagrat talent, but something else as well. A mixed legacy she could almost taste, but didn't recognize. No doubt some leftover of an illegal cross-mixing. And no doubt lethal, given his trade. Unlike Aron, this part-Fae knew how to control his talents.

When she joined with him in such a fashion, cooperative, lending her energy to his, the Stone Brother would know who and what she was. If he had a strong legacy, as she suspected he did, he would be able to remember this joining, and use the sense of it to locate her, if he had a mind to do so. If she made it out of this nightmare alive, if she made it home, he could find her. He could expose her people. All of Eyrie might learn that Furies stronger than the Sabor had survived the mixing disasters—and those wars might start again, so intense was Fae fear of anything with more powerful *graal* than they possessed.

Perhaps she should just kill the Stone Brother.

Either way, the boy Aron would be free to take shelter, if she could make him understand what had happened. Yes. Killing the Stone Brother would be the safest course for her people, and his death might help the boy as well.

After all, Dari thought, falling back on childhood teachings, *only a fool thinks it takes two to keep a secret.*

Aron gave a loud bellow, shifted his stance, and sliced through a mane who had nearly reached Dari. Its screech nearly made her ears bleed.

Little time to spare. She needed to act. At nearly seventeen years of age, Dari had seen and done her share of killing. Such was survival in these treacherous times.

She lowered her hands, braced herself, and touched the Stone Brother's heart to still its beating.

Stormbreaker's lids fluttered open.

Dari had seen them from a distance, those searching, almost glowing green orbs, but nothing prepared her for the jolt of meeting his gaze at close range.

She saw lightning in those depths, and the raw force of thunder and rain and wind. She saw honesty and fear and anger, and worst of all, a touching openness, not unlike her missing twin's guileless eyes.

A boy with an ancient graal.

A High Master of assassins with the unstained essence of a child.

A dynast lord turning his Guard against his most loyal and simple charges.

Into what madness have I fallen?

Stormbreaker's voice rang through the other side of the Veil as Dari slowed the normal rushing of his blood. *Kill me if you must, but save the boy.*

Aron shouted again, as if in answer, and stabbed another mane. Dari glanced at the boy. His essence burned brightly, but his skin had taken on a frightful pallor.

Aloud, Stormbreaker said, "*Cha.*"

A term of respect, for the Fae ladies of a dynast.

Dari cursed his gentle, pleading address. He probably took her for a Ross pigeon, some bastard child of the Fae line. Well, let him. Another few seconds, and he would be dead. This kidnapper. This enemy. This part-Fae killer, with his strange, dangerous *graal* and his robes full of knives and who knew what other weapons.

"Save the boy," he urged her once more, then closed his eyes with no attempt to fight her.

Swearing with more force, Dari jerked her hands away before he died. His eyes. She saw them when she closed her own. His eyes and her sister's eyes, and she could hear the kind way he called her *Cha.*

A ploy. A manipulation.

He was *Fae*, for the sake of all the heavens.

But with her awareness on the other side of the Veil, she sensed no deception from Stormbreaker, who seemed to be the opposite of his traveling companion in the shelter.

Beside Dari, Aron staggered, almost caught by a vicious mane in the shape of a rock cat. She shot out a hand, grabbed the mane, and dispatched it with her touch. Then she grabbed the Stone Brother's head and poured her energy into his healing.

His essence twined around hers, grateful, desperate, almost as hungry as the onrushing spirits of the dead. For a moment, she feared he had tricked her, that he would drain her until her heart stopped beating. Dari tried to pull away, but a storm surrounded her, held her—then suddenly let go of her.

She came back to her senses staring into his eyes once more, only now he seemed suffused with energy. Lightning skittered across his skin and blazed in his eyes. From somewhere all too close, Dari heard the ominous rumble of thunder. She moved deeper into the other side of the Veil, and had to bite back a shout of surprise at the Stone Brother's appearance.

Cayn's teeth. Is he made of weather?

Dari had seen bastard *graal* before, but this—this was something entirely *other*. Her mind tried to add and subtract combinations of Fae and Fury genetics that might have created Stormbreaker's mind-talents, but she couldn't work the equation. Not now. She knew her deep shock reflected on her face—and she could tell from Stormbreaker's stunned expression that he had sensed the truth about her as well.

"*Cha*," he murmured. Then, "Shape-shifter. Fury!" And, "By the gods. A Stregan—but with Ross legacy, too. How?"

Dari could tell he wanted to ask more questions, hundreds of questions, but their situation became apparent to him. Instead of wasting time, he struggled to his feet, then helped her up as well. They turned to face the murderous sea of manes.

Don't touch the boy, Dari warned. *He's dangerous.*

Spare him, Cha. *He doesn't understand his power.* Stormbreaker spoke to her reverently, as she knew all Fae once did before Stregans were stripped of nobility and murdered in droves along with most of the other shape-shifters. He reached into his robes and withdrew two silver blades. *The boy intends no evil.*

I know. Dari stepped past Aron without making contact. She and Stormbreaker advanced into the manes, scattering them, driving them back and dispatching them two at a time. Dari murmured blessings to each spirit. She heard Stormbreaker doing the same. A few would get past them, but the boy was still standing, still fighting. He could handle a few until he fell, and Dari felt certain she would sense the loss of such a powerful energy.

Stormbreaker appeared to share her sentiments. Occasionally, he glanced back toward Aron, but kept moving forward, taking the battle to the manes.

Minutes later, minutes that seemed as long as summer days, they had thinned the ranks. Stormbreaker whirled and sliced and cut. His body temperature hovered just below their awareness threshold, and Dari kept her temperature the same. She was so tired she could feel the fatigue in her eyes, her teeth, her fingers, but she sent each mane she touched onward, onward to Cayn's cold welcome.

At last, when no more manes rushed from the woods, when no more manes crowded around her or crossed her field of vision, she looked toward Stormbreaker, who was lowering his daggers.

He gave her a respectful bow, which somehow did not seem sarcastic or condescending, coming from him.

Together, they turned to Aron—who was standing beside the barn, surrounded by no less than five manes. He held out his dagger to cut into the smallest and closest, the image of a small girl who was holding up her arms as if she wanted him to lift her from the ground. His hand shook. Sobs tore out of his throat.

To Dari's great horror, Aron threw down his silver blade and reached for the child.

Stormbreaker got to him before he made contact, which surely would have been fatal. Stormbreaker, too, hesitated, but only for a moment. With a flourish of his blades, he dispatched the child's spirit, and two of the nearest manes, as well.

The boy had temporarily lost his senses, Dari felt certain. Battle madness. She rushed to the barn to help with the remaining manes as Aron collapsed beside Stormbreaker.

Dari thrust her hands into the nearest mane, and went rigid with shock. Images flooded her, of Aron and other children and a farm burning. Hogs being slaughtered. This mane, this mother's screaming, rang through her mind almost as powerfully as Aron's thoughts had done when she touched him.

Oh, gods. His mother. His family . . .

But she couldn't let them kill the boy all the same. She dispatched Aron's mother with a firm touch and blessing, and an older boy, too. A brother. Stormbreaker dispatched the last mane, another tall, long-haired brother of Aron's, whispering, "Seth. You did get to fight a great battle after all, boy. I'm sure you fought bravely."

As he watched the mane he called Seth turn to sparkles of energy and drift away, Stormbreaker said, "Did your father refuse to believe my warning? Did your family tarry too long before fleeing your farm?"

Dari had no idea what Stormbreaker meant, and she had no time to puzzle it out. Instead, she worked to deepen her presence on the other side of the Veil, and prepared herself to kneel beside Aron and join with him, to force his body through a basic healing process, but a loud thunder of wings brought her up short.

She wheeled away from the barn and ran forward, Stormbreaker at her side.

Openmouthed, the two of them watched as the moonlit sky filled with huge, powerful flying beings. Not mockers, these. No. The outlines were unmistakable—bodies of lions, the heads, wings, and claws of giant eagles. Gryphons, blotting out all the stars with their size and numbers, moving in defensive V-formations, heading due south.

Dari's entire essence fell back from the other side of the Veil so fast she almost vomited. She needed no enhanced perceptions to understand what she was seeing, but she didn't want to believe it.

"The Sabor are withdrawing from Eyrie," Stormbreaker murmured, obviously as shocked as Dari that the servants of Cayn would leave their hired posts in castles, temples, shrines, and manors all over the northern lands. "Lord Ross must have called them to close and guard his dynast borders."

Dari clutched at her own tunic, twisting it, tearing it in little patches as she went. Images of home filled her mind, with its welcoming mists rolling outward. The Ross border was between her and those mists, and now that border would be so closed and well defended even a single mane couldn't slip through without most of the dynast hearing the alert.

"Oh, gods. Grandfather!" Dari pulled at her tunic again. "How will I ever get home?"

CHAPTER NINE

DARI

When the sun at last found its place in the sky, the travelers from the shelter dispersed in many directions. Stormbreaker held back his group and bade Windblown and Zed to feed themselves and prepare the animals for journey, then took Dari and the stumbling, stupefied Aron away from his companions for breakfast. He gave Dari a soft gray robe of his own, along with a dagger to cut it to a length that suited her, then apologized for not having clothing more appropriate for a lady.

While she numbly worked on the robe, he built a strong fire in a nearby forest clearing, which Dari figured was more for warmth and cooking than protection from mockers or other predators who might move in the light. Stormbreaker knew animals and even the shape-shifting half-animals would keep a respectful distance. Dari was Stregan. Now that she was free of sleeping potions and able to broadcast a bit of her true essence, no beast would approach her without invitation. Stregans had no natural enemies, save for themselves—and of course, anyone with Fae blood.

Stormbreaker had not asked her about her heritage, perhaps to keep Aron from overhearing it. Shielding her people or being courteous— Dari had no idea why he kept his questions to himself, but she was grateful. The Stregans had no wish to be revealed. The Fae had betrayed them once, driving them near to extinction. She didn't intend to give the landbound remnants of her enemy's bloodlines another chance.

Dari was also grateful that Aron had regained consciousness, just before sunrise. The wiry boy with sapphire eyes had spent the waning hours of night trancelike and raving, seeming to talk to some injured, dying child he thought should be the king of the world. Aron had begged the child to live long enough to kill their mutual enemies and to restore Aron's family to him. After a time, Aron had lapsed into grateful sobs and more ranting.

Listening to Aron had torn at Dari's heart. Even though she knew he was part-Fae, he seemed no more and no less than any child of her own people. So small, so slight to be so bereft. She wanted to shut out his cries of agony, but she couldn't. She wouldn't, any more than Storm-breaker, who had sat for hours on his knees, keeping vigil beside Aron.

Now that Aron was awake, he huddled beside the large fire without making a sound, covered in a drape of two travelers' blankets. His light brown hair hung about his pale, freckled face in disarray, and his unusual eyes seemed dull and blank. Dari had used her *graal* to examine him as much as she dared, as had Stormbreaker. The Stone Brother's Vagrat blood gave him healing skills almost equal to Dari's, after all. Neither of them could find serious physical injuries affecting the boy. The damage had been done to Aron's mind, from encountering so much he didn't understand, from spending far too much time deep on the other side of the Veil without the training to manage such a journey, and no doubt from the overwhelming grief and shock of seeing his dead family rendered into carnivorous manes.

By the time Stormbreaker finished preparing a restorative meal of toasted nuts, quail eggs, and bacon, Dari had washed her face in a nearby stream, wound her hair up in several thick braids, and changed into the freshly shorn robe. As she walked back into the clearing, passer-ines filled the morning sky. Some moved in message flocks, while others flew alone, carrying private notes in every direction.

One of the larger flocks, the sadly wheeling group of tiny white birds, conveyed a clear and disturbing message. The last Mab heir, the hobbledehoy, was dead. Mab had none of the true ruling bloodline to take the throne when the mad queen died.

Tears in the sky, bringing a sense of dread and doom to all who saw them.

Even though her people had and always would keep themselves separate from the Fae dynasts, Dari wasn't immune to the dread. The hobprince's death would be more than enough to plunge Eyrie into chaos. She held up her dark hand and watched the birds through her fingers, wondering how the death might be connected to the massacre in Dyn Brailing—for surely it was. The timing was too great a coincidence. Her skin still glistened with the oil she had worked through her hair after waking, and she wished she had enough mint and tea balm to cover her body and soothe her nerves in the face of such dark news and such dreadful musings. Such were the luxuries of home, though. And she was far from home, with little to no hope of returning anytime soon.

From what Dari could surmise from visiting the other side of the Veil, where unguarded thoughts moved freely even over great distance, Lord Brailing had broken the Watchline, then turned his forces due north, intending to march on Eyrie's ruling dynast with the help of neighboring Lord Altar. Dyn Mab, seemingly oblivious to this threat, had its soldiers committed to pushing their way south, perhaps to strike a preemptive blow against Lady Mab's imagined enemy, Lord Ross.

Dari didn't know if the Mab forces had learned of the flight of the Sabor, if they knew yet what they would find when they reached the Ross borders, but someone would inform them soon enough. Perhaps they would be shocked into reconsidering, and withdraw back to Mab to address the threat from the west.

Perhaps her grandfather intended exactly that effect.

She plowed into her breakfast, desperately needing the fortification of protein and oils to restore the energy she had lost the night before.

A few bites later, however, her mind returned to a set of lingering questions.

"I don't understand why Lord Brailing failed to dispatch his dead." She interrupted herself with a bite of nuts, then swallowed back a caustic remark about Fae cruelty and poor judgment, considering her present company. "Many of them had to have *chevilles*. It would have taken more time for word of his pogrom to spread if he had sent the spirits to their afterlife. Did he leave evidence of the slaughter of his own people simply to intimidate his foes?"

"Or his allies." Stormbreaker offered Aron a slice of bacon. The boy snatched it away and chewed, his eyes still distant. "Lord Brailing is beyond treacherous. He has his own designs, throwing in with Altar, but I'm sure he wants to keep Altar aware of his power and ruthlessness."

Dari downed more nuts, and followed them with eggs. She washed down the nourishment with sweet-tasting water from one of Stormbreaker's flasks. "But Lord Brailing has killed his staunchest supporters. His most loyal citizens—many of his own distant relatives."

Stormbreaker nodded. "When I asked his permission to Harvest from the Brailing blood along the Watchline, he refused me. He feared these people. That much was obvious."

And that much, at least, Dari could understand. She glanced at Aron, who grabbed some roasted nuts from Stormbreaker's hand and thrust them into his mouth. Lord Brailing must have realized some of his relatives were producing offspring with powerful *graal*. Throwbacks to better days for the Fae—but threats to Lord Brailing's power. Even on this side of the Veil and less than sane, Aron's essence pulsed a brilliant sapphire. The color outlined his entire body, even lighting up his clothes. Indeed, Lord Brailing must have seen it, or someone close enough to him to be heard and believed. A completely Quiet idiot might sense something about this boy.

Still, somehow the Watchline farmers had been keeping their

legacies a secret. They weren't trying to intrude upon the recognized Fae ruling bloodlines or force places amongst the privileged.

Well, of course they could keep their graal *a secret.* Dari took another swig of water to temper the salty bacon. *In the oldest times, Brailing ruled Eyrie because the Brailing* graal *could bend the universe to its will. Animate matter, inanimate matter—a trained Fae with the Brailing mind-talents could force a rock to comply with his wishes.*

Stormbreaker fed Aron a bite of eggs and nodded, as if following her thoughts. "I suspect it was a simple matter for these folks to keep a testing cup from smoking, or force a rector not to notice how loud the blood was speaking when they presented their children for legacy screening after birth. I only saw Aron's abilities because he wished it, to save his younger sister the pain of my blade."

Dari swallowed a bite of eggs that had turned leaden in her mouth. Was this the same girl whose mane the boy almost embraced the night before? She studied Aron's face, but saw no flicker of emotion. His expression remained empty.

"Either some observer noticed what the rectors missed, or Lord Brailing got a taste of Aron's legacy when the boy saved his young talon from the Scry." Stormbreaker shook his head sadly. "His family took the bequest of the little talon as a gift. In truth, I fear Tek was a marker, to make certain Aron's family died when the time came."

Dari finished her meal and wiped her hands on a cloth the Stone Brother provided to her. "Do you think Lord Brailing is behind the rumored poisonings in Dyn Mab's capital—in the Tree City? Is Lord Brailing the reason Mab now has no true heirs?"

Stormbreaker took back his cloth and cleaned his own hands before responding. "That's anyone's guess. No doubt Lady Mab blames Lord Ross, in the madness of her grief. She always turns her suspicions southward and misses the treachery closer to her home. Dari, what relationship have you to the Ross line?"

Dari clamped her teeth together, every drop of her blood and will rebelling against the thought of answering that question. She sat quietly, feeling her body rebuild itself thanks to Stormbreaker's meal, and debating what she should say. The Stone Brother didn't press his question, but instead busied himself by removing daggers and knives from his robes, laying them before him on the ground and cleaning the soiled blades in the fire. He even took off his swords and laid them with the rest, disarming himself as she had seen few Stone Brothers do. This High Master, Dunstan Stormbreaker, was something she had not encountered before. True of heart, despite his Fae heritage, and intelligent beyond what most of his peers might understand. She suspected his fellow Brothers saw him as a good leader and teacher, though a bit impulsive, with a tendency to risk his own life in a reckless fashion, protecting the innocent and weak, as the first tenet of the Canon of Stone dictated. Dari, however, suspected that Stormbreaker did nothing without tremendous thought and calculation. He simply kept his factoring and figures to himself.

These thoughts made her feel ill at ease. The complexity of the man, the boy, the whole situation—it did not sit well with her. She had never considered what it might feel like to take any Fae seriously, outside those few in the Ross and Cobb dynasts that she had known since childhood. Those few, they were the only exceptions to Stregan prejudice against their enemies—or so she had believed until she met these two.

Were they truly exceptions to the brutish stupidity of Fae, or had she let down her defenses too far in the heat of battle?

Another period of silence ensued, until Dari grew so tense she could hardly continue to sit inside her own skin.

"Lord Ross is my grandfather," she admitted at last. "Though that relationship remains as secret as my Stregan nature. His eldest son wed my mother—twice, in fact. Once they joined as promise-mates in the custom of my people, and later they wed again as band-mates in the custom of your people."

Stormbreaker didn't ask his questions aloud, but Dari could read them on his tattooed face. What rector would give his permission for an illegal cross-mixing and formalize an oathbreaking union? How in all of Eyrie did Lord Ross find a rector who would add those second *chevilles* to the ankles of her parents, crystal born of the same fire, so the two could always find each other, no matter how the wind blew?

"My parents *were* true band-mates," she said. "The union was sanctioned by the Ross rector. Gloster is his name, and he's very, very old, and also very skilled in the making of *chevilles*. He could do the work himself, without having to commission a stone mason to do it—well, you know most in Dyn Ross have some skill with working rock and stone anyway. Needless to say, Gloster does not hold tightly with his allegiance to Thorn." She sat back, surprised at the sense of burdens lifting from her as she shared some of her secrets, and surprised by the flicker of darkness that crossed Stormbreaker's features at the mention of Thorn.

"I suspect the writ of acknowledgment of that marriage has never found its way out of the walls of Gloster's Temple of the Brother," she said. "Probably never will, unless need demands it."

Stormbreaker looked appeased, and once more light and focused. "Loyalty in Dyn Ross runs strong to the Ross bloodline—stronger than in any other dynast, except perhaps for Dyn Cobb. If Lord Ross had asked it, I'm sure any number of his people would have kept this secret."

Dari nodded. "Those in Ross were the only Fae who refused to betray their Fury brothers and sisters during the mixing disasters. They saved the Sabor from extinction, and in the end, they offered shelter and secrecy for Stregan survivors as well. I suspect a number of Ross citizens know, or have guessed, that my people reside nearby to their dynast borders, and that sometimes, we come amongst them. Yet no rumors of our existence have spread."

"Rumors will not spread from me, either," Stormbreaker assured her. "No rumors of you, and no rumors of this boy's origins."

Dari gazed once more at Aron, at his distant, vacant expression,

and wondered if Stormbreaker's efforts on his behalf—and her own—
had been in vain.

Would Aron's mind heal from the blows he had suffered?

Could he?

It didn't take Dari long to add up that Stormbreaker had come to
Brailing on purpose, probably sensing some shadow over the dynast, or
maybe even the growing doom hanging above the Watchline. The
dynast lord had refused him permission to Harvest from the dynast
bloodline, but Stormbreaker had Harvested Aron anyway, despite
potential ill will from Lord Brailing. The guild could take such an
action by law, if it suited their purposes, but they rarely did so. And if
she wasn't much mistaken, Stormbreaker had tried to save Aron's family from the coming massacre.

She eyed the *dav'ha* marks lining the Fae's arms.

Perhaps Stormbreaker even had some debt of honor to Aron's
father. Perhaps Aron's father had made *dav'ha* with this Stone Brother,
somewhere back in time.

Dari's gaze returned to Aron.

Did the boy realize that Stormbreaker had saved his life? That the
Stone Brother had tried to spare his family from Lord Brailing's attack?
What did this isolated boy from an isolated Watchline farm understand about the workings of Eyrie? Their talk of politics and allegiances and betrayals were likely lost on him, beyond the fact that his
family was dead and the only home he had known had probably been
burned to the ground.

Her mind turned over the night's events one more time, and a new
coldness flooded through her. "Lord Brailing couldn't interfere directly
with your Harvest, Stormbreaker, but he could be relatively assured of
your death if he filled the woods between the Watchline and Triune
with manes."

Stormbreaker, who had finally arranged his blades to his satisfaction, let out a sigh that told Dari she was correct.

She jammed her hands against the ground on either side of her, to ground herself. "He thought you might disobey his wishes and Harvest one of the Watchline families. He left the essence of all of those people in torment, in hopes they would do murder for him. Lord Brailing sent this boy's family to kill him!"

In response, Stormbreaker selected a dagger covered with ceremonial marks and lifted it. "I don't know for certain, but, yes, I believe you're correct. Either he came for Aron and his family in person, or his soldiers had orders to break their *chevilles* without dispatching their essences. The numbers were too great for any other explanation."

Aron still gave no visible response. The boy just stared at the fire, but somehow Dari knew he was listening.

"When you took Aron, were you interfering with the course of a dynast's history?" Dari asked, knowing the question might offend Stormbreaker. Eyrie's guilds expressly swore never to interfere with the workings of a dynast, and to do so would be cause for expulsion and execution.

Stormbreaker gave no visible reaction save the slight inclination of his head as he continued to study the dagger he held. "I was saving a boy, the child of a man to whom I owed a personal debt, nothing more. I urged Aron's family to leave the Watchline, but apparently, they couldn't make their escape in time."

Aron continued to sit so still he might well have died as they spoke, but for the steady rise of breath in his chest, and the bright, living focus in his eyes as he gazed at the flames. Dari lifted her hands from the earth and brushed away the dust on her fingers. As the faint clouds of brown wisped past Aron and dissolved in the light breeze, she decided to risk another question, one that revealed much about her own increasing disquiet. "Fae and Fury have known many wars across many worlds and lands, fighting with one another and against one another. But this—this attack on the Watchline—it has a different feel to it. Do you sense it?"

"I do." Stormbreaker lowered the dagger in front of him and placed the blade reverently on the ground as he shifted his full attention to Dari. "I sense . . . I sense this war could mean the end of my people."

"The end of your people?" Dari heard herself echoing Stormbreaker's words, but she couldn't stop herself. Her blood had surged at his words, because, yes, that *was* it, that *was* what she had been sensing, though she couldn't for the life of her understand why.

Stormbreaker touched the dagger he had placed on the ground, then stared at it as if the blade might contain answers to questions even he feared to ask. "The land itself might remain intact, but society could collapse and come to nothing."

"The Fae always manage to survive." Dari couldn't wrap her mind around what he was saying, or imagine how such a thing could come to pass. "Even if the conflict rages too long, some will escape, move on to new territories if necessary."

Stormbreaker shook his head, then glanced at Aron. "With the strength of the Fae bloodlines so depleted, if our society collapses, I doubt we can recover again. There will be no migration, no rebuilding." His frown grew deep and sad, like the tone of his voice. "If we ruin what's left of our strength, if we kill our youngest and brightest and strongest, Eyrie will belong to your people once more."

Dari stared at Stormbreaker, pondering his words with a mixture of shock and trepidation. Her rational mind tried to argue that such an outcome would be desirable, fantastic in fact. If the Fae destroyed themselves, her people would have no reason to remain in hiding. Surely they would be able to reverse whatever damage was done to the energies of the land and make Eyrie fertile and welcoming again. There would be no more hiding, no more fear.

But the loss of so many lives—and how many would be innocent? Cut down because of proximity, or starvation, or other tragedies?

Somehow, it seemed unfair and wrong. Murder and mayhem—

those weren't the ways Dari wanted her people to reassume their right-ful place in this world, even indirectly. Who was to say that the conflict wouldn't spread and grow until every living thing in the land suffered and perished? The mixing disasters had almost produced such devastat-ing madness, hadn't they?

We start the battles, her grandfather always said, *but it's Cayn who ends them.*

Only death, destruction, and perversion came of war. Her grand-father was committed to that belief, as was her cousin Platt, who was the leader of her people. She knew that Eyrie's guilds, by charter, were supposed to hold the same values and refuse to participate in wars no matter how great the incentives or pressures.

"You saved my life, *Cha* Dari, of—" Stormbreaker broke off after interrupting her internal struggle. He waited, then, and Dari realized he was protecting her privacy, that he wasn't sharing what he had learned on the other side of the Veil. He wanted her to supply the answer she wished Aron to have, rather than simply reveal her identity, even though Aron might remember it on his own, from his own contact with her, as he healed.

"Ross," she said, deciding to be at least that honest. Let all the other Fae think she was some lord's pigeon, far down the dynast bloodline. It wasn't like she could hide the shade of her skin, or her talent for dis-patching the dead. "Dari of Ross."

"*Cha* Ross." Stormbreaker held his dagger toward her, hilt first. "Were it not for your bravery and Aron's, for your determination and his, I would have died beside that barn. The two of you fought a battle wor-thy of any soldier—of a legion of soldiers. In honor of your courage, I offer to make *dav'ha* with both of you. If you consent, I will join us with the mark of Cayn, to commemorate the army of dead we dispatched."

Dari stared at Stormbreaker once again. Her mouth opened in sur-prise.

A day ago, this man had been her captor, and now he was offering to bind himself to her with a blood-promise? To stand beside her in any conflict, and to keep her interests always close to his heart? Those who made *dav'ha* gave each other total honesty, total support, whenever and however possible. They became *la'ha* and *li'ha*, sisters and brothers of the heart, evermore. It was a promise, not an oath—not binding in any legal sense. But it was a promise independent of dynast allegiances. Independent, even, from guild duties or bonds of marriage and birth families.

What would *her* family say about such a promise with a Stone Brother? They might think it wise, to have allegiance with a man who might rise to great power. But a blood-promise with a Fae—a man not even of the Ross dynast?

She shivered with distaste—and interest.

It would seal his silence about my origins, would it not?

Once more, her eyes found Aron.

And his as well.

Yet if she made this promise, she would be bound to this devastated, broken boy. To the awesome and frightful abilities he might one day learn to use, if Lord Brailing didn't manage to kill him or have him killed.

And if Stone isn't forced to dispatch him for failing to control himself.

Did it bother her, to think she might be shackled to a child who would never recover from the wounds to his heart?

She thought of how he stood over Stormbreaker, slaying mane after mane after mane, even though Aron probably believed it would have been better for him if the Stone Brother died. She thought of how he almost embraced his dead sister, no matter the consequences. She also thought of how alone he was, and about her own twin sister. Dari had come north to search for Kate, poor confused Kate, who could not keep her thoughts and actions in order.

Thanks to my negligence. Were it not for me, Kate would still be safe in the mists.

But now Kate's frailty would place her at the mercy of whatever captor might run across her. Kate was just as alone as Aron, at least in her own troubled mind.

The similarity was too much for Dari to bear.

"I will do it." She moved herself closer to Stormbreaker and held out her left arm, to signify her first *dav'ha*. "These promise ceremonies are not common to my people, but I will honor the mark you make, Stormbreaker."

Stormbreaker retrieved his dagger from the ground and touched her arm with the hilt, then held it toward Aron.

"When I claimed you, I called you Aron Frosteye. You have distinguished yourself beyond such a casual designation, so I ask you now, do you choose another name for yourself?"

Dari thought Stormbreaker was being formal, or foolish, to offer such a choice to a boy mute from shock, but to her surprise, Aron's mouth opened. His voice wavered and broke as he spoke, but as he formed the syllables, she understood him perfectly, with a rush of painful memory from the night before.

"I am Aron, son of Wolf Brailing of Brailing," he said in a hoarse whisper. "And I will be Aron Brailing when I die."

Stormbreaker's eyebrows arched. The blade in his hand twitched, as if he considered withdrawing it before Aron could extend his arm.

Dari knew Stone well enough to know that the guild did not allow the keeping of family names, of family ties forged prior to Harvest. She didn't think Stormbreaker could grant such a request, but when he owed the boy his life, when he was offering to make *dav'ha*, how could he deny it?

After a pronounced silence, Stormbreaker steadied the dagger he offered Aron. "If I had the power to allow you to keep your family name, I would do so—and it's obvious that you'll hold that name in your heart until you breathe no more. I respect that, and do not challenge you."

Aron glared at Stormbreaker, unmoving.

"I propose a compromise, to honor both our traditions and your request, a name taken from the oldest ruling lines of Brailing. Will you accept Aron Weylyn?"

Son of the wolf, Dari translated in her head. From a dialect even older than the Language of Kings, brought to Eyrie when the Fae and Furies first migrated to this planet through the great channels of power, swapping their old world for a new one. Did the boy even know what the word meant?

By the flash of his sapphire eyes, he did know, and he was appeased, though he spoke no more. Instead, he extended his left arm, and Stormbreaker touched it with the hilt of his ceremonial dagger.

Aron and Dari sat and watched as the Stone Brother heated his blade in the fire. He waited until the tip changed color, removed it, then, before the silver could cool too much, used it to burn the downward triangle of Cayn's face into his own arm, followed by the upward twist of Cayn's horns, which formed a pentagram. Anyone who saw the mark would know it as a glyph representing the great horned god of death, the terrifying winged stag.

Stormbreaker reheated the knife, removed it from the fire, and gestured to Dari. She leaned forward, arm still extended, and closed her eyes.

The moment the hot blade touched her, she wanted to scream. It made a sound, a sickening sizzle she had heard only a few times in her life and didn't care to hear again. Then came the smell, sickly sweet, not unlike the bacon Stormbreaker fried, yet completely different. Dari had to swallow repeatedly to keep from retching from the pain and the stench. Face, horns—each line burned new agony into her flesh, and when Stormbreaker finished, Dari wanted nothing more than to thrust her arm into an icy mountain stream.

The Stone Brother let her go, and Dari opened one watery eye to look at his work. A perfect raised face of Cayn gazed back at her, pink and angry against her dark skin. The mark was small, no bigger than the pad of her thumb, carved just above her wrist. Typically, first *dav'ha* marks were made near the inner bend of the elbow, but Stormbreaker would have filled that spot long ago. He placed their marks where they would match, even as the skin moved across the years.

As soon as his blade heated again, Stormbreaker turned to Aron.

The boy held out his arm and didn't move as the Stone Brother carved the *dav'ha* mark into his flesh.

Dari imagined that Aron had been frightened and angry when Stormbreaker Harvested him. She figured he had planned a dozen escapes, maybe even a few that would have worked. Now the boy knew he had nowhere to run. Whether he wished to be a professional killer or not, Aron would shed his old identity, learn to live by the Canon of Stone, and become an assassin.

Perhaps he now wanted the training Stone had to offer. In his place, she would want those skills. How else could she ever hope to bring her family's killers to judgment? What better way to learn to strike down the enemies who crushed the people she loved?

Even now, Aron Weylyn, the newly named Son of the Wolf, might be etching the title and face of Lord Brailing across his broken heart. One day, he would learn the name of the guardsmen who did the killing on their lord's orders. And one day, as a fully trained Stone Brother, apprentice to a High Master, Aron Weylyn might draw a stone on one of those murderers, and when he did, the horned god Cayn himself would smile.

Stormbreaker's eyes flashed.

Had he caught a trailing of her thoughts?

If he had done so, he seemed to agree with her assessment. Maybe he even looked forward to the day he might put that stone in Aron's hand.

The Stone Brother brought the ceremony to a close with a pledge, repeated by Dari and mouthed silently by Aron.

"By this mark and the memory of our battle, I pledge my heart to you."

It was done, then.

Dari looked at Stormbreaker and Aron, at the man and boy she would call *li'ha* for the rest of her life, which might be shorter than she planned if the borders to Dyn Ross remained closed. She had actually bound herself to two people with Fae blood.

For now, she would have to trust herself to these two former enemies, and even, in part, to the likes of Windblown and the Altar whelp he apprenticed. Dari didn't care for either of them, but even if she went to Stone as a person in need of shelter instead of a Harvest prize, she would have to find a way to make peace with many who struck her as arrogant or deceitful or dangerous.

And, in truth, how different would they be from her? She had her own secrets to keep, and her own battles to pursue. Most of them, she wouldn't like any more than they liked her.

Stormbreaker stood. "Dari, you and I must teach the boy what he has to know about his legacy to make us all safe. Then we need to ride out and cover the leagues quickly." His green eyes flickered as he glanced east, in the general direction of Can Rune, where Lord Brailing held his seat. "With dynast lords turning on their own people, the only safety in all of Eyrie may be behind guild walls, and we'll be sorely pressed to reach Triune before trouble reaches us."

Dari thought about the irony of seeking safe haven in the stronghold of professional killers, but she kept such thoughts to herself as Aron Weylyn got to his feet. His sapphire eyes blazed as he looked toward Can Rune and nodded, seeming to give himself over to the idea of becoming a Stone Brother.

"Perhaps," Dari dared to say as she stood and carefully took Aron's hand in her own, "there is such a thing as killing with honor, after all."

PART II

Elhael

FATE WATCHES

CHAPTER TEN

DARI

Time was short.

Dari felt that in her depths, though common sense could have told her the same thing.

War had begun. Borders were closing. Allegiances were being forged, and the lay of Fae lands might already be shifting. No doubt the byways were becoming more treacherous by the hour.

Yet she and Stormbreaker still had work to do with Aron, no matter what was happening outside the clearing. It wouldn't do to evade soldiers and looters, to survive the surges of displaced citizens and refugees wars always produced, only to die by accident in battle because the boy didn't understand his own power, or couldn't control it.

He could kill us as we ride, as we sleep—it wouldn't take much.

She helped Stormbreaker settle Aron on the ground a few paces away from the cook fire, then sat facing the boy. The spot Stormbreaker had chosen was sun-warmed and soothing, close to a nearby pond. It was perfect for going through the Veil, especially for Fae who needed structure and inducement to achieve a meditative state. Dari and her people never needed such help, but she knew those with Fae blood often did, especially if they had little practice at the craft, or if they were distressed or unbalanced.

At the moment, Aron would meet all those characteristics, she thought, then had to fight off a surge of dread.

Stormbreaker's face softened, and when he spoke to the boy, his voice was measured and kind. "What do you know of the Fury races, Aron?"

The boy shrugged, indicating very little.

Dari figured he knew what most Fae without extensive guild education could grasp. Perhaps the names of the races, general ideas about Fury abilities, and something about how all the Furies but the Sabor came to perish during the mixing disasters.

Stormbreaker must have made the same assumption, and he began the boy's instruction simply enough. "Furies have a natural ability to go through the Veil, whether or not they've been trained to the skill. Since you and I are of Fae heritage, we have only a fraction of the understanding Dari possesses."

Aron's gaze shifted from Stormbreaker to Dari, and she could tell the boy believed what Stormbreaker was telling him. "My people often refer to being on the other side of the Veil as seeing the world-carved-over-the-world," she said. "Everything has more detail, and though it isn't solid, it can be seen at such greater depth, in such greater detail, like the most intricate woodwork imaginable."

At this, Aron brightened a fraction, which surprised Dari.

Was the boy already so talented with his meditating that he had perceived this in his time on the other side of the Veil?

Indeed, someone in Aron's former life must have had some knowledge and skill, and made an attempt to pass these gifts on to the boy. It was fortunate for Aron and for them all that she and Aron would not be starting at the absolute beginnings, at least. Still, it was the next bit that Stormbreaker had to say, the part that was coming, that she most feared Aron would reject. And it was the most essential, if they were to let the boy live.

Stormbreaker's green eyes brightened, and the spirals on his face seemed to move as he worked his jaw. "You have noted, I'm sure, that I possess a dangerous and unusual legacy."

Aron's arms twitched, and he nodded.

"Good." Stormbreaker spoke more quietly, likely to command even more of the boy's attention. "You believe this because you have seen it and felt it."

Again, the boy nodded.

Stormbreaker glanced at Dari. "We have seen and felt, Dari and I, that you have a *graal*, too, Aron Weylyn. It is nothing like mine, but it is no less dangerous."

As Dari had feared, the boy's expression went from rapt to incredulous. He waved a hand as if to dismiss Stormbreaker's words, but Stormbreaker wouldn't be put off. "Your father and mother must have possessed a touch of it, and perhaps some of your brothers and sisters. You, however, have much more than a touch."

The boy's relaxed posture and bemused countenance suggested that he gave this assertion no weight at all.

Stormbreaker pressed onward, obviously planning to convince as he educated. "Aron, I believe you have the Brailing legacy, and not the weak sort left to the bloodline after the mixing disasters. I believe you have the old, true *graal*—a full measure of it."

Now the boy laughed outright, the first sound he had made since the *dav'ha* ceremony—only the resonance wasn't happy, or even sarcastic. More pained and harsh, as if the noises were torn from his throat.

Stormbreaker held up his hand for silence. "Throwbacks occur, random returns to these true mind-talents. We don't know why. We can't predict or control these phenomena, but I think perhaps these throwbacks have been happening along the Watchline, in families far from the diluted and mingled legacies found in the cities."

Aron straightened somewhat, and Dari figured that as a child raised on a farm, he had some grasp of breeding principles. Aron probably knew how to keep stock of pure and strong blood, how to weed out culls and join sires and dams for strong traits instead of weak ones. Now Aron was listening more closely.

And perhaps beginning to worry.

"I know you were tested at birth like all children who bear the name of their dynast bloodline," Stormbreaker said. "The rectors wouldn't have seen your mind-talents because your parents didn't want them to discover your legacy and take you from your family. I doubt your parents even knew they were influencing the testing-cup results. I don't believe they could employ their mind-talents deliberately, or else they would have influenced my testing-cup results as well."

Aron's expression went distant, as if he might have been remembering something.

"Your parents weren't influencing the results," Dari said, correcting Stormbreaker as she assumed he wished her to do. After all, he did bring up her greater understanding of the Veil, and by dint, the workings of legacies. "Your parents influenced the *perception* of the results."

Stormbreaker nodded and looked relieved by her assistance. "Yes. Thank you. And that's the core of it, Aron. I believe that with training, you'll be able to sense when people speak the truth and when they lie, and also influence the perceptions of others about what is true and what is not—either individually, or on a larger scale. And those skills are both a great gift and a terrible, terrible curse."

Dari knew that without the education offered by guilds, Aron had no way of hearing the old stories, of learning the atrocities of mind and body that the Fae and Fury races had once committed, both against themselves and against one another. In a way, that was a mercy, or he might have drawn his daggers and cut his own throat when Stormbreaker told him the nature of his *graal*.

Stormbreaker retrieved a twig from his left and used his right hand to remove some grass until a patch of dirt lay between him and Aron. In the dirt, he drew a line with a dot beside it. "Imagine a man standing on the edge of a precipice."

Aron's uncomprehending stare became more focused and a bit uncomfortable.

Stormbreaker tapped the dot. "Now imagine that this man 'sees' or become convinced of the truth of a pack of mocker rock cats here, advancing upon him."

For a moment, Aron did not move. Then his thin faced pinched. Horror spreading slowly across his features as he looked at the line of the precipice and the dot representing the man. He reached down, hand trembling, and erased the dot.

"Yes," Stormbreaker agreed, shifting beside his diagram until he was leaning toward the boy. "Most men would jump to their deaths rather than be torn to shreds and eaten, or worse yet, burned alive by mocker poison."

Aron's stare remained fixed on the line in the dirt.

Now he was clearly waiting for the next blow, and Dari hated to know it was coming.

"Let us take that a step farther." Stormbreaker restored the line and the dot. "Let us say that instead of seeing the image of mocker rock cats, the man had a thought that he should jump, that he must jump, reason or no reason. And let us say that he believed this thought absolutely and without question to be true."

Air hissed from between Aron's teeth.

Once more, he rubbed out the dot.

Stormbreaker erased the line with his palm and blew the dust off his hand. Then he used the end of the twig to place many dots in the dirt. "With the true Brailing *graal*, and with some training, it will be nothing to you to convince a mind that it should stop its own heart." He blotted out a dot with his fingertip. "You could invade a man's thoughts and cause him to believe he should plunge his dagger into his own chest." He erased another dot. "And if your legacy is full, without any limits or fettering, you could do this to large groups of people at the same time."

Stormbreaker smeared away all the dots with a fast, harsh swipe of his hand.

"And if you follow the path of the assassins who once roamed your dynast, for hire to those with the fullest purse," Dari added, "you could become so efficient that you could kill in moments. Slaughter crowds with only a few thoughts—perhaps even one thought. There are rumors and old tales that the first Brailings could even bend inanimate material to their will."

Aron raised his hands, covered his ears, and stared at the ground.

Please, Dari said to the horned god Cayn, hoping the great stag would hear her plea and show Aron some mercy. *Do not let this boy's mind break like my sister's did. Do not let me have to gaze into the mad, vacant eyes of someone I care about a second time. Leave him his sanity.*

Stormbreaker gave Aron a moment, then tapped his wrist.

The boy lowered his hands to listen.

To Dari's great relief, the light in his eyes hadn't become the gleam of one no longer residing in the tangible world. At least not yet.

Stormbreaker's face also reflected some relief, even some hope, and the motion in the rank spirals tattooed on his cheeks and forehead increased. "I don't have to tell you that this legacy is amazing, Aron, but to use the Brailing mind-talents against another living creature even if you think you're acting for the greater good, that would be a monstrous thing."

Aron looked away, first at the grass, then the trees, then the sky. He shrugged, seemed to think better of such a casual gesture, and nodded instead.

Dari took a deep breath and assumed responsibility for delivering the next bit of bad news. "You have already done harm with your *graal* at least twice."

Aron's mouth came open. His eyes blasted denial and anger, but Dari carefully and patiently reminded him of the battle the night before. She recounted how Aron felled Stormbreaker with a single thought on the other side of the Veil, and how Aron injured her in similar fashion.

"If Dari had not been Stregan and very powerful in her own right, she and I would be nothing but ashes smoldering atop our funeral blaze." Stormbreaker's tone remained gentle, but Aron twitched with each word, as if the man were striking him. "Your body would be burning, too, Aron. None of us would have survived the attack of the manes."

This realization seemed to drain the fight and denial right out of the boy, and he slumped over, hugging his own knees.

Dari wanted to stroke the boy's arm, but thought it best not to quell his emotions. She needed him to be raw and ready, unable to battle against her next statement. "So now you understand why we must begin to teach you how to use your skills on purpose, so that you do not use them by accident."

Stormbreaker nodded. "If you do employ your legacy, you must do so without emotion, with deliberate thought and decision, and much, much discussion of the potential consequences. The only exception would be to save your own life, directly and in the moment, if you're threatened. Truly threatened." He grimaced and rubbed the side of his head, as if remembering great pain. "Not just when the danger from others is imagined."

Aron still didn't speak, though Dari saw the boy's throat working. She was fairly certain it was his mind and emotions blocking his words and not some physical malady, but she resolved to check the moment they were on the other side of the Veil.

"I will train you until no one will be able to discern your *graal*, except those to whom you reveal it." Dari nodded to Stormbreaker. "He can't help you with that. No Fae that I know of has that level of skill on the other side of the Veil, so this won't be easy."

"You must learn to manage and conceal your legacy," Stormbreaker said before making any move to walk away. "If you do not, I fear you will do great harm. And there are those like Lord Brailing who would kill you for your mind-talent, no matter how you choose to employ it. Others would be tempted to take you, even enslave you and force you to breed to propagate it, or worse yet, mix it with other mind-talents to make it even more efficient and deadly."

Dari reined in her own emotion and managed to assume a relaxed seated pose across from Aron. As he hurriedly brought his posture in line with her own, Dari said, "Once I've helped you handle the visible essence of your *graal*—the color around you that others with legacies might be able to see—and contain your talents on the other side of the Veil, you will learn more. The simpler things like healing and long-range communications, and of course, spying on enemies and friends alike."

She glanced at Stormbreaker to see if he would contradict her, but he merely gave her a bow and moved back toward the cook fire, clearing the area for their work.

"I know you're distressed, but we have no more time to lose, Aron." Dari held out her hands to him. "Come with me. I'll take you through the Veil, and we'll begin our training here, now, today. I think we must, to avoid any repeat of what happened to Stormbreaker and to me last night."

The guilt written on the boy's face punched at her insides, but there was too much at stake here to be gentle and kind at every turn. One day, Aron would grasp such intricacies of emotion, and perhaps much more than any living Fae about the power available to him on the other side of the Veil.

For now, though, Dari would feel fortunate just to succeed in teaching this boy how to keep his abilities concealed.

And maybe, just maybe, how to keep himself from murdering her the next time they faced adversity on the other side of the Veil.

CHAPTER ELEVEN

DARI

Dari kept the first training session simple. She sat Aron down, helped him calm himself, and took him through the Veil. Once there, she gave him an initial lesson on focusing his attention, on "seeing" the visible evidence of his own legacy. Everything had gone as well as Dari could have hoped. The boy did seem comfortable on the other side of the Veil—and she had found no physical reason for the silence that had gripped him since he saw the manes of his dead family. Time would heal his lack of speech. Time, and force of will, and necessity.

Better yet, the boy had done a fair job willing the color of his *graal* from that mind-numbing sapphire to a dull, dusty bluish gray, even to her well-trained eye. To anyone who checked on this side of the Veil or the other, Aron would appear to have just the faintest kiss of Brailing ability.

If he knows someone's looking.

She sighed to herself.

Next, she needed to teach him how to maintain that illusion all the time, just in case. Or at least how to sense if someone was trying to see his legacy.

So much work to be done.

When she brought Aron back to this side of the Veil, Stormbreaker was ready to leave the clearing and return to Windblown, Zed, and the wagons. Dari led Aron behind the Stone Brother, surprised that her arm still smarted from the *dav'ha* ceremony. As they traveled through the dim, thick forest toward the travelers' shelter and their waiting companions, the daggers Stormbreaker had returned to her before they left the clearing tapped against her waist and hips, secured by loops in her makeshift rope belt. The scent of rotten leaves and fertile forest dirt made her nostrils flare and reminded her of home, as did the occasional shriek of birds and the distant cry of rock cats seeking shelter against the day's light.

They walked directly behind Stormbreaker on the path he had cut with his swords when they first separated from Windblown and Zed to have their private meeting. Stormbreaker didn't look back, and he had made no attempt to tether Aron to keep him from fleeing. Dari also didn't think the boy needed watching any further, but he seemed to cling to her for comfort. If she had to admit the truth, his touch comforted her as well.

As they walked, she used her own mind-talents to ease the pain from her tattoo, and to heal the flesh around it before sunlight could make a pink-and-white horror of the scars. They would be a faint but definite gray now, and stand out against her darker skin—but not overly so.

Stormbreaker's stride was long and deliberate, but before they broke free from the tree cover, he turned to her. "Be cautious, making full use of your *graal* as you did just now. There are many amongst Stone who can sense such immense mind-talents, and some who could move far enough through the Veil to see the truth of who—of what—you are."

In the shade of so many large-leafed *dantha* trees, his expression remained unreadable, but his voice was kind. Dari let go of Aron's hand and dismissed the urge to trace the whorls on Stormbreaker's face to see if they possessed an energy of their own. They seemed to move again, bright and flickering in the semidarkness, those three complete spirals that marked him as First High Master in the Stone Guild, but perhaps it was only to her eye.

Despite his indeterminate appearance, Dari's encounter with Stormbreaker on the other side of the Veil last night had shown her how young he was. He had not yet seen his twenty-fourth birthday, yet he had already earned rank befitting a man twice his age. To do so, he had to be very talented and trustworthy. And very strong.

Or was he cunning?

Ruthless?

Dari gazed into the endless light green of Stormbreaker's eyes and knew better. After all, she had shared her thought-essence with his, and in battle, no less, when defenses and deceptions tended to fall away. If he were secretly some monster without morals, she would have sensed it last night.

Unless, said a tiny warning voice in the back of her consciousness— a voice that sounded damnably like the grandfather she knew she might never see again—*unless he is very, very good at the lies he tells.*

Color flecked Stormbreaker's pale, marked cheeks, as if he heard her thoughts directly. "So long as you practice your mind-talents only in small measure, *Cha,* you should remain undetected."

Aron coughed with surprise at the proper term of address. When Dari glanced at the boy, she saw that he had moved up beside Storm-breaker. The two of them stood like a last bastion between Dari and the tree-break and the uncertain world beyond. Aron seemed to shake off the shock of hearing Dari addressed as a dynast lady and began to remember who and what she truly was, for he would have seen it on the other side of the Veil just like Stormbreaker, during the battle and then again just now, in their training session.

"Stregan," Aron whispered, speaking for the second time since his family died, as the totality of his memory seemed to return to him.

His eyes widened, and for a moment he looked like a young child, untainted by the horror of Harvest, his lord's treachery, or the deaths of all those closest to him. It was clear the boy was awed by meeting and finally accepting what was to him nothing but myth or legend come to life.

Stormbreaker stared at Aron, but left it to Dari to speak.

She reached for the boy and once more took his slender hand in her own, gratified when he did not pull away from her

"*Li'ha,*" she said, careful to keep her voice neutral. "Will you keep the secret of my true essence?"

"H-how," Aron began, gripping her fingers. Then he switched to, "Why did you come here, back to Eyrie? If some of your people escaped slaughter during the mixing disasters, why would you ever come back?"

The boldness of the question impressed her, and Dari considered that Aron had a right to the answer before he pledged himself to protect her identity, promise-sister or not.

"My twin sister, Kate, has been soft in the mind since an illness in our childhood, unable to truly care for herself," she explained as Aron let go of her. She was careful to keep from looking at Stormbreaker because she was worried about how he would receive this news. "Many of my people have such an affliction. Kate escaped our protection—*my* protection." The words seemed to knot in Dari's throat, but she knew she had to untie them and tell the truth, if she could. "I—I lost her. I wasn't cautious enough, and now she's somewhere in Eyrie. I intend to find her, and when travel into Dyn Ross is once more possible without attracting attention, I'm going to take her home."

"Cayn and the Brother," Stormbreaker murmured. "Your sister is lost in these lands with a war beginning? A Stregan who does not understand her own power or how to manage herself? She'll be little more than—"

"A dangerous weapon," Dari finished for him as a cool morning breeze struck the perspiration on the back of her neck. She shivered at the sensation, and at her own words. "My sister is a dreadful prize to be seized and used instead of rescued, should anyone outside the three of us and those we carefully choose learn of her existence. Many of my people will be wanting to hunt her—maybe even people in my own family—but I don't know how she'll react if anyone other than me tries to control her. If they come after her and find her first . . . That can't happen. I have to do it. I need your silence, and I need your help."

Aron and Stormbreaker remained silent and still.

Dari took a slow breath and waited, growing more tense with each fraction of a moment. The words had come easily enough, but now her destiny and Kate's rested on the honor of an assassin she scarcely knew and a boy so damaged she had wondered just hours ago if he would ever speak again. *Dantha* leaves rustled gently above them, making the shadows dance, occasionally allowing flashes of sunlight to touch Stormbreaker and Aron in equal measure.

To Dari's surprise, Aron acted first.

He extended the arm with its fresh, angry *dav'ha* tattoo, kissed the fingers of his other hand, and pressed them against the raw burn mark even though the pain of the action brought immediate tears to his sapphire eyes.

"I will raise my blade to protect you and help you find your sister," he said in perfect, formal *Sidhe*.

Now it was Dari's turn to feel a deep sense of shock. Aron had the dynast name of Brailing, but she knew how he was raised and that he had been taken from a farming family. So where had a common boy reared by goodfolk learned to offer a pledge of fealty in the Language of Kings?

"Wolf Brailing," Stormbreaker said in answer to her quizzical expression, "was a man of much depth and wisdom." As he finished, he reflexively touched a tattoo farther down toward his wrist.

At the mention of Aron's father, the boy's shoulders slumped as he lowered his arms. His expression remained hard and determined. Almost too much so, by Dari's reckoning. It would not serve Aron well to cleave to her and Stormbreaker only to close out the rest of the world—but she feared that might be happening.

Stormbreaker repeated Aron's gesture of loyalty and fealty, and it eased the last of Dari's worries about being revealed as a Stregan, and about compromising her twin more than was already in fate's hands. *Elfael,* she thought, only the word once more came to her in her grandfather's voice. Fate was in the air. It meant that fate watched, that fate was always watching.

Dari answered Stormbreaker and Aron by paying homage to her own tattoo, and their first loyalty-based bargain was sealed. No one would be telling the others' secrets.

At least these two take dav'ha *as seriously as they should,* she thought. *Already, they stand out amongst their more treacherous Fae fellows.*

"When we reach Triune, we'll use maps to set up searching grids, and I'll assist you in locating your twin." Stormbreaker bowed to Dari again, then turned his attention to Aron. "We may meet many travelers on the road. More than would be normal, given the tragedies that have come to pass." His expression grew even more solemn, and the marks on his face more lively in the light filtering through the *dantha* leaves overhead. "It would not do for any to realize that you once bore the Brailing name, or to notice the color of your eyes. Do I make my meaning clear?"

Aron nodded, and more of that cool anger Dari sensed at the fringes of his essence enveloped him and seemed to turn his nerve to ice as she watched.

He can keep himself concealed. After our session this morning. I'm sure. Dari paused a moment to wonder how much more the boy knew, and how fast he might learn. After all, before she had even begun to assist him, he had survived an unusually long stay on the other side of the Veil.

What did *his father teach him?*

She found herself wishing she could have met the man, as Stormbreaker apparently had, at some point back in time.

"There, now, *Cha*," Stormbreaker said, once more studying Dari with his grass-colored eyes. "We should all be safe for the time at hand."

She laughed. "Not if you call me *Cha* or *Lady* in front of your friends."

At this, Stormbreaker frowned, and Dari could tell he would be profoundly uncomfortable treating her as an equal, or as a woman of less status than he possessed. Nevertheless, he seemed to resign himself to the fact that such treatment was necessary for her safety. When the three of them left the forest in a straight line, Dari walked in last position, placing herself in the lowest order against her two companions.

They covered the open ground between forest and shelter in just a few minutes. Outside the barn, talon-side, Zed sat atop his seat in the front wagon, seeming full and pleased, and Dari sensed the young man might be one of the rare folk who possessed a generally cheerful disposition, irrespective of circumstance or challenge.

Not so his master.

Windblown's disapproval began almost the moment they re-formed as a traveling party. He was already readying the three talons for departure, but he paused to frown first at her braided hair, as if the upswept style did not befit a female who was little more than ground-hatched in his eyes.

She ignored him and did her best to watch Stormbreaker and Aron as they took over readying the saddles and bridles of their mounts.

When Dari next looked at Windblown, he was focused on the somewhat butchered robes she wore.

"Damnation, Dun," the man said to Stormbreaker. "That's expensive cloth you've given her."

Stormbreaker gave Windblown a smile, though the expression

seemed forced. "You would prefer she bare her flesh to the world in that torn rag she was wearing when we found her?"

"Zed has extra tunics," Windblown grumbled as he cinched his talon's saddle.

"They would be indecent on one as slight as she," Stormbreaker argued back as he cinched his own saddle.

Windblown gave a sniff, then switched tactics. "With the state of things, who knows what dangers we'll encounter on the road. We should stop in the next village and fashion her a *cheville*, in case—"

Dari bared her teeth at the man and snarled, "I will not be banded."

Windblown's scowl pinched his round face until it looked like a dried red grape. "At Triune, our stoneworker will see to you as quickly as all the rest. You'd do well not to forget you're no better than the rest of us."

"You are not the only one who can deal in death, Stone Brother," Dari said before she could contain herself. "You'd do well not to forget how quickly breath can cease."

Windblown's face turned an ugly purple, but Stormbreaker cleared his throat and brought all eyes to his own face.

"She is not returning with us as a Harvest prize," Stormbreaker said in a flat tone that brooked no argument. He looped his reins over his bull's head. "She will be sheltered. And we will not waste time in debating that point. We should be on the road, and quickly, if we're to survive this journey."

Windblown's purplish color deepened and his mouth came open. He gripped the reins of his talon and pulled down so hard that Dari feared he might tear the bridle straight off the animal's large head. "She has no status to ask asylum with the Stone Guild, Dun. Even you must clear such decisions with the Lord Provost."

"Lord Provost Baldric will grant her shelter, I have no doubt." Stormbreaker never looked at Windblown as he swung himself into the talon's saddle. The big bull playfully butted at Dari, ignoring his rider, and she had to give the beast a quick mental command to attend to its business.

To Dari, Stormbreaker said, "You may ride with me if you wish, or there is plenty of room in the wagons."

Again, Windblown nearly barked with frustration. If his color progressed to deeper hues, it was possible his heart might explode on the spot.

Aron frowned at Stormbreaker's offer, and so did Dari.

He was doing it again. Giving her too much deference. It would be a great mark of respect for Stormbreaker to allow Dari to share seat on his talon, but she thought it best not to invite too much scrutiny. So she thanked him and politely refused, gave Windblown her frostiest smile, then climbed into the front buckboard beside Zed.

Zed grinned and scooted over to welcome her. Oblivious to Windblown's mutterings, Stormbreaker's low-level agitation, and Dari's worry, the young man started to hum to himself. He looked eager to get on the road, as if he didn't realize they might find any number of disastrous situations awaiting them.

Another chill breeze eased across Dari's skin, putting her mind on fall, then winter in a climate much colder than she usually endured.

Stormbreaker waited for Windblown and Aron to mount their talons, then said, "Henceforth, Aron will be known as Aron Weylyn, with no further mention of his previous name."

Dari glared at Windblown and his sour expression, but at least against that command, he made no argument. So far as she knew, that was well within Stone customs anyway, and it didn't seem to bother Zed.

Stormbreaker gazed at the byway, turning his head in both directions, then looking slightly disturbed at their isolation. "We'll make for the Brailing Road, as quickly as we can reach it."

Windblown adjusted his bulk in his saddle. "There . . . will be soldiers on a great road."

Dari could tell he wasn't challenging Stormbreaker, but rather thinking aloud.

"Yes," Stormbreaker agreed. "And refugees, travelers, rectors recalled to their monasteries, and tradesmen on the move, hoping to offer wares to the amassing armies."

To suppose that Stone Brothers returning from Harvest would need to worry about ambush or outright attack, especially from dynast forces—it was nearly unthinkable. If nothing else, Fae usually clung to traditions with a blind fervor that often annoyed her when she encountered it. In war, though, especially a conflict started with such wicked betrayal, she supposed anything could come to pass.

Stormbreaker moved them out along the overgrown byway at a trot, due west this time. Dust boiled up from the talons' clawfeet and the rattling wagon wheels, and Zed's affable expression turned to an intense stare of concentration as he struggled to guide the mules in a straight line behind the Stone Brothers and Aron.

Dari cursed the slowness of landbound travel. Even if they kept at this unsustainable pace, riding from daybreak until as near to sunset as they dared, it would be more than three weeks before they reached the safety of Triune. Three weeks before her own safety and Aron's was assured. Three weeks until she could plan, determine methods, and make a more organized search for her lost twin.

Forever.

Too long.

Yet there was no point shouting about problems. Problems had no ears to hear, no minds to change. Instead, Dari let her palms slide to the hilts of her daggers and decided to watch the edges of the woods, because her eyes were sharper than any Fae's.

Perhaps she would see trouble before trouble saw them.

CHAPTER TWELVE

ARON

"Get up, boy." Stormbreaker rattled Aron by the shoulder the next morning, and when Aron pried his eyes open, he saw that his guild master was already dressed. "We have an hour for breakfast and weapons practice; then we ride, as hard today as we did yesterday."

Weapons practice?

Stormbreaker left the tent in a fluid rush, leaving Aron to blink as the ashy scent of doused tallow reached his nose.

Aron turned his head toward where the other boy had slept in the tent beside him, but Zed's bedroll was already bound into a tight bundle, and Zed himself was already out of the tent.

Aron yawned, then grimaced. His entire body hurt from riding yesterday, and the insides of his legs were chafed. His mind felt chafed, too. After a few seconds, he remembered that they were camped with a few other parties below a small travelers' shelter that had been too full to accommodate them. He managed to pry himself from his bedroll, sit up, and scoot from the tent he had shared with Zed. Near their small camp circle, several lines of tallow still burned near tents that remained tied tight against the night, though the flames were low now.

In the Stone camp, no tents still stood, save for Aron and Zed's.

A few yards away, Stormbreaker, Windblown, Dari, and Zed were already eating. Between Stormbreaker and Dari, a plate of bread, honey, bits of cheese, some nuts, and dried fruit awaited Aron.

He allowed himself one stretch to soothe his pains. Then he reminded himself of his new purpose, the one he had settled on in the clearing yesterday.

I'll train with Stone. I'll do whatever I'm asked, learn whatever I can. Then one day, when I'm ready and able, I'll avenge my family.

Those thoughts were enough to fuel him, and he hurried to pull on his new gray tunic and breeches, lace his leather boots, and belt on the silver daggers Stormbreaker told him to carry during their journey. Almost as fast, he rolled up his bedroll, set it out with Zed's, then took down the tent as his father and brothers had taught him to do on their hunting trips to the Scry.

No one spoke when Aron joined the group, but the silence was friendly enough. He ate with some haste, cleaned his dish when the others did so, then followed Stormbreaker's lead into the tree line, and to an unfamiliar clearing.

To Windblown, Zed, and Dari, Stormbreaker said, "Give us a safe berth."

To Aron, he said, "Wait here," and strode toward the nearest tree.

Aron watched the others move away without comment.

Windblown and Zed had swords today, though Zed's blade was considerably smaller than the older man's blade. Several yards away, Windblown and Zed stopped, and Windblown pointed out some trees and rocks that Aron assumed would form the boundary of their fighting area. Dari went farther, off to herself, and began what looked like a dance, stretching her long body this way and that, as graceful as any bird on the wind.

Her movements did something strange to Aron's chest. He felt his ribs tighten and his heart beat faster, as if she were somehow pulling the air from the clearing with each sweep of her hands and legs.

Stormbreaker came back to Aron's side, and for a moment, he, too, watched Dari as she swayed and bent, stepped and spun. Aron glanced up at his guild master and he saw that Stormbreaker's green eyes had a distant cast, as if he might be remembering something, or maybe someone.

Seeming to sense Aron's gaze, Stormbreaker came back to himself and looked down. "Normally, Stone begins its day with *fael'feis*—the celebration of the air—but you'll learn those movements better in a group. So it's weapons training that begins today for you. I've carved a target on the nearest *dantha*. Draw your daggers and show me your throwing stance."

If Aron thought riding on talon-back all day was difficult and tiring, it was nothing to what he went through in that first long set of minutes. Stormbreaker corrected his grip time and again and had him throw the knives over and over and over, even though Aron missed the target each time.

Most throws, he even missed the tree.

"At Triune, the weapons master will show you no mercy," Stormbreaker warned, picking up the daggers. "You'll be hauling buckets of water to the forge, adding trips for each miss. Again."

"Again."

"Again."

Aron's aches from yesterday's ride began to deepen, first in his shoulders, then his upper arms, and finally across his ribs, robbing him of deep breathing.

"Watch the target." Stormbreaker's voice remained calm as he demonstrated once more, hurling a dagger directly into the soft wood of the *dantha*. "See my marks in the bark and nothing else."

Aron narrowed his gaze and tried to shut out everything but that target, though he remained too aware of the blur that was Dari occasionally flicking past the corner of his eye.

Why had he never used daggers on hunting trips? He was fair with bow and arrow, good with his shovel in the hog pens—but this?

"Again, Aron."

"Again."

But the *dantha* tree remained safe from Aron that morning.

By the time Aron got to the barn to clean and saddle Tek, every part of him was throbbing. The little talon whistled and butted at him as he pulled on her harness and bridle, and he kissed her rough scales.

"We can do this," he assured her, just in case her legs were as sore as his. "We'll get used to it."

She butted her nose against him and snorted until he had to wipe the fluids off his chin. Her whistles were light and loud, but Aron could have sworn he saw doubt in the beast's orange-red eyes.

• • •

Over the next two weeks, Aron's new life took on a predictable rhythm. They rose with the first light, and each morning, Aron practiced with Stormbreaker on daggers, then short swords, then bow and arrow—which was the only skill Aron could demonstrate with some precision, especially with his muscles so taxed they ached at the slightest movement. Meanwhile, Zed and Windblown worked with their own weapons and Dari performed what Aron now understood to be a ritual, part for exercise and part for spiritual soothing.

Then they rode, as hard and fast as they could push the animals and wagons, with only two breaks for meals and personal respite. Most of the time they rode in silence, but Stormbreaker and Windblown occasionally required recitations from Aron or Zed—the Code of Eyrie, the Dynasts and their lords and ladies, the dynast capitals and other great cities, the Canon of Stone, or some other set of facts they were expected to know as well as their own fingers and toes.

In the late afternoon, they found a travelers' shelter and, more often than not, made camp because the shelter was full.

As soon as the tents were pitched, Dari and Aron retired to Stormbreaker's larger gray shelter for Aron's *graal* training.

Which, unfortunately, was no easier or more natural than his acquisition of skills with weapons—as he was once more demonstrating on the fifteenth evening of their ride toward Triune.

"No, Aron. Don't go through the Veil. Stay on this side." Dari shifted until her left elbow bumped the tent wall. "I think you're trying too hard."

Aron snorted with frustration and opened his eyes. "Sorry," he muttered as he shook his wrists and arms, which were now numb on top of sore, from sitting so still. "I never tried to see . . . you know, extra stuff on this side of the Veil before."

Dari opened her eyes as well, and Aron felt the release of the privacy she was able to give them for their training sessions, almost like a real cloak lifting from the top of his head. He didn't know how she could do such a thing, pull what felt like actual cloth around them so no one could hear their thoughts or see what they were doing, even on the other side of the Veil, but Aron figured he might learn that one day, too, if he could.

They were both sitting on Stormbreaker's blanket inside his large gray tent, legs folded, hands resting against their knees. Outside, all across the massive travelers' encampment, afternoon cook fires crackled. The scent of stews and roasting meats and vegetables gave him a gnawing sensation in his belly, though so far, the Stone Brothers had made sure that he never went hungry.

"Few Fae work with their mind-talents on this side of the Veil." Dari gave a little shrug. "In fact, few can. Only those with very strong legacies like yours. Rest a moment and we'll try again. Stormbreaker wants you to learn this skill by day's end."

The skill of seeing a legacy, or the colors that show a person has a legacy. I'm never going to do it.

Aron wanted to groan, but held back so he wouldn't embarrass himself in front of Dari. It was hard for him not to study the small space between them and wonder what it might be like to brush his knee against hers, or maybe his wrist. The muted sunlight washing through the tent fabric made Dari look so soft, even though he thought of her as strong and tough and brilliant.

"My father told me that in the old days, each Fae bloodline had its legacy," he murmured, doing his best to keep his attention on a spot in the tent wall just over Dari's shoulder. "And that most were telepaths. He said some could move small objects without touching them, adjust wind currents to facilitate flying—that there were hundreds of small talents."

"There was a basic skill set that everyone with legacies trained to use—nothing spectacular." Dari lifted her long arms above her head and stretched, dragging Aron's focus back to her face, then her arms and fingers. "Just practical, useful things like basic healing, basic mind-speaking across short distances, and sometimes, yes, moving small objects. Those with more powerful mind-talents received more extensive training on how to use their *graal* to its fullest."

The idea of what Eyrie might have been like when the Fae could fly, when the Furies still lived, and when Fae families had strong mind-talents intrigued Aron. "What could the Furies do? What kind of legacies—"

"We don't have legacies," Dari said before he could finish. She lowered her arms too quickly, and Aron heard the tension in her voice. "Not in that simplistic sense."

Aron wished he could kick himself for his stupidity. "I—I'm sorry. It's just, you look like us, and I forget that we're as different as you say."

Dari sighed. "No, I'm sorry. We *are* more the same than anything, but my skills are broader. I have bits and pieces of all the legacies—you've heard me call it *graal*."

"Gray-al," Aron repeated, knowing the word was *Sidhe* even though it was new to him.

"Yes. Good. Fury *graal* is stronger than Fae—but we're all different from one another, too, just like all Fae are unique to themselves."

Dari settled back into her meditative sitting pose. "I might be good at this or that skill, while the next Stregan may have a completely different set interests, and different strengths and weaknesses."

"But you're all telepaths," Aron asked quickly, before she redirected them to their lessons.

"Yes," Dari said, but Aron could tell from her tone that she didn't intend to discuss it further. Dari didn't seem to want to reveal too much to him, which he supposed he could understand. Still, Aron wondered if there were libraries at Triune. His father had taught him to read *Ogham*, the common spoken language of all the dynasts, first used by traders and couriers. He could even read a little in *Sidhe*, so maybe there were records of the Furies. Maybe he could—

"We've got only a few moments before dinner." Dari closed her eyes, and Aron felt the cool sensation of her protections descending upon them again. "Now try again to see my essence. Think of it like—like studying a pond while you've got a baited string waiting for a tug. Look past the string in the water. Gaze at the ripples, then the trees beyond, but all the while, keep some awareness of that string, in case it should move."

That was an example Aron could better understand.

He closed his own eyes and fixed an image of fishing firmly in his mind. Fishing in the pond near his family's farm, on the Brother's Day, when his mother allowed no work in the fields or barns. He slowed his breathing and gazed at the glittering image of the water, at the imaginary string with its bit of wood tied at the top for a bob. He could almost feel the bite of the old twine wrapped around his fingers, almost smell the fresh water and the life of the trees beyond.

In his mind, Aron moved his eyes to the ripples, to the trees, then opened his eyes to the hazy image of Dari before him.

She was ringed with a soft greenish hue, a faint flicker of color, touching her everywhere, yet not touching her at all. It was . . . muted, somehow. Pretty like she was and yet . . . and yet . . .

It's not true.

I'm seeing what she wants me to see, not what's truly there.

He glanced down at his own hands to ponder this.

The brilliant sapphire rising from his own skin startled him so badly he clambered to his feet, holding his wrists and hands away from him like they might be diseased.

Seconds later, the colors vanished, and Aron became aware of Dari's soft laughter.

His cheeks immediately started to burn and he looked away from her, fumbling with a stray thread in the tent wall.

"Ah, now. Don't be like that. It scares everyone the first time." Dari got to her feet. "You did very well, Aron." She turned loose the protections shielding them once more, and Aron forced himself to look at her despite his flaming face. He also managed to lower his arms, which to his relief looked like normal arms again.

Dari came closer to him.

Aron wanted to step away from her, but didn't.

She smelled like flowers in springtime, just touched with fresh rain. The scent of her fixed him where he stood.

"Perhaps you have some idea now why you must learn this skill," she said.

"So . . . so I can change my color." His voice broke again. "Tone it down and hide it."

Dari nodded.

"Like you're doing," he added, watching her face. "Like you've been doing since I met you."

Dari's eyebrows arched. Then she offered him a quick bow, which only made his face burn hotter. "Soon, seeing *graal* will be as easy to you as noticing the size of a nose, the shape of an ear, or how many teeth a man has when he smiles. Then we can begin working on the other skills—such as changing your own color all the time. Yes, like I've been doing."

CHAPTER THIRTEEN

ARON

On the sixteenth day of their traveling, Aron found himself limping as he helped to ready their new encampment for nightfall. He had been assigned with Dari to help traveling parents get their smaller children into the raised shelter, while the Stone Brothers helped to build tallow circles and secure pack animals.

The insides of Aron's legs had been rubbed as raw as his mind, and his skin was no longer responding to quick efforts to heal it or the use of a salve Zed had given him. His talon saddle did some to shield him from Tek's scales, but she seemed to be growing a thicker set with each passing day.

She was also growing more rambunctious. Aron could hear her squeals over the noise of the shelter encampment, even though she was in the farthest stall of the barn's talon-side. He had to work to ignore her and to force his legs to cooperate as he carried a little girl toward the ladder into the travelers' shelter. He focused on the pain, welcomed the burn, because anything was better than looking at the child in his arms. She had dark curls like his dead sisters. No doubt her eyes were brown, too, but her sobs had no effect on him. He paid no heed to her when she reached back for her mother, who would be taking her chances in the tallow circles this night.

Some part of Aron's mind scolded him, insisted he should offer the crying child some comfort, but no words came to his lips. Better that he make certain she didn't snatch at the daggers belted to his waist until he could hand her off to Dari, find Stormbreaker, and get his next set of instructions. There was still much to be done before sunset, with the shelter too crowded for all who had come seeking its safety.

Aron elbowed past dozens of cook fires and tents, and dozens more milling travelers and refugees. Some were merchants on the move, while others seemed to be farmers displaced by battles, or village goodfolk fleeing ahead—or behind—the fighting. Most of them looked away when he passed. Aron knew they thought it might be ill fortune to deal directly with a Stone Brother, even a boy like him, who was just in training.

A small bunch of travelers near the shelter's base actually turned away from him as he approached with the girl, and he realized they wore the black robes and *chevilles* of rectors. Rectors were sworn to the service of the Brother of Many Faces—but all rectors were trained by the Thorn Guild before they went into service with elders at a Temple of the Brother.

Nearby, Aron noticed Stormbreaker standing and staring at the Thorn-allied group, his hand on the hilt of his sword. From his position, he might have been keeping watch, as if Aron and the other children needed protecting from the rectors.

Does he think I still dream of running away with weak fools like that? Aron shifted the girl in his arms and frowned as he reached the ladder.

The very air around those rectors radiated disapproval.

Well, fine.

Aron disapproved of them, too.

His mother had been deeply devoted to the Brother, but where was he, that great god of love and protection, when Lord Brailing sent his guardsmen against the Watchline?

"Aron," Dari called. "All your scowling frightens the little ones."

When Aron looked up at her as she reached for the girl, he felt the slightest lifting of the ever-present anger that bubbled in his blood like some dread poison or infection. Low blue hues from the late-afternoon sun highlighted Dari's beauty, which reminded Aron of how she looked on the other side of the Veil. In her human form, anyway.

Dari took the girl from him and climbed with the child as if the little girl weighed nothing at all. For all Dari's fighting skill and sharpness of wit and tongue, her tall body was so graceful each movement seemed to flow, and her features remained delicate. Aron thought her wide black eyes were close to perfect, and he liked the dusky red color of her lips, outlined by the dark, glistening skin of her face. For a moment he stood like a ground-hatched fledgling, staring after her, wishing she would turn back to him and give him one of her gentle smiles.

But of course, she didn't.

Dari was never lazy from the day's business.

Aron shook himself out of his glazed staring and made his way back through the crowd, searching for Stormbreaker. As he walked, he caught snatches of conversation.

"I heard Lord Altar's on his way down from Can Olaf, bringin' most of his warbirds to meet Lord Brailing's guardsmen. . . ."

"Warbirds ain't like normal soldiers. They can live off sand and rocks. . . ."

"They'll threaten Lord Cobb until he joins them against Lady Mab. . . ."

"They'll be at the north borders by winter, and they'll fight until we all die or starve. What do nobles with strong Fae blood care for goodfolk? We're worth nothing to them. . . ."

Aron cataloged each detail, weighed it, and tried to use his legacy to sift out what was accurate and what was only rumor. His *graal* told him that the warbirds really were marching down from the northwest to join with Lord Brailing's forces. That was bad, in his estimation. The combined armies of Altar and Brailing could exert considerable pressure on Lord Cobb to the east, and maybe force one of the greater dynasts to join their campaign against Lady Mab. The wings of the great bird that was Eyrie might be smaller than the body, but wings could guide the bird if they moved together.

When Aron reached the spot farthest from the travelers' shelter, he saw that Stormbreaker, Windblown, Zed, and six other Stone Brothers who had joined them on the road were digging another trench for the tallow circle. Hopefully, the flames from the lit tallow would keep them safe this night. Though none but Aron and Stormbreaker knew it, Dari's presence in the shelter would assure that the children and infirm would be unharmed, for that's all who would fit in the shelter. The rest would have to risk sleeping on the ground with fire, weapons, and hourly watches to keep them safe.

Inside the circle Stone was digging, there were four tents, each large enough to sleep four men. Three boys, Harvest prizes who had yet to accept their destiny, were shackled to one another beside the center tent and under guard from two Stone Brothers. The Brothers spoke kindly to their charges, and gave them water and food. They even took them for brief walks one at a time, without their restraints, to make certain no harm came to them.

Aron climbed over the dirt trench and headed for Stormbreaker even as the boys glared after him like he was some sort of traitor.

Hadn't their fathers taught them that anger without power was folly?

Didn't they see?

In the end, Stone's training would give them power to right whatever wrongs had been done to them.

"High Master Stormbreaker," Aron said as he approached Stormbreaker, feeling the tap of the sheathed silver daggers Stormbreaker had given him on the outside of both thighs. "What would you have me do now?"

Stormbreaker, who was still hunkered over his shovel, grunted, then stopped digging and wiped his face. Windblown, Zed, and the four other Stone Brothers continued their work without so much as a glance toward Aron.

Aron stood still as Stormbreaker appraised him, then nodded. "You have worked hard and well." He gestured to Aron's breeches. "But your legs are bleeding from your riding sores again. Go and take yourself through the Veil for some concentrated healing."

"Yes, High Master." Aron tried not to look too eager.

"There's a pond just inside the tree line." Stormbreaker pointed to the eastern edge of the shelter encampments. "Take no more than half an hour, or sunset may catch you unaware."

"Yes, High Master Stormbreaker." Aron gave a quick bow of respect, turned to do as he was bade, made it about four steps—and came up short as shouting broke out in the camp circle adjoining their own. About ten yards from Aron, a big man, long-haired with a red, bushy beard, bellowed at a scrawny ginger-haired boy who stood next to a spilled bowl of porridge. Several other men moved away from the chaos. They looked much like the yelling man, perhaps older sons, or maybe relatives, six or seven in all. Aron noted the heavy, muscled arms, and that several held mallets or hammers, and he realized they were blacksmiths plying their trade on the road.

The yelling man had no hammer, which Aron thought fortunate for the child, who seemed no more than eight years, maybe nine, and not well fed. The little boy cowered away from the force of the man's rage, lifting his hands like he feared the man would strike him.

"Clumsy, dirt-eating cull," the man shouted, his words slurred from too much drink. "You killed your mother in the birthing, and you'll be my death, too!" He pointed to the spilled porridge, which to Aron stank of aged cabbage even at a distance. "Don't think you'll get another bowl this night."

Then, before Aron could cry out to stop it, the man swung his massive fist and caught the little boy in the side of his face.

The ginger-haired child crumpled like a doll thrown to the ground.

Aron barked his surprise and grabbed his own face, almost feeling the blow crushing his own bones.

Breezes blew by him, one, then two, then more, so fast he wasn't certain what was happening. Not until Stormbreaker seemed to materialize in front of the angry man, both of his gleaming saw-toothed swords drawn and ready. Windblown stood immediately behind Stormbreaker, his broadswords drawn, too. Five of the other six Stone Brothers quickly formed a ring around Stormbreaker, Windblown, the man, and the downed child, facing outward, toward the others in the man's traveling party. The blacksmiths had raised their hammers and mallets to come in defense of their own, but Aron saw awareness dawn as they studied the gray-robed men and their fearsome swords, never mind their blank, battle-ready expressions.

One at a time, the blacksmiths lowered their weapons.

Somebody nudged Aron, and he jumped.

It was Zed, only not the typical jolly, smiling Zed Aron was coming to know from their hours on the road. This was the reckless, mad Zed who had tackled a rock cat the first night Aron knew him— and Zed had his own daggers drawn.

"We fight with our Brothers," Zed whispered, not as chastisement. More teaching. Encouraging.

Aron's pulse quickened, and he cursed his own slow mind. As fast as he could, he drew his own blades.

Zed gave him a solemn nod, and they walked forward until they were in striking range of the blacksmiths, should Stormbreaker and Windblown require assistance. From the insane blaze of anger on Stormbreaker's normally calm face, Aron thought it unlikely he would need any help at all, but kept himself ready nonetheless.

Seemingly everyone within earshot had gone totally quiet. Most people were moving away, even if it meant abandoning their camp circles.

See, their frightened faces seemed to announce. *We know this is Stone business.*

Aron didn't know if law-abiding respect drove their decisions, or fear of the drawn swords, but he didn't care. Blood pounded in his ears now, and his breath came short as he gripped his daggers.

Would the drunken animal of a man be foolish enough to fight?

Aron glanced at the other men. Would they interfere?

There were strong customs about avoiding conflict in or around travelers' shelters, not to mention the Code of Eyrie, which forbade disrespecting Stone or Thorn.

Overhead, thunder rumbled in a completely clear late-afternoon sky, and Aron knew the sound rose from Stormbreaker's agitation.

"Pedia i'ha Sten," Stormbreaker said to the drunken man, his words laced with the force of that thunder.

The second tenet in the Canon of Stone, to which Aron had lately sworn himself each time he recited it. Children and the infirm were to be kept close to the heart. To harm children or the weak was Unforgivable in the eyes of the Stone Guild.

From behind Stormbreaker, Windblown added the next and related tenet. *"Pedia n'ha du'Sten."* His voice didn't carry the untamed power of Stormbreaker's words, but his tone held the weight of righteousness. "By the third tenet of our Canon, those who harm children or the weak answer to Stone immediately, outside any pronouncement of the law. You have harmed this child before our eyes—and I'd lay bets this isn't the first time."

The man snarled a curse in response.

Aron could see the truth on the faces of the other blacksmiths. Two of the men actually turned and walked away, and Aron wondered if they, too, had suffered at this brute's hands, with no Stone Brothers to witness their pain.

Almost as one, the Stone Brothers and Zed intoned, "Abuse of an innocent is Unforgivable," as if those words were all the reading of charges and sentencing they would offer before they took action.

The drunken man finally seemed to grasp what was happening,

what the Stone Brothers intended to do, and he made a ham-handed grab for the unconscious boy.

Stormbreaker smashed his elbow into the man's chin so fast Aron barely perceived the motion. The man almost fell, righted himself, and howled as he raised both hands to his now-bleeding face.

"Step away from the boy," Stormbreaker commanded, already back in ready stance with his swords. "Don't tempt me to kill you. I'm already too eager to see your blood on my blades."

The man recovered himself enough to spit at Stormbreaker, who didn't move so much as a fraction. Then the man growled, "What right have you, interfering between a father and his son? Get out of my camp circle." He rubbed his chin, then seemed to think better of his attitude. "We've plenty of coin. I'll see that you're paid for your troubles over this useless bit of skin and bones."

He made as if to kick the child, but Stormbreaker blocked the blow with his own foot.

The man staggered.

Stormbreaker didn't.

Aron squeezed his daggers so hard the silver handles felt like they were burning into his palms. It might have been his imagination, but he thought he could smell the sour-rag scent of the drunkard's belligerence and fear.

Fight, he willed, hoping the man would attack. Hoping his remaining friends and family would attack.

Fight.

Fight!

Aron wanted his first real chance to battle beside his guild master. He wanted to yell and scream and stab, and let out some of the anger steaming through his bones. But the man wasn't moving. He once more got his balance and stood staring at Stormbreaker. After a tense, silent second, he moved a step away from the ginger-haired boy.

Lightning rippled along Stormbreaker's forearms, and the man moved again, this time several steps away.

When Stormbreaker spoke, his words were tight and harsh. "The flesh of your flesh is your son no longer."

Aron flinched as he recognized the ritual words he had heard his father speak only weeks ago, though it already felt like years.

The man's eyes went wide. "You can't—" he sputtered, but Stormbreaker continued.

"He is dead to you, to his mother, to his brothers and sisters. He is disinherited from you, before these witnesses." Stormbreaker paused, and more lightning traveled across his shoulders. Wind whistled around the camp circle, but dissipated when he spoke again. "I lay foul any claim he has to your lands or name. He will go from this place, never to return. If he should return, you will give him no welcome."

"Is it binding?" Aron murmured to Zed, risking a quick glance at his companion. "Can Stormbreaker speak those words for the man?"

Zed nodded, his eyes shining. "Stone can claim an abused child at any time, just like they claimed us at Harvest."

"What is the boy's name?" Stormbreaker asked, and when the man lunged forward and tried to grab him, he smashed the man's eye with another blinding-fast turn of his elbow.

This time, the man went down heavily on his knees and didn't try to get up.

"Raaf," the man said, as if at last realizing he was overmatched.

Windblown moved in to stand over the drunkard as Stormbreaker sheathed his swords. When he knelt to retrieve the boy's limp body, he said, "I'll call you Raaf Thunderheart until you earn some other distinction." Stormbreaker kissed the boy's forehead, and Aron saw what looked like tears gleaming in his green eyes. "You must have thunder in your essence to have survived the likes of this."

To Aron's surprise, Stormbreaker didn't proceed with the rest of the ritual, the words that would have pledged Raaf Thunderheart to the Stone Guild forever.

As if reading the question in his expression, Zed murmured, "Raaf will be given the opportunity to join the guild when he's older. For now, he'll be healed and sheltered at Triune, with others like him."

When Aron didn't respond, Zed continued, keeping his tone so low only Aron could hear him. "Stone takes all wounded children who need their assistance, plus child-criminals and incorrigibles. Orphans go to the Thorn Guild. Or they're supposed to. We get a fair lot of them, too."

Aron pondered this new information.

His father had taught him some about both guilds, but clearly, there was more to know, far more than he ever expected. A new emotion competed with that all-gnawing anger inside him, a wider, broader sensation. Maybe something like pride, that he might one day rescue a child himself, and take the child safe away from some drunken monster.

"Back away with your weapons raised," Zed told Aron as Windblown, Stormbreaker, and the boy moved away from the kneeling man. They flowed past Zed and Aron, heading for the Stone camp circle. "If that dirt-eater or his people come after us, cut first and consider later."

Aron did as he was told, giving ground but keeping his eyes fixed on the man and the other blacksmiths. When he tried to swallow, he found his throat dry.

The other five Stone Brothers were withdrawing in similar fashion, swords still at the ready.

No one made a move to follow.

Moments later, Zed and two of the Brothers were running toward the barn to retrieve horses.

Stormbreaker placed the child on the ground in front of the nearest tent and began to minister to the wounded boy. Aron sheathed his daggers and stood at Stormbreaker's side in case he was needed. Three more of the Stone Brothers began digging the tallow circle again while a fourth posted himself as guard between the hostile camp circle and their own.

Meanwhile, Windblown unlocked the cuffs on one of the shackled boys. "Gather your things and help your guild master," he told them. "You'll ride out tonight."

"But it's less than an hour until full dark," Aron said, then smacked his hand over his own mouth.

Windblown gave him an icy glare. "You'd do well to learn when silence suits you."

"A few of our Brothers have to leave with Raaf, and they have to let the boy's people see them ride out." Stormbreaker sounded distracted as he rubbed a bit of salve on the boy's cut cheek. "As the night grows long and they drink more, those men might be tempted to try to take him back."

Stormbreaker let out a breath, and his next words sounded tired, as if the conflict had drained all the force from his will and body. "You did well, following Zed's lead, but don't be too eager to fight, Aron Weylyn. Spilled blood always comes at some cost."

At this caution, Aron had to force himself not to frown—and he barely got his body to bend in the bow of acknowledgment.

Stormbreaker nodded at Aron's bloodstained breeches. "Go now, as I instructed before, while you still have a bit of day left to you. Clean up and do what you can toward your own healing—but pay heed to the time and the angle of the light."

CHAPTER FOURTEEN

ARON

I can do it.

It was a bold plan, but possible.

And this, more than anything, might grant him some relief from the turmoil always lurking at the edges of his own mind. All else in his life remained little more than a blur, as it had for all the hard days of riding and training and failing and knowing only small successes. Paths, byways, finally now a wide section of great road clogged with so many travelers Aron could scarcely keep track of it all. But it was hard for him, where they rode now.

The Brailing *Road.*

Seeing those words carved into a pylon a day ago had set him to his current line of thinking, and brought him to the realization that he couldn't wait until his training with Stone was finished, until the war ended, until he had a legal chance to address his family's murderers.

Aron scowled at the thought of the name he had carried from birth until his claiming by Stone.

Brailing.

His rising anger forced him to hesitate as he tried to slip through the Veil. His fists clenched in the grass beside him, tearing out thick green blades. Violet hues of sunset played off the surface of the little pond and turned Aron's reflection into a horror of waves and lines. When he thought of being divested of the name "Brailing," he now felt nothing but a fierce joy mingled with relief.

Behind him, a thin line of *dantha* trees swayed in the light breeze as in the distance travelers finished boarding their animals, cleaned up from dinners, and lit tallow lines circling encampments.

May Raaf Thunderheart and his keepers travel safely, Aron thought, though he didn't direct that plea toward the Brother of Many Faces. He was through with the Brother, just like he was through with the Brailing name.

Aron took a centering breath, and his nose stung from the chilly air. The nights were getting cold now, colder each night that they traveled. They were almost out of the dynast forests, close to the flatlands. Smells had changed from loam and leaves to dust and cooking from increasingly more frequent villages and towns Aron couldn't name and didn't care to. The sooner they got to Triune, the better. Once at the Stone stronghold, he would gladly surrender the hated bit of sapphire circling his left ankle. Anyone who bore that blue *cheville* should feel the shame and disgrace of Lord Brailing's treachery.

Murderer. Fiend.

Aron glared at his face in the pond and imagined the ripples to be wrinkles, willed his hair to darken, commanded his body to grow and change to its man-weight and man-size. *However long it takes, I will be the one to seek out Lord Brailing, or his sons, or his sons' sons.* One day, that monster would pay for the blood he spilled along the Watchline.

It took Aron another few moments to regain control of his temper enough to slow his breathing and use the light on the water as a focus point. The *tap-lap*, *tap-lap* of wavelets against wet dirt helped him ease into a mental rhythm. The world around him fell back a pace, then two, as Aron's consciousness at last settled enough to slip through the Veil.

As Dari had taught him across their training sessions, he made no attempt to shift his focus, but instead took stock of his enhanced perceptions. The water before him now glittered like dazzling purple diamonds, so bright he had to narrow his eyes to bear the gleam. The pop and whish of fish breathing and feeding filled the air, along with the rustle of grass moving beneath the cool winds and the loud rush of *dantha* leaves behind him. Travelers spoke in shouts and whispers, and if Aron chose to, he could concentrate until he eavesdropped on any conversation he chose. Often, he did so, but tonight, he had other purposes in mind, and he needed to hurry before sunset.

First, to be true to his word and charge, Aron let his thoughts dwell on the ache and burn of his legs. He stretched his mind's power into the broken skin and the few weeping sores that remained near his knees, urging his body to heal the rents and stave off infection. He gave the tissue warmth and blood flow, and at the same time, eased his own pain enough that he would be able to walk without pointing his knees east-west and waddling like a waterfowl.

When he felt like he had done enough to ensure another day's riding, Aron turned his consciousness to the essence of his *graal* and made certain that it seemed dull and weak.

That was getting as easy as breathing, just as Dari had promised.

Now, he formed a filmy "cover" of thought around himself, which would shield his audible thoughts so that anyone more than an arm's length from him couldn't easily ascertain what was in his mind. Dari said he had learned that trick better than most Fae, and his *graal* likely gave him a natural affinity for it.

When Aron completed these precautions, he eased his awareness away from his body, the pond, and the travelers' shelter. This part of being on the other side of the Veil was a lot harder. Movement, or more specifically, controlling movement. Most of the time, when people meditated, their awareness hovered right next to their tangible self, so close they could still hear their own heartbeat. His own body, his immediate surroundings—that's usually all Aron could see.

Tonight, alone and unchecked, he intended to move so far away from himself that he couldn't even catch a glimpse of his own body. He kept going, aiming for someplace high above the people and trees, where he could see for endless leagues and search out his targets. A small amount at a time, he moved forward and upward, seeing first the shelter and nearby woods, then more. Forests and roads. Huts. Villages. Towns.

At first he moved south, slowly.

East, slowly.

His perspective blurred and a wave of nausea almost sent him spinning back into his waiting flesh and bones.

Careful.

Slow.

Careful.

He breathed in time with his own internal cautions.

Slow. Slow. Take your time. Look.

He paused a few breaths to glance back at himself and make certain his heart was still beating. The image of his body seemed no more than a faintly glowing speck on the ground, very far below him.

Then he moved on. Farther. Higher.

This was dangerous, he knew that, but he had survived such a journey once before, during the battle with the manes. And he had done *that* by accident. Surely it was much safer taking such a trip on purpose.

Soon he could see that the roads of Eyrie teemed with people. Fires blazed along dozens of byways. But Aron was searching for one byway in particular. A small one, insignificant to most, far in the middle of nothing.

He let his heart guide him, let his instincts pull him, until gradually his surroundings seemed a bit more familiar. Then very familiar.

These woods, he had traveled before, hunting with his fathers and brothers. If he flew east, he'd be over the thick part of the forest, and soon at the dark, deep trenches of the Scry. If he flew south, he'd find the small mountains between Dyn Brailing and Dyn Ross, and farther south, he'd see the mists of the Deadfall.

He was almost home. Almost back to tiny spot in the scrub grass and dirt that he knew so, so well—and then he was standing in the muck of his own hog pen.

And standing.

And looking.

And blinking away startled tears.

A cry of rage rose in his depths, and before he could stop himself, he loosed the fierce noise on the other side of the Veil.

The shout blew out of him like an urgent howl of ear-crushing proportions, rattling Aron's senses as if a boulder had exploded right beside his head.

As his essence vibrated from the error, he was pretty certain that his cry had been audible to anyone on the other side of the veil. His "cover" contained thoughts, not actual noises.

Stupid. Stupid!

He tried to get hold of himself, tried to shake off the failure as best he could, and somehow managed not to curse aloud and add to the mistake.

The essence of Aron's feet rested on black, dry mud, so brittle it snapped at the slightest movement of his toes. It was as if some unimaginable heat had scorched the moisture from the earth itself, consuming hogs, slops, fence, and all.

Everything.

Everything was burned.

The barn—gone.

The house—nothing but sticks and ashes.

Except for a bit of burned detritus, all traces that a family had lived in this small space, deep in the reaches of nowhere, had been totally erased.

Aron found breathing difficult as an inner pain claimed him.

Dari's people called the other side of the Veil the "world-carved-over-the-world," and Aron now grasped that description more than he wished. Each charred bit of his family's barn, his family's ruined home, seemed so vivid it almost had a life of its own. He could see each blackened furrow in the bits of wood, sense the patterns of smoke and burn on nearby trees, and even trace the crumbling tracks of a wagon in the dirt near where he stood.

His gaze sharpened on the track, and he mentally compared it to what he remembered of his family's wagon.

Then he followed the track away from the ruined house.

It moved in the opposite direction from the path Stormbreaker had taken with Aron and their party on Harvest, almost directly toward the woods and the Scry.

Cayn's teeth. Aron sobbed quietly to himself. *They ran to the Guard, not away from them.*

Surely his father had known better.

Aron remembered the conversation between his father and Stormbreaker, and added up the fact that Stormbreaker had warned Wolf Brailing to take his family and flee. Stormbreaker had gestured, had shown Aron's father the direction from whence the soldiers would come.

But Father would have realized he could never move fast enough to outstrip mounted guardsmen, not with small children and a wagon pulled by one old ox barely worth its feed.

Aron kept following the wagon tracks, until they turned off the byway onto a hunting path.

You tried to take them into the woods.

Aron realized he was speaking as if some ghostly remnant of his father could hear him, but he couldn't help himself, or the awful, queasy misery roiling through the essence of his body. He drifted forward, needing to see, but not wanting to see.

You tried to take them into the woods, to hide them away, but here—Aron paused next to the burned husk of his family's wagon—*here, the axle broke because of the rough terrain.*

A little farther into the woods, he discovered the carcass of the old ox. *And here, the ox gave out, and you cut its throat to quell its suffering.*

Aron knew if he was following his family's tracks so easily, guardsmen would have had little difficulty doing the same, especially when the trail was fresh. Wolf Brailing knew how to disguise his movements, but a wife, six sons, and two daughters did not.

So it was that Aron was only mildly surprised to discover the partially burned bones of his family, piled together in a clearing, *chevilles* still attached to their skeletal ankles.

Though he knew what he was seeing was only an image, only a reflection of what lay on the "normal" side of the Veil, Aron reached out and brushed his fingers against the bones of the tiniest hand. Then a larger bone that might have been his mother's wrist, protruding from the pile.

At least they seemed peaceful enough in posture, as if they were all dead before their bodies had been stacked and burned and mingled.

Had they understood what had happened when they rose as manes and fled mindless and hungry down the byway toward where he waited? Had they known even a moment of awareness?

The rage inside Aron bred more rage and more, until the feeling seemed to grow teeth and claws of its own to dig out of his consciousness and eat the world.

He let his hands wander across the smooth and grooved bits of his brothers, his sisters, his parents. Something nudged at his awareness, something out of place or not quite right, but beyond the obvious horror of seeing them all dead but still banded, undispatched, their spirits doomed to rise so terribly, he couldn't grasp what his enhanced senses were trying to tell him.

All he knew for certain was that this sight would live in his mind forever.

He would etch it there, his own private world-carved-over-the-world.

He would let this image guide him this day, and every day to follow.

My promise—no, my oath—*to you,* he thought, drawing back his hand even though he didn't want to surrender the contact.

Time was passing.

Time was running out, and he wanted—needed—to act now, with this picture fixed firmly over his other thoughts.

Aron gave himself over to the clawed thing inside him, that thing made of fury and single-minded vengeance, and left his family behind.

This time, he moved much faster. East, then north. East, then north.

In due time, Aron saw little ginger-haired Raaf Thunderheart and the Stone Brothers who took him away from his family, riding hard along the Brailing Road below. The boy was awake now, face bruised, eye swollen closed. He clung to the waist of one of the Brothers as they galloped down the Brailing Road, horses' hooves kicking up stones as they hammered around curves and over small smells. The Brother he was riding with carried a flaming torch, just enough light to cast off the growing shadows on the byway. The other Stone Brother carried the Harvest prize, but that boy was too busy clinging to the horse's neck to offer much resistance.

Aron moved on, still hoping for the best for Raaf, though that hope was distant now, just a shapeless blob, nothing in size against Aron's thickly clotted anger.

He shifted the force of his own will once more, north another fraction. Then west, a smaller fraction.

And finally, *finally* saw a clump of soldiers who looked to be guardsmen. Their banners bore the yellow and sapphire blue of Dyn Brailing, and their shields carried the symbol of the ruling seat of his former dynast—the head of an eagle with its wide, all-seeing eye.

Was this Lord Brailing's rear guard?

Aron ground his teeth, or rather the essence of his teeth, but it felt real enough.

Just the sight of that banner, that shield, made the fire in his blood more painful.

And now the question he hadn't been able to answer.

Was it possible to strike at people from the other side of the Veil?

In moments, Aron would know the answer to that question, no matter what it might cost him.

CHAPTER FIFTEEN

ARON

Aron knew all too well that he could hurt someone who had gone through the Veil with him, or anyone whose essence hovered near his own. He *had* hurt Dari and Stormbreaker, the only two people now left in Eyrie that meant anything to him.

And they believe it's wrong, using my mind-talents to harm someone else, except under threat, to defend my own life in case of attack.

Below Aron's awareness, the Brailing guardsmen went about making their camp safe for the night, oblivious to rock cats prowling nearby, and even some mocker foxes and hoards of rats displaced by village fires. They were certainly oblivious to Aron, too, and his vengeful intentions, or they'd be drawing swords to defend themselves.

Stormbreaker had insisted Aron should use his *graal* only to defend himself from an immediate threat, if at all.

Lord Brailing's Dynast Guard wasn't attacking him now.

But wouldn't they set upon him soon enough, if they found him?

He brought forth the image of his family's bones to answer his own question.

If Lord Brailing or anyone loyal to him realized Aron had escaped the slaughter along the Watchline, the soldiers would hunt him until they killed him, too. He was within bounds and ethics to see to his own safety.

So why did this line of reasoning seem shabby to the point of being threadbare?

Stop it. Just concentrate, and do what you came to do.

When Aron thought these things, the audible manifestation of the words sounded much like his father's voice.

His dead father's voice.

Aron took that for an omen that Wolf Brailing would approve of satisfying this blood-debt. If he were alive, he might even help Aron complete the task.

Besides, what were Aron's lessons with Dari for, if not to make him more powerful—and ultimately, a better killer, just like his weapons training with Stormbreaker was designed to accomplish?

Drawing strength from the fresh, vivid picture of his murdered loved ones, and more strength from the memory of his father's approval when he showed strength and competence, Aron focused on the soldiers and counted them. Close to a hundred—many, but not enough to be the rear guard. Lord Brailing's dynast army numbered in the tens of thousands, and Aron couldn't imagine a rear guard any smaller than a few thousand.

So this was a patrol.

Perhaps one of the patrols who broke the Watchline.

The essence of Aron's fists flexed.

If he imagined the soldiers dead, if he put enough power behind the thought, would they die?

No. It's not that simple. I have to convince them to die. To kill themselves or one another.

He thought about the example Stormbreaker had given the morning he and Dari first explained Aron's legacy. A man on a cliff, surrounded by mockers—

But there weren't any cliffs here.

And would the effort Aron exerted trying to plant some dangerous "truth" in the soldiers' minds kill him, too? It might, he figured. Especially if he tried to take down more than one life force.

Spilled blood always comes at some cost, Stormbreaker had told Aron only minutes ago. And Dari and his father had taught him that time on the other side of the Veil, simply staying in the altered state of meditation, especially farther and farther through the Veil—such journeys had a cost, too, in energy and health.

Why hadn't he thought of these things before?

So foolish.

He should have come up with something truly terrifying to "suggest" to the soldiers before he ever crossed through the Veil. But there was nothing for it now. He was here and they were here.

Aron's attention shifted back to the rock cats and rats near the soldiers.

How much would it cost him to stir the animals toward the camp?

Could he even manage such a feat?

That might be more fair. At least the guardsmen would have a chance to defend themselves, a fair shot at survival.

Which is more than they gave my family.

Aron's consciousness leaned toward the rock cats, but at the last second, he reeled himself back and cursed to himself.

This isn't wrong. Just reach for the rock cats. Imagine something for them to see. A wounded stag, perhaps? Help them imagine the scent of fresh blood. They'll go into a frenzy, and—

And—

And . . . this is wrong.

It was all Aron could do not to shout again.

How could it be wrong? As far as he was concerned, he had a blood-debt owed to him by the entire Dynast Guard of Dyn Brailing, not to mention Lord Brailing himself.

But Dari and Stormbreaker said this was wrong. The Stone Guild would probably judge it wrong.

His essence tightened and seemed to hum with frustration inside the "cover" he had established for himself.

For killers, Stone has damnably many rules about how to take a life.

The Code of Eyrie contained a law against random murder, but no prohibitions about harming people from the other side of the Veil. The Canon of Stone, however, was a different matter. Aron was pretty sure the last of the six new tenets he had memorized and recited, *Libra i'honore*—judgment with honor—somehow prohibited what he was considering.

Yes, that's what was troubling his mind. That, and his father's teachings. Kindness, honest labor, honor, and truth. Where was the honor in this? The honest labor? Never mind the kindness, or even the truth.

I'd be judging these soldiers without a proper reading of charges and sentencing—the justice all of the Judged receive. I'd be executing them without offering them a chance at combat, and the innocent would die with the guilty.

His entire being twitched with heat, with rage made manifest on the other side of the Veil, barely contained by his cover.

No soldier carrying the banner of Brailing is an innocent, and they don't deserve kindness. That *much is the truth. And there is honor enough in doing away with murderers.*

Aron gazed at the prowling rock cats again, feeling the blaze of that angry, angry heat covering his body, feeling the claws of his need for vengeance scooping out his guts.

Suddenly, he was closer to the rock cats, seeing them more clearly, and the cover around his thoughts and essence evaporated. His eyes fixed on the big fangs. The bloodstained paws. He could almost reach out and touch one of the tawny, spotted coats.

Is it you? called a voice, as loud and sonorous as a bell from a Temple of the Brother. It rang across the Veil like a living thing, snatching hold of Aron and yanking him completely away from the rock cats and the soldiers he had been planning to destroy.

Wind seemed to strike him from all directions, blowing him upward, sucking him past anywhere he intended to go. He flailed the essence of his hands as if to grab hold of something, anything that might slow his mind-jarring ascent. On the other side of the Veil, there was nothing to hold. It was a place, but not a place. A realm of pure spirit, not substance.

A pressure formed behind Aron's eyes, then pain. The essence of his ears filled until he heard nothing but the squeezing thunder of his own heartbeat. Pound and pound and pound, and he couldn't breathe, couldn't feel anything but ice forming around him, on him, freezing his toes and fingers until he feared they would snap from his thin arms and legs.

Here, said the voice, still a boy's voice, but mingled with a girl's voice, too.

Aron stopped so suddenly his guts almost heaved through his eyeballs. He shook his head, tried to clear his mind, loosen the leather bands that seemed to squeeze his ears, and found his essence standing—no, *floating . . .* somewhere.

A tall, beautiful woman in silver robes stood before him. In the nowhere-nothingness Aron now occupied, she seemed so vivid she couldn't possibly be real. Her blond hair spilled in waves down her shoulders, and her cornflower-blue eyes narrowed as she studied him. Silver light blazed off her skin, laced with what looked like fine strands and shimmers of copper. Aron didn't know whether to embrace her or cry out in fear of her.

Goddess . . .

The thought blended and swirled through Aron's mind against his own will, and he barely managed to keep the word inaudible on the other side of the Veil. Guilt stabbed at him as he realized he had just betrayed his own mother's beliefs about the Brother and the heavens above, but he couldn't help it.

Goddess . . . and yet . . .

There was something fearsome in her presence.

He had never seen one of Dyn Altar's great white Roc birds, a predator even rock cats and mockers feared, but Aron imagined a Roc's gaze would look as shrewd and hungry as this woman's stare.

With one graceful, terrifying hand, the goddess-monster reached for him.

Aron let out a shriek and tumbled backward, away from her, flying, spinning, falling, and crying out until—

Until he was floating again, somewhere too close to the stars and too far from level ground.

Somewhere on top of the world.

This time, the figure before him was a large, pale boy with golden curls and eyes so brightly blue they might have been made of sparkling light and pure water. The boy's skin glowed a brilliant ruby, or rather the essence of the *graal* that hovered above the boy's skin like a beacon.

Snowflakes tumbled around them, imaginary yet real at the same time, and Aron's teeth chattered. When he looked at his feet to see if he still had his toes, he saw pebbles and rocks and scrub plants he had never seen before, but knew from his father's descriptions to be mountain vegetation.

Behind him, there was nothing but a terrifying void, blacker and emptier than any hole Aron could imagine.

He forced his awareness back to the boy. *Where am I? How did I come here?*

Shadows loomed, and Aron thought he could make out a rough travelers' shelter and a small stable behind the boy. Smoke issued from the shelter's chimney, shimmering silver puffs in the moonslight, almost overrun by the snow. He couldn't smell anything at all, or sense anything beyond the bone-shattering cold, and he wondered if that was because he was perceiving his surroundings through the boy's thoughts instead of his own. Perhaps this was the boy's method of answering one of his questions—where he was. Perhaps the boy was telling Aron all he knew of his surroundings.

I was looking for you, the boy said, as if that answered Aron's other question, about how he arrived. *It's me. It's Nic. It's been so long since I've seen your glow. Where did it go?*

The boy, who had called himself Nic, smiled and reached out a pudgy white hand, offering it as a dynast noble would, to have the knuckles touched with respect. Aron stared at the ghostly fingers, at the rounded wrist, uncertain of what to do even though he knew from his father's teaching.

Nic's smile faltered, and he lowered his hand slowly back to his side. *My apologies if I offended you. I'm not sure why I did that.*

Aron felt too dizzy and enraged at the interruption of his plans to respond.

I don't know why we've come here, Nic admitted. *Perhaps I ran away from my home. Or . . . flew away.* His expression shifted to one of puzzlement, as if he was rifling through his own memory and finding nothing but vague impressions. *Yes, that seems closer to the truth.*

Aron pondered in silence for a moment, then shivered as the boy regarded him with those bright blue eyes, the loudest eyes Aron had ever seen save for Stormbreaker's. That more than anything else calmed the clawing beast inside him, and made him focus on the situation at hand instead of dwelling on the disruption of his plans.

Will you meet me when I come? Nic asked, quiet and sincere.

Something in the boy's demeanor reminded Aron of where he had seen him before, or a boy very much like him. The first night after his Harvest, before the manes attacked—wasn't this the dying spirit he encountered on the other side of the Veil?

Will you meet me when I come? Nic repeated.

Aron felt a flicker of surprise. *Come where?*

The boy hung his head, and for a moment Aron was painfully reminded of his younger sisters—though he was fairly certain Nic was older than he was. There was something soft about him, yet something strong, too. Something unforgettable.

Curse him for making me think of my sisters, Aron thought, managing not to broadcast the thought across the Veil where Nic could hear it. He wanted to slap the boy, or grab him and hug him like a younger child. The conflicting urge was untenable, and Aron felt his essence waver.

I'll meet you, he said, more to stop Nic's suffering than anything else, and hoping the boy might let him go, send him back, somehow undo whatever he had done to bring Aron to this place.

Do you give your oath that you'll meet me? Nic whispered. *Not your promise, but your oath?*

The boy would never stop, never release him if he didn't answer. Aron knew this deep inside his own instincts, and he felt trapped.

Give your oath, Nic said again.

Yes! Aron mind-shouted, just to make the boy turn him loose. Nic flinched away from him as Aron kept ranting. *Now go—and let me go!*

The boy's image vanished, just winked away from Aron like a snowflake that landed in a flame.

The vague image of the travelers' shelter wavered and disappeared, along with the weather, the ground, the rocks. Aron realized he was standing in that blacker-than-black void.

No.

Not standing.

Falling!

He cried out and flailed the essence of his arms.

Something stung his face once, then twice, drawing quick tears to his eyes.

Scaly, clawed hands reached into the nothingness and grabbed him, as if the beast inside him had become completely real. The hands yanked him down so hard he was sure every frozen bone in his body— real or spiritual—would splinter when he landed.

"Little fool!" he heard, and the voice was female, yet not. Deep and growly and so powerful it blasted away all the fullness in his ears.

A minute later—or was it only a second?—he blinked his eyes, his real, physical eyes, and saw the purpled rim of the setting sun reflected back to him, broken into prisms by ripples and wavelets.

The pond. Noises from the shelter encampment behind him. The faint smell of burning tallow . . .

Was he back on this side of the Veil?

Someone slapped him so hard his head snapped to the side, away from the blow. He shouted and grabbed his cheek against the sting. Fluid ran out of his nose and eyes and ears, and his teeth danced and jittered together, fighting off what felt like dead-of-winter chill.

"*What* were you thinking?" Dari's angry hiss made Aron turn his head back toward her, his fingers still pressed against his throbbing cheek. "Were you *trying* to die? Fool. Fool!"

She gazed at him, mouth open, dark eyes burning with anger and concern.

Aron couldn't look away from her.

She was just so pretty.

No, more than pretty.

Dari was as beautiful as a rare, perfect jewel, and her fury only made her more so.

He pulled his palm away from his face and realized the warm fluid he felt was blood.

Dari moved so quickly Aron perceived nothing but a blur. He felt the pressure of her palms against the sides of his head, then a white-hot light burned through his mind, searing his awareness, blasting heat through every inch of his flesh.

Somehow she knew what he had been planning to do to the soldiers, didn't she?

And now she was killing him because he was too dangerous. He couldn't be allowed to live.

If anyone else had attacked him, Aron would have fought back, but not against her. Not against Dari.

She was killing him, and maybe it was for the best. He tried to think, to form some logical resistance that wouldn't harm her, but he was dying and he couldn't even fight her.

After a long, agonizing moment, Aron knew nothing but darkness deeper than the void he had seen on the other side of the Veil—and pain worse than anything he had ever experienced.

CHAPTER SIXTEEN

NIC

The woman sitting above him smelled of almonds, which frightened Nicandro Mab beyond reason.

Torchlight from several dancing flames staked around the wagon set her shadow to dancing like some wine-maddened fool. If he could have shifted away from her, he would have, but spikes of pain nailed him to the wagon in which he lay.

Where am I?

Am I dead?

A cool breeze chilled his burning skin as he tried to raise his fingers and touch his own cheek, but his arms had been pulled straight and bound to heavy pieces of wood. Torch flames hissed as he realized both of his legs had been treated in similar fashion, and cloth straps held him to a wide, smooth board. Even the thought of movement brought tears of agony. Nic groaned before he thought to hold back the sound.

"Be still, boy," the woman said without turning toward him. "You have many wounds and broken bones."

Nic blinked at the stars and twinned moons above him.

Since he first began waking, an hour ago, maybe longer, he had been expecting the woman's voice to sound rough and harsh, but this—this was the sound of ancestors gone to the Brother, wings restored, singing joyous praises on a hilltop at sunrise. This was a voice that dulled minds with its sweetness, that stole awareness even as a hidden dagger crept toward its target.

Nic's chest ached more fiercely.

Had the woman moved?

He didn't think so.

She continued to sit motionless, some sort of silvery statue bathed by the frenetic torchlight, holding her hands and the reins in her lap.

He couldn't see her face for the cowl pulled up to hide her features. He wasn't certain of the color of her robes in the darkness—but he thought they might be gray.

I'm giving myself night-scares.

His mind struggled to gather the pieces of his life and make sense of what was happening, but he could not. The last thing he remembered was speaking to a boy on a mountaintop—a boy who glowed sapphire blue, almost as bright as the midday sun.

Had that conversation truly taken place?

I flew.

I think I flew away from the castle, from my mother in Can Rowan. I flew away because . . . because Kestrel died.

The sound of wind in cloth startled him, and when he turned his eyes to where the woman had been, he saw only the reins from their team of oxen, knotted around the wagon's board seat.

"I'm here," the woman said from Nic's other side.

Brother save me. She's in the back of the wagon with me now.

And he couldn't move.

Fiery bolts of misery traveled through his face and head as his teeth clamped together.

The woman knelt, head bowed, attending to several small leather goatskins belted at her waist. She selected one, then lifted her hand and her head as she offered it to Nic. Torch shadows and moonslight played off her face, but he thought he caught glimpses of black marks beside her eyes and white-blond hair brushing the sides of her chin.

When Nic made no effort to open his mouth, when he pressed his lips together so tightly it would have taken murderous force to open his mouth, the woman laughed.

Once more, the sound nearly wrecked Nic's nerves, because it was so mellow and beautiful.

But what had he been expecting instead? Some sort of deadly hiss?

This woman could be some rector's errand runner, ferrying him away to the Thorn Guild for healing.

Or maybe she's Cayn in disguise. If I could sit up and shove back her hood, I might find the god of death's terrible stag horns, waiting to gore me until manes come to feast on my blood.

For some reason, Nic found himself more comfortable with thoughts of Cayn than the idea that he might be going to Thorn to be nursed by rectors and their apprentices.

The woman offered the goatskin to him again, but that ever-present hint of almonds in the air made Nic shake. He whimpered from the pain of the movement, but still refused to open his mouth.

"I'm not offering you Mercy, boy." She raised the skin to her own lips, took a sip, swallowed, then offered it to him again. "It's a mix of water and nightshade wine, proportioned for you. Drink. It'll ease your pain."

Mercy.

As in, a peaceful death extended to those who suffer.

Nic squinted at the woman's robes again, and he decided the cloth might be gray after all.

He was in the company of a Stone Sister.

No wonder the air seemed thick with the scent of poison.

But she drank from the goatskin she was extending toward him, and she told him she wasn't offering him Mercy.

Nic wished he could see the woman's eyes, to judge her trustworthiness for himself.

As if hearing his silent plea, she pushed back her cowl. The darkness around them seemed to lighten, as if clouds had cleared away from the moons, and Nic saw the woman more clearly now. She was small-boned, thin, with dark blue eyes that studied him without mirth or judgment. At the corners of both eyes, reaching down to her cheeks, two black spirals had been tattooed into her brown skin.

Brown skin—like she might be from Dyn Cobb, but her white-blond hair, cropped at her shoulders, looked more like Fae bloodlines from Dyn Vagrat. This puzzled Nic. An unusual combination of traits, but then, he had met many Fae of mixed heritage.

Even in the semidarkness, Nic could see that the woman's arms were lined over with *dav'ha* marks.

A woman?

Tattooed like a soldier?

On impulse, or maybe out of sheer awe and confusion, he sipped from the goatskin she offered. The thick sugar-potato taste of nightshade flowed over his tongue, burned down his throat, and rushed into his aching, growling belly. Moments later, relief edged outward, touching first his spine, then his arms and legs, then his fingers and face. First a warm, soothing tingle, then a blessed partial numbness that helped his tears stop flowing.

The woman nodded her approval, then hung the skin back on her belt. "You're feverish, or I'd offer you more." Her teeth flashed white in the moonslight, a quick smile, and she tapped a goatskin on the opposite side of her belt. "This is the one with the poison, in case you continue to wonder."

Nic gaped at her, and she shrugged. "Some can smell the almond scent, some can't. I rarely use it anyway. I prefer hand-to-hand combat when I deal with my Judged. Most men—and women, too—underestimate me."

"S-stone," Nic managed, trying his voice for the first time, and grateful to find he still had the capacity to talk. Then his thoughts and education combined to tell him the rest of what he should have known. "*Benedets.*"

The woman touched one of the spiral marks, then the other. "Yes. I'm marked with two full *benedets.* That's because I'm Tiamat, Third High Mistress of Stone, though most call me Tia, or use my guild name, which is Snakekiller. And you are?"

"Nic—" Nic broke off before giving a full response. His mind raced over possibilities, finding many, settling on none, but he was suddenly certain of one thing more than all others. He did not wish to be returned to the castle. To his mother. To the destiny that awaited him there.

He closed his eyes—and seemed to fall.

Fly . . .

Nic cried out and lurched against his bindings. Confusion hit him so hard, so fast he wondered if the Stone Sister had given him Mercy after all.

"Easy." Her smooth tones broke through the rattling in Nic's skull, and her cool touch to his shoulder cooled the raging heat on his face, in his mind. "Breathe slowly when the pain hits you, boy. Nic, if that's your name. Just keep your mind on the flow of air, nothing else, nothing outside of that motion."

Her words made concentration possible, and Nic did as she instructed, moving air in through his nose and out through his mouth. The pounding, tearing throb in his muscles and bones eased, then eased a bit more, until he once more opened his eyes to see the woman called Tia Snakekiller kneeling by his side. Her small, graceful fingers rested on his shoulders, and the light that had allowed Nic to see the details of her features had receded, but not completely died away.

She was gazing at him, not smiling, but not coldly or harshly either. Her expression seemed kind, and somewhat concerned.

For a time, they sat in silence.

When Nic thought he could speak coherently, he said, "I'm Nic Vespa," borrowing a surname he had heard on one of his many trips to the castle kitchens.

Snakekiller raised one eyebrow, then seemed to accept this offering. "Vespa. I know many Vespas in Dyn Mab. Goodfolk, one and all. That's a fairly common family name, is it not?"

"Yes," Nic said, since he couldn't nod with his head barely mobile.

"It's a serviceable name. We found you on a deserted side street while riding to Harvest, Nic Vespa. You were broken and bleeding, as if some brute beat you within an inch of your life. Did someone beat you?"

Her gaze was so intense Nic wished he could roll away from it. He didn't know what to say, what to tell her, so he said nothing. Some things were so clear, and others, so muddled. He might have been beaten. Was he beaten after Kestrel died?

Or . . . did he fall?

Trip and plunge from the castle?

I flew.

The thought stuck in his mind and he almost closed his eyes again. Only terror of that terrible plummeting sensation kept him from making that mistake twice.

Snakekiller's tone was both soothing and accepting. "It's no matter if you don't wish to explain. You're a child and you needed aid, and Stone gave it. The low-town rectors wouldn't take you for healing, as your wounds were well beyond their abilities, so we didn't ask them."

She paused and looked off into the night, and Nic couldn't help shuddering at the realization that he had been so near death. So close to breathing his last breath that only the dangerous medicines of Stone could help him. Then the rest of what Snakekiller told him penetrated his mind. Low-town. How had he wound up so far from the castle? The rectors who pushed him wouldn't have looked for him there. They must have assumed him dead, and by now passed another body off as his own. Since Snakekiller asked no one's permission, no one in Can Rowan knew he had survived.

When Snakekiller once more gave him her full attention, he shifted his eyes to hers, though that took more courage than he thought he possessed. "Am I a Harvest prize, then?"

"No. We've secured our Harvest in the other wagon, the one pulled by mules." She pointed into the night, to a spot Nic couldn't see. "We've been on the road nearly three weeks since we found you, but—well, I suppose you may as well know. War has begun."

Nic once more hurt himself by trying to sit up, and Snakekiller gave him another sip of relief.

As he swallowed the sweet liquid, trying to focus on the taste rather than the burning throb of his entire body, Snakekiller said, "Lord Brailing has joined his forces with those of Lord Altar. Rumor says they're both marching on Mab's western border—but Mab seems to be turning the bulk of its forces south and east, as if to make a charge toward Dyn Ross. We had to flee into the Wenhorn Mountains to avoid the armies. Now we're making for the border of Dyn Cobb, where rumors and whispers hold we'll be given safe passage back to Stone."

"Why have we stopped?" Nic asked, his words slurred from the nightshade wine. "Because it's night?"

"We ride through the night whenever we can. Even with mockers and manes, travel is safer." Snakekiller once more glanced into the darkness, but this time, her smile gave him a fresh set of chills. "We've stopped because my companion Hasty—Hastling is his proper name—believes one of his Judged has squirreled himself away on a cousin's farm nearby. I gave him and his apprentice leave to hunt for an hour. Strange times, strange measures, of course, but for Stone, duty continues even with soldiers skulking behind every tree trunk."

Nic shuddered again, this time at the image of gray-robed assassins stalking their human quarry. Once a Brother or Sister drew a stone on one of the Judged, that Judged became their personal responsibility until either the hunted or the hunter died.

Nic had never seen any part of a hunt, but his brothers had told him stories of great chases. The Judged could choose immediate combat on the grounds of Triune, which most did, or they could choose flight. Those who opted for flight were given two days' lead; then Stone came after them. Sometimes the hunt took days. Sometimes it took years. But in the end, Stone always seemed to prevail. The Judged would be found dead, arms folded over their chest, the image of Cayn's antlers burned into the flesh of their forehead. In their left hand would be the white pebble, the one the Stone Brother or Sister had drawn on the day of Judgment, with the quarry's name etched into the rock's grain.

"If I'm not to be a Harvest prize," Nic whispered, speaking to erase his terror at the thought of the hunt more than any other reason, "then what am I?"

"That will be up to you, Nic Vespa. You'll go with us to Triune, where you're welcome to stay until you've healed. When you're well, you're free to return to your people, and we'll let you leave on any convoy bound to your home territory." Snakekiller sounded earnest enough, and Nic realized that despite his education, there was much he didn't know about Stone, past the myths and stories he had gleaned from rectors and his brothers.

"If you'd rather learn a skill and petition to join a trade lodge, you may do so," Snakekiller continued. "Some of our rescues eventually seek shelter or training with Thorn, though they turn away most without bulging bags of godslight these days. Others elect to take vows with Stone."

Nic wished he could sit up so that his next words might carry some force. "I want to take vows with Stone. Can I do so now?"

Snakekiller looked surprised, then bemused, then worried. She shook her head. "With so many of your bones broken and drunk on

nightshade wine? No, Nic. Making vows to Stone is serious business—
and lifelong. Once spoken, there's no oathbreaking."

She left off with that heavy word sitting between them.

Oathbreaking.

Nic remembered hearing from his brothers that a Stone Brother or
Sister who tried to flee guild services would be hunted by their own
guild mates, not to mention the Dynast Guard—from every dynast.
Oathbreakers had no home, no family.

Oathbreakers were enemies to all.

"Give your body time to heal, Nic Vespa." Tia Snakekiller climbed
out of the back of the wagon and settled herself on the board seat in
the front, above him. He could barely see her hands and one of her
sides from his position, tied down as he was.

"Allow your mind time to clear," she said as she untied the reins
from the board where she had secured them. "When you're well, you'll
be free to make your own choices about Stone or Thorn or the trade
lodges, or some other path. Don't be so quick to seal your future. The
Mother has blessed you with many options. I suggest you consider
them all."

The Mother? Nic stared at the moons and stars above him, surprised. *Then this one is from Dyn Vagrat, or she was raised by a parent
from Vagrat, at least before she took her vows and the name of
Snakekiller.*

Only citizens of Dyn Vagrat worshipped the Mother of Mystery.
In the other dynasts, nobles and goodfolk alike prayed to the merci-
ful Brother, except in Dyn Ross to the south, where many still followed the old ways and looked to Cayn the horned god for their
relief.

How had a woman from Dyn Vagrat come to reside in Triune,
with Stone? Had she been Harvested? Run away?

Perhaps rescued, like me.

Nic tried to work up the courage to ask her, but voices rose in the distance, and Nic realized this would be her companion Hasty, return-ing from his hunt with his apprentice. From the laughter and shouts, Nic supposed the Stone Brother and his helper had been successful.

And somewhere in the darkness, a man lies dead, clutching a white pebble and wearing the mark of Cayn on his brow.

That was the custom of Stone, for sanctioned kills.

Nic felt a rush of something like power. It combined with the lin-gering effects of the nightshade wine, making him dizzy, almost giddy. He knew he should have been horrified, but all he could think was, *Well done. One less criminal to terrorize the goodfolk.*

Snakekiller's silky voice slipped into his euphoria. "Our companions are earlier than I expected. I'll ask you this once, and only once." She was speaking rapidly, as if to get out the words before the approaching men drew within earshot. "And you must answer me now. Are you cer-tain you don't wish for me to take you to the nearest Thorn guildhouse, so the rectors can take you to Eidolon for the rest of your recovery? I have no love for the men who wear black, or the Thorn Guild either, for that matter, but they would give you the respect and honor due your station in life."

Nic's heart seemed to skip and stutter, sagging into his ribs from the shock of her knowledge. "No," he said, his voice cracking with each word. "No rectors. Please."

After a moment of silence, he saw Snakekiller shift on the board above him. "Then it might be prudent if you didn't reveal the extent of your education—knowing *Sidhe* words like *benedet*, for example. And keep your speech less proper, or better yet, speak little, if at all."

Nic wanted to close his eyes, but didn't, fearful of falling in his mind, of losing what little ration he possessed. *I'm such a fool.* He started to promise to be cautious on this point, but Snakekiller plunged ahead. "Last night, you made contact with someone on the other side of the Veil. A boy with a very powerful legacy—and at least one powerful enemy. Both have mind-talents as bountiful as your own."

Now Nic's mind spun with a wildness he couldn't control. *I don't have a legacy. The rectors said I'm Quiet. I've always been Quiet. . . .*

But he had spoken to that boy on the mountaintop, hadn't he? Tia Snakekiller had just confirmed that. He had been on the other side of the Veil. How she knew that, he couldn't begin to guess, and he sensed he didn't have time to ask.

"I think it might be safer if you don't go through the Veil again until we reach Triune," she said, and this time her movements seemed to free that terrifying scent of almonds, of poison, waiting to find its quarry. "Until you have some training and some protections so no one will recognize you by your *graal*. Do you take my meaning, Nic *Vespa*?"

At that moment, Nic could do little but wish for another mouthful of nightshade wine. He wanted to drink the goatskin dry and slip into nothingness, where he couldn't make such ridiculous errors. Where there was no chance he'd be sent back to a life of treachery and murder—or the vicious madness of his mother.

"Yes, High Mistress," he whispered, hoping he was telling the truth, that he could be as careful as she was ordering him to be. "I understand."

CHAPTER SEVENTEEN

DARI

Afternoon sun cast greenish hues over the tiny Dyn Brailing village as Dari stood with Stormbreaker, Windblown, and the tearful, sag-shouldered man who had fetched them from this area's main byway. They had left the wagons, Zed, and Aron a few yards out of the town's limits, under guard of what was now a traveling group of more than twenty Stone Brothers, plus their Harvest prizes.

An agitated traveling group who knew they were moving all too slowly.

Dari glanced at the sun's position in the sky and shared the group's unrest.

Time was passing.

She could almost feel the crawl of hours across the back of her neck and shoulders. When they were finished with their business here, they would skirt the town and join the byway again as soon as possible.

But would that be soon enough?

Could they possibly be fortunate enough to avoid soldiers and bat-tles all the way to Triune?

"We're leagues from the Brailing Road now," Windblown mut-tered, and Dari took his meaning immediately.

They were alone in this abandoned place, except for the man who had fetched them. Here, there was no great crowd of witnesses, save for whatever type of goodfolk populated this bunch of dirt farms. Though she had to admit, having a small army of Stone Brothers positioned within shouting distance gave her comfort. It would take an army of fools to risk combat with such a large contingent of professional killers.

"Are you sure we should do this, Dun?" Windblown's whispered question echoed Dari's thoughts exactly.

"We'll see to our duty." Stormbreaker lifted his cowl against the wind. "Those who need Mercy don't choose the time. The time chooses them—and war or no war, we'll not leave a child suffering."

Brisk, cool breezes stirred dust down a handful of hard-packed roads little wider than paths. The sag-shouldered man picked at his tunic for a moment, adjusted the traveling pack on his back, then gestured toward one of the path-roads.

They followed him, mindful of his slowed steps, though he was young and apparently of able body. This journey must have been unspeakably hard on him, fetching Stone to minister to his only son. His pack held several days of dry rations and water, and he had been planning to walk five towns to the north, where the nearest Stone guildhouse was located. Fortunately for the man, and for the man's son who lay dying in one of these shacks, his journey hadn't taken that long. When he encountered the party of Stone Brothers returning from Harvest, he had been able to stammer out his name, Gund Zeller, and make his formal plea for Stone's intervention. Other than that, he hadn't made a sound beyond an occasional sob.

As they walked in the swirling dust, Dari kept her eyes wide and her senses on full alert. Though she had determined she could not launch an organized search for her sister until she reached Triune, there was always the chance Kate could turn up in some unexpected spot—or that someone might have seen her or heard of her.

If she's still alive.

Dari winced at her own thoughts, then let her consciousness

drift into the scent of burned cornmeal and stewing vegetables. Here and there, meat was cooking. They passed doorway after doorway, and people came to stand and watch the procession. Thin people, wrapped in thin clothes, with thin, pinched expressions. This was a poor and hungry place.

After another few steps, Dari felt a tickle in the back of her thoughts, a jangle in the mental connection she had established with Aron to save his life.

"He's awake," she murmured to Stormbreaker as they passed another shack full of scrawny, staring people. "He's getting out of the wagon to follow us. Zed's with him."

Stormbreaker kept his cowl up and seemed to be looking straight ahead. "Let them come. It won't hurt Aron to see this."

Windblown gave a sniff that Dari had learned to associate with his perpetual disapproval—of everything. Windblown thought Aron had fallen by the pond and struck his head, and that the boy was taking his own lazy time recovering. This was a perception Dari and Stormbreaker hadn't corrected.

The truth would have been too dangerous to tell.

Dari briefly closed her eyes against the grit trying to find purchase on her face.

Aron tried to murder Brailing guardsmen from the other side of the Veil.

He made contact with someone else who possesses a dangerous, powerful legacy—someone we don't know.

He overreached his training and may have damaged his own mind.

And the rest of it?

Dari had managed to forge a healing connection between them just in time to save the boy's life. If she had let Aron die, he would pose no further risk to other living creatures, accidentally or on purpose—but Dari had never been able to take that belief or habit into her own heart. Not with Kate in her life. Not with so many that she had seen, damaged, different, yet with something to offer their world, often in ways no one could foresee.

For his part, Stormbreaker had been grateful for her intervention, and more grateful still that she could use the healing connection to keep a watch on Aron's activities on both sides of the Veil. For the four days Aron had been only partially conscious, Stormbreaker had tended the boy like his own son, keeping him clean and forcing him to take soup and water whenever his level of awareness allowed. He showed Aron every kindness, despite what amounted to a betrayal of his trust few men would have tolerated.

Dari couldn't help remembering Stormbreaker's image on the other side of the Veil. A towering creature made of lightning, thunder, and rain. If he had been allowed to survive, and he had learned to control such an unusual and powerful *graal,* surely Aron could do the same.

Gund Zeller finally brought them to a halt in front of what looked like a two-room cabin at the far end of one of the little streets. The structure was in fair repair, and Dari noted a few struggling trees and plants in the small yard. Someone had tended to watering and cultivating. There was even a small stone walkway leading over dried patches of mud, to the well-carved but simple entrance.

The front door opened to reveal another man, this one much older, with a bald head, a craggy face, and an uneven white beard. He wore a leather tunic and breeches that looked like they might have been tanned and hammered during the mixing disasters. This older man glanced from their sag-shouldered guide to Dari to Stormbreaker and Windblown, and a wild white light seemed to flicker in the depths of his cloudy brown eyes as he returned his attention to Stormbreaker.

Dari's breath hitched.

Stormbreaker always seemed to catch people off guard, just by his very appearance—and anyone with a hint of *graal* could sense the roiling energy inside him. What if this man judged Stormbreaker to be some sort of Brotherless demon?

Windblown tensed, and Dari saw his hands flex as if readying for sword work. Stormbreaker remained calm as always, letting the man grow accustomed to his hair, his rank-marks, his green eyes.

The older man bowed his bald head.

"Thank the Brother you've come," he said in voice much deeper and firmer than Dari expected. "I'm Dolf Zeller, the boy's grandfather."

Stormbreaker introduced himself with a polite bow, then named Windblown and Dari as his companions. No one seemed surprised or put off by Dari's presence, and she knew the color of her skin caused them to assume she possessed the Ross *graal*. Death vigils were the one place outside of Dyn Ross where those with her presumed legacy of being able to dispatch spirits were always welcome.

Dolf Zeller stepped aside to admit them, and Dari filed in behind Gund Zeller and the two Stone Brothers.

The heat inside the room struck her like a fist and she coughed. Sweat broke immediately across her forehead and the back of her neck. She squinted because the light inside the cabin had been shuttered to almost nothing. A few candles revealed basic furnishings—chairs, a table, all hand-carved. A small bedchamber stood empty toward the back. On a pallet beside the hearth, which had been stoked to its capacity, a small brown-headed boy lay shivering beneath a stack of rough blankets. A woman, presumably his mother, sat by his side, stroking his pale, wet face with her fingertips.

As Dari watched, the boy's body arched and contracted into a rigor so unnatural it seemed all his little bones might break. This posturing, along with his unmistakable grimace of pain, lasted a few seconds; then he collapsed back to stillness, save for his rapidly heaving chest.

"There," said the woman, as if the boy could hear her. "The worst of that fit's past now."

"There are two more of our party on their way," Stormbreaker told Dolf Zeller. "They're young ones. Apprentices. They need to learn."

Dolf Zeller nodded and kept the door open a crack, glancing down the road. Dari wondered if he was watching for Aron and Zed or expecting trouble from his neighbors, who had looked none too comfortable at the presence of Stone Brothers walking their dirt streets.

More Fae foolishness and short-minded fear.

She caught herself and sealed off her quick-rising disgust as Stormbreaker went immediately to the ailing boy and knelt beside him. He was so focused on the child that he gave little heed to the distraught mother, whose pale face and sunken cheeks suggested she might have been awake for days. It was Windblown who settled himself beside the boy's mother. He reached out his hand. "There, now. You've had a long and heartbreaking watch over your boy, I'm sure. Talk to me while my companion examines your son."

The woman stared at Windblown with wide brown eyes, taking in his round face and pleasant expression. Dari realized his gentle appearance was a great strength, and of significant use in situations where a soft touch was needed for the Stone Brothers to see to their duties. Perhaps this was why Stormbreaker and Windblown had chosen to travel together, or been paired by the Lord Provost of Stone. One to do the harsh work, and one to soothe. Dari was beginning to suspect that Stone did little by chance or accident.

The woman beside the boy couldn't look at Stormbreaker at all, and in the end, she reached out to Windblown and allowed him to comfort her.

"What is your name?" Windblown smiled as he asked the question, his expression now even more welcoming and encouraging.

"Frega," the woman said, and at the cracked sound of her words, Dari instinctively moved to the small table in the room, picked up a wooden pitcher with a bit of water still in the bottom, selected the cleanest-looking wooden cup, and filled it.

As she handed it to the woman, Dolf Zeller opened the door once more, this time to admit a flustered Zed and a sallow, starved-looking Aron. Both boys were frowning. Their gray tunics were wrinkled, as if there had been grabbing and snatching, and both boys had mussed hair and dirty faces. Zed had a bruise starting on his left cheek, and Dari could tell from Zed's expression that he would very much like to bruise Aron back for coming here without permission.

Dari straightened beside Frega Zeller, catching the attention of both boys. She gestured for them to come to the small table and sit, and to remain silent. To her relief, they complied quickly, and with no violence or noise as they moved. She sat across from them, where she could easily watch them or Stormbreaker. Then she used her mental connection with Aron to check his emotional state.

Tired. Hungry. Angry. Confused. And now intrigued, too. Wondering what was happening here, and giving his full attention to the matter. *Good.*

If he was engaged with the events in this room, his thoughts wouldn't wander elsewhere, at least for a time.

Windblown patted Frega Zeller's arm to return her focus to him. "Can you tell me about the boy's sickness?"

The woman sipped the water Dari gave her, then placed the cup on the board floor beside her. She gazed at the child, somehow managing not to look at Stormbreaker, who was systematically flexing the boy's limbs. "Kristoff has been ill for almost eight weeks. He rallies, then sinks, worse each time, with shorter periods between wellness and sickness."

Dari's shoulders tightened. Zed's frown told her that he had likely seen such cases before, but Aron's confusion only deepened.

The boy seized again, stretching, arching, his eyes closed, his mouth open from the force of his pain. This time, the attack lasted longer, almost a minute, and Dari wanted to cry out for what the boy must be going through in such a state.

"We have no rectors here," Frega explained after the boy once more collapsed back to panting stillness. "But our healer said—she said she thought—"

"Wasting Fever," Stormbreaker confirmed in a low, tight voice. He folded Kristoff Zeller's skeletal arms over his frail, heaving chest, then pulled his blankets back up to cover him.

Dari could barely stand to hear the words. It was all she could do not to make a sign against ill fortune, like some ground-hatched Fae. She had lost far too many friends and relatives to this disease in childhood, and she hated even the mention of it.

Dolf and Gund Zeller had no such inhibitions. They came to stand behind Frega and Windblown, to the side of Stormbreaker and the boy. All three quickly touched both of their own cheeks, to invoke the love and blessings of the Brother.

At the table with Dari, Zed looked down, and his posture drooped in understanding.

Aron continued to look confused, and this was the primary emotion Dari sensed from him. So he hadn't had a sibling die in this fashion. Fortunate for him, and for them. Perhaps their family line wouldn't be plagued by the disease unknown before the mixing disasters.

None of the Zellers seemed able to speak for a time, and it was the boy's father, Gund, who found his voice first. "How can this be the Wasting? Our people have no legacies. No one in this village even bears a dynast name—we don't even get sent for testing at birth."

"Everyone in Eyrie originally came from Fae bloodlines, or Fury," Windblown said. "Sometimes combinations of traits line up just the right way, and legacies can reappear even in families who have no other hint of mind-talents."

"Kristoff's eyes are brown," Frega Zeller protested. "There's no color in them. They're Quiet. We're all Quiet."

"Eye color isn't a reliable indicator of legacies, not like in older times," Stormbreaker said. He remained beside the boy, keeping his hand atop the blankets. He spoke as kindly as Windblown, yet the ever-present power in his voice made him seem more stern. The woman leaned back from him as he spoke. "Since the mixing disasters, anything is possible."

Dolf Zeller, who seemed somehow more aware of the workings of the world than his son or daughter-by-marriage, pulled at his beard until Dari realized this habit was probably what made the growth so uneven in the first place. "I thought it took a strong legacy to bring the Wasting," he said. "I only hear tell of it when the Ross heirs die."

Dari grimaced at this, then hoped no one noticed.

Windblown shook his head. "Any amount of mind-talent can trigger the illness. We've never understood why some children take sick and others never show signs. We just know it runs in some Fae bloodlines more than others."

And the bloodlines of my people, too. Once more, Dari was seized by an unwelcome but powerful sense of kinship with the Fae, at least the ones in this room.

That sense of sameness only deepened when Gund Zeller let out an anguished curse. "If we'd lived in a city, if we'd known and the rectors could have seen to him—"

"It would have made no difference," Stormbreaker assured him. "The best anyone could have done was keep him comfortable. Only one child in a hundred survives the Wasting—and those survivors often keep the minds of young children forever, even as their bodies grow."

Now Dari saw understanding on Aron's face, and to her relief, a mix of fear and unhappiness at realizing the boy was dying.

He's not gone cold inside, and his reason is still with him. That's something, at least.

Frega leaned down to her child and kissed his brow. "If Kristoff survives, we'll care for him. We'll—"

"Frega." Dolf's tone was gentle, and very, very sad. "If the boy were going to live, there would have been no third bout of fever. He's on his sixth bout now. His last."

Stormbreaker confirmed this with a nod, and Windblown squeezed Frega Zeller's wrist in his big hands. "After the third bout, no child lives. I'm sorry. If this is his sixth fever, he won't wake. It's down to how long you wish to leave him in this state. It can last for weeks, and soon he'll begin to moan and thrash."

That truth struck Frega Zeller like a blow, no matter how sweetly Windblown tried to speak it. There was no getting around the fact that Wasting Fever was painful. Agonizing, in its last reaches.

Gund Zeller was crying as hard as his wife, but he said, "You sent me to Stone so Kristoff wouldn't starve and drown in his own fluids. You said you couldn't bear to see him go to the Brother screaming."

Frega Zeller kept her eyes on her boy and didn't respond, not until Dolf Zeller murmured, "We treat beasts better than that."

At this, Frega Zeller collapsed, sobbing like her heart was tearing from her body.

Windblown caught her and held her, saying nothing. Dolf and Gund Zeller stood behind them without speaking, as if standing watch for Frega, too.

Aron dug his ragged fingernails into the wooden table, but Zed kept himself straight and still, giving nothing but sadness away in his expression. Dari knew Zed had more training, but she also figured that his feelings were more straightforward than Aron's. Zed had a guileless quality, almost too basic and trusting for Dari to imagine him ever becoming a Stone Brother.

She looked at Stormbreaker, remembering how fresh and innocent he had felt to her the night they made mind-to-mind contact battling the manes. She saw the open, full grief flowing across his tattooed face now, the tears glistening in the corners of his green eyes. In that moment, there in front of the hearth, tending to a dying child, he reminded Dari of carvings she had seen in temples.

He should have wings, and no cares in the tangible world. He's too beautiful to be landbound.

Her heart stirred in funny ways, as much for Stormbreaker as the boy and his family, and she wanted to cry, too. As it was, Frega Zeller sobbed for some time, then went quiet in Windblown's careful embrace. When the woman was able to sit up, Dari thought about taking her more water, but there was none left in the pitcher. She wished she had something to do, something to offer this woman, but her skills would be put to use soon enough, if the determination in the woman's expression were any measure.

Then Frega let go of Windblown, who moved away so the boy's father and grandfather could kneel beside Kristoff and lay hands on him, too.

Now Frega seemed focused only on Stormbreaker. Her voice held an eerie dignity as she said, clearly and without a break in her tone, "On behalf of my son, Kristoff, I ask for Mercy."

Zed took a breath and let it out, almost a sound of relief. Aron's bright blue eyes shifted from Zed to Dari to Stormbreaker, then back to Dari. Then they went wide as he understood the word "mercy" used in such a context.

Dari nodded to Aron, who then looked at the table, the wall, the ceiling, anywhere but at the dying boy and his grieving family.

When she looked back at Stormbreaker, his eyes were fixed on Gund Zeller.

The man nodded, then hung his head as his father gripped his hand.

Stormbreaker swiftly removed a small goatskin from his belt. In only seconds, he had lifted the boy and tilted his head back, positioning him so that his family could still touch him, but so that his swallowing would be reflex more than conscious action.

"The peace of all the heavens be with you," he said, and tipped the goatskin against the boy's parted lips.

Dari caught the scent of almonds and sugar-potatoes, strong and heady and so deadly it made her insides contract.

Stormbreaker stroked the sides of the boy's face, then his throat, until the boy swallowed.

Everyone seemed to take a breath at the same time, and hold it as

Stormbreaker eased the boy back to the mat, made sure his arms were crossed, and once more resettled his blankets until they were snug about his waist.

His parents kept their hands on his head and arms, and his grandfather stroked his shoulder.

Stormbreaker stood and retreated, along with Windblown, moving back smoothly and silently to give the family privacy.

Dari wanted to look away because she had watched death too many times, but she found her gaze riveted on Kristoff. Zed and Aron were just as captured, staring as the boy's chest lifted once, held, then eased into stillness and moved no more.

Without pain. Without screaming. At least there's that. Dari's fingers curled and uncurled as she remembered her sister's Wasting. Kate had recovered after her second bout of fever, but her body had been left so frail, and part of her mind was forever gone. Dari had lost her twin to that illness, so long ago—and yet Kate still lived, somehow, somewhere. Dari knew she was fortunate, and that the Zellers would trade all their wealth and their own health and lives if Kristoff could have recovered.

For a time, no one moved or spoke, and there was no sound save for the soft weeping of Kristoff's family.

Dari gave them some time, a few minutes, as did Stormbreaker, but finally, he spoke the words. "Be easy. This watch has ended."

At that signal, Dari got up to do the duty expected of her. Stormbreaker and Windblown could have done it, but she knew it would seem more natural to everyone if she took the responsibility.

Aron's stare felt like a force pressing on her back.

Dari eased herself down until she was kneeling at the boy's feet. His parents, teary-eyed but still determined to see this through, gave her permission with gestures and nods.

Dari lifted the blankets to expose the boy's feet.

On his left ankle rested a clear crystal *cheville*, probably rock-glass or some equivalent, but it was enough to hold his spiritual essence close to his body.

Dari let her fingers rest on the *cheville*, tracing the energies inherent in all rocks and stones, until she found the pattern of this particular piece. Her mind saw it as a whole, like a small map. After a few centering breaths, she went through the Veil and let her own energy sink into that small map. Then she expanded her power slowly, slowly, pushing outward into the pattern, finding its weak spots and pushing harder, until the *cheville* burst into pieces.

Bits of rock-glass and dust tumbled into her palm. She caught it, and at the same time felt the cool rush of Kristoff's essence sweeping upward. She could see the boy's image, shimmering and winged, like a silver and gold shadow.

Go, she instructed. *Upward. Outward. Find the stars. They'll take you to the heavens.*

As always, once the spirit had direction, it took off, leaving behind the shell of its existence.

Dari gathered the pieces of his *cheville* and presented them to his father, as was custom. In the calmest voice she could muster, she said, "Kristoff Zeller's essence has departed."

Gund Zeller choked out a fresh sob, then gave the bits of glass to his wife, who kissed them and cried all the harder.

Now would come the rougher time for these people, Dari knew. The funeral pyre, then the emptiness of returning to a life with no child, sick or otherwise, to fill their time and hearts.

Stormbreaker turned to Aron and murmured, "When innocents die, it should always be in this fashion. Peacefully, and with consent of those who care most for their welfare."

Aron's cheeks colored, and his gaze dropped to the floor.

From Stormbreaker came a jumbled mix of emotion—sadness, worry, reservations—and she realized with a start that Aron's punishment for his transgression was far from over.

And perhaps not completely within Stormbreaker's hands.

Will he tell the Lord Provost when we arrive at Triune?

What will Stone do to Aron then?

The thought of any harm coming to the boy made her angry and sick at the same time, but in this, she had no real say, did she? Aron was the province of Stone and Stone alone now. She was, at best, an ancillary in his care.

As I was with my sister—and look what happened there.

Dari's fists clenched as Stormbreaker walked away from Aron, moving toward the door, and Windblown indicated to Zed and Aron to follow. She joined the boys at the table as they got up, but Dolf Zeller caught them all at the doorway before they pulled open the carved wood handle.

"I'll escort you to your traveling party." He didn't meet anyone's eyes, or look back at his dead grandson and grieving family. "I can show your group a faster way back to the main byway, to make up for some of the time we've cost you."

Dari could tell by the old man's expression that doing this was important to him. Like many, he needed to give back in some small way, since Stone would take no coin for offering Mercy.

Stormbreaker bowed to the elder Zeller. "Your kindness is much appreciated."

Once more, he went to open the door, but Zeller held up a hand to stop him. "You—you should know this. There's a man asking after you, after Stone Brothers with apprentices traveling in their company. I heard it from our traders, up from the Brailing-Ross boundary. They said this man's tall and keeps his face wrapped like he's just out of the deserts in Dyn Altar."

"Many people are distressed after Harvest—" Windblown began, but Zeller cut him off with a fierce glare.

"This man isn't one to be taken lightly. The traders say he slaughtered five Brailing guardsmen as they made camp a few days back."

Zeller shook his head. "Isolated them from their fellows somehow, then left them headless and knife-torn until their own families might have trouble putting this part with that one. A pack of mocker rock cats couldn't have done more damage."

Aron swayed on his feet, but Dari managed to catch his elbow before he fell.

Zed and Windblown looked confused and mildly irritated, as if they had no understanding or concern for what bearing this might have on them. Stormbreaker's expression never changed, but Dari sensed the surge of power inside the man. Something like dread mixed with anguish. From somewhere in the distance, thunder rumbled.

Aron.

No.

Dari didn't want to believe Aron was responsible for such an evil, but she had seen what Aron was planning. She had known, sensed, and touched what he had planned to do to that contingent of guardsmen.

But he didn't do it . . . right?

She felt like swaying herself as her mind raced over the minutes since she first had an inkling of Aron's plans on the other side of the Veil. She'd been with him. Right on him, physically—and mentally, even when he was out of her reach.

He didn't do it.

But if he did . . .

"Excuse me for my intrusion," she said, letting the words ease the terrible gnaw of that doubt. "But have you heard of a girl like me being found? A girl of the Ross dynast? Even a whisper or rumor would be welcome."

It was a risk to ask him, especially in front of Windblown and Zed. Dari trusted that Stormbreaker would bind his companions to silence, and she felt a natural trust of Zeller. She didn't think his family would repeat her words. In a day, her question would be so overshadowed by their grieving that they likely wouldn't even remember her asking it.

"No, I'm sorry. I haven't heard anything of that sort." Zeller gave her a kind smile, which Dari tried to return despite a wave of disappointment.

His response had been so quick and sure she had no doubt it was as open and honest as all else he had shared. Zeller nodded once to her as if to apologize, then opened the door and headed outside.

He stopped before taking more than a step.

Windblown and Stormbreaker went out behind him, and Dari came to stand in the doorway behind Aron and Zed, still feeling ill from the heat, from the boy's death, from the realization that many might argue for Aron to be given Mercy for his own good and the good of everyone he might harm—the same arguments that had been made against her sister. The sister who remained missing, vanished, with no word at all, though Dari had allowed herself to hope that Zeller might know something.

The moment she reached a point where she could see outside, all other thoughts and feelings streamed away from her as if her mind had been tipped on its side.

The dirt street outside the Zeller house was filled with the blank-faced people Dari had noticed earlier. They held pitchforks and other farming tools—but that wasn't what made Dari's chest clench like someone had a fist on her heart. The sight of those scared farmers wasn't what made her pull Aron and Zed close to her, as if she could shield them from the murder and violence that had crept upon them while they brought Mercy to a dying boy.

Behind the people were three ranks of mounted soldiers, thirty in all, in full battle uniforms of sun blue and yellow. Their standard, an eagle with an all-seeing eye, flapped in the breeze above the lead horse.

"Dyn Brailing's Dynast Guard," Zed whispered. "Brother spare us. Now there'll be more than one funeral blaze this night."

CHAPTER EIGHTEEN

DARI

Dari bit her bottom lip as Aron and Zed pulled away from her grasp.

The afternoon now smelled of horse and sweat and manure, even the coppery panic of some of the farmers attempting to look stern with their tools.

Aron and Zed kept their eyes on Stormbreaker and Windblown, who made no attempt to draw their weapons. The boys moved in behind them like thin shadows, ready to pounce if they received the slightest signal from the Stone Brothers. Aron's face was a mix of wrath and readiness, of horror and rage, and Dari could see how he shook head to toe.

She didn't think the shaking was from fear.

Zeller, who stood in front of their group, flushed a wicked shade of red. He fumbled at his waist, as if he were once accustomed to having daggers at the ready, or maybe a sword.

The captain of the Guard contingent, obvious from the large metal eagle wings mounted on the sides of his silver helmet, moved his gray horse even with the standard-bearer. His face was hidden by his visor and nose plate, but his build was that of a young, fit man.

I could change, Dari thought as blood pounded behind her eyes. *If I took my true form, they would scatter like dust in the breezes.*

And her sister might be lost forever, and her people revealed and betrayed, much more than she had already done by revealing herself to Stormbreaker and Aron.

If she even used her *graal* beyond the small connection she maintained with Aron, even just to reach outward and summon help, one of those guardsmen or townsfolk might recognize her mind-talents for what they were.

Aron. What about his legacy—?

Dari could have kicked herself the moment she thought it. Here she was, almost wanting to nurture the fury inside the boy, to turn him into an oathbreaker, a weapon for her own purposes. What kind of person was she?

"Dolf Zeller," said the guardsman with the big wings on his helmet. "I am Captain Fen Brailing. We're told you're the town elder."

Zeller stopped reaching for his nonexistent weapons and slowly lowered his arms. "I am. You've come with poor timing. My grandson—"

"On behalf of my uncle Helmet, Lord Brailing of Brailing, we extend our apologies for your loss." The captain did at least sound a little chagrined, but he plowed straight into his own purpose. "Also on behalf of our Lord Brailing, my men and I lay claim to the food and stock of this village, and any male child less than a year from Guard service."

Many of the farmers, male and female alike, now looked wary and angry instead of menacing, and Dari slowly realized she had been deceived by her own prejudice against those with Fae blood, especially those who remained uneducated. These people hadn't brought weapons to attack Stone at the behest of the Brailing Guard. They were here, armed to the best of their meager abilities, in case Zeller gave the order to resist.

Which Dari could see from the old man's posture and expression, he deeply wished to do.

"We have scarcely enough grain and stock to see ourselves through the winter," Zeller said, speaking slowly as if choosing each word with care. He pulled at one side of his beard. "I freely offer you our excess, what little there is, and any goods that might ease your travels or enhance your fighting. As for the children—"

"This is not a trader's bargain, old man." The rough voice to Dari's left made her turn her head. She saw a bigger man than Captain Fen Brailing, this one heavier and rounder, probably older by the sound of him, edging his brown mare up to join the captain. This one had wings on his helmet, too, but smaller ones, made of silver.

"My promise-brother is too kind in his command," the big man went on, and Dari decided she didn't like his tone at all. Sarcastic. Condescending.

She frowned, then remembered it was probably best to keep her expression neutral, like the Stone Brothers and Aron and Zed.

The big man spat on the ground, then started up again. "We're at war now, with threat from the north and south alike. The Guard takes what it needs, and you should count yourself fortunate to help the dynast's finest defenders."

Dari almost grabbed Aron at the end of this diatribe, but somehow the boy kept himself from moving, speaking, or slaughtering the oaf in his saddle. Aron's sapphire eyes blazed, and his color went as dark as Zeller's. Nevertheless, he was keeping cover over his legacy, hiding its true essence from any who might be able to see it.

Good boy. Keep it up. Hold on to yourself.

She didn't think Aron could hear her mind to mind, but maybe he could sense her encouragement.

Zeller clenched both fists. "I'm a Guard veteran, retired now fifteen years. I gave my youth and the better portion of my life to the service of Brailing, and now I wish only to see to the needs of my friends and family." He raised his chin. "No principled soldier would starve the very people he claims to defend."

Murmurs broke through the clump of armed farmers, and Dari saw expressions brighten as the big man bellowed at the insult and started to heft himself down from his saddle. Only a stern grab from his captain kept him in place, and this with some struggle.

"Please do not challenge the honor of my men, Dolf Zeller," Captain Brailing said as he kept a grip on his second in command. "Least of all Lieutenant Hoch, who has twenty years' service himself. We've been long on the road to meet up and form ranks, and longer still in search of grain and stock to build our own stores."

Stormbreaker eased over to Zeller so fluidly Dari was surprised to realize he had moved. Aron now stood exposed, glaring at the Brailing Guard, shaking, fists clenched like Zeller's. Dari realized Zed had Aron's arm much as the captain had hold of his promise-brother Lieutenant Hoch.

Before anyone could react, Stormbreaker spoke to Zeller in a voice so quiet she figured only Zeller could hear.

Zeller looked briefly surprised, then seemed to relax a fraction.

"Very well, Captain," Zeller said as Stormbreaker moved back to Windblown's side and once more shielded Aron. "Take what you will, but we have no children old enough to send with you. Our village has been hard struck with Wasting Fever, and I fear we have nothing to offer but those you see and a few babies and little ones not yet old enough to wield a blade."

At these words, some of the guardsmen actually yanked back on their reins. Dari could see only their frowns and open mouths, but her spirits rose like a spirit on its way to the heavens.

She knew old, dark fears were stirring in the depths of the fighting men now. Despite years of education about the condition, many in Eyrie raised outside of dynast bloodlines and education still believed Wasting Fever was somehow contagious. Common superstition held that men exposed to Wasting Fever had their very loins polluted.

Forever.

Zeller's flush was receding and his tone grew even more earnest as he continued. "We were considering posting plague warnings on the town's boundaries, but I was sorely distracted by the death in my own house."

Captain Brailing cleared his throat. "I see. If you'll appoint someone to show us to the stables and granary—"

But his request was drowned by the mumblings and grumblings of his own men. Horses pranced nervously beneath equally nervous riders. Some mounts actually broke a lather in response to the rising distress all around them.

The captain had to shout, then finally bluster, pull off his helmet, and draw his sword to regain control of his own ranks. The well-crafted blade flashed in the low afternoon light, giving its smooth edge a menacing glint.

Dari noted with some unease that his second in command wasn't among the soldiers showing fear and a desire to make haste out of the village. Lieutenant Hoch's big head was turned solidly toward Storm-breaker and Windblown. His visor hid his eyes, but Dari felt certain the brute was glaring at the Stone Brothers.

Or was it Aron?

Had the dirt-eater caught sight of the boy?

Did he know something?

Suspect?

It took all of Dari's self-control not to find out.

The farmers began to disperse, satisfied that their town elder had defended at least their children, and likely their winter supplies as well.

Indeed, a few moments later, Captain Brailing took Lieutenant Hoch and the rest of his men, and they rode away without making another address to Dolf Zeller. Dust swirled in the wake of the horses, and Zeller and the Stone Brothers didn't move until that rolling cloud was a street or more away.

"Come," Zeller said, once more patting his waist as if searching for a weapon. "You must get far from here, and quickly."

Stormbreaker's only reply was a bow, and Zeller led them away from his home with a brisk, purposeful stride.

Dari fell in beside Aron and Zed, who looked as tense and mistrustful as she felt. "You did well," she said to Aron, who didn't acknowledge her.

Zed gave her a fast grin. "I'd say High Master Stormbreaker did the best."

"They haven't gone far," Aron muttered, looking left, then right as they plowed past a set of dirt-packed cross streets. "Men like that—they'll be back after sundown, at least some of them. And they won't be kind."

"Their commander ordered them off." Zed sounded genuinely surprised. "How could they come back against his command?"

Aron gave Zed a sharp look, but his expression softened after a few more steps. "Not everyone is as honorable as you, Zed."

Those words, coupled with a tone that suggested genuine respect for Zed's good heart—not to mention a bit of guilt over his own actions—gave Dari a little more hope that Aron might not yet be lost to his own rage.

Zed grunted, as if not quite believing Aron, and she was left wondering once more if Zed was more brawn than brains, and not cut out for the life of a Stone Brother.

"Dolf Zeller seems like a capable elder," Zed said, apparently to soothe away Aron's unpleasant suggestion that the town would suffer this night, despite this first small victory. "I'm sure that once he returns, he'll post lookouts and keep the families and livestock someplace safe, if he thinks they're in danger."

Dari didn't try to correct this perception, and she was relieved Aron left it alone, too.

Dari estimated that they had less than three hours before full dark. She hoped Zeller had been truthful about the quicker route back to the main byway. She truly didn't want to camp in the nearby woods, so close to the Brailing guardsmen, and risk the manes or other havocs some of them might create in vengeance for their humiliation. She also didn't want to think about Zeller being away from his town should some of those soldiers return under cover of night.

Zeller let out a whistle when he saw the large group of Stone Brothers, Harvest prizes, wagons of supplies, goats, oxen, and mules collected along the road. Dari saw that the group was larger still than when they left it. A covered, barred wagon now stood in the back—a wagon of accused, likely collected from nearby towns and villages, heading to Stone to be judged.

Even in war, the law must continue, she realized.

"This group will move as slow as snails," Zeller said, and Storm-breaker agreed with him. "If you'll give me a mount, I'll see you to the first turn, then explain the rest. I think it best if I'm back in the village before full dark, though mockers and manes are few around here."

"Thank you for your assistance," Windblown said, beckoning to a nearby group in possession of a few horses. "Any guidance will be much appreciated."

Dari watched as Zed took command of their two wagons and hitched in tandem so he and Dari could ride together comfortably in the lead buckboard. She climbed aboard as Aron went to Tek, and Dari heard the affection in his voice as he stroked the little talon's scales, gave her water, and checked her straps. When he mounted, Tek gave a whistle of delight, and Dari felt a rush of the creature's joy at Aron's presence. The boy must have treated the talon well, to have such affection and loyalty from her.

Zeller took his borrowed mount to the head of their column, waited another few minutes, then stood in his stirrups and gestured toward the road before him. On horseback and talon-back, in wagons and on foot, the column of bound for Triune lurched slowly forward.

Dari glanced at the sun as unease rose anew in her belly.

"I hope we get back to Triune before the first snow," Zed said.

When Dari glanced at him, he was grinning, but she thought he might have realized how long it would take them to cover the distance at this pace. A single horseman could probably reach the Stone stronghold in a day, maybe two. But this unwieldy column—it might be days upon days, even weeks yet.

Aron, who rode beside them, keeping Tek under careful rein and back from the bull talons, grumbled his agreement.

Dari studied the boy and thought how hungry he must be, and how stiff and sore his muscles must feel after lying in a stupor for so many days. She also thought of the perpetual chafe on his tender legs, still toughening over the weeks of riding. He couldn't possibly be comfortable, yet Aron rode without complaint or question.

A mixed bag, this boy. One minute, he's fast at work on becoming an oathbreaker, and the next he's training to be a strong, silent hero.

What is his true nature?

Minutes plodded by, seemingly at the same slow speed as the mules and oxen walked. Zeller led them over several hills and around a large turn. At the next fork, he took them in the opposite direction from what Dari expected, into a wide bunch of fields that spread away from the tree line like fine spun rugs of the purest green. He explained to Stormbreaker and Windblown about a traders' route over the next rise that would take them directly to the byway, saving almost half a day's travel.

The Stone Brothers thanked their guide and were just about to discharge him when the sound of hoofbeats hammered away the polite good-byes.

"Horses," Zed said, handing her the reins and standing, hands on his daggers. "A lot of them. Coming fast from the northeast . . . and from the west. Behind us, too."

As he spoke, Dari saw a dull ripple of copper rush over Zed's skin, and knew it as the sign of a weak Altar *graal.* Tracking, sensing of prey and predators—no doubt this boy was a formidable hunter and fighter, even with such a small measure of that mind-talent.

Aron pulled Tek up behind the bull talons and steadied himself in his stirrups.

Up and down the column, Dari heard the mutterings of Stone Brothers giving instructions to apprentices and Harvest prizes, and even the rattle of weapons being readied. Her heart took the rhythm of the approaching horses as they ran, galloping with them, wondering what she should do, if anything.

She could reach out to the horses and turn them from their task— but that would likely get the animals killed, and it wouldn't delay the arrival of their riders for long. They were too close already, if they could be heard so clearly.

The horsemen broke into the open, and cold fingers of fear gripped Dari's heart.

She caught her breath as she saw the banners flapping at the head of the columns. Banners showing an eagle with an all-seeing eye.

"Brailing Guard," she said aloud. "Only in twice the numbers we saw in the village."

CHAPTER NINETEEN

DARI

Moments later, their traveling column was surrounded by Brailing guardsmen who had burst from the tree line beside and behind them. Mixed into their ranks were soldiers wearing the steel and copper colors of Dyn Altar. Dari saw at least two standards with the Altar symbol of sword crossed with arrow, held in the talons of a great white Roc—the giant birds who made their home in the stone outcroppings of Altar's deserts.

Still more hoofbeats bore down on them from the northeast, no doubt to reinforce the Guard's already superior numbers.

She quickly picked out the two helmets sporting eagle wings, and the build of the men confirmed her suspicions. Once more, Captain Brailing and his promise-brother Lieutenant Hoch had them at their mercy. They wasted no time coming to the head of the column, where Captain Brailing addressed Stormbreaker from only a few horse lengths away.

"You were clever in the town, robbing us of our necessities." He tapped the hilt of the sword at his side. "Since my men will have none of their grain or livestock, we'll relieve you of yours—and as permitted by law, we'll take the accused for conscription."

Stormbreaker's jaw clenched and unclenched once before he spoke. "You would interfere with the Stone Guild as we return from Harvest?"

The captain snorted. "Wartime law allows my men to claim supplies and conscription from any within our borders, Stone or otherwise—as you well know." He glanced toward Hoch, who pumped a fist as if urging him onward. "You could fight us and perhaps even win, but you would make an enemy of Lord Brailing and his heirs, as well as Lord Altar and his. I doubt that's a price you'll pay."

Dari ground her teeth. They had so many innocents to protect in this column—how many Stone Brothers would die because they wouldn't leave their charges?

Too many.

And yet if they surrendered their supplies, could they make it to Triune without starving along the way?

Stormbreaker seemed to be considering this, and since he was the guild member of the highest rank, the rest in the column awaited his decision.

It came swiftly enough.

He lifted his reins to his teeth, never taking his eyes off Captain Brailing or the treacherous lieutenant. With his hands free, Stormbreaker drew his swords and lifted them above his head.

At that signal, the rest of the Stone Brothers drew their weapons, as did Zed and Aron, who had his talon's reins in his teeth as well. Responding to his distress, Tek's neck scales flipped up into a battle ring almost at the same time as the bulls raised their neck scales.

Tek whistled.

The bull talons bellowed.

Some of the Guard horses, likely animals confiscated from farms and without proper battle training as yet, sidestepped nervously away from the big predators, leaving their riders to struggle for control.

Zeller wheeled his horse toward Zed and Aron, his wordless request obvious on his angry features.

Zed changed his grip on one of his daggers and held it out, hilt first.

Zeller hurried over to grab it, then wheeled about and once more took position beside Stormbreaker.

Now the captain seemed less certain.

He had yet to draw his own sword and give his soldiers the signal to ready for battle, but Hoch seemed to have no reservations as he yanked his blade free of its scabbard.

Many of the Brailing soldiers followed his lead.

The rest looked from Captain Brailing to Hoch in confusion, then at the Stone Brothers. This was obviously not the response they had been led to expect.

Stormbreaker let his reins fall to his lap. "It's nearing sundown," he said to Captain Brailing, the cold resolve in his voice no doubt obvious to anyone within earshot. "Let's finish this so the dead can be dispatched before full dark, shall we?"

Captain Brailing's hand moved toward his sword. Hesitated. Rested on the hilt.

"Don't be spineless," Hoch growled at the captain, yanking his mount's reins until the horse's head bobbed. "Don't slight our honor a second time this day."

Dari wished she had a bow so she could fire an arrow directly into Hoch's mouth. Listening to him strangle to death on the tip of her arrow would have given her immense satisfaction.

If it comes to a fight, I can't let these innocents die.

She slowed her breathing, readying herself to go through the Veil and make the change to her true form, if it came to that.

There would be consequences, dark ones, but she couldn't watch murder, even Fae murdering Fae, and do nothing.

The horses from the northeast burst into view over the nearest hill, dozens of them, and dozens and dozens more, some manned, some bare but charging along nonetheless. They rode so hard into the fields that the grass and dirt seemed to explode around them.

Dari experienced a moment of disorientation.

The colors were wrong.

The uniforms and standard should have been blue and yellow, but instead she saw the obsidian and ruby of Dyn Cobb—and banners that bore the emblem of a great black stallion, winged and rearing.

Beside her, Zed didn't seem to know whether to lower his daggers, attack something, or slit his own throat. Tek let out a whistle of surprise and confusion, and Windblown shifted his bull talon to get a look at the new arrivals.

"Dun," was all he said, and all he had to say.

Stormbreaker's gaze moved to the newcomers, now less than two miles away and closing ground fast.

The Cobb soldiers had weapons drawn, and their attack column wheeled on the Brailing Guard without the slightest rein or break in ranks.

Dari couldn't draw a full breath. There had to be a hundred of them, maybe more—but how? And why? What in all of Eyrie would make Lord Cobb risk his forces in Dyn Brailing?

Though deep in her heart, she thought she knew the reason.

Over the madness of the approaching army, Dari heard Windblown shout to Stormbreaker, "I suppose we know better where Cobb's allegiances lie."

And that was enough for Captain Brailing.

"Retreat!" he shouted to his men, who could see nothing but doom streaming toward them, or awaiting them at the tips of Stone Guild swords. They were outmatched, and now outflanked, and they didn't have to be urged twice. Even Hoch wheeled his animal around so fast he almost lost his seat.

Seconds later, the marauding guardsmen thundered away, shouting, almost in complete disarray.

Less than a minute after that, the Cobb Guard reached the traveling column.

Two captains broke away from the main group, leading their men in a chase of the fleeing soldiers. Cobb's rear contingent, at least fifty strong and paired with saddled but riderless horses, pulled up short in front of Stormbreaker, Windblown, and Zeller.

Their captain urged his ebony mount to the forefront, his black helmet shaped in the form of a stallion's head. Something about his size, his posture, and bearing struck Dari as familiar, but at first she couldn't place him. When he removed that helmet, though, she almost slipped straight off her wagon seat in surprise.

She knew that face only too well. Older than most soldiers, lined with a few battle scars. Dimpled chin, thick brown hair with white streaks at the temples, and a rogue's gleam in both eyes.

The captain nodded to Stormbreaker first, then let his eyes move immediately to Dari.

Stormbreaker sheathed his weapons and spoke calming words to his snorting bull talon, then leaned forward in his saddle and bowed. All the Stone Brothers followed his lead.

"Lord Westin, Cobb of Cobb." Stormbreaker made his formal address to the dynast lord who held more physical territory than any other in Eyrie. "Once more in my life, you arrive at a moment of great need. I am surprised, but most grateful, to see you here."

Lord Cobb continued to gaze at Dari, but when he spoke, his words were to Stormbreaker. "It's good to see you again, too. What has it been since you last visited Cobb? Three years?"

"Four, *Chi*," Stormbreaker corrected, using the formal honorific for a dynast lord and keeping his gaze averted despite Lord Cobb's friendly familiarity.

"Four." Lord Cobb nodded. "I remember now. During Lady Vagrat's last visit. I'm glad I reached you in time. Some promise-brothers called on *dav'ha* and asked that I see Stone and Stone's Harvest prizes safely back to Triune. We've set up supply lines across Cobb lands to help those trapped in other dynasts, and we have riders searching Altar,

Mab, and Vagrat for parties in distress. Lord Ross—" He broke off, finally looking away from Dari, to her great relief. "Lord Ross is assisting the Stone parties in his dynast."

Stormbreaker didn't respond, and Dari didn't dare speak a word. Zeller remained rigid on his mount, like a soldier at full attention who had not been given leave to relax. Windblown seemed too shocked to make a sound, and Zed and Aron were both sitting, wagon-side and talon-back respectively, openmouthed. Dari would have laid odds that Zed had never been so close to a dynast lord.

Lord Cobb gestured to the horses. "I know it will be a hardship, but you must abandon your livestock, wagons, and supplies. My soldiers will see to getting the accused and any infirm safely to Stone, but the rest, all who can ride, should move out now. I have torchbearers at the ready to accompany you, along with my personal regimen."

Stormbreaker bowed so low his head neared the neck of his bull talon. When he rose again, he shifted in his saddle until he could look directly at Zeller. "This man is Dolf Zeller, *Chi*. A Dynast Guard veteran, and the elder of a nearby village those Brailing soldiers attempted to raid. Can some of your men clear his path home, and help him to claim our supplies? I'm hopeful the food and clothing and livestock might make their winter easier, and give them some excess to fall back on should the soldiers return later to scavenge."

Lord Cobb immediately gave orders to a man on his right, and the man barked out a set of names. They rode out of formation and surrounded Zeller like an honor guard. The older man barely managed to return Zed's dagger and express his thanks to Stormbreaker before they swept him away.

The next moments were a whirl of activity as Stone Brothers exchanged wagons and oxen and mules for mounts, loaded Harvest prizes into the saddles with them, and readied themselves to depart and ride hard for Triune across the night.

In the chaos, Lord Cobb managed to steer his mount close to

Dari, who was now on foot, stroking the nose of the horse who had come out of the pack at her quick mental call.

The horse's name was Toronado, and she didn't think anyone but her had ever been able to ride the stallion. Unlike all the other mounts, this horse wasn't saddled, and he had only a lead rope and halter—how most Dyn Cobb soldiers trained, and the way Dari had always preferred to ride.

"The beast has missed you," Lord Cobb said beneath the din and clamor. "As do others, who act almost as beastly when their hearts are wounded."

Dari met the man's warm brown eyes for a moment, then looked away to find Aron's gaze fixed on her, like she was a puzzle he was struggling to piece together. There was worry on the boy's face, and something like fear.

He's afraid I'm going to leave him. He doesn't want me to go.

And what did she want?

Dari knew she could part company with the Stone Brothers now, head for Can Lanyard, the massive Rope City on the plains of Can Cobb, under the dynast lord's protection. That might be a safer place for her to pass the war, certainly a more stately and comfortable location, and Lord Cobb might be able to smuggle her home after she found her sister.

But finding Kate . . .

And now there was Aron, too, and Stormbreaker. Two Fae, bound to her by promise.

She sighed and pressed her face into Toronado's neck. The horse gave a snort and whinny, and she knew the creature meant it as a greeting.

Lord Cobb shifted close to her again. "Of all people to have taken up with a group of Fae—Stone Brothers at that—I wouldn't have thought it would be you." He shook his head. "Now I know for certain you'll do anything for your sister. Everything isn't your responsibility, child. *She's* not your responsibility."

"Who will help Kate, then? My cousin Platt?" Dari took her face from the horse's neck. "He'll have her hunted and killed."

Lord Cobb's expression flickered between sternness and pity. "Kate has always posed a danger to your people, but Platt hasn't moved against her out of respect for your wishes. And his own mercy."

Dari chose not to respond to his statement. She was as loyal to her people, as protective of their separation from Eyrie, their secrecy, as anyone—but Kate's right to live had been settled long ago. If necessary, Dari would defend it with sword and claw and tooth, with her own breath and life. Her grandfather would defend it with all his armies, if it came to that.

"Tell my grandfather . . . tell him I love him very much." She swallowed hard, having trouble with a tightening lump in her throat. Being around this man, thinking so much about her family—it made her feel like a little girl again. "And tell him that I'm sorry for losing Kate, and I'm sorry I haven't found her yet."

"He doesn't blame you." Lord Cobb's expression went soft, like Dari remembered from so many times in her childhood, and that feeling of being a vulnerable little girl doubled, then tripled. "A moment's lapse—it could have happened to any of us. Your grandfather isn't angry over you coming north to look for Kate, though he's beside himself with concern for both of you. I fear there's little time left for searching. Platt has sent representatives in your grandfather's dynast, and they've already begun their own hunt for your sister."

The world flew back from Dari. She tried to grab for her own maturity, but she was still lost in that small-child sensation. She couldn't get her bearings. She lost track of her surroundings, the soldiers, the Stone Brothers, the horses—everything. Heat raced along her muscles, tearing and pushing, and her blood blazed so hot sweat broke across every inch of her skin. The horse she was soothing yanked his head against her firm grip on his rope, his eyes rolling back, showing white terror as he stamped the ground beside her.

"Curse him," she snarled, not caring that she was speaking ill of her own cousin, the man who was her Stregan regent, and the leader of her people in exile. The resonance in her voice was almost enough to overcome the noise around them. "You tell Platt that if *anyone* harms Kate, that *someone* will answer to me."

Lord Cobb didn't shy back from her, but the black and ruby essence of his *graal* flared brightly about his shoulders.

Don't shift. Don't change. His directed thought rushed across her mind, as if from great distance, speaking to that animal part of her as those with the Cobb legacy could do so well. *Not here, little one. All would be lost.*

But her muscles were already growing. Expanding. Pain stabbed at her back and jaws and neck. She was changing, and there was nothing for it. Even Lord Cobb's successful attempt at animal-speaking couldn't ease her instincts or stifle her rage over the implied threat to her sister. It was species-deep, instinctual, flowing through her like a molten river.

Dari knew she was getting taller.

She squeezed her eyes shut and tried to force herself to remain in fully human form.

Her breathing wouldn't slow. Her heart wouldn't stop its pounding beat in her temples, and she was still growing. Claws formed on her fingertips. Horses close to her began to twitch and whinny.

In moments, everyone would notice.

Dari swore to herself and tried again to keep a grip on rational thought, to hold her form—and failed. She was changing. She was—

Stop!

The command blasted through her awareness, seemingly from nowhere, so firm and loud Dari staggered against the panicked Toronado. The stallion reared, and she barely managed to keep hold of him, to bring him down before he trampled her. Images fired into her mind, of herself, looking normal and calm. She drank in the urgency of those thought-pictures, letting it flow over her intense wish to protect Kate.

She couldn't have fought against the images even if she wished to. They were absolutely true, those pictures. Undeniable. Right.

The flaming agony of her transformation ceased abruptly, leaving her cold and still, teeth chattering, fighting to regain mental purchase and an understanding of what had just happened.

The first thing she noticed was Lord Cobb looking shocked instead of worried.

Dari turned to follow his gaze and blinked against the sapphire blaze of Aron's full Brailing *graal*. The color quickly muted and shifted to a dull dollop of blue, allowing Dari to see the concern etched across the boy's face. Aron's eyes were wide, and his fists clenched Tek's reins. The little talon stood frozen beneath him, as if caught by the same command that had stilled Dari's angry shift to her Stregan form.

Aron's eyes got wider.

He looked almost as scared and frozen as his talon.

Stormbreaker edged his big bull closer to Aron. "Is all well in this quarter?" he asked, his voice quiet but firm.

Aron looked even more horrified, and Dari understood that the boy didn't know if he had done right or wrong in her eyes. He also didn't know if later, when apprised, Stormbreaker would approve of his decision.

"All is well," she said, looking at Aron, hoping he grasped her meaning.

"As well as it can be," Lord Cobb amended. He gave Aron another measured stare, then guided his mount away from Dari before any further trouble ensued from their contact.

Before Dari had quite recovered from seeing her grandfather's best friend, from giving up a chance to return to familiar territory and familiar people at his side, and from almost revealing her true nature to hundreds of Stone Brothers and soldiers, the traveling column was preparing to move out again.

This time, there was nothing to slow them. There would be no thoughts of night or shelters or dangers along the road.

As the soldiers escorting Zeller herded livestock into a circle and began to push southwest toward the town, Lord Cobb galloped forward, hesitated to allow his torchbearers to form ranks around the travelers, then shouted, "Triune!"

"Triune!" his soldiers echoed, and Zed, and many of the Stone Brothers, too.

Dari noticed Aron remained silent at Stormbreaker's side. The boy kept glancing at her, and she resolved to thank him properly at her first opportunity. Perhaps that would help him understand that he had used his mind-talent well this time, that he had saved her and perhaps her sister, too, not to mention protected the anonymity of her people.

Lord Cobb led them forward, trotting at first, then quickly shifting to a gallop.

Dari wrapped her fingers into Toronado's mane and tried not to let herself feel the weight of a day that had already been too long and far too eventful. She let her thoughts flow into the movement of the horse as the stallion tensed, then bolted forward.

As the cold night wind hit her full in the face, as her eyes began to water and her skin began to chill, Dari allowed herself only one thought beyond keeping her own body in rhythm with Toronado's gait and shifts.

Let us find safety before the sun is full in tomorrow's sky—and let me find a way to search for Kate before it's too late.

CHAPTER TWENTY

ARON

The small hours passed outside Aron's awareness, and dawn came only at the fringes of his perceptions.

Had the torchbearers doused their flames?

Yes.

He could see better. More shapes than moonslit darkness or gray mysteries. Still, villages blurred into woods into hills into rocks as they passed. He no longer even took the effort to look at them. The packed dirt byway was wide now, and mostly empty but for their traveling column.

How long had they been riding at this streaking-arrow pace?

Hours.

But it seemed more than days.

All he could hear was the thunder of hooves and the thump of clawfeet. All he could taste was dust. His arms and hands and fingers had gone numb, along with his feet. He wished his legs and belly and back would deaden, too, and leave him in peace. Perhaps he should tie himself to Tek's neck, as Stormbreaker had done during his Harvest, just to be certain he didn't slip from his saddle and get crushed to death by other talons and horses.

Tek's scales were so lathered from her fatigue that the oozing, smelly oil dripped on his cramping legs, and her battle ring kept flipping upward. Over and over again, he reached up to stroke her neck and restore her focus, which got harder as his own slipped away.

Beside him, Stormbreaker and Windblown kept their eyes forward, expressions flat and determined as they thundered toward Triune. Soldiers on horseback surged up and back, sometimes ringing them, sometimes falling away to leave the talons clear ground to run. Aron clenched his jaw as he twisted his burning neck and checked behind him. Zed and Dari were riding close at his flank. Neither were shouting complaints from the backs of their horses, and nor would Aron. Even if his thighs bled. Even if his back broke.

"Halt!" came a cry from the front of their column.

At first, Aron wasn't certain he heard it, but the motion ahead began to settle into stillness.

Others picked up the call, and bit by bit, the traveling column slowed.

He tried to haul back on Tek's reins. At first his arms wouldn't respond, but Aron managed to put his weight into the pull and get the little talon's attention. She came to a restless halt beside Stormbreaker's bull, her sides heaving, oil sliding from her scales and spattering against the well-trampled ground.

"Come with me." Stormbreaker glanced at Aron and Dari as he steered his talon forward, into the ranks of lathered mounts and drooping heads.

Aron pressed his heels into Tek's sides.

The talon squeaked, but didn't move.

He nudged her again, and she let out a hiss—but she stumbled forward, making her way behind the bull. The *clop-clop* of Dari's stallion's hooves let Aron know she was following, too. He hadn't had time to wonder at how effortlessly she rode, and without saddle or bridle, but he was growing accustomed to the endless stores of mysteries related to Dari.

On they went, weaving through exhausted riders, until they

reached Cobb's standard-bearers and the front of the traveling column. Lord Cobb had moved his mount to the edge of the rise, and he had his helmet off, gazing into what Aron assumed would be the vale or gorge below. The dynast lord's horse didn't move at all as the talons approached, and Aron figured the creature had been through much training and many mock battles. It probably wouldn't shy from a falling boulder or flee a spiraling arrow unless its rider directed it to do so.

The sight of such a well-trained animal chased away some of Aron's fatigue. *One day, I'll be able to train Tek like that, and other talons, and horses, too.*

"Here." Stormbreaker gestured to a spot on the rise beside him. "Come and look, boy."

Aron's muscles tensed. After all they had seen and been through since his Harvest, his mind shrank back from more surprises, more chaos and destruction—but he made himself hold his head level. At the nudge of his heels, Tek moved forward.

Dari moved her stallion until it drew even with Aron and Tek as he gazed over the edge of the rise.

"Oh," Dari said, but Aron couldn't say anything at all.

In the far distance, yellow sands that had to be from the Barrens reached toward bare rock and gravel Aron recognized as Outlands from hunting excursions with his father. Both formed the upper boundary of a green valley crisscrossed by bright blue rivers and streams. The valley's southern edge was obscured by columns of blue-gray mists.

I'm looking at the Deadfall for the first time.

His blood seemed to hesitate in his veins, then grow cold at the thought of the horrors slithering through those mists. Daylight or moonslight, it didn't matter in the Deadfall. Manes walked those poisoned lands at all hours.

But even that realization paled inside Aron, lost to his awe at the castle filling the habitable portion of the valley.

It was magnificent. Scarcely believable.

"Triune is larger than Can Lanyard in my dynast," Lord Cobb said. "It's as self-sufficient as any great city—any dynast, even. And an absolute marvel of construction. There has never been a successful breach of Stone, from without or from within. I doubt any army could successfully lay siege to that fortress, even if they were foolish enough to try."

"Stone never makes war or joins it, *Chi*," Stormbreaker said, "so no one makes war on us—except errant Brailing soldiers on the road. Look there, Aron." He pointed to the right corner. "That's the main gate and keep, where we'll enter."

Aron tried to take in the magnitude of the keep, but failed. Instead, he fell to counting the outer structures beside the main gate and keep, the tall stone buildings connected by what looked like a massive wall. The structures seemed too plentiful, as if his eyes were playing tricks on his mind.

"How many towers?" he asked, after losing count for the third time.

"I've been trying to count," Dari murmured, and to Stormbreaker's right, Lord Cobb laughed. It was a tired sound, but somehow relaxing and inviting at the same time.

Stormbreaker's tone was indulgent when he responded. "Twenty-six. Brothers and Sisters live in those towers, and inside the curtain itself. It's as thick as the length of five grown men laid head to foot."

Aron felt even smaller than he usually did. He couldn't imagine how such a structure had ever been built, but the massive wall stretched the length of the diamond-shaped enclosure on all sides, the spiked battlements connecting the towers. As for the towers, Aron counted three rows of windows top to bottom. *Like three cottages, stacked atop one another.*

He couldn't judge the depth and girth at this distance, but they looked spacious, especially the ones on each corner, which were wider.

On the west side were fields with grazing livestock, stables, paddocks, woods, and ponds. On the east he saw crops and gardens being harvested or cleared from harvest, streams dotted with wooden or stone bridges, a few buildings that looked like forges, or maybe armories, or both. There were barns—even a Temple of the Brother with its bell tower clearly visible. And at the back of the massive city, the north tip, there was a mill, many collections of cottages, and what looked like a separate castle-within-a-castle, with its own keep and a set of four towers at the corners of the square building.

At last, Aron's eyes watered from staring. He blinked away the moisture, then noticed a strange structure near the front, something that appeared to be a large, ornate stone barn, only without doors sufficient to allow for livestock. To the barn's left were what looked like stacks of stone steps joined by pillars.

Stormbreaker gestured to the spot. "That's the House of the Judged."

Lord Cobb made a quick sign against ill fortune, and Dari coughed.

Aron wondered if he should avert his eyes out of respect for the condemned people awaiting death in that structure, but decided against it. He was a Stone of Stone now, after all. Sooner or later, he would have to look the Judged squarely in their eyes, face them in combat, and hunt them if they chose flight instead.

I'm not spineless. Better I grow used to the thought now than fight it when it's inevitable. He swallowed hard and wished his hands would stop shaking.

"If all goes well with the Lord Provost, you'll spend many an hour in that arena." Stormbreaker adjusted the reins on his bull talon's neck until he gripped them in his opposite hand. "Sometimes as a witness, other times in training—and after you're fully vested, you'll see combat there, more often than you can imagine."

Aron didn't want to imagine it. Looking at the House of the Judged and that arena was all his stomach could take for the moment.

His mind worked over Stormbreaker's words for a moment, and then his stomach really lurched and churned. He met Stormbreaker's gaze even as everyone else studied the scene below them.

"You'll have to face him, for your actions with the Brailing Guard." Stormbreaker kept his voice quiet, and Dari and Lord Cobb didn't seem to notice him speaking. "You understand that, don't you?"

Aron felt himself sink against Tek's powerful neck, but he nodded. He had suspected something like this would happen, but there had been no time for questions or discussions. Aron wanted to ask Stormbreaker if everything would be all right, if he had a fair chance with the Lord Provost, but Stormbreaker's sad expression gave him answers he wasn't sure he wanted to hear.

Dari pointed to what looked like a portion of a small tower outside the main enclosure, a tiny building that seemed to be positioned at the intersection of Barrens, Outlands, and the Deadfall. "What is that?"

Stormbreaker remained silent for a moment, and Aron couldn't help the sense that the High Master was trying not to make his own sign against ill fortune. "The Ruined Keep."

Lord Cobb shifted his saddle and rolled his shoulders forward and back, as if to relieve his comfort. "Where Stone Brothers and Sisters go for their final trial and become full members of the guild. I've heard tales about that place. Folly and exaggeration, I'm sure."

Once again, Stormbreaker didn't answer right away. When he did, his words came out uncharacteristically slowly. "It would be difficult to form lies worse than the truth about that place. I've had my own dark experiences there."

Aron chilled so deeply he felt his bones creak in the saddle. He couldn't tear his eyes from the tiny, broken building in the mists and sands and rocks, and when he spoke, his words came out in a scratchy whisper. "If I'm allowed to continue at Stone, how old will I be when I face my trial?"

Stormbreaker's expression remained mostly neutral, but Aron

thought he saw a flicker of something like concern. "At least sixteen—but we have no set age after that. It's up to the apprentice to ask for the privilege when they believe they're ready, and up to the master to grant permission. Since men and women can petition to join Stone at any age, we've had apprentices go to trial as old as fifty and sixty years of age."

Aron immediately set about worrying that it would take longer than two years for him to become ready for the trial. What if it took three years, or five? What if he became the oldest apprentice to complete the trial ever? What if he couldn't possibly learn all that Stone had to teach—or what if he didn't want to learn some of what he'd be forced to absorb? His gaze shifted back to the House of the Judged and the arena standing beside it, and he imagined the brown surface took its color from old blood.

How many men and women had died between those rock pillars?

Did anyone at Stone keep a record of terrors like that?

Did he even want to know?

"We've but a few miles to go to the shelter of Stone," Lord Cobb said, pulling his mount about to take the lead behind the standard-bearers. "Let's not be caught sky gazing by the Brailing Guard this close to safety and relief."

Stormbreaker turned his talon toward the rise's downward slope. Windblown went by, and so did Zed, but Aron couldn't stop staring into the valley below.

Triune was impressive. Breathtaking. But he couldn't help comparing its beauty to the dazzling way scales of venomous snakes glistened in the sun.

I can't enter that viper's den. He gripped Tek's reins in both fists. *I can't begin to make myself move.*

But he was Aron Weylyn now, not Aron Brailing, and destined to become one of the vipers he feared. He was the son of the wolf, with a wolf—and his family to avenge. Ruined Keep or not, House of the Judged or not, he knew he had to ride down the slope and make his way into that monstrously splendid enclosure. Then he would face the Lord Provost, and somehow convince the man that he was worth the apprenticeship Stormbreaker had bestowed upon him.

"Home is a matter of choice," Dari said from behind him. "For now, *li'ha*, we're both choosing this place."

Choice.

Do I truly have a choice?

Aron cast another glance at the city-castle in the valley.

Was he choosing Triune? Had Triune chosen him?

Both, perhaps.

Whatever the case, the words helped him press his feet against Tek's sides, gently, almost hoping she wouldn't respond.

The little talon let out one whistle. Then, oblivious to her rider's wishes, she followed like a puppy after Stormbreaker and his big bull.

CHAPTER TWENTY-ONE

ARON

Aron had to tilt back his head to take in the height of the gates as the traveling column mustered to ride through them. Just the sight of the massive wooden structures set his blood to rushing again, shoving warmth into his clammy feet and hands. The air smelled of horses and sweat, of fields and manure, oil and leather and rock—and from somewhere, the scent of baking bread and frying meat tortured his senses.

Bells rang all along the battlements, first close, then moving quickly away, as if running the length of the big stone wall that enclosed the stronghold. It sounded like a signal. Maybe an announcement. Aron squinted, but couldn't see where the bells were located.

"They're announcing the arrival of a dynast lord." Stormbreaker gestured toward the top of the battlements. "So appropriate meals and quarters will be readied. It won't take you long to learn all the patterns and messages carried by the bells."

The tone and rhythm of the bells shifted, and Aron saw the relief and pleasure on Stormbreaker's face. He suspected the bells were now spreading the good news that one of Stone's High Masters had made it safely back to the stronghold. Tonight, Stormbreaker probably would sleep in a real bed, after a real dinner.

Would his apprentice enjoy the same treatment?

Aron's entire body ached with anticipation, despite the fact that it would be hours before the sun made its way across Eyrie's skies.

At the moment, I'd settle for breakfast. A handful of nuts. Anything.

Yet the desire to eat battled against a queasiness at the size of the gates, at the enormity of Triune, and the thought of going inside.

Lord Cobb and his personal regimen formed up behind his standard-bearer, and Stormbreaker, Aron, Dari, Windblown, and Zed gathered behind them. After that came the remainder of the Stone Brothers and Harvest prizes, and the Cobb Guard protected the rear from any last-minute attacks. Aron heard the call of, "Heave!"

Wood popped. A great grinding sound followed, and a few inches at a time, the massive wooden gates swung inward to reveal what looked to Aron like an endless courtyard crowded with people. The smell of food grew stronger, making his belly twist and growl. Aron actually checked to see if any of the people milling about on the cobblestones ahead might be holding a plate—but he was disappointed.

Lord Cobb and his Guard entered Triune to the rhythmic ringing of bells, and as he drew closer to the gates, Aron saw Stone Brothers in gray robes lined up on either side of the entrance, obviously prepared and waiting to see to the dynast lord's every need.

As he passed beneath the arched entrance behind Stormbreaker, the bells stopped.

Aron found himself in a huge walled courtyard large enough to accommodate a small army—which was fortunate, since they had arrived with just such a contingent. Hooves rang against the cobbled stone surface, and Tek's claws clacked and scraped with each step. People clogged parts of the big space. Some were male, some were female, all ages, some in gray robes, some in simple tunics, gathered in groups, all watching the procession. Beyond them rose a formidable-looking stone building, larger than any structure Aron had seen before. Water flowed in front of it and a drawbridge had been settled into place, providing narrow but sufficient passage across the water.

From what Aron could see, there were . . . things in the water. Maybe fish. But larger than any fish Aron had ever seen. On either side of the big keep, Aron saw thick wooden screens extending down into the water, as if to keep the giant fish swimming only in the small channel in front.

Mocker fish?

Cayn's teeth. Would the guild keep mockers so close to people on purpose?

Aron couldn't believe that, not even of the Stone Guild, yet he found himself edging a few steps away from the water, until he couldn't see the shadows swimming through it.

Lord Cobb and his Guard were soon surrounded by a frenetic cloud of gray-robed Brothers and at least one Sister dressed in similar fashion. Aron reined Tek beside Stormbreaker as Lord Cobb and his party dismounted, then allowed their horses to be led away across the drawbridge, then into and through the central arched space running the length of the keep. On the other side of the long arched hallway, Aron could see a road, with grass and trees to either side.

The rest of the traveling column poured in through the gates behind him, going right and left in large groups, and people moved to meet them and assist with their horses.

"Here," said a voice below Aron, and he looked down to find the ginger-haired boy, Raaf Thunderheart, raising his hand to take Tek's rein. The boy couldn't have been at Triune more than a few days, if his riders carried him with scarcely any rest, yet he already looked thicker, taller, and healthier. Some scars marked his little face, but otherwise, only the bruise on his cheek gave any hint to the little boy's harsh past.

"Don't worry," Raaf said. "I've been working with talons and horses since I was near born, since my people where smiths and all—and she's a little 'un. Give her over to me and I'll see that she's cleaned and fed and stabled, proper-like, in the talon barn, and away from those bulls."

Aron looked to Stormbreaker, who had already dismounted. So had Windblown. Helpers took control of the bull talons immediately, but Zed was leading his own horse away. On all sides, Aron saw other Harvest prizes being instructed to take and tend to their own mounts, yet here was this boy offering to take Tek—and another boy was helping Dari down from her stallion as well. Aron wondered why they were getting special treatment.

Stormbreaker strode over to Aron, glanced at Raaf, and smiled. "Pleased to see you, young sir." He nodded to Aron to give his talon into the boy's care. "You will enjoy some privileges as a High Master's apprentice, but you'll also know more hardship in exchange."

A moment later, he went back to searching the crowd again and again, as if seeking something he couldn't find. "All Harvest prizes are kept close to their guild masters in the first weeks," he murmured, sounding distracted and beyond fatigued. "You'll be no exception. Come with me now. No tarrying."

Stormbreaker strode away from Aron, and Aron had to scramble down from Tek. "Thanks," he said to Raaf as he tossed Tek's rein to the boy. Then he followed Stormbreaker at a run. A few steps later, he stumbled from being so long in the saddle and almost crashed to his knees, but strong hands caught his filthy tunic from behind.

Dari.

She lifted him back to his feet, dusted him off a bit, then frowned at the blood seeping through his breeches around his thighs. "It's good that we'll have some time on our own feet instead of riding. Those saddle sores need to heal."

Aron didn't answer. It irked him that his body kept showing weakness even as his mind commanded it to be strong. Did his precious Brailing mind-talent work only on others? Why was it he couldn't use it on himself?

"I should follow Stormbreaker," he muttered, then forced his aching muscles to move, to follow the High Master, first at a trot, then at a run. Dari hurried to keep up with him, and the two of them passed by Windblown in a whirl, leaving him to grunt with surprise and frustration.

A few seconds later, Stormbreaker once more stopped and searched the crowd.

Aron had no idea what the High Master was looking for, but he stopped beside Stormbreaker and searched, too. So did Dari. Aron wondered if they would instinctively know their quarry when they saw it.

Against a far wall of the courtyard, he spotted a few men preparing to mount fresh horses—men not from their traveling party. From their bright silk tunics and breeches, each in dynast colors, he knew them for messengers. An honorable occupation, and fairly safe in its own way, even in wartime. Those who harmed messengers knew swift vengeance from dynast lords, especially since most were the younger sons of families high in the dynast ruling lines.

Aron watched the messengers line up to ride out, and wondered what they carried in their leather pouches. Good tidings? Ill omens? Acceptances, refusals—the possibilities were endless. His father had taught him that some communications were too complex or sensitive to be sent fastened to the legs of lone passerines, even though that method was the fastest. Flash signals, like the flocks of passerines that called dynast lords to the Circle of Eyrie, or the bells that rang to announce their traveling party's arrival at Triune, were effective only for simple notifications. Aron hadn't thought about how active messengers would become during times of war, or how active they might be even during peacetime for a place as large and busy as Triune. Probably dozens of messengers came and went every day. Maybe hundreds.

For now, though, he watched ten or so ride out from the courtyard, through the gates, and onto the byway Aron's traveling party had taken on their trip down from the rise. Then he jumped at the shout of "Heave!"

The loud *crack-pop* of wood echoed through the stone courtyard as workers labored at the ropes to pull shut and secure the huge gates with equally huge, thick wooden bars, one at the top, one at the bottom, and two at the center. The finality of the castle's entrance slamming closed, sealing him away from the world outside, made Aron's gut clench even as he permitted himself to be relieved that he was now safe from threat.

Threat from the Brailing Guard, at least.

"I wish I knew what he was searching for," Dari mumbled from behind Aron, returning his attention to the milling crowd.

About a yard from Dari and Aron, Stormbreaker kept up his vigil, but his brow had furrowed and his lips had pinched together until he seemed to have no mouth at all. To Aron, the man looked worried, or perhaps it was sad. He couldn't tell. The tattoos on Stormbreaker's face made his expression seem severe even when he wasn't radiating displeasure or anger.

Another boy in a brown tunic came up to them, this one with short blond hair and a very dirty face. He glanced at Aron and Dari, gulped, reached out a trembling hand, and tugged Stormbreaker's robe.

When Stormbreaker looked down, the boy squeaked, "Lord Provost wants you. Now, he said. Tell Stormbreaker right now, no guff."

When he quoted the Lord Provost directly, the child used a growly, loud voice, imitating the man who had given him the summons to deliver. Stormbreaker reached to pat the child's head, but the boy was already gone, elbowing through the crowd as if he had urgent business elsewhere.

After one last glance around the crowd, Stormbreaker gestured to Aron and Dari to follow him, then set off across the drawbridge into the massive building.

Aron stood still until Dari shoved him, then moved slower than he should have toward the stretch of wood. He didn't know what scared him more, crossing that stream with only a bit of wood between him and whatever unnatural creature was swimming below, entering a keep larger than any building he had ever seen in his life, or coming face-to-face with the Lord Provost of the Stone Guild.

Aron's knees wobbled as he stepped up on the rough planking, which was wide enough to accommodate two horses, no more. He briefly wondered why Stone would make it so difficult to move large groups out of the castle, but it occurred to him the same design made it difficult to move large groups into the castle. An assailing force might breach the courtyard, even manage to drag down the drawbridge—but they'd still be able to move across only a few horses at a time, while defenders picked them off from the main battlements and the keep battlements, too.

Dari started to give him another push, but Aron wheeled on her and grabbed her wrists. "Don't play. I think they have mocker fish in this stream."

Dari's eyebrows lifted. She glanced over the edge of the drawbridge, then stepped back and noticed the wooden screens. After a moment, she put out her hand for Aron to grasp. "Let's not linger here. Fish are difficult to control, even for me, and I have no desire to be some monster-carp's breakfast."

Dari's discomfort propelled Aron forward. He gripped Dari's soft fingers as they crossed into the maw of the square, turreted keep, and Aron noted that the gray stone walls and floors of the open, arched center section were clean and without decoration save for sconces and candles, and a pair of gray banners hanging down the rock on either side. On the banners was the symbol of the Stone Guild, the entwined antlers of Cayn, rendered in darker gray than the background cloth. Aron had that clutching sensation inside again, like each step he was taking was sealing his own doom tighter, and tighter yet, until he couldn't breathe, until he would die before ever leaving this place. He glanced toward the other side of the arched space, to the road and grass and trees beyond, to that first bit of Triune he could see, the Triune that existed on the inside of the massive walls.

To Stone go the Stones. Well, I'm a Stone now, and I'm here.

Stormbreaker was disappearing around a set of circular stairs on their left. Aron and Dari clambered up the steps behind him, both groaning as their exhausted muscles protested the climb. At the top of the stairs, they entered into a closed section of the keep, which was just as clean and sparse as the open passageway below. Moments later, they jogged together down the smooth stone hallway to where Stormbreaker stood in front of another large wooden door, which was partially open.

From inside came the scent of a meal.

Aron's thoughts jumbled and he imagined himself eating through wood and rock to get to the delicious-smelling food, if it came to that. His mouth watered. His stomach bellowed, and he thought he heard Dari's belly make a similar noise.

Stormbreaker knocked on the door.

In his single-minded pursuit of breakfast, Aron almost forgot to be terrified about meeting the Lord Provost. The moment a voice called, "Enter," he remembered his fear. His legs turned first to wood, then to reeds, trembling and bowing and refusing to move forward even as Stormbreaker pushed open the door enough to enter.

"There, now." Dari squeezed Aron's shoulder. "He's a Lord Provost, not a rock cat. The man won't eat you."

Aron flushed and shook off her grip. He didn't want to look at her, to see the pity or humor on her pretty face. He wanted her to see him as quick-learning, brave, and powerful, not as some terrified little boy.

Yet he didn't quite believe her about the Lord Provost. The man was leader of the Stone Guild. He was the chief killer in a city full of assassins. Where was it written that he didn't eat people who displeased him?

Fighting the blush he knew was coloring his face, Aron kept his eyes away from Dari.

"Go on," she said, sounding less patient. "Inside. We have no choice, Aron."

A different sort of heat surged through Aron. "Leave off talk of choice," he snarled. "You have plenty of options. It's me that has none."

Dari looked pained at his sharp words, and the heat seeped out of Aron so fast he could do little but curse himself and wonder why he spoke harshly to Dari when he really just wanted to hold her hand again.

A new despair settled across Aron's shoulders.

"Sorry," he muttered, wondering how many more times he would find himself apologizing to Dari because he couldn't keep his fool mouth closed in her presence.

"All right," she said, still not smiling, but no longer looking like he had wounded her with a dagger. "I'm sorry, too, for slighting the truth of your situation. *Now* will you go inside?"

Aron snorted and turned away from her again, this time managing to bite back the annoyed comments trying to burst from his throat.

He lifted his chin. Doing his best to control his galloping nerves, he shoved open the door. Without glancing back at Dari, hoping she'd see that he wasn't afraid now, Aron marched into the room behind Storm-breaker.

CHAPTER TWENTY-TWO

ARON

Aron stopped inside the room, flushing all over again as his legs once more started to wobble.

He had expected to find a room fit for a dynast lord, decked in silks and rugs, with soft furnishings, a lit fire, and servants standing silently along the walls as some flabby, ancient man spouted orders to any who would listen. What he found instead was a big stone chamber, cold, with embers barely flickering in the fireplace. A huge desk sat near the fireplace, and scattered over the rest of the space were a bunch of rough-looking wooden chairs and a few tables.

Lord Cobb was seated at one of them, without any soldiers protecting him, gazing at Aron, obviously taken aback by Aron's bold entrance.

Stormbreaker was regarding him, too, his marked face still and unreadable. Aron wished he could fade back to the other side of the door and try again, this time with less fanfare.

Lord Cobb smiled at him the way his father used to do, when he had done something particularly silly but not desperately harmful. The heat in Aron's face deepened.

The dynast lord had paused in the act of dipping his hand into one of several platters heaped with meats, breads, cheese, fruit, and eggs— more food than Aron had ever seen on a table, even on feast days, birthdays, or other celebrations. Several tankards sat on the table as well, along with two large silver flasks and a wooden pitcher of water.

"Join me." Lord Cobb gestured to all of them as Dari came in behind Aron, though his next smile seemed to be for Dari alone. "There's far too much here for one man, though I appreciate the kindness of Stone in seeing to my legendary appetite."

Aron still wanted to fall through the cobbled floor, but his embarrassment quickly gave way to desire to fly to the trays and stuff bites of everything in his mouth at the same time. Somehow, he managed to wait for Stormbreaker's nod of permission. Then he walked to the table with deliberately slow steps, sat at what he hoped was a respectful distance from the dynast lord, and grabbed only a few slivers of cheese and apples. It didn't seem proper to take the meat or hot bread, not until he was certain Lord Cobb had eaten his fill.

What were the protocols involved with eating at the same table with a dynast lord? Aron had no idea, though he knew there had to be customs, traditions, and rules. What if he broke one of them? Would the Lord Provost or Stormbreaker cast him out for such an offense?

"Don't hold back on my account." Lord Cobb pushed a tankard and the heaviest tray toward Aron as Stormbreaker and Dari sat across from him. "Take what you will, though I suspect when the Lord Provost returns, he will demand we tidy up our own mess."

Stormbreaker selected a sugared bun as Dari picked out fruit and nuts. "Lord Provost Baldric would not ask a dynast lord to perform menial labor, *Chi*," Stormbreaker said.

Lord Cobb laughed as Aron poured himself some water with unsteady hands. "Baldric would have me scrubbing floors if he thought no one would notice." The dynast lord helped himself to some sausages and hard bread, biting and chewing between words and more laughter. "He used to pound me on a regular basis in our youth—or hasn't he crowed about his propensity for abusing dynast rulers?"

At Stormbreaker's stunned silence, Lord Cobb added, "His mother was my mother's lady-attendant." To Aron, he said, "Dynast lords are not made of rock-glass and straw. Most of us can take a punch, if fairly delivered. And what might your name be, boy?"

Aron almost choked on his overlarge mouthful of bacon. His gaze darted to Stormbreaker as he fought to swallow the food. His father had taught him much, including the proper fashion of speaking to a dynast lord, but Aron wasn't certain what Stone's rules were in that respect. Was he supposed to respond directly? Wait for his master to direct him? And what would happen if he accidentally spit out the pork he was chewing because he couldn't recover from the surprise of being directly addressed by the ruler of a greater dynast?

"Aron Weylyn." Dari set a partially eaten strawberry on the table in front of her. "He's High Master Stormbreaker's new apprentice."

Lord Cobb's expression remained light, but he said to Stormbreaker, "You took him from the Watchline."

Stormbreaker retrieved a tankard and poured a honey-colored liquid from one of the silver flasks. After a long few seconds, he said simply, "I did."

"Fortunate for him—and you as well, if he can learn to manage himself." Lord Cobb took hold of his own tankard, and Aron saw the man's knuckles go white. He was surprised the cup's handle didn't bow from the force of that grip. When the dynast lord spoke again, the warmth had gone from his rich voice, replaced by cold anger. "There will be no place in the heavens for Helmet Brailing. I curse him here and now, in front of any who might listen. Turning on those he swore to protect—if I could reach him, if I thought the Circle of Eyrie would permit it, I'd kill him myself. I may yet, and curse the consequences."

Stormbreaker and Dari agreed by banging their cups on the table.

Aron found himself losing his taste for the bacon he had claimed, but he finally managed to swallow what was in his mouth.

Lord Cobb regarded him with a mix of sadness and lingering rage. "I am truly sorry for the madness Lord Brailing unleashed against those you knew and loved. Would that I had known what he was planning, I would have thrown every soldier I command into Dyn Brailing to prevent the slaughter."

Aron had no doubt Lord Cobb was telling him the truth, that the man's anger and pain at the suffering of those on the Watchline was genuine.

Is that instinct or my graal *giving me such information?*

He would have to ask Dari, but for now, Dari seemed lost in her own thoughts. She hadn't touched her strawberry again, but stared at it instead. It wasn't like her to be so unsettled, and it worried him.

"You have a very powerful legacy, and bless the Brother for it," Lord Cobb said to Aron, startling him all over again. "Thank you for helping Dari control herself when I first met your party and upset her."

Once more, Aron looked to Stormbreaker to see how he should respond. He couldn't fathom engaging in casual conversation with a dynast lord, especially about issues he was supposed to keep secret. Yet Stormbreaker didn't seem distressed by the fact Lord Cobb knew about Aron's Harvest, or about his mind-talents. And the dynast ruler seemed very familiar with Dari. It was obvious she trusted the man, so Aron decided it might be permissible to trust Lord Cobb as well.

"You're welcome, *Chi*," he whispered, then repeated himself louder, so he could be heard.

Neither Stormbreaker nor Dari gave Aron a crosswise look, so he figured he must have done passably well with his answer. His stomach ached, demanding more food, overriding his nerves and even his sadness at the mention of his family's deaths. He selected a biscuit and some sausages from the proffered tray, and moments later, he was once more shoveling down the nourishment. The sausage tasted of sage—and other spices, real *spices*—he had rarely had the good fortune to enjoy. His tongue and mouth tingled from salt, from garlic, from something so hot it made his ears buzz and his nose run. He wiped his mouth and nose with his sleeve, then took another big bite of the tangy meat. Aron had no idea what that hot taste was, but he wanted more of it.

Stone must be wealthy indeed, or perhaps their soil allows for growing such expensive treats.

"Where is the Lord Provost?" Stormbreaker asked as Dari continued to poke at her strawberry without eating it. Her dark eyes remained on the table, and she was frowning.

Lord Cobb pointed toward the chamber's door. "He had to step out to resolve a spat between a Mab messenger and an Altar messenger. Not certain of the details, but I heard they were threatening daggers or swords over some slight or the other."

Stormbreaker sighed. "This will only get worse. Even in times of simple border disputes, we're flooded with messengers full of demands, wanting reassurance about Stone's neutrality, or how we view this issue or that issue. It takes inordinate time, and it's not worth the trouble."

Lord Cobb worked on a bit of bread for a moment, then said, "You should know that Baldric knows all that I know about your traveling party, save for a few details." He seemed pained by his admission, but continued nonetheless. "My apologies, but at least half the *dav'ha* marks I bear are shared on his arm, and it was his urging and Lord Ross's that sent me thundering out of Can Lanyard with a good portion of my dynast force."

Dari didn't react, but Stormbreaker shifted in his chair, as if his nerves might be twitching as much as Aron's at hearing these words. "We would have had to tell him most of it, in any case. Let's hope he'll remain in good temper for the duration of our meeting."

Now Aron really didn't want the Lord Provost to return. He couldn't imagine a man severe enough to cause Stormbreaker discomfort. Didn't even want to imagine such a monster. He forced down his mouthful of nuts, bread, and jam, and stared openly at Stormbreaker, hoping to catch his eye and read his intentions.

Will you tell him about my crime at the travelers' camp? Will he judge me here, now, for my intentions?

"Lord Cobb, when did you last see Platt?" Dari's interruption came out rapid-fire, as if she had been battling the question until it exploded inside her. Aron's attention shifted to her so abruptly that he almost couldn't remember his own last thoughts.

"What did my cousin tell you about his plans to find my sister?" Dari seemed to realize Stormbreaker and Aron were confused, because she added, "The Cobb line knows *who* we are, my sister and me, but only Lord Cobb and his eldest son know *what* we are. Platt is my mother's sister's son, the leader of my people—and until this last year when I came of age, he was my regent."

Dari's expression reminded Aron of Seth spatting with the two brothers closest to him in age. Most of the time Seth was—well, he had been—quiet and of measured temper, but taunting from Davyd and Cairn could turn Seth into a raving beast, barely human, frothing at the mouth and searching for weapons. Aron saw hints of such a transition in Dari now, from the way her voice tightened and the corners of her eyes narrowed.

"I saw Platt during the last moons cycle, when I traveled to Can Elder." Lord Cobb's voice grew softer, more gentle as he spoke to Dari, and his gaze softened to something close to apologetic. "I went to pay my respects to your grandfather after I heard his twin boys had succumbed to the Wasting."

Dari's mouth came open, and tears immediately filled her black eyes. "Both of them? Both of my tiny little uncles? Tell me that's not true. They can't both have died."

Lord Cobb's sadness was obvious. "That makes nine children lost in all, counting your father." He glanced at Stormbreaker and Aron.

"I know most of Eyrie believes Kembell Ross's eldest perished in his teen years because of damage done to his lungs by the Wasting he survived in childhood. In truth, he left Can Elder to marry and died in a fire a few years after that, along with his wife."

Stormbreaker assailed another sweet bun, then allowed, "Yes. Dari explained about the marriage, but I didn't know her father had indeed lost his life, or her mother."

Dari once more stared at the table, and Aron could tell from the tremble in her shoulders that she was crying, perhaps for the deaths she had just been made aware of, or perhaps for her father and mother. He wanted to kick himself even harder over his snappish words to her in the hallway.

She has lost family, too. Hers to a tragedy—a fire. That's as unfair as losing them to murder, isn't it?

He wanted to get up and go to her, put his hand on her shoulder like she so often did when comforting him, but he didn't think it was proper to rise from the table without the dynast lord's permission. He wished Lord Cobb would comfort Dari, or even Stormbreaker, but neither man did.

Lord Cobb gestured to Dari. "As you can see, the union of Dari's father and mother was against the Code of Eyrie. A cross-mixing. She can never take the throne at Can Elder in Dyn Ross—but thank the Brother the girls were born, and that they lived, or I fear Lord Ross would break apart altogether. Too much death, even for such a strong man."

"My cousin Edrian is all my grandfather has left to him now, since his mother died in the birthing." Dari's voice shook, but she looked up, clear-eyed, at Lord Cobb.

"Save for you and your sister." Lord Cobb reached for her hand then, and covered it with his own. "Your grandfather is mad from worrying about you both. He battled Platt fiercely on the subject of what to do about Kate's escape from her protections, but in the end agreed that perhaps it would be best if you returned to Dyn Ross and let Platt find and tend to Kate in his own fashion."

"No!" Dari jerked her hand back.

Lord Cobb blew out a breath, obviously expecting this fight, and ready for it. "Platt is sending out more of your people to locate Kate. Trained soldiers."

Stormbreaker went very silent, motionless, as if removing himself from the conflict. Aron's insides twisted with the need to help Dari, stick up for her, defend her, but he, too, said nothing.

Dari sat up straight in her chair, dark eyes burning with conviction. "I'm trained! As good a fighter as any of those men—maybe better. Besides, Kate might not respond peacefully to their attempts to help her. She doesn't trust anyone but me."

"Dari, listen to reason." Lord Cobb reached for her hand again, but Dari wouldn't let him touch her. "If your sister resists you, or if she's being held in some fashion that doesn't allow for escape, you'll have no choice but to . . ." He broke off, obviously searching for the words. At last he came up with, "You'll have no choice but to offer her Mercy. Could you do that, if you're left with no option?"

"There will be another option." Dari spoke through her teeth this time, and Aron couldn't help but notice the brilliant flares of red and green all around her body. Her *graal*, more the truth of it than the illusion she cast, was so powerful he didn't have to focus his vision in that certain way to see it. In fact, he had to blink against the force of it, and convince himself not to look directly into the green brilliance, lest it claim his senses, and maybe his sanity.

"No matter the circumstance, I'll get her out," Dari said, glowing more brightly than ever. Lord Cobb and Stormbreaker averted their gazes as she insisted, "I *will* get my sister home safely."

"You can't know that," Lord Cobb countered, driving Dari to her feet.

She slammed both palms against the table and leaned toward Lord Cobb. "If Platt acts to harm my sister, I'll—"

"You'll do nothing." Lord Cobb stood as well, arms at his sides, his voice loud enough to command all the attention in the room. His gaze was as stern as any Aron had ever seen from his own father, and it took some effort not to scoot his chair back from the table to get more distance from the man. "Platt is a king, Dari. The king of your people, and he and your grandfather have kept all of you safe for years. If Platt acts, it will be to save your people, and to save *you* from further danger. You know he has more to attend to than the workings of one heart—even if that heart is yours."

Dari removed her hands from the table, turned away, and finally lowered her head. "I can find Kate. You tell Platt and my grandfather I can do it."

"I see that you intend to, and I hope that you'll be successful." The sternness was gone now, and Aron saw nothing but kindness in the dynast lord's weathered face as he approached Dari and rested his hands on her shoulders. "I have my youngest sons dispatched as messengers in every dynast, keeping ears open for any word, any hint. I'll give you whatever help I can, child, but there's no promise Kate is even alive."

Dari moved away from him, but not rudely this time, and sat down once more. All the air seemed to rush out of her in a single breath. "My twin still lives." Her voice was thin now, her tone almost desperate. "I'd know it if she died."

Lord Cobb remained on his feet, but he looked at Stormbreaker, as if he didn't know the mechanics of what Dari had just claimed.

Stormbreaker placed a portion of sweet bun on the table in front of him. "Twin connections are very strong, Dari. Why can you not see Kate on the other side of the Veil?"

Dari went back to staring at her fingers in her lap, which made

Aron want to slip around the table and sit beside her, just in case his presence might offer her solace.

"It's always been difficult, since Kate's mind and awareness aren't consistent," she said, "but usually, I would have caught a hint of her by now. I don't know. It's as if her essence is hidden from me. Being hidden, I mean."

Stormbreaker's brow furrowed. "To hide a twin from a twin, that would take a powerful force indeed. I can think of only a few who could manage such a feat."

"A few that we know of," Lord Cobb corrected, once more sitting down, then shifting his attention back to Aron. "Aron Weylyn, here beside us and eating his weight in sausage, is proof that many rogue legacies, both true and mixed, may be running about the country-side right under our very noses."

Dari clenched her fists on the tabletop. Aron could tell she was holding back a fresh tirade, or maybe another round of pleading with Lord Cobb, but she never got the chance to speak.

The chamber's wooden door bounced open, and in strode a big, muscular man in a gray robe. He looked to be the same age as Lord Cobb, perhaps a few years older, and just as fit—only this man had no hair. Not on his head or face. Not even eyebrows. Aron couldn't help thinking he looked a bit like a brawny brown egg. An egg with four full black spirals tattooed on his face, one at the forehead, one on each cheek, and one on his chin as well.

This rank-marked egg could darken a room with the magnitude of its frown.

Lord Baldric.

Aron needed no formal introductions, and his mind moved auto-matically to the proper address of a Lord Provost—his title and his first name, to distinguish him from a dynast lord.

It was as if the man's title and his fury had stormed into the room before his body ever broke the plane of the entrance.

Aron got to his feet at the same time as the others and lowered his gaze from the Lord Provost.

It's time for my first judgment. I feel it in my blood. He stared intently at his feet, willing the man not to notice him, but knowing that he would.

Aron wished his *graal* would tell him something, give him some small hint of the truth, but his mind remained absolutely and completely silent.

He was on his own with this one, no matter how it ended.

CHAPTER TWENTY-THREE

ARON

Aron's body reacted of its own accord, tensing, as if his muscles expected that he might have to flee for his life before this meeting ended. The trays on the table once more lost all appeal, and he wished he hadn't stuffed himself so thoroughly that he might not be able to run as fast or as far, from the sheer weight of meat in his belly.

Aron let his gaze shift in the fashion Dari taught him, and noted the touch of black and ruby coloring drifting about the bald man's shoulders and head. A hint of Cobb legacy, though nothing as strong as the dynast lord's.

Lord Cobb nodded first, though even at Stone in Lord Baldric's own chambers, he remained of higher rank. "I trust you avoided bloodshed, Baldric?"

"Dirt-eaters." The Lord Provost's frown grew more thunderous. "Stone observes the sanctity of messengers like every citizen in Eyrie, but if the cursed fools want to duel each other, they can swap sword blows until they bleed to death for all I care. Off Stone grounds. Away from Stone's walls. I sent them away under guard of the Stone Sisters. Let's see them get away from *that* before I wish it."

Lord Cobb opened his mouth as if to offer commentary, but Lord Baldric kept up his tirade. "And Pravda Altar has lost her senses, if she ever had any to begin with. For the twenty years since she's been elevated, Thorn has ignored every orphan they could shunt to Triune. Now she wishes to discuss the possibility of transferring 'any unclaimed children' to Eidolon. In the middle of a war."

"Pravda is Lady Provost of Thorn, Baldric," Lord Cobb said quickly, as if to make sure to get his words in before the next explosion. "She's not an Altar now, or allied with them any further. And she's not the girl-child we used to tease and leave behind in the barns and fields."

Lord Baldric snorted. "Don't be fooled. She's the same conniving little—"

"Baldric." Lord Cobb gestured to Stormbreaker, Aron, and Dari.

Lord Baldric grumbled for a moment, then wheeled on Stormbreaker without so much as a small bow to Lord Cobb. "And what have you brought me? A Brailing stolen from the Watchline without consent of his dynast lord—and her. Some pigeon under the direct protection of Kembell Ross, and him crazed with grieving the loss of two more children."

"Darielle is Kembell's granddaughter," Lord Cobb said from behind Lord Baldric, whose mouth came open from the shock. "And she's no pigeon. I'll not explain more, and you won't ask, and you *will* see to her comfort and safety while she's in residence at Stone." After a moment, he added, "Please. For the sake of all the three of us have shared, you and Kembell and me. It's a small thing to ask, Baldric. Truly."

The entire land seemed to slow to perfect stillness for Aron. He noticed that Stormbreaker and Lord Cobb weren't moving, and Dari wasn't even breathing deeply enough to make her chest rise and fall.

Lord Baldric glared at Stormbreaker. He didn't seem to be able to process Lord Cobb's announcement, or willing to turn on Lord Cobb and refuse his request. When he spoke, his words were still directed at Stormbreaker, this time in a strangled whisper. "Are you *trying* to incite the wrath of two dynast armies and bring them directly to Triune's gates?"

Stormbreaker didn't meet Lord Baldric's furious stare or even answer his inquiries. Instead, he proffered one of his own. "Where is my sister? Has Tia returned?"

Both Aron and Dari raised their heads at Stormbreaker's words. Aron was relieved to see that she looked as confused as he felt—so he wasn't the only person surprised by the question.

Lord Baldric stopped ranting, but the furious hue stayed in his cheeks. "We've had no word from Snakekiller, for good or ill. I'm sorry, Dun." The shift in his tone was nothing less than unsettling, and Aron set his teeth to keep them from chattering.

"We do know that Seventh High Master Uldin and his youngest apprentice were killed at the Brailing-Ross border. Stray arrows, Lord Brailing claims." Lord Baldric smacked a fist against his open palm, the color on his face expanding to cover his neck, too, red creeping over sun-baked brown. "The old fool is trying to blame some shadow-man with a cloth-wrapped face—said the same man butchered a bunch of soldiers, too. The Brailing Guard has dubbed this mystery fellow Canus the Bandit."

Stormbreaker looked both sad and uncomfortable as Lord Cobb laughed outright at this announcement.

Dari turned her head to avoid Aron's eyes.

Aron felt a queer unreality sink about his awareness. As it had back in that village, in the Zeller home, his mind seemed to split into two pieces, one that remained engaged with the real world, the now world—and one that shot back to the night he sought the Brailing Guard to avenge the deaths of his family.

I didn't kill them. Dari stopped me. Or the glowing boy with the bright red legacy. I didn't do the murder.

Did I?

But what if he had, somehow?

Were his thoughts powerful enough?

Maybe he, Aron, was this heinous outlaw, this Canus the Bandit.

And maybe Lord Baldric will know it and kill me now.

Yet even if Aron had managed to do harm to the soldiers, he couldn't fathom how he would have also sent an arrow through a High Master of the Stone Guild so far away from his targets—much less manifested as the image of a wrapped man fresh from the Barrens. Those things couldn't be possible.

At least he didn't think they were.

Brother help me.

Lord Baldric paused, then swore to make clear his opinion of what he obviously considered to be Lord Brailing's lies and excuses about the High Master's death. "Cayn take the Brailing Guard and Altar's warbirds with them—I've demanded a full granary load in repayment for Uldin's death on their watch, and I'll judge the archer myself when he's caught. Canus the Bandit, indeed."

Aron felt a surge of surprise at Lord Baldric calling the name of the horned god inside his own walls, then thought himself foolish. Of course a killer wouldn't fear the god of death. Hadn't Stormbreaker used an image of Cayn to make their *dav'ha*, after all?

"Uldin's oldest apprentice—what's his name—Galvin? Yes, Galvin Herder. He isn't ready to take the duties and may well never be, so I've decided to elevate Windblown to Uldin's position." Lord Baldric pointed at Stormbreaker. "That's a favor to you. You know I'm not fond of Windblown, but he's acquitted himself well these past years as your companion."

Stormbreaker seemed to gather his emotions, and he gave a little bow.

Before he straightened back to his full height, Lord Baldric had caught site of Aron, and his brown eyes crackled with energy and disapproval.

Aron swallowed. He didn't insult the Lord Provost by looking him directly in the face, but he wouldn't let himself cower either, no matter how his muscles tried to pull him to the chamber floor and curl him into a tight ball.

"Now, as for this boy," Lord Baldric said, his gaze still firmly fixed on Aron. "Westin says he may have the Brailing legacy. Is this the case?"

"Yes, Lord Provost," Stormbreaker said, remaining in his tense, stiff stance. "We believe he might possess the full and true measure of the old Brailing mind-talents."

Lord Baldric grunted in acknowledgment, maybe surprise as well. "And has he done anything with his mind-talents that I should know about?"

Dari's breath hitched along with Aron's. She shot a desperate glance at Stormbreaker, but the High Master didn't acknowledge her unspoken plea. Stormbreaker ignored Aron's worried look as well. As if oblivious to the damage he might be doing, Stormbreaker plowed ahead with telling the Lord Provost and Lord Cobb about Aron's attempt to attack the soldiers, and how Dari thwarted it and brought him back to this side of the Veil. He didn't make any excuses for Aron, or discuss his lack of training or understanding—nothing of the sort. He just laid bare the facts, and left them in the hands of Lord Baldric.

Aron didn't know whether to shout or run, or kick Stormbreaker right in the shin like one of his little sisters might have done. He had known the information would be shared, but the way Stormbreaker told the tale seemed so stark, so cold. Anger took Aron's breath first, followed fast by a pained sadness and a sense of betrayal. For a dark moment, he was standing outside his home again. He was listening to his father disown him, and he wanted to kill Stormbreaker just as he had then.

Lord Baldric approached Aron, moving slowly, and Aron's eyes darted all over the man's gray robes, wondering where his weapons might be hidden.

Aron knew he should probably run now. Yes. Running would be wise. But for some reason, his legs locked into place, and all he could do was shake and stare at the floor.

"Look at me, boy." The demand was simple, and spoken in low tones, but it sounded like a thunderclap to Aron.

He had to use all of his strength and courage to lift his head and do as the Lord Provost had ordered. When he did, he felt like the Lord Provost was glaring directly into his *graal*, his very essence—and like he might never stop. Like he could hold Aron there for as long as he pleased, while Aron squirmed and screamed under the merciless scrutiny.

"I have taken in children with legacies as dangerous as yours, Aron Weylyn," Lord Baldric said, his tone neither friendly nor cruel, "though admittedly none with a dynast lord actively seeking their murder. Why should I keep you here? Why should I even take the risk of letting you live, when you've already tried to become an oathbreaker?"

Aron couldn't help glancing at Dari and Lord Cobb, who didn't seem inclined to save him from the Lord Provost, especially not in the man's own chamber, in his own keep, behind the walls of his own castle. Aron's gaze moved to Stormbreaker next, and there Aron saw more truth, and his wish to kill Stormbreaker began to ebb.

Aron understood now, just from the expression of respect and deference on Stormbreaker's pale face. Here was the man who had allowed the High Master to stay at Stone. Here was the man who had protected Stormbreaker despite his powerful mind-talents, who taught him the control he now employed to not hurt anyone with the bursts of weather he could command. Lord Baldric had been one of Stormbreaker's teachers and masters and champions, and that told Aron all he needed to know.

It went without saying that Aron wanted to live. That didn't surprise him. What did surprise him was the stirring of emotion at the Lord Provost's words. The lightning-bright realization that for all of his doubts about coming to Triune, about entering the castle, about becoming a Stone Brother, Aron desperately wanted to stay. He had nowhere else to go, nothing left but these men and the training offered so that one day, he might have the chance—the legal, ethical chance—to right the wrongs done to his family.

When he looked back at Lord Baldric, Aron did his best to let this desire to remain show on his face, in his eyes. Let the old man probe into the depths of his thoughts. Let him take him apart layer by layer, if that's what he sought to do.

"To Stone go the Stones." Aron willed his voice not to crack under the strain. "I'm a Stone now. Look into my heart and find the cold, smooth rock at its center."

Lord Baldric laughed.

Aron had expected many reactions, but not that one, and the rich sound of the man's amusement dug at him down deep inside.

This was serious to him. His life, his future—it was no folly, nothing to be taken so lightly.

"Aron with the heart of stone, what of your grudge against the Brailing Guard?" Lord Baldric laughed again, and Aron wanted to bite him. Hurt him somehow—do anything to make that sound stop.

"What of it?" he snapped before he could calm himself. His fists clenched at his sides. "There is nothing I can do about my grudge now, but if I'm true to my training, and if I follow everything my father taught me about kindness, honest labor, honor, and truth, I'll earn my place in the Stone Guild. Then, after the war is over, when criminals are called to task for their war crimes, perhaps I'll draw a stone on one of the dirt-eaters who murdered my family. That alone would make my life have purpose."

Aron couldn't see anyone around him anymore. The world had narrowed to Lord Baldric, to his brown, tattooed face, and the gleam in his bark-colored eyes.

"Vengeance." The Lord Provost sounded thoughtful. Maybe even impressed. "That's as good a motive as any, and as good a motivator, one Stormbreaker knows well. As for all that about kindness, honest labor, honor, and truth—not bad aims and goals for a guildsman of Stone. I suppose you'll do."

Aron's mouth opened, but he closed it before he could say anything to reverse the Lord Provost's decision.

"Thank—" he started, but the Lord Provost silenced him by grabbing his collar just below the neck. The man's grip was forceful, and he was so strong he lifted Aron from the ground with only one hand and pulled him close, close to that brown-egg face of his.

All Aron could do was kick and sputter against the choking sensation, but he stopped moving altogether when he realized he was just hastening his own loss of air.

"In the matter of dangerous legacies, judgment is mine and mine alone as Lord Provost of the Stone Guild." Lord Baldric held Aron suspended, speaking to him in a calm, yet terrifying tone. As if he were instructing him to set the table, or sweep away some crumbs. Black spots danced at the fringes of Aron's vision, but he didn't struggle. "If you ever use your mind-talents to harm anyone, if you even attempt it again, I'll kill you. I'll kill you before you ever know another night's sleep, or another morning's waking, and I'll do it with cold steel, not gentle poison. Do not use your *graal* at all, except at my bidding, or Stormbreaker's, or those training you in the arts of the mind."

With that, he set Aron back on the floor and released him—though he still wasn't finished.

Aron gulped a mouthful of air even as he lifted his hands to his belly, imagining the slice of a blade in his guts and the way Lord Baldric's eyes would blaze as his blood spilled on the man's boots and breeches. He would watch Aron die with the same cold detachment Aron had heard in his voice.

"Using unfair advantage, that's not the way of Stone." Lord Baldric actually smiled at him, but there was no way Aron could take the expression for friendly, or the least bit kind. "We hunt, fight, and kill with hands, feet, and teeth. We employ weapons and wits and wiles, but never mind-talents the Judged can't learn for themselves, even if they choose to dedicate themselves to the task. Do we have an understanding about that—and the consequences of disregarding me on this point?"

"Yes, Lord Provost," Aron said, then clamped his teeth shut again.

Lord Baldric's tone remained pleasant, but his eyes grew more deadly with each sentence. "You will have none of the leeway given other apprentices. If you're to remain here, it will be on my terms, and my terms are this: you will serve me whenever I demand it, however I demand it. And if ever once you're brought before me for your conduct, you will be culled from Stone, then immediately sent to judgment for your attempted crimes." He leaned close to Aron, so close Aron could almost feel the man's big hands choking him again. "I'm asking for nothing short of perfection. Think hard, boy. It might be better to take your judgment now and have done with it, because I assure you, I *will* be watching you."

Aron knew his eyes had gone as wide as milk saucers, but he could do little to suppress the lightning jolts stinging his insides. What the Lord Provost asked—Aron was no fool. He knew it was impossible to be perfect. But what chance did he have at judgment? Even a first-year apprentice could cut him down in a battle.

But Lord Baldric was not his father, and deep within Aron's raging depths, he knew he had done more than speak back to his mother or upset his little sisters.

What he had tried to do to the Brailing Guard, that was no childish misbehavior.

Oathbreaker . . .

The word hung in his mind, thin as a woman's fancy hair ribbon, as if showing him the impossibly slim difference between what he was, and what he had almost become.

Lord Baldric didn't seem inclined to rush his decision, this choice Aron now found himself making between immediate death and one more day, one more week, one more cycle of life. Between no chance, and a small chance. A chance likely purchased by pity inspired by the slaughter of his family.

Aron fought down a ragged breath, then found himself searching the face of Stormbreaker, then Dari. Both seemed very worried, and very invested in what he might say next. The corners of Stormbreaker's eyes glistened as if he might be battling back tears. As for Dari, she looked ready to use her bared teeth to kill something.

"I accept your terms," Aron said, bracing himself for the Lord Provost's next arguments or pronouncements.

Lord Baldric turned to Stormbreaker instead. "I don't like this, Dun. The fact we'll have to hide his abilities from the others or risk attack from Brailing. I don't want secrets between Brothers and Sisters. Secrets could destroy the Stone Guild faster than any army could lay siege and bring us down."

This time, Stormbreaker did lift his head and met the gaze of his mentor. "Thousands of secrets live within Stone's walls, and thousands more are buried with the bones of those Brothers and Sisters dead before us. What will two more matter?"

Aron rubbed his tight, aching throat as the High Master spoke, slowly realizing this battle had been won, that Stormbreaker's honesty and silence might have been the very tactic that ensured the victory.

Dari shifted from murderous to impressed.

Lord Cobb looked amused, and the food trays on the table once more seemed to beckon to him. He kept glancing at a pile of dates near his left hand, and finally claimed one and popped it in his mouth.

"You'll keep a close watch on the boy," Lord Baldric demanded of Stormbreaker. "Her, too." He pointed at Dari as he glanced toward Lord Cobb. Aron realized Lord Baldric didn't want to call Dari's proper title and name or acknowledge Dari's status aloud, as if that might make her presence more real, or more dangerous.

Lord Baldric returned his gaze to Stormbreaker. "She'll have to reside here as if she is a Ross pigeon. Others will make the same assumption I did, which is all the better for us. Just a sheltered pigeon, nothing more. Even though she's sheltered, she'll house inside the walls of the High Master's Den with the boy. We'll make whatever explanations we must, but I'll have it no other way. And I want them both to keep quiet. No standing out, no gathering attention."

"I'll stay far out of the way and assist with Aron's training," Dari said, then seemed to regret speaking as the Lord Provost glared in her general direction.

"Dari has great talent with managing legacies," Lord Cobb said around his chewy mouthful of date. The smell sent bile up the back of Aron's throat. "She can bring Aron along faster than most teachers."

This seemed to help sway Lord Baldric, who waved one hand in front of his face. "Fine, fine. So be it, then. In the morning before archery and knives, and in the evening after dinner, work with the boy, Dari. That will be one of the tasks you do to earn your keep here, and I'll hold you accountable for his mishaps."

Aron rubbed his sore neck. This threat, even more than the fear of a sword through his belly, would hold him in check.

Don't worry, he tried to tell Dari with his eyes. *I won't let you down.*

She nodded as if she heard him, word for word.

"She'll have to be banded," Lord Baldric said as he pointed to Dari's bare left ankle. "An unfettered legacy, and all that from the third law of the Code of Eyrie. The dynast lords will be calling me an oathbreaker if they hear I'm breaking that law and letting a girl with no *cheville* practice her legacy within these walls."

Dari's eyes narrowed and her mouth came open, but Stormbreaker spoke before she could say anything. "We'll arrange something, Lord Baldric." To Dari, he added, "Something for show, easily removed at your discretion."

Aron watched as Dari calmed down, but Lord Baldric grew more tense. His smile seemed more predatory than friendly as his gaze swept over all of them, one at a time. "Now, do any of you have any more surprises or bad news?"

Lord Cobb grinned, then picked a bit of date from his teeth with his fingernail. "Just one. I suspect Dari's personal protectors will be arriving any moment."

Aron looked at Dari, puzzled, but she squeezed her eyes shut and rubbed the sides of her head like her mind might explode.

"They won't be admitted," Lord Baldric blustered, starting to turn red again. "I'll not have—"

"What you'll have is no choice, not in this matter, unless you want a battle that costs you much of your guild." Lord Cobb seemed to be enjoying himself overly much at Lord Baldric's expense, and Aron was once more powerfully reminded of his older brothers, and how they sparred and spatted. "Her protectors are Sabor, two of them, and one's bound to her by a birth-promise. The other's on some sort of spiritual mission. You can either let them in or let them fight their way in. They won't be kept from her."

Lord Baldric's jaw went slack even as Aron felt a cool rush of surprise.

For a time, everyone stood without speaking.

Aron managed to forget his own predicament as his mind raced through the possibility of meeting his first Sabor, of actually talking to one of the powerful shape-shifters he and some of his brothers used to imitate when they played at battle. He wanted to know if they really had yellow eyes. He wanted to see one . . . change. He wanted to see a Sabor take somebody on in a fair match, to know if they really were as unbeatable in single combat as all the stories made them out to be.

Why did no one else seem thrilled by this prospect?

When the Lord Provost regained his voice, he addressed himself to Stormbreaker with, "Sabor. Cayn's *teeth*. With Lady Mab and the cursed Thorn Guild waiting for any hint we're taking sides in this conflict." He let out a fresh string of curses, some of which Aron had never heard before, but the tone made the meaning clear. "I've had dozens of different messengers between Thorn and Mab, the two of them making demands, asking for concessions, pledges of neutrality. Thorn is turned on its ear because the greater dynasts are marching into Dyn Vagrat without so much as a fine greeting or an if-you-please— and we're to have Sabor sheltered behind our gates? They'll accuse us of harboring spies, of siding up with Lord Cobb, here, and our old friend Lord Ross."

Stormbreaker kept his own counsel, as did everyone else, though Aron wondered if that wasn't exactly what Lord Baldric was doing, by taking in Dari and letting him stay as well.

"Low profile, my left cheek, and not the one on my pretty face." Lord Baldric shook his head as he gazed first at Dari, then at Aron, until Aron's heart tried to squeeze itself to death, and finally at Stormbreaker. "Very well. Our Sabor guests will be your responsibility, too, and you'd best start thinking of a first-rate explanation for their presence."

Stormbreaker continued his silence, and Dari and Lord Cobb remained just as quiet. Aron wondered if this was the best way to handle Lord Baldric when the man was in a temper, then hoped he would never try the Lord Provost's patience again and have to find out.

Lord Baldric ran his hand across his bald pate, then down across his face, touching each tattooed spiral as he went. "May fate favor the foolish, Dun, and I fear that you—or perhaps we—are very much in that category now."

PART III

Elfael

FATE CIRCLES

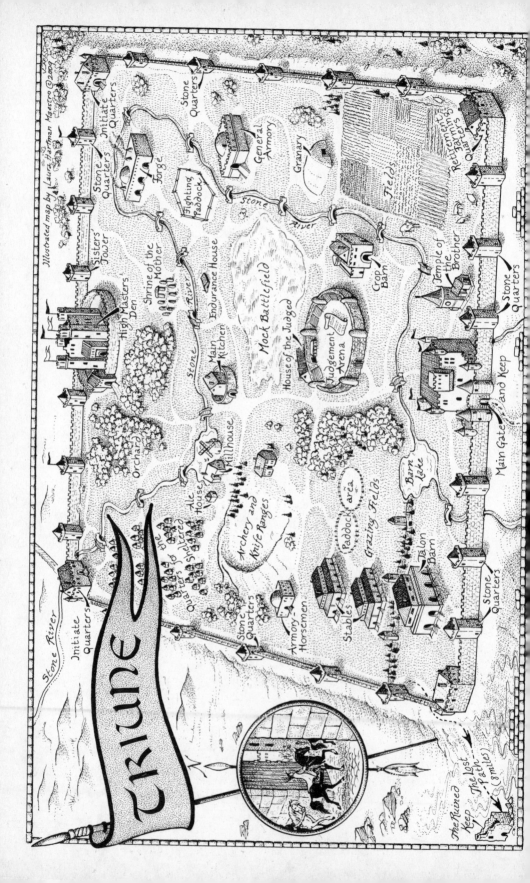

CHAPTER TWENTY-FOUR

ARON

Late the same day as his arrival, Aron found himself trying to drag his heavy, aching limbs up Triune's main road, due north toward the strange keep-within-a-keep he had noticed on his arrival. He didn't bother to ask Stormbreaker what it was. He was too afraid the High Master would question him about it, and that he might have to endure more walking or running, more weapons practice, or more hauling water and grain to increase his strength and bulk. That, or something else equally exhausting.

Aron had expected to be shown to his living quarters after Lord Baldric dismissed them, perhaps be allowed to clean himself or see Tek, or even sleep after such an exhausting ride the night before. As it was, Dari had parted company with him just outside the main gate and keep, and gone off to make her farewells with Lord Cobb. Then, without regard to how long they had been awake and on the road, Stormbreaker had walked Aron all over the sprawling castle grounds. For hours. Stopping only to "rest" by having Aron throw daggers at various targets, run sprints to buildings he couldn't remember to name, or carry pots or bags for people they passed on the roads.

"Carrying and hauling is good for the muscles," Stormbreaker told him each time he stopped a traveler and had Aron relieve them of their burdens. "You need much work in that respect."

Aron had complied and done his best, and all the while, Stormbreaker pointed out structures and areas Aron was responsible for knowing—the first time he was told, without any repetition—unless Aron wanted to run a bit more. There were stables to the west, and talon barns, grazing fields, the horseman's armory, and the archery and knife ranges. When Aron failed to immediately remember a site, Stormbreaker had him run sprints, and doubled them, sending him up and down the well-kept graveled byways again and again, until Aron felt the impressions of a thousand small stones across the bottoms of his feet, straight through his leathery boots.

"No. Again. Run to that tree." Stormbreaker's voice grew as monotonous and grinding as the tasks.

"Here, Aron. You must do better. Sprint to the edge of the talon barn and return to me."

"You were slow. Run the route again, and make it smart this time."

Endless. It was endless. The day would never finish itself, Aron was convinced as he stumbled back from a flying run to the mock battlefield beside the main byway. He reached Stormbreaker and had to double over, hands on his knees, holding himself up as he tried to breathe, had to breathe, yet couldn't quite seem to do it properly.

"Your life, your success in a hunt, will depend first on the choices you make, and second on what you see and how fast you see it," Stormbreaker told him as he waited for Aron to stop wheezing. "Details. You must notice every last one, and commit them all to memory. The Judged will give *you* no second chances, no reading of charges and sentencing—nothing but a swift blade to the heart. The time will come when you're carrying ten stones on Judged who have chosen flight, or twenty, or more." He patted a pouch tied around his waist, and the rattle from the bag made Aron wonder how many death sentences traveled with Stormbreaker everywhere he went, every step he took. "At any moment, a man could spring at you to save his own life, to win back his freedom. Never let your mind or your eyes be idle. Even here."

Aron had scarcely gathered in that thought when Stormbreaker moved them east, past the House of the Judged and the arena, to the Temple of the Brother, the crop barn, fields laden for harvest, the granary, and the general armory. Aron's feet tried to drag as he walked, but he managed not to stumble. Sweat coated his skin despite the cool afternoon air, and his muscles burned so badly he wondered if his body could catch fire with no flame to ignite it. In his mind, he tried repeating the list of places they passed five times to himself, then six, then seven, adding on each area Stormbreaker identified. That worked for a few names, but not all of them. When Stormbreaker quizzed him on which crops lay in which fields, he got to dash to each one, and to three of them several times.

In desperation, Aron moved to using first letters, then associations—like *crop-fields-harvest-granary*—that made sense and led his memory from one thing to the next. To the north, he was introduced to the quarters for the sheltered, the millhouse, the main kitchens, the fighting paddock, and the forge.

A few steps away from the pungent sulfur odor of the forge fires, Stormbreaker stopped them. "What was the last structure we passed, Aron?" He gestured to a huge wooden enclosure near the forge.

Forge-fight, Aron's exhausted mind flung at him. *Forge-fight!*

"The fighting paddock," he said aloud, his voice forceful enough to surprise him, given the screaming ache throughout his entire body.

Stormbreaker paused, seemed about to smile, and a wave of elation almost made Aron whoop. For the first time, he had supplied the correct answer and avoided another rib-crushing sprint to a structure he failed to name.

Stormbreaker turned him toward a well-formed path off the main road. Aron could see the river that ran through the grounds, rock bridges to cross it, and a small stone building. From behind him, meaty smells rose from the main kitchens, but he was too tired to feel hunger. He had taken enough drinks to keep his thirst slaked, so the river held little appeal for him, too. He did feel a touch of curiosity about the small building, because it seemed to radiate darkness, like some sort of *graal* he had never heard of before. It had to be a trick of the light, of shading from the nearby bridges, but the bleakness seemed to ooze out of the stones of the building itself. If Aron hadn't been too tired to take extra steps, he might have moved away from the sight.

"Endurance House," Stormbreaker said, pausing to let the title sink in to Aron's mind.

Endurance bridges rivers, Aron told himself, hoping he would remember the association.

Stormbreaker seemed tense as he gazed at the building. "I hope you avoid it."

Aron didn't understand, and Stormbreaker seemed to realize this. He turned away from the building to face Aron. "Even Stone needs methods to deal with incorrigibles in our own ranks. Those who break major rules or refuse authority spend additional hours at Endurance. I pray that will not be your destiny, for Lord Baldric will give you no quarter."

Aron pressed his hands to his aching ribs.

"He gave me none," Stormbreaker added, gazing at Endurance House again, this time with distaste.

Of course Stone would have to have such a place, especially if they took in child-criminals. It followed, too, that since many children were Harvested as he had been, they might remain angry about their own losses and require persuasion to do their duty for the guild. Aron supposed there was no magical force preventing older guild members from committing minor infractions, too. His father had taught him that wherever men and women congregated, there would be brawls, drunken moments, or even hasty words. Outside the walls of Triune, such problems would be the business of the Dynast Guard—but inside Triune, offenders would be brought here.

Endurance House.

The sound of it made the pain in Aron's chest worse. He studied the building with new understanding, realizing that the bleak energy he sensed might be coming from the people inside it—or what was being done to them. No need for memory association now. He would never forget the name of this place, no matter how well he avoided it. Just the sight of it—or rather the sight of the strange essence that seemed to surround it—bothered his awareness.

His senses swam as he tried to look away from the building, instinctively moving his gaze toward the rush of the river, the solidness of the rock bridges. Yet that same darkness, that same . . . wrongness . . . seemed to creep out of Endurance House, polluting the river, crossing those bridges, sliding back toward . . .

Wait.

Was the shadow he was seeing coming from somewhere else?

Aron's knees felt weak from more than exhaustion. Perhaps he had been too long on his feet, or without sleep. Had it been so many hours since the opulence of breakfast in the Lord Provost's chambers, or the bread and hardtack Stormbreaker had shared with him at lunch? Why was he growing dizzy?

His head lifted as if some hand had slipped beneath his chin, and he caught sight of a ring of small monoliths beside trees that seemed heavy with brightly colored fruits.

The blackest aspect of the shadow radiated from that spot, but the harder he tried to stare at it, the more elusive it became.

"That's the Shrine of the Mother," Stormbreaker informed him, though his voice seemed to reach Aron across some distance. "We placed our Shrine beside the orchard because the Mother's children prefer the peace of the woods—and the orchard that rings the High Masters' Den is lightly traveled."

Aron tried to shift his attention to the orchard, or to the keep-within-a-keep he now knew to be the High Masters' Den and the place he would be residing, by order of Lord Baldric.

His head wouldn't turn.

His arms wouldn't lift, and his mouth wouldn't open to say anything to Stormbreaker, who continued to talk about how most citizens who weren't from Dyn Vagrat or Dyn Ross had never seen a Shrine.

A Shrine that to Aron's senses now seemed . . . overly bright. Especially in contrast to the harsh grays and blacks of Endurance House. It wasn't dark at all. There was no shadow there, or anywhere.

I imagined it.

But hadn't he felt that darkness? Almost like a real and thick cloud, settling over the building, the bridges, the river, the stones?

No, that couldn't be.

Because now, the monoliths were white.

They seemed to have a glow in the late-afternoon sun, blazing, yet also somehow soft and inviting, like moonslight on the motionless surface of a pond.

The symbol of the Brother was the bowed head of a fair-haired man with the sun's light behind him. But what was the symbol of the Mother?

The moons, his own mind told him, remembering some lesson from his father. *The moons, twinned and full.* Aron had never troubled himself overly much with the workings of faith past a basic understanding of signs and practices. He had always leaned more toward the mundane habits of his father than those of his devout mother.

"Boy?" Once more, Stormbreaker's voice seemed to drift toward Aron from very far away. "Aron?"

Aron blinked at the moonlit stones, glowing from night's silvery brilliance even as the sun remained in the sky. The sight was so entrancing, so perplexing, he could do little but sink to his knees and stare at it.

More light flared from the circle of monoliths, and more still, until the brightness of it reached out to him, covered him, bathed him in its unusual coolness.

Thunder rumbled above him, around him, but he didn't care. He didn't fear the lightning. Nothing could touch him so long as that light stayed with him.

Was that Dari inside the Shrine of the Mother?

The tall woman with the full moons spinning above her head?

At first she seemed dark, but now she seemed lighter, silvery white like the stones, and much older.

It had to be Dari, because she was touching his thoughts and essence like Dari did when they practiced going through the Veil. That, and he had never known anyone else so beautiful. He assumed the creature had to be mortal, flesh and bone like himself, because his father taught him that gods were more a belief in people's minds and hearts than actual beings. Aron had always known that when he prayed to the Brother, he was praying to a good thing, a true thing, but not necessarily a thing he could ever see or touch or speak to in the way people talked to one another.

Someone was trying to grab him, but no fingers touched him.

Lightning and thunder exploded in every direction.

Then . . . that bright, bright light, moved into the sapphire Brailing *cheville* he still wore about his ankle, then all through his body even as he welcomed its chilling presence.

There's a blond man with the lady, and a stag. Such a stag!

Aron had never seen such antlers on a real beast in the forest. He didn't even know if a rack of that size was possible, and the way the horns tangled together at the top—

The lady of the moons stepped away from her companions and favored him with a glance.

Aron felt her eyes like stakes through his lungs.

She looked . . . familiar to him.

I've seen her before. I've seen her in a dream? Where?

The longer he stared, the more terrible she seemed to become.

His mind brought him an image of a great white Roc bearing

down on him, talons open to snatch him straight from the ground. His breath wheezed out of him, but he was smiling.

He kept right on smiling as he pitched forward and his head met the ground so hard it knocked all images of the real world straight out of his awareness.

CHAPTER TWENTY-FIVE

ARON

Aron's head throbbed.

He wanted to lift his hand and rub a particularly painful spot above his left eye, but his arm ached as badly as his skull.

Did I forget to latch Tek's stall again? Did Seth hit me?

He blinked, trying to focus in the semidarkness and make out the familiar lines of the room he shared with his six brothers. There should have been bedrolls and arms and legs and lots of snickering, maybe even another punch to send him silly again—but nothing happened. There were no bedrolls. There were no brothers. Just a dancing yellow light. A fire. In a stone hearth. Stone walls.

He was in a small chamber with a bed, neatly made, beside him on his left.

Aron pressed the cloth beneath him and understood he was in a bed, too, a real bed with a stuffed mattress, pillows, and linens. The cloth felt soft against his bare skin, nothing like the rough-spun blankets his mother usually made.

I'm not at home.

Because . . . home is gone.

The truth came back to him, full and pummeling, and he cried before he could stop himself. He called out for his father, squeezing his eyes closed and wishing the fire and the stone walls away from him. He'd give it all up, his future, his life, anything the Brother might take or want, just to hear his father answer him.

A hand stroked his head, warm, with long fingers. "Our quarters are small, but we spare no expense on bedding," Stormbreaker said from his right. "At Stone, we work hard. Men and women should be able to rest in comfort, if nothing else."

Heat blazed through Aron, and humiliation that he was sobbing in front of his guild master, but he couldn't stop the tears. He felt as if his heart were ripping into pieces, like someone had stuck a blade into his chest, twisting, twisting more. He only wished the blade were real enough to kill him.

Stormbreaker made no comment about his emotions. He didn't laugh at him or smack him like his brothers would have done. He only offered the comfort of his hand on Aron's head, and after a time he said, "I won't tell you the pain will heal. You'll never forget what was taken from you, and it will never hurt less when you focus your thoughts on that loss."

Aron gulped for air around his sobs, willing his body to stop shaking beneath the cotton blankets. At least Stormbreaker thought enough of him to speak the truth. He couldn't imagine how he would survive this hurt, moment after moment, night after night. How could he continue to be in this world when his family was gone? How could he sleep in a soft bed in a castle with his own fire in its grate, when the bones of his people lay scattered in some forest clearing?

"I can tell you that you'll find new focus, that you'll learn to manage the pain." Stormbreaker's voice soothed Aron's raw senses, seemed to reach into the agony and lessen it just enough to make it bearable. "I can tell you the loss will become a part of you, like a scar. With time, the scar won't pull and bleed each time you stretch."

Aron got hold of himself enough to glance at Stormbreaker, who was seated on the edge of his bed. The High Master pulled back his pale hand and let it rest in his lap. Candles in sconces ringing the small room illuminated Stormbreaker's face and the moisture in his own green eyes. The spiral rank-marks, the *benedets* on his face, gleamed as he shifted, and Aron wondered if he had been crying.

Stormbreaker met Aron's gaze directly, and Aron had no further question about whether or not the man had been shedding tears. "If I could have saved them all, I would have," Stormbreaker said.

For a moment, Aron assumed Stormbreaker was speaking about the massacre along the Watchline, and he remembered how Stormbreaker had argued with Windblown, how he had gone back to Aron's father and told Wolf Brailing something that sent him running into the house—then into the wagon with his family, and out onto the byway.

Aron swallowed, tested his own voice with a hum, then whispered, "You tried. I know that now."

Stormbreaker looked away from him, into the fire. "Trying matters little when failure is so complete."

Aron started to offer reassurances again, his own comforts, as best he could think them up, but his instincts held him silent. In the stillness, he realized Stormbreaker might be remembering something else entirely now, some other failure or tragedy. His thoughts moved to the reality of Stormbreaker's sister, and the fact they couldn't both have been Harvest prizes. So how had they come to Triune? Aron wanted to know, felt like it might be very important in his understanding of Stormbreaker, but he couldn't dredge up the courage to ask him about it. Instead, he looked into the fire, too, and wondered if fire gazing helped with pain that came from the heart.

Indeed, a few moments later, the shaking in Aron's body subsided, and he could breathe without sobbing anew.

"I'm not the mother who birthed you." Stormbreaker kept his focus on the hearth. "The next time you reach the limits of your endurance, you'll tell me before you pitch to the ground and crack open your foolish head."

Aron cringed away from Stormbreaker's words, but he didn't miss the concern. It was like taking a reprimand from his father, or from Seth, after Seth's time in the Guard.

"A Stone Brother who can't attend to his own body and his own needs is a hazard to us all," Stormbreaker added. "We're a guild, not a stable of wet nurses with infants to be tended."

Aron hadn't considered his actions in this light, and now that he did, he felt new prickles of embarrassment. "Yes, High Master. I'll be more cautious in the future."

"Choices. It comes first to that, as I told you yesterday. In the end, you'll be nothing more than the sum of choices you've made." Stormbreaker still seemed obsessed by the fire, but the tension in his muscles eased a fraction. "Aron, did something unusual happen to you outside Endurance House? Something that drained what was left of your energy?"

Aron tried to put his mind on what happened, made it up to the point of seeing Endurance House and the shadows—but, really, those creatures he saw in the Shrine, they couldn't have been real. It was his exhaustion that caused him to imagine fancies and nightmares, maybe his hunger and thirst.

And his fear.

He pushed himself into a sitting position, then hung his head. "Endurance House bothered me, the thought of it, that's all. And the Shrine of the Mother. My imagination ran wild with me, and for a moment I imagined I saw—that I saw a goddess, or maybe a god, or both, inside the monoliths."

Stormbreaker gave a noncommittal grunt disturbingly like a sound Lord Baldric might make. "You would be the envy of everyone who worships the Mother, then. Take no shame in visions, especially of visitors from the heavens. Those are usually good omens."

Aron tried to absorb that interpretation, but nothing about his vision felt like a good omen. He didn't know how to keep talking about what had frightened him, and his embarrassment over his weakness and his shortsightedness was still too fresh. He slipped out of bed, wrapped a blanket around his waist, and eased past Stormbreaker, to the room's only window. In some part of his mind, he knew the blanket was scant cover, but the room was passably warm, and he assumed Stormbreaker would offer him clothing soon enough. In the moonslight, he could see the stone wall of the keep-within-a-keep, and some of the orchard beyond it. Even though he squinted, he caught no hint of that Shrine, or of the dark little building across the river from it.

"You're in the west-facing tower of the High Masters' Den." Stormbreaker came to stand beside him, gathering his gray robes close about his tall frame. "The Shrine is on the east side. Dari could see it from her room in the east tower, positioned opposite your own, just down the hallway outside your door."

Aron gave no response, but he was both relieved and disappointed that he had no view of the Shrine.

"Zed will be coming to the Den now that Windblown has been elevated to Seventh High Master," Stormbreaker said as he placed a hand on the sill. "He'll share this room with you, since the two of you will be the newest. You'll mix only with other apprentices from the Den. It won't be easy, and you'll have much ground to cover, but I trust you and Zed will help each other in that task—if, that is, it was no dread contagious illness that caused your vision and fainting this evening."

Aron felt yet more foolish for his behavior over Endurance House and the Shrine. He dared to look up into Stormbreaker's expressionless face, feeling like he owed some explanation beyond a simple apology. "I didn't want to complain or be some spineless slackard."

Stormbreaker nodded, and he didn't look angry at all now. "It's never cowardly or lazy to speak up for yourself. You may speak up to me, Aron, always, if you do so respectfully and accept my judgment when I offer it."

For a moment, Aron scarcely could remember his initial urges to hate Stormbreaker. He wanted to listen carefully to everything Storm-breaker said. Learn fast. Answer all the question put to him—

"Dari's room," he muttered, putting together what Stormbreaker said about seeing Endurance House and the Shrine from her window. If he could study the building and stone monoliths from above, perhaps he could understand what happened earlier in the evening when he collapsed, if it was anything beyond the addled workings of his own mind.

Yes. That would be best, to look, to try. Then, no matter what he saw, he'd do his best to explain the shadows and figments to Storm-breaker, and trust the High Master wouldn't think him insane.

"Aron?" Stormbreaker called after him as he hurried from his chamber, turned in the direction Stormbreaker had indicated Dari's chamber would lie, and took off down the stone hallway. "Aron!"

"I'll be back," he shouted, letting go of his blanket as he counted doors to be certain he could estimate the position of Dari's room, if it truly was exactly opposite to his own. "I just need a moment, truly."

Aron's bare feet smacked against the smoothed rock as he left the rounded portion of the tower and entered the hallway. He passed only sparse furnishings, nothing more than chairs, some bookcases, some wrought armor, and pikes and staffs hanging in racks on the wall. Then he once more reached a rounded section. And Dari's room would be—there—but—

But a huge boy stood outside her door, arms folded.

The boy was wearing a brown tunic, breeches, and boots.

And his skin was blue.

Aron was running so hard and fast he stumbled at the shock. Forward. Toward the door. Toward the boy.

Who wheeled to face him and glared with fierce, slitted yellow eyes.

Aron fought to control his balance, then fell in what felt like a slow, dreamlike motion. The boy's image shimmered in his awareness, blazing yellow, then blue, then yellow again. He seemed to be getting taller. And wider.

The boy opened his mouth and let out a roar that would have sent rock cats fleeing in terror.

Aron struck chest-first against cold rocks, screaming even as breath crushed out of his body. He couldn't speak. Couldn't move at all, save for fishlike gasping to recover the air he lost. When he lifted his head, he saw four huge golden paws directly in front of him. Paws with claws larger than his own forearms.

Then he heard running feet, and Stormbreaker's call, and more running feet. Aron coughed and managed to suck in a breath as Dari's door opened.

"Iko," Dari said, laughter barely contained in her words, "be easy. Aron poses no threat to me. He's the one you came for."

By the time Aron looked at Dari, the blue boy was just a boy again—no paws, no claws, just those bright yellow eyes and a smile that seemed like a taunt. "Him?" The boy's voice sounded nothing like the roar he had managed before. "Is this some jest, Mother?"

Another blue person, this one female and large and older, with her ebony hair swept into a knot atop her head, stood beside Dari, one protective hand on Dari's arm. This woman wasn't smiling, and in fact, looked as if she might never have smiled in the length of her existence.

"Visions never jest, my son," the woman said, her tone confirming that laughter wasn't part of her constitution.

But other people started to laugh.

Aron rolled over to find Stormbreaker, Windblown, Zed, and a small collection of Stone Brothers and apprentices—at least two female—standing over him. The tallest of the boys hung back from the rest. He looked to be about Seth's age, with reddish hair and brown eyes. His arms were folded, and unlike everyone else in the hallway, this tall, brooding boy wasn't laughing at all. His cold gaze moved first to Aron, then to Windblown and Zed, then back to Aron.

Aron shivered, part from outer cold, and part from inner.

Despite the tall boy's fiery looks, he seemed to have ice in his heart. This was the type of person Aron had expected to find at Stone. Someone devoid of emotion. Of conscience.

"Thought we were supposed to keep all this quiet, Dun." Windblown shifted his eyes to Stormbreaker, who looked both amused and chagrined. "Brother spare us. You'd think the boy never heard of Sabor before."

I'm . . . naked. The thought hit Aron hard, driving away all thoughts of the tall boy with the icy eyes. A flush colored his entire body redder than Dyn Mab's finest ruby. He needed to get up, flee back to his room for a tunic and breeches, but he couldn't seem to move, save to cover the most important parts.

A moment later, Zed elbowed his way out of the little crowd, bumping the tall boy, who bared his teeth as if he'd like to shift to a mocker and spit poison in Zed's face. "You have no place here," the boy said in a too-calm, too-controlled voice.

"Leave off, Galvin," Zed muttered as he pulled off his own tunic. "We serve the same master now, so you might as well get used to me."

Zed threw his tunic at Aron, who snatched it, stuffed his arms into the large sleeves, and scrambled to his feet as the fabric fell to his knees.

Shirtless, Zed looked almost as large as the boys snickering behind him, but he was far more muscled about the chest and arms. The older boys seemed to take stock of this when Zed turned to regard them with one of those wild Altar hunting looks he got before he tackled rock cats with bare hands and dagger. The crowd started to disperse. Even Galvin and the older Stone Brothers, who were all marked in one fashion or the other to indicate status in the guild, began to walk away, most shaking their heads.

Windblown gave Zed a disapproving look. "Fight no one else's battles, boy. You robbed Aron of a chance to test his own mettle against Galvin—and Galvin could have used a proper combat to vent some of his rage and grief over the loss of his master."

"Aron will have many chances to test himself when the day hasn't taken such a toll." Stormbreaker's expression remained neutral, and he looked more at Zed than Windblown. "And against a more fair opponent than Galvin. I think you and Aron will work well together, Zed." His gaze shifted to the blue boy at Dari's door. "Or will it be three, Iko?"

The blue boy frowned, but said nothing. Aron could make no sense of Stormbreaker's question to the Sabor, and wasn't sure he wanted to.

"Come on," Zed said, taking Aron by the shoulder and steering him back toward the east-facing tower. "We have a fresh, long day awaiting us tomorrow."

Aron didn't protest or look back at Dari. He didn't care to see the laughter still in her dark eyes—laughter at his absurdity.

"Aron," she called as he walked away, and he stopped without turning around. "After you've dressed, will you return for a moment? Zed can come, too, if you'd like. We need to set a schedule for your training, and discuss a few other things."

Aron swallowed. The heat in his cheeks was almost painful, but he made himself nod before he started walking again.

Zed moved beside him, arms rigid at his sides, and he kept looking back over his shoulder. Finally, when they reached the door of their chamber, Zed muttered, "What's he want, you think?"

Aron shook his head, confused until Zed nudged his shoulder and pointed behind them. Aron turned to see that Iko had followed them from Dari's room to their own. Aron couldn't help moving toward the chamber door, and Zed opened it. They slipped inside, never taking their eyes off the Sabor. Then they both peered out at Iko through the partially open doorway.

Iko refused to meet Aron's gaze, but he moved forward, showing a grace and fluidity definitely not human. Each step communicated power and absolute control.

How old is he? Aron wondered. *How much training did he need to proceed so surely, so quickly, without making a sound?*

He thought about Lord Cobb's assertion that if Lord Baldric had chosen not to admit the Sabor, they would have fought their way to Dari, taking much of the Stone Guild down as they proceeded. Now Aron could believe that bit of warning. Even in human form, without the paws and claws, Iko was fearsome.

The Sabor boy stopped a distance from the door, turned, and took up a position similar to his stance outside Dari's door.

"He's protecting you, I think," Zed muttered.

Aron slammed the door as much from surprise as denial. "I don't know him. I've never even met a Sabor. Why would he bother with the likes of me?"

Zed gaped at him, then shook his head. "Aron Weylyn. You're not exactly a normal arrival at Stone. You were stolen from a dynast lord's vengeance, chosen as the first apprentice to the First High Master. You rode through the gates of Triune under guard of Lord Cobb himself, and you've been assigned for twice-daily tutoring with a girl like Dari—don't you grasp any of that?"

"But that was because of Stormbreaker, and the war, and Dari!" Aron glanced at the closed door. "I didn't—I don't—" But he trailed off, uncertain of what to say next.

Zed's gaze was steady and unusually serious. "The Sabor and my former people in Dyn Altar share a few beliefs about fate. Mainly that fate is really another word for the will of the gods—for us, the Brother, for the Sabor, Cayn."

Aron looked Zed in the face, startled to hear him speak the name of the horned god of death inside—in their *bedchamber*, for the sake of the Brother—seemingly with no fear at all about bringing them ill fortune. He started to touch his cheek to ward off the bad omen, but wondered if he would look foolish following his mother's traditions before the older boy. His hand shivered from the wish, but remained at his side.

"In desperate times, fate watches, fate circles, then dives like a hungry hawk, striking people who will be important." Zed's eyes lost some focus, and he seemed to be reaching beyond himself, back to what his own mother might have taught him. "Fate chooses who will affect what's happening in Eyrie, who will rise up and shift the winds. I sense fate circling above you, Aron Weylyn. Dari and Stormbreaker, too. Great events may be drawn to you, and you to them, whether you wish it or not. I bet Iko thinks the same thing, maybe even had a vision of it as Sabor are prone to do, and that's why he came here with his mother."

Aron's mouth came open again. He could hear Zed's words, but he couldn't allow them any space in his heart or mind. "That's—that can't be. Me being important like that, I mean. It's foolish."

"Is it?" Zed's easy smile reflected no offense at Aron's disagreement. "Well, foolish or not, for me and for the Sabor—for a lot of people raised with older traditions—if we truly think we're in the company of a person fate is circling, we have a spiritual duty to help them if we can. So even though you're a bit strange, and more than a bit annoying, I'll draw my blade in your defense."

Zed lowered his head and spread his arms as he said this, in the gesture of an old-style promise of fealty, as formal as the one Aron himself had sworn to Dari back in the woods, at the first of their journey to Triune. Aron had played at such oaths dozens of times with his brothers, but this—this was no game. Zed was as serious as Aron had been when he gave Dari his own promise. Zed was truly pledging his service, as if Aron were some dynast noble.

All Aron could do was stand stupidly and dredge through his mind for some return of Zed's offhanded kindness. He finally came up with, "Uh, thank you. And thanks for helping me in the hall."

Zed looked up and shrugged. "*That* was no spiritual duty. It's work together now or be talon-meat for the older apprentices. They'll take whatever liberties we give them—and I suggest we give them none at all." He gestured toward the unmade bed. "You'll find your tunics and breeches and underclothes in a trunk that slides beneath the slats. Best give me back my tunic and get dressed, unless you'd like to go before such a pretty girl in nothing but your skin again."

Aron flushed all over again, pulled off Zed's tunic, and went to gather his own. The whole time he was dressing, he tried not to think about the big, silent blue boy outside his door, or anything Zed had said about fate, and the will of the gods, and fate striking people destined to rise up during desperate times. In his opinion, all the madness they had encountered since his Harvest, that had been happenstance and offshoots of Dari's presence in their traveling party. If anyone was chosen by the gods to be important in this world, in this desperate time, it was her, not him.

Yet was it not his legacy that had caused Stormbreaker to select him?

As Aron pulled on his breeches and tied the waist-string tightly for a good fit, the *dav'ha* mark on his arm smarted. He glanced down at the shape, now a well-drawn set of raised, reddened lines, a scar in the perfect form of a downward triangle, topped by an upward twist into a pentagram.

Cayn, the horned god.

Aron felt wicked just looking at the image, at thinking about the horned god in his bedchamber. Then a snatch of conversation from that jumbled day after his Harvest drifted through his mind.

He left the essence of all of those people in torment, in hopes they would do murder for him. Lord Brailing sent this boy's family to kill him. . . .

Was that real?

Had he heard that, or dreamed it?

Aron reached into his mind, prodding with his legacy, caring nothing for who might sense the workings of his mind, or notice the color of his *graal*. The blood in his veins moved more slowly, chilling him even as he pulled his tunic over his head.

Those words were true.

His legacy made him certain of that fact.

The words were true, and Dari had said them, and he had the memories now, of everything that was spoken in the clearing.

Stormbreaker said, "Tek was a marker, to make certain Aron's family died when the time came."

More images flew at Aron, of Wolf Brailing gathering his family and fleeing into the woods. Of the pictures occupying his father's mind before the Guard bore down upon them and killed them all. It was almost like he was dreaming his father's dreams, or reliving his father's last moments in complete, painful detail.

His father didn't get far enough away because he didn't want to put too much distance between himself and the route the Stone Brothers took. He had wanted to hide the others, and then—

And then he was planning to come after me.

The certainty of Wolf Brailing's motives for the route he took, the choices he made, pummeled Aron like fists.

His father hadn't surrendered him at all, Harvest or no. Wolf Brailing never planned for Stone to get away clean with Aron.

He told me I'd always be his son, and he meant it, and he died for me.

They all died for me.

Aron wanted to beat himself with his own fists, but Zed was pulling at his arm again, leading him forward toward the chamber door. "Daydream later, dunderhead. Dari won't be patient forever, and me, I wouldn't keep that girl waiting."

Aron couldn't respond, because his senses were slowly leaving him. The warmth he had drawn from waking safe in a room, from crying out his losses, from Stormbreaker's comfort and Zed's kindness, all of it, every bit of it, rushed out of him as if his essence had sprung a dozen leaks.

They passed by Iko, and Aron didn't so much as glance at the Sabor. Didn't notice if Iko moved to follow, didn't care in the least. He was turning to ice, inside and out, because now he knew what he should have known since the day after Stormbreaker claimed him.

My family's bones lie like sticks in the woods because of me.

CHAPTER TWENTY-SIX

DARI

Blath stood in silence, keeping herself between Dari and the room's window as Stormbreaker helped Dari fold marked maps and load a traveling pack. Moonslight gave the Sabor's skin a soft look, and Dari knew it to be that soft and more, from the many times Blath had held her since she could first remember.

The only mother I've known. I'm fortunate, and more than blessed that she's here.

Yet having Blath so close again brought Dari's emotions and worries perilously close to the surface. It should be three of them, Blath, her, and Kate. Three, as it had always been, since the deaths of her parents. Three, and sometimes four, when Iko decided to take up with them for a few days.

It was all Dari could do to focus on folding the blanket she would use to shield Kate from the night's chill, assuming they were fortunate enough to find her this night.

Was that possible?

Would fate finally cease its watching and circling and let her bring Kate safely back under her protection—before her cousin sent his own brand of assassins out to find her?

Stormbreaker handed Dari a spare dagger, sheathed and wrapped with leather straps she could use to tie it about her waist. "I know you have little need for such a basic weapon, but it would please me to know you have it, just in case."

Dari took the knife and belted it across her hips, letting the tip tap against the leather breeches Blath had brought her. Her loose white tunic covered the hilt as she thanked Stormbreaker, but she kept her gaze averted from his.

If she found Kate tonight, she would leave and try to smuggle her sister into Dyn Ross, then back home.

But how could she just . . . go, after making *dav'ha* with Stormbreaker and Aron, and assuring the Lord Provost she would help to train the boy?

Before making this journey, Dari never would have believed she could feel such fierce loyalty and concern for anyone outside her family and their small circle of allies, much less two people with Fae blood. An image filled her mind, of Aron in all of his naked embarrassment a few moments back. He was still such a boy, yet there was much to him already, with all he had suffered. At least the damage seemed to be healing enough that he took the silliness in the hall with some grace. That was a promising sign.

If she could find Kate and get her safely across the border to Dyn Ross, she could return to Triune and see to her duties with Aron. Though if she didn't return, Dari was fairly certain Lord Baldric and Stormbreaker would not fault her. Her grandfather might even arrange to have a tutor located and sent for Aron, someone with suitable strength of *graal*. Yes, everyone would understand, except—

Except Aron.

It would be more pain for him. More loss. And what would he make of that? Never mind the fact that the thought of never seeing Stormbreaker again left Dari feeling empty and at odds in ways she never expected.

She stole a glance at him.

He didn't notice, but Blath did. Her dark brows arched upward, but otherwise she gave no outward reaction. Dari wasn't fool enough to take that for approval, but she knew Blath wouldn't interfere. That wasn't Blath's way, or her role in Dari's life.

Dari almost wished Blath would charge forward like an angry mother or some Fae dynast lord from Altar or Vagrat or Mab, where the "properness" of women remained so important. She wished Blath would roar and forbid any further association between her and Stormbreaker, because everything would just be simpler, then, wouldn't it?

Dari glanced at Stormbreaker again, at the handsome line of his face, at his white-blond hair pulled tight against the nape of his neck.

If Blath forbade me to notice him further, would I disregard her? Probably.

Cayn's teeth, this was complicated. She wasn't some lark with loose morals—and the last thing she needed was closer association with the Fae. The need to find her sister crawled like bugs beneath her skin, mingling with concern on top of worry until Dari knew that if someone shouted behind her, she'd probably shriek and break into pieces.

"I—I'm being selfish. I'm sorry." She wet her dried lips with her tongue and wished she had thought to bring more water to the room. "The day has been long, or I would have remembered to ask about your sister. You mentioned her in Lord Baldric's quarters. Tia Snakekiller? She's still missing from Harvest, is she not?"

Stormbreaker answered with a silent nod and frown. His bright eyes dulled immediately, and Dari could sense the tension building in his emotions.

"Then we should search for her, too," Dari said. "We can inquire about her just as easily as we can speak with your sources and the other guild houses about Kate."

Stormbreaker looked horrified, then gained control of his expression, once more becoming calm, almost blank, before he spoke.

"That won't be necessary. Tia took her vows and survived her trial long ago. If she wants my assistance, she'll find a way to send for it."

"But what if she's injured?" Stormbreaker's attitude puzzled Dari. She squeezed the folded maps in her hands, but caught herself before the paper crumpled. "What if she can't get word to you?"

"Tia isn't my twin, but I would know if her peril were dire enough to risk disgracing a Stone Sister by suggesting she needed any man's help to complete a task." Stormbreaker's gaze was clear now, firm and decided, and understanding sank across Dari's shoulders.

She tucked the last maps into her pack without further comment. Though she had never met Tia Snakekiller, she felt some kinship with the woman, who no doubt had to battle twice as hard as any male to earn her place in a stronghold like Triune. Though Dari's people allowed women complete freedom, even they held on to prejudices about which gender made for better soldiers, and who ought to have rights of leadership and command.

"How did both you and your sister come to be at Stone?" she asked, distracted by her own thoughts, too much so to censor the question. "Isn't that unusual, siblings taking vows?"

Stormbreaker's expression shifted again, this time to a look of granite stillness. "That tale is long and perhaps not worth repeating."

Dari's insides heated at her breach of manners, intruding on his privacy so deeply. She had obviously wounded him just by asking. As she fished in her mind for the proper apologies to offer, her eyes met his, and she sensed his pain in her own heart. The ache made her want to weep and throw her arms about his neck.

A knock sounded at the door, and she startled.

The connection between her and Stormbreaker fractured like bit of rock-glass slammed against stones, and Dari felt its absence so acutely she had trouble taking a breath.

Blath moved quickly to see who wished to enter as Stormbreaker placed a hand on Dari's arm. "*Cha*, are you all right?"

His touch ignited heat along the back of her neck. It was hard not to stare at the spot where his fingers met her skin, and harder still to swallow. "Don't call me *Cha*. We've discussed that."

"With your Sabor protectors in attendance, I think the battle to keep your status completely secret has been lost." Stormbreaker smiled, and the expression made his face even more handsome. Staring at him helped her keep her mind off Kate for one moment, and away from her many growing dilemmas.

The effect was incredibly pleasant. She feared she could grow too used to it.

Dari was vaguely aware of Aron and Zed being admitted to the room and Iko taking up his post outside her door before Blath closed it again. Aron stared from her to Stormbreaker, then at Storm-breaker's hand. The flash of anger in the boy's sapphire eyes was unmistakable.

Stormbreaker let Dari go, but he didn't seem uncomfortable because of the boy's scrutiny. More . . . concerned.

Dari studied Aron, feeling her own level of worry rise.

He had left her doorway a little while ago embarrassed, blushing, but seemingly intact. Now he had that haunted look about him again. His expression had become blank, almost slack, and other than his irritation at seeing Stormbreaker's hand on her arm, he seemed utterly devoid of feeling or interest in the world about him.

"He's likely exhausted to the point of illness," Dari said to Storm-breaker, and Aron didn't react. "Two hours of recovery after fainting wasn't nearly enough."

Stormbreaker addressed himself to Aron instead of responding to her. "Remember our agreement, Aron? Are you fit enough for this meeting?"

Aron's expression hardened yet more, though Dari hadn't thought that possible. "I'm fit," he said in a voice so low it was almost a growl. The tone sounded deeper, older than she expected, and more powerful.

"If you require further rest—" Stormbreaker tried again, but Aron cut him off before the sentence finished.

"I'm fit. Have you established a plan for the search?" Aron folded his arms, staring intently at the pressed *dantha* leaves on Dari's bed. He likely could see the ink marks standing out against the smooth folds.

Stormbreaker eyed the boy with caution, then concern, then seemed to accept Aron's assertion that he was well enough to proceed. To Zed, Stormbreaker said, "Dari's sister is lost, and we'll be searching for her until she's located. Your master has been informed, and the boy Iko, and the Lord Provost and Lord Cobb. Otherwise, only the people in this room know this fact, and you'll keep it that way—even if questioned by one of the other High Masters."

"Yes, High Master." Zed dipped his head. "How may I assist in the search?"

"This night, you may look after Aron in my absence." Stormbreaker gestured to Aron. "That will ease my mind, since Lord Baldric will no doubt be checking up on him."

Aron's mouth came open. Closed. His eyes widened as he said, "But I want to go with you. We both swore to aid in the search once we got to Triune. Are those maps? I can learn how to read them, help to form a searching grid like I used to when I hunted in the Scry with my father and brothers."

Stormbreaker went to the boy and knelt down before him, putting himself eye to eye with Aron. "Not this night," he said, and his tone was infinitely patient and kind. "I've laid out an initial path for us that covers the area immediately surrounding Triune, and Dari and I will do what we can to explore it with Blath's help—while you rest and regain your strength. I'm very sorry this other duty is taking me away from you on your first night at Triune. I shall be very concerned about you until I return."

Aron seemed to shrink away from Stormbreaker's care, but he allowed Stormbreaker to put a hand on his shoulder. "You need your rest for training, too. Tomorrow, after you confirm that Dari and I have returned, you'll join our morning celebration for the first time, then go to the stoneworkers at the forge and receive your new *cheville*. After that, it's legacy training, then weapons training, sessions at the armory, time in the granary to build your muscles, work with your talon, lessons in the library—you'll be grateful to see the sunset. And grateful that I made this decision."

Aron responded with a glare, and Stormbreaker sighed as he stood. "We'll be going out twice per week with the assistance of Blath and Iko, or more if we happen upon credible rumors or tips. You'll have plenty of opportunity to assist Dari once you're a bit better with defensive weapons."

Dari noted no change in Aron's stance or attitude.

"Aron, this is not a debate," Stormbreaker said. He pulled another *dantha* leaf from the folds of his robe and extended it to Aron, who frowned, but took it. "Our path is marked. Should we not return before morning, you'll give this to the Lord Provost. If we cannot be located, you and Zed should continue the search for Dari's sister with Iko's aid until the Stone Guild can get word to Lord Cobb and Lord Ross and seek their counsel."

Dari moved around the bed to Aron, barely aware of her own purpose until she gripped his folded arms with both hands and met his angry gaze. "If I die tonight, you do everything you can to find my sister before my cousin Platt takes matters into his own hands. I call upon our *dav'ha*, Aron, and ask you to keep Kate safe if you can."

Aron didn't pull away, and his expression softened as he stared at her. After a long few seconds, he swallowed, slipped his arms through her grip until he caught both of her fingers in his, and dipped his head in acknowledgment. "Of course I will. But you won't die tonight." He gazed at her once more, his eyes now bright with what she took for worry. "You'll be back by morning, perhaps with Kate, or with information that will lead you to her."

Dari once more heard that surprising ring of force in Aron's voice, and saw a glimmer of the strong man he would one day grow to be.

Strong and kind—or strong and cold?

The dueling images struck her as she let Aron go, but she made herself sweep them from her mind. Dari focused instead on what he said, hoping his words would prove to be prophetic.

This time, when Stormbreaker told Aron to go and restore himself, Aron left with Zed, offering no complaint.

Blath closed the door behind them, and when she turned to Dari, Dari could tell Blath's opinion from the narrowing of her dark eyes and the tight purse of her lips.

That one could be trouble.

She heard the words as if Blath spoke them aloud. It was no mental connection that allowed her insight into Blath's thinking, but rather endless years of experience, and relating comments to expressions.

Even without the benefit of those years of knowledge, Stormbreaker acknowledged Blath's discomfort by clearing his throat. "We've a ways to go with Aron. I have hope."

"So does my son," Blath said. "Though for my own part, I have doubts." She gestured to the open window behind Stormbreaker. "Will we leave by way of the trellis, or take stairs and risk being seen by others in the guild?"

"Trellis," Stormbreaker said. "It's set in stone and reinforced with rock cement, and it leads directly to the courtyard. That's why I selected this room for Dari."

"I see." Blath's tone was cool as she moved toward the window. "I trust you'll not use this manner of entrance or exit for any other purpose than our search."

"Blath!" Shock suffused every inch of Dari. What would possess Blath to interfere with her life in such a fashion?

"I will respect Dari's honor every moment of every day," Stormbreaker declared as he stepped aside to let Dari follow Blath.

"I wasn't speaking to you, Stone Brother," Blath said as she nimbly climbed over the sill and began to climb down toward the courtyard. "Your safety is no concern of mine—and Dari is well capable of defending her own virtue."

Dari heaved herself over the sill and started down herself, going hot-cold with embarrassment at being spoken to like a wayward girl-child in front of Stormbreaker. "I won't leave Triune without your escort for my protection," she said through her teeth, hoping that would appease Blath.

It seemed to. For the moment, at least.

The tension in Dari's muscles grew with each inch and foot she descended. The reality of renewing her search for Kate and the increasing urgency of finding her twin began to ball up inside her, and by the time her boots touched the stones of the courtyard below her window, she was desperate for any distraction.

"Do you think Aron is troubled by the attraction we share?" she asked as Stormbreaker touched down beside her and pulled his gray robes tight about his waist to tie them in preparation for their journey.

He halted in his motions and glanced at her. There was no surprise on his face. The expression was more . . . humor? Amusement? Confusion gave way to irritation, and Dari thought about slapping the man just to erase the strange smile from his lips.

To Stormbreaker's far left, in the moonlit courtyard of the High Masters' Den, Blath began to change. Dari saw the telltale zigzag of golden fur appear across the woman's face. Blath's tunic and breaches seemed to melt to her ankles, but just as fast, her body grew taller and wider until no human shape was left to it. The golden zigzag spread like wildfire across her blue skin. Her shoulders burst outward, now covered in downy yellow-brown fur. Feathers emerged from her mid-section as she dropped to all fours.

Stormbreaker was clearly captured by the process, and Dari realized he had never seen a Sabor shift.

Good.

At least in this experience, *she* had the upper hand with this man.

Dari let him watch, let him become yet more enraptured as Blath's knees and hands became paws, one of which clutched her shed clothing in claws the size of a human child's arm. Blath grew a furry tail and sprouted wings that increased in size, fast enough that Stormbreaker tensed with alarm, no doubt wondering if there would be room between the keep walls and the keep itself to accommodate her. The knife belt Blath had been wearing expanded as she did, becoming a leathery band around her girth. Her green boomerang knife swung gently in its scabbard, coming to rest in front of her left wing.

Blath's change finished with a rush of air, and Dari took in the blessedly familiar sight of her surrogate mother, a creature with the head and wings of a giant eagle and the body of a huge lion. Blath's back and wings had heavy, thick white feathers, as did the crest of her head, and a mane circled her broad neck. The remainder of her body had soft, downy fur that more than once had absorbed hours of Dari's tears.

"Amazing," Stormbreaker murmured. Then he focused his attention more directly on Dari, her sensitive vision taking in how his green eyes seemed alight with amusement. "Now, to what you were saying before—Aron, and the attraction. *Is* there an attraction between us, Dari?"

As he spoke, he managed to move closer to her, until she could feel the warmth of his body only inches from her own.

"Stone Brothers are not required to be chaste." She had to work to make her mouth cooperate, and she found she couldn't look him directly in the face—which he no doubt found as amusing as her words. "I have known you more than a cycle of the moons now, and I'm a few cycles shy of my seventeenth year, close to full adulthood by both Fae standards and Fury. As a Ross female, and a Stregan, I'm allowed to select my own companions."

"I wouldn't have expected you to be interested in anyone with Fae blood." Stormbreaker's tone was matter-of-fact. Dari wished she could see his expression, but not enough to risk a glance at him. "From the moment we first joined our essences during the battle with the manes, I've known you haven't much regard for my people. Only yours, and those related to or loyal to you."

Dari stared intently at her feet and the night-darkened cobbles below them. "By my estimation, you're as loyal to me, to protecting my people, as anyone I know. You and Aron and even Lord Baldric—you have given me reason to rethink many of my beliefs about the Fae."

Nothing but silence from Stormbreaker in response to that. But at least he didn't move away from her.

"Cross-mixing is illegal, but only an issue should we choose to wed or bear children—neither of which I plan to do." Dari focused on his wrist, on his long-fingered, graceful hands and wondered why, after having such a hard time beginning, she couldn't stop talking now. "Despite your high station, you're only a few years my senior. Similar rank, similar station, similar age."

She gestured to Blath, who slapped a forepaw against the courtyard stones as if to express irritation at the delay. "And we do have a chaperone whenever we need one, though Dyn Ross and my people put little stock in such nonsense. All in all, it's an acceptable situation."

"An . . . acceptable situation." Stormbreaker's teasing tone made Dari really, really want to slap the *benedets* right off his pale, chiseled cheeks.

She raised her hand. "Cease toying with me, or I'll—"

Stormbreaker gently caught her wrist as her palm swung forward, and the contact jarred her into looking at him.

There was a light in his green eyes, and, yes, he was smiling, but he wasn't laughing at her. She knew that for certain when he bent so close to her he could have touched her lips with his own.

For one heart-clenching moment, Dari thought he might, believed he might, willed him to do it, move that last little inch—but he spoke instead, his voice quiet and husky. "You are most attractive, and I do see you as a woman grown, or nearly so. If my heart were my own to give, you would tempt me, Dari Ross."

His breath smelled of mint and winter, and the hand holding her wrist was so, so warm.

Had he just refused her?

She wasn't certain.

Maybe her feelings should be hurt, but at the moment, Dari's heart thumped and bounced until she thought her knees might knock together. She trailed the fingers of her free hand along the spirals tattooed on Stormbreaker's face, and he didn't stop her. His expression was a strange mixture of interest and pain, much the same as she felt in the pit of her own belly.

Too soon, he let go of her wrist and pulled back from her, leaving her chilled in the evening air. "We can discuss this later," he said in that low, ragged voice. "When we're once more safe behind these walls."

"What makes you think there's safety here?" Dari murmured, surprised she could speak at all.

Blath growled low in her massive throat.

Stormbreaker laughed and bowed too deeply, teasing her again. "*Cha*, it seems our chaperone objects."

Dari let out a breath, exasperated by the fact she wanted to lean in to him again, to get close to those lips once more and this time share a kiss, but she knew he would only laugh at her anew—and this time, she *would* slap him. Instead, she turned away from him and marched over to Blath, letting Stormbreaker keep up if he could.

"Here," he said as he moved up beside her and took hold of the leather strap in front of Blath's wings. "Let me help you. That's a long way up—two men's heights, at least."

Dari gaped at him for a second. "One kiss that never even happened, and I become some helpless slip of a girl in your eyes?"

Stormbreaker looked confused, but Dari ignored him and leaped upward with all her strength, springing toward the moons and stars and dark sky above her. In that one jump she doubted any Fae—even him—could make, she released a rush of tension. It cleared her senses better than she would have done by jamming her head beneath the surface of a cold lake. She landed neatly on her feet behind Blath's neck, then slid into familiar riding position, wrapping both hands into Blath's wiry golden mane.

Stormbreaker was reduced to clambering onto Blath's lowered wing, then pulling himself onto her back using the leather strap and fistfuls of fur.

Dari felt no pity for him, but she did wince for Blath, who stamped a hind paw as Stormbreaker dug the toe of his boot into one of her ribs.

"You might have given me a few instructions," Stormbreaker grumbled as he inched up Blath's back, toward Dari.

"Don't blame me for your shortcomings." Dari tried to sound light, as if talking to the man were as effortless as the jump she made. "Were it not for you, I'd fly myself, and none of this clumsy riding would be necessary. I'm Stregan, and if almost brushing your lips against mine for a few seconds hasn't addled your brain too greatly, I'd thank you to remember that fact."

Stormbreaker clamped his mouth shut. He settled behind Dari, and his muscled arms ringed her as he, too, gathered handfuls of Blath's stiff mane for balance. His nearness and warmth unsettled her, but she wasn't about to give him further amusement at her expense.

"Go," she said before he noticed any reaction.

At her command, Blath ran forward, digging her claws into stone and dirt to gain more power in her stride.

Stormbreaker lurched against Dari, swore, and would have slipped off had she not grabbed both of his elbows and helped steady him.

"Careful, now, big, strong man," Dari said. "Falling from a Sabor is a good way to earn a broken neck."

The look Stormbreaker tried to give her was wry, but it quickly shifted to worried as they plunged toward the high stone wall of the Den.

Blath's wings unfurled behind where they sat. In one powerful pump and sweep, they were aloft.

Dari faced forward again. Wind blasted across her cheeks even as Stormbreaker tightened his grip on the mane and pressed his arms yet more tightly into her sides.

I'm free again.

I'm flying!

She wasn't certain which sensation stole her breath more completely, but just this once, she didn't feel compelled to sort it out.

It lasted all of five seconds, maybe ten, and then reality came smashing back against hers, hard as the rushing wind.

Kate.

Her belly clenched with the knowledge that they were sailing high over Dyn Brailing, so high the air was near to ice itself, to avoid the threat of arrow shots or detection by soldiers who might be fighting battles beneath them. They were heading out from Triune, into the woods between the stronghold and the formidable walls of Can Rune. Dyn Brailing first—and if they didn't find Kate as the search progressed, they would move farther north, to Dyn Altar.

If she's in the lair of the enemy, we have to extract her with haste, Stormbreaker had said as they marked the maps. It was the first time he had stated so bold a position in the conflict between Eyrie's dynast rulers. Guilds were supposed to remain neutral in all political dealings, always a balance, a control set against the political powers that rose and fell in Eyrie. Nevertheless, Dari knew Lord Brailing's actions had forever destroyed loyalties and darkened the name of his family line, perhaps forever, even in the eyes of Eyrie's professional killers.

The enemy. Yes, that's how Dari saw the rulers of Dyn Brailing and Dyn Altar, and she rued the thought of Kate being captured or harmed by the lords or forces of either dynast.

But what if Kate had journeyed east, into Dyn Vagrat, or all the heavens forbid, farther north, past Dyn Cobb into Dyn Mab? Those flights would take much longer. Several days of journeying, even with Blath's powerful flying.

Stormbreaker tensed behind her as if the man could read her thoughts, or maybe her growing anxiety.

I've got to find you, Kate. Dari pulled hard against Blath's thick, rough mane as Blath began her first descent of the evening. *Please, let it be this night.*

CHAPTER TWENTY-SEVEN

ARON

Aron lay wide-awake in his bed, feeling alternately chilled near to death and warm from the fire in the hearth and the blankets he had pulled up to cover himself.

In his own bed, Zed was chattering away, though Aron rarely answered. "Wait until you see a Judgment Day. It'll be a few cycles before you're allowed to witness combat, but there's a fair lot of work to do just to get ready for the reading of charges and sentencing. You'll be able to help with that right away; then later you'll manage weapons during the combats."

Aron remained silent, trying to imagine what would happen at the Stone Guild each cycle, on the day following full moons. There would be wagons of the Judged arriving from local jails, already found guilty and sentenced in their towns or cities. Spectators were permitted, representatives from the dynasts, and families and friends of victims of violence, to see justice served and find peace from the fair dealings.

How many would it be?

And would the war change anything with respect to the sentences meted out by the Stone Guild?

"Master Windblown should have his chain by now." Zed shifted in his bed, making the wooden slats creak. "They don't mark Seventh High Masters, not until they move up, except by a thick silver chain and medallion. That's the only position a regular Stone Brother or Sister can be elevated to, you know. Usually when High Masters die, their oldest apprentice takes over, unless the Lord Provost thinks the apprentice isn't up to the task."

"Oldest apprentice?" Aron moved in his own bed until he could see Zed. "I thought Stone Brothers and Sisters chose only one apprentice."

"They only select one, yes, but if a guild member dies, whoever takes their position usually takes on the orphaned apprentice, if no one else speaks for them." Zed kept his eyes on the ceiling. "It happens a lot. Life at Stone isn't easy. Most apprentices dread the night of their trial in the Ruined Keep, but they come out ready for independent duties in the guild. If they survive, of course."

Aron didn't want to think about "trials" or the Ruined Keep, whatever that was. He mentally counted the boys and girls in the crowd that had gathered in the hall earlier, to witness his humiliation outside Dari's door. He was fairly certain he had seen nine in all, and he and Zed would make eleven. That meant four of the apprentices had been "orphaned" in the past, assuming there weren't more he didn't see.

He swallowed, feeling a strange lump in his throat. "Do High Masters die often, Zed?"

"No more often than any other guild member." Zed yawned, then picked back up as if he had never paused. "Sick people come here for Mercy, and sometimes guild members become ill from transferred infections. We lost one High Master to illness about three years ago—that's when Stormbreaker took his position. Then there's the poisons and weapons—mistakes claim a lot of apprentices and even full Brothers and Sisters. There's Judgment Day combat and pursuit, and now the war and battles, too. Who knows how many Brothers and Sisters might not even make it back from Harvest?"

Aron's mind moved quickly to Dari and Stormbreaker, flying with Blath over the darkened countryside, searching for Dari's sister.

What if some stray arrow knocked Stormbreaker from the sky?

Then Aron would wake in the morning to learn he served some new master or mistress, who might be kind or cruel or anything in between. Aron shivered beneath his blankets. He had barely grown accustomed to the idea of answering to Stormbreaker. The thought of plunging back to uncertainty and total aloneness gave him a bitter taste in his mouth. Whatever his issues with Stormbreaker, Aron wanted the High Master to return safely.

That he wanted Dari to return unscathed went without saying.

He had been angry with them for leaving him behind, yes, and angry with them for reasons he couldn't put into words—but he didn't wish them harm. His mind knew that, but when he searched inside his heart for some emotion, some feeling of worry, he felt little beyond a blaze of pain for his lost family. The rest was only a queer numbness, as if part of his spirit had been torn away from and discarded, or maybe walled away forever.

Aron squeezed his eyes shut and tried to ignore Zed, who was now prattling about the other apprentices. "Master Windblown will have Galvin Herder as an older apprentice now. We'll have to watch out for him. He came up hard—one of the incorrigibles who chose to take vows. I think he's ill with Lord Baldric for not promoting him to Seventh High Master, even though he hasn't finished his training."

When Aron didn't respond, Zed continued with, "The Third High Master, Tiamat, Stormbreaker's sister—if she doesn't come back, she has a female apprentice who is through with training and ready to step into her position. The Second High Master, he's got two apprentices, and the Fifth High Master and the Sixth, too, and those boys and the one girl are nice enough. The Fourth High Master has only one apprentice, but he's friends with Galvin, so likely no friend to us."

Trying to keep track of so many new people was too much for Aron, rather like the vastness of the stronghold's grounds and this new "family" of his, though he couldn't yet see any of them in that light. "How many apprentices are there in Triune altogether, do you think?

"Hundreds." Zed yawned again, twice this time, and Aron couldn't help yawning with him, even though his eyes remained wide-open. "And that's not counting sheltered children, who can train with us if they choose, or the incorrigibles and child-criminals, who have to train with us until they come of age. Some of them will end up taking vows, but I don't know many who are older or younger than me."

Aron turned more fully to Zed, suddenly curious about something else. "Where did you live before Windblown was elevated?"

"For the first few cycles, I stayed in the initiate quarters with Master Windblown and all the other Harvest prizes and their masters. Once Master Windblown was certain I wouldn't bolt or hurt myself or make a fool of him, we moved to a tower like all regular apprentices and masters." The always-pleasant expression on Zed's tanned face faltered for a moment. "We were in the eighth tower, near the quarters for the sheltered. I'll miss some of them, the men in the eighth tower. There weren't any women. All the Stone Sisters who aren't High Masters or apprentices to High Masters live next to the Den, in the Sisters' Tower."

The sadness in Zed's expression made Aron frown, even if it didn't erase the numbness in his chest. "But you'll see the people from the eighth tower every day in training, right?"

"No." Zed let out a slow breath. "Well, maybe from a distance, or in passing. But we're apprentices to the High Masters now. We'll train separately."

Aron's thoughts niggled at him, and he realized Stormbreaker had told him something like that, that he would mix only with the other apprentices who lived in the Den. "Why?"

This time when Zed spoke, he sounded more tired and still a bit sad. "I suppose because we have to learn to get along with one another and work together. But also it's like any army, I guess. It's hard to give orders to people who share your table and toilet, so officers usually stay apart from other soldiers."

This made some sense to Aron, and he thought he might have heard something similar from his father, when his father talked about his Guard service. Still, it made him uneasy that he would be kept away from so many and given different treatment. He might end up with a great many enemies, other boys resenting him when he didn't have any say about what living quarters he received or what training schedule he had to follow.

"Don't think they'll take it soft on us," Zed said as he rolled away from Aron and pulled up his blanket. "All the training masters are worse on apprentices from the Den. We don't even get two days off in the week. Only one. And really just part of that one, if you count Den cleaning chores."

Aron didn't think he wanted to hear any more. Not tonight, at least. It all seemed so much larger than him, and he had no idea how he would face any of it. Were it not for his resolve to avenge his murdered family, he might have planned an escape, tried to run from Triune and see how far he could get. But as it was, he wanted to check to see if Dari and Stormbreaker had returned. If they hadn't, he wanted to look from Dari's window to see if he might catch a glimpse of the Shrine of the Mother.

He closed his eyes and made his breathing even and regular, as if he had drifted off to sleep. Soon enough, Zed's breathing matched his own, and when Aron peeked at the other boy, he saw that Zed's cover rose and fell in a predictable rhythm. Zed turned to his back again, and his face had relaxed, returning to a semblance of a smile.

Relief at the silence spread through Aron. He settled deeper into his own bed, and once more let his own eyes close.

The image of his mother's face danced through his mind.

Pain stabbed at his chest and throat, and Aron jerked his eyes open again. He blinked in the low light of the fire, using most of his strength and focus not to cry out, or burst into sobs. His teeth clamped together as his mind fled back to his earlier realizations about his father's plans to rescue him, and about how his family died. His fists doubled, yanking at the soft covers of his bed.

Where is the Brailing Guard now?

The voice in his mind sounded much like his own, yet also different, in ways he couldn't describe. He slowed his breathing, tried to find his center, find some focus, at least enough to slip through the Veil. He could just check for the Guard. Search the nearby countryside, no farther than the fringes of Triune and Dyn Brailing.

No. If I see them, I'll kill them all.

He was panting now. The fire seemed far too hot.

And if I kill them all, Stormbreaker and Lord Baldric will kill me.

"Maybe death would be better," he whispered, directing his words at the high stone ceiling.

Where would the Brailing Guard be now? With the ranks mixed with soldiers from Dyn Altar, could he even tell them apart if he found a group of them on the other side of the Veil?

Stop this.

But he didn't think he could stop it. His mind felt like a bull talon out of control, lowering its head and charging in whatever direction it pleased. Light blazed through his consciousness, not real, yet incredibly real, and this time his thoughts spoke to him in a voice that sounded like his mother, or maybe his dead sisters, grown to the womanhood they would never know.

Find the Guard. Find your own power. Show everyone what you can do. Aron pressed his fists into his ears to block the sound, but still it came, this time in Seth's voice, and his father's. *Who could blame you? Who could stand against you?*

He wanted to do it. No matter his promises to Stormbreaker and Dari, no matter Lord Baldric's warning, Aron wanted to find those guardsmen and watch them all plunge to their deaths from the side of some cliff, or tear one another apart, or run mad into the woods, screaming until rock cats hunted each one for prey. He wanted it so much that he could almost see the Veil. He hungered for the enhanced perception he'd know on the other side, reached for it, almost moved through to that un-time, that un-place—

No! Leave me alone!

Sounds fractured.

Light splintered.

The totality of his bedchamber seemed to slam into his eyes, and his ears roared against the sudden silence.

Aron threw back his blankets and leaped from the bed.

The sudden shock of hard stone against his bare feet brought him a few paces back toward reality and the force of his beliefs and promises. His hands shook. His legs shook. He could hear himself gasping like an old man who had run too far, too fast. But he was still in his new room at Triune, all of him, body and consciousness as well. Flickers of light and whispers seemed to hover at the edges of his awareness, as if to draw him straight back into temptation.

Zed's expression remained placid as Aron gathered himself and shoved away the fringes of the Veil, then pulled on his tunic and breeches. Still barefoot, he padded across the fire-warmed stone floor to the doorway, eased back the handle, and let the heavy wood swing open just enough to allow him to slip into the hallway.

Chilly air brushed against his hands and face as he settled the door behind him—and found himself standing shoulder to shoulder with the big, muscled Sabor Zed believed to be Aron's new—what? Guard? Chaperone?

Aron stood very still, staring straight ahead into the stone hallway, which was lit by clusters of candles in sconces. He took a deep breath of dusty rock and tallow, and caught a whiff of some spice, exotic, not at all unpleasant, but different. He thought it might be clove, maybe with a touch of cinnamon.

He glanced at Iko, who kept his arms at his sides and his dark gaze on the hallway.

In the low candlelight, the boy's skin seemed an even darker, richer blue than it had before, and the furry golden blaze across his face, traveling down his neck into his brown tunic, seemed to catch the dancing golds and yellows of each little flame.

"Dari and Stormbreaker have not returned," Iko said in a low voice. "Nor has my mother."

Surprised, Aron spoke before he thought better of it. "Will you know when they do come back?"

Iko's response was immediate. "Yes."

Aron considered this and didn't find it strange. Perhaps the Sabor had mental connections with family members, if Fury races really had the powerful *graal* Dari claimed they did. Fine. Fortunate, in fact. "And if there's trouble?"

"I will know," Iko said without ever changing positions. "Are you well? A moment ago, I sensed . . . energy. I was close to entering the bedchamber when it ceased."

"I'm fine. A bad dream." Aron tried to sound confident, even though he was fairly certain he had almost lost his sanity a few short minutes ago.

Iko didn't challenge him, and for a time, Aron continued to stand in front of the closed door, battling between anger at the interruption of his plans and curiosity about Iko's presence. He didn't think he was afraid of the boy, but then, he could feel so little at the moment, it was hard to tell.

"Do you know of any rules to prevent me from walking about at night?" he asked, more to test his own nerves than to receive an answer.

"I do not," Iko said with no hint of irritation. "But I have been here even less time than you."

Aron waited, but the boy didn't add anything more helpful to his response. When it became clear that Iko would be content to stand as they were, perhaps until morning, Aron tried again. "If I go walking about, do you plan to raise any alarms?"

Iko's jaw clenched, then relaxed. "It is not for me to judge your actions. Do as you wish."

"And you'll follow." Aron watched Iko's expression, though he wasn't sure why, since it never seemed to change.

Except for his jaw. It was clenching again. "Yes. If you go walking, I will follow you."

Zed's earlier words drifted through Aron's mind, about fate and the will of the gods, and people . . . and Sabor . . . who might feel like they have a duty to those fate has chosen. He still thought that was ridiculous, at least the aspect of Zed's belief that made Aron one of those people—yet here he was, in the High Masters' Den of the Stone Guild at Triune, in the middle of the night, trying to have a conversation with a Sabor who seemed to be standing guard outside his bedchamber.

Aron forced himself to select a better question this time, and decided upon, "Why are you here, Iko?"

Iko seemed to consider his inquiry seriously, but when he spoke again, he said only, "I am here because I should be here."

This time, it was Aron who clenched his jaw, and his fists, too, but he made himself calm down and proceed further. "Do you really believe I'm important to Eyrie somehow, that my actions could shift the winds in one direction or the other?"

Iko finally moved enough to look at Aron, and he lifted an eyebrow at him.

That was the extent of his response. He didn't answer more directly.

Resisting an urge to pull the boy's long black hair, Aron grumbled, "So are you going to swear to protect me or something?"

Iko kept up his steady regard, and once more, he seemed to consider Aron's question seriously and carefully. "I have sworn to do so already, but the oath was not to you."

From the firm set of the boy's face, Aron could tell Iko wasn't planning to reveal any more information.

He's a lot like Seth, Aron thought, and the realization finally brought forth some emotion from the numbness inside him.

The emotion was sadness.

Aron launched himself away from his door and into the hallway, walking quickly away from the bedchamber, this time in the opposite direction from Dari's quarters. He had abandoned the idea of trying to get a view of the Shrine of the Mother the moment he discovered Iko still outside his door, so he had no real idea where he was going, only that he needed to move, to walk off the misery battering at his insides.

Perhaps he should leave the High Masters' Den and try to find the talon barn. Some time with Tek might ease his mind. Yet even behind the walls of such a fortress, it was nighttime in Eyrie, and his instincts shied away from venturing outside without benefit of a tallow circle, or at least a torch.

With every step, tears gathered in Aron's eyes and spilled down his face. He didn't look back to see if Iko was following him, but his better sense told Aron that this was the case. He wove out of the tower and into the Den's wider section, then into another tower, around and around until he lapped past his room twice, then started using the staircases he found. His mind registered a few details—a rug here, a table there. A library on the top level. A kitchen on the lower level. Weapons on the walls, decorations mostly, as they seemed very old. Here and there, he turned a corner to find moonslight spilling through grates or small arched windows.

When he once more reached the level of the Den where his own room was located, though in the tower opposite his own, he was moving so quickly he almost didn't see the tall boy with the reddish brown hair step from his bedchamber.

Aron pulled his stride before he smacked into Galvin Herder.

Galvin, who was dressed in tunic and breeches and boots, as if he might be planning to head out into the darkness, paused to stare down at Aron just as he had done earlier, outside Dari's bedchamber. "Little children should be in bed."

That brought the heat to Aron's face quickly. "I'm not a child. I'm fourteen years, and I'll be fifteen in a few cycles."

Galvin regarded him with absolutely no emotion at all, and Aron fought a sense of being a rabbit in the eyes of a fox. "I would have thought Master Stormbreaker would pick a strong apprentice, or at least one of normal size for his age."

Aron bit back a rush of angry responses and made to move past Galvin, but the taller boy blocked his path. Galvin's flat, unreadable face unnerved him and though he hated himself for doing it, Aron glanced back to see if Iko really was behind him.

The Sabor was there, a few paces back, standing with his arms folded. He was watching. Just watching, with no apparent intent to intervene.

Galvin seemed to notice the direction of Aron's glance. He smiled, but the expression seemed twice as cold—even frightening. "You can't count on savages like the Sabor. They have their own purposes, and you'll receive their kindness only until they're finished with you."

Aron managed to swallow, though his throat was so tight the movement caused him pain. His heart was starting to beat too fast, and his breathing turned jerky. He wasn't afraid of taking a beating. His own brothers had given him plenty of those. No, it was something else, a rank meanness ingesting this boy like a plague on the spirit, or the heart. It set Aron's instincts buzzing, as if he were standing right next to a prowling beast, or a mocker about to make its deadly shift.

Aron wanted to get far away.

Now.

Before something happened that caused Lord Baldric to send him straight to judgment.

"I'll go," Aron said, trying again to skirt Galvin and continue down the hallway.

Galvin moved so quickly Aron didn't see his arm or hand before he felt the boy's fingers clamp on his shoulder. Galvin gripped him so hard Aron feared his bones might come through his flesh. His face and chest burned as he struggled, but he couldn't extract himself. White-hot bolts of pain traveled down his right arm, making his fingers tingle.

"If I want you to stay, you'll stay." Galvin sounded matter-of-fact. Almost . . . happy. As if he could sense Aron's hurting, and enjoyed it.

Aron pushed his shoulder upward into the bigger boy's grip to ease the pressure, a trick he had learned from fighting with his brothers so many times. "I don't have any quarrel with you, Galvin Herder."

"Where is Master Stormbreaker?" Galvin's voice was barely above a whisper, but it carried threat and force. "Did he leave you all alone on this, your first night at Triune?"

Aron ground his teeth against the pain and tried once more to get himself free. There was no way he would tell this boy where Stormbreaker had gone, or why.

Galvin tightened his grip until Aron yelped and habit took over. With all the force he could muster, Aron launched a kick. His toes crumpled as his bare foot slammed into Galvin's knee. More pain blossomed like hot coals pressed against Aron's skin, but he barely felt it as the older boy swore and turned loose his shoulder. Aron started to hobble past Galvin, but Galvin grabbed his good ankle.

From the corner of his eye, Aron saw Iko start to move, but somebody in a gray tunic stepped gracefully in front of the Sabor.

"This will cease," said a woman's voice, and Aron felt himself freed once more.

He toppled forward and barely managed to catch himself on both hands. As fast as he could, he righted himself and turned to see who had spoken.

It was one of the girls he had seen in the hallway outside Dari's door. One of the girls who had seen him naked and making a fool of himself. She was tall, willowy, and she seemed older, more a grown woman than a child. Aron noted the yellow-blond hair and bright blue eyes usually found in the Mab dynasty, but her gray robes and *cheville* marked her as a Stone Sister.

Aron bit at his lip at the throb in his shoulder and foot as Galvin managed to stand and lean against the wall, massaging his knee. "Stormbreaker has abandoned his prize, Marilia," he told the Stone Sister. "He might escape."

Marilia's lips curved into a frown, but Aron could see from her narrowed eyes that she didn't trust the boy, or like him much at all. "Stormbreaker knows his own business, Galvin Herder. I suggest you leave it—and this boy—to him."

Galvin stopped nursing his swelling knee and managed to stand up straight. His height allowed him to stare down at Marilia much as he had done with Aron, but Aron saw that Marilia wasn't intimidated.

Galvin seemed to notice this, too, and that coldness Aron felt from the boy increased like a building winter storm. "May Stormbreaker's judgment prove better than Snakekiller's. When your mistress doesn't return, we'll learn what Lord Baldric truly thinks of your abilities."

Marilia's features hardened, making her look older and more regal as she stepped closer to Galvin, moving her face very near to his. "Snakekiller will come back to Triune in her own time, and I'll thank you to remember I'm no longer an apprentice needing a mistress. If I had wanted to, I could have claimed you when you were orphaned, and put you to work scrubbing latrines in the Sisters' Tower."

Galvin stood his ground, but his answering smile was more frigid poison. Aron realized the boy really wanted to throw himself at Marilia, but didn't want to risk outright defeat at her hands. No. This boy would wait. He would choose his moment and strike, perhaps even from behind, like a brazen coward.

Aron swallowed as he flexed his shoulders and toes, trying to make certain they would move at his bidding.

Cowards were always the most dangerous, weren't they?

From behind Marilia, Iko fixed his dark eyes on Galvin. Aron wasn't certain, but he thought he saw something like anger or dislike in the Sabor's stare.

"Your charge is to find peace and learn to respect each other, for the good of the guild," Marilia said, addressing herself to Aron and Galvin. "If you cannot do so, you'll be spending long—and unpleasant—hours at Endurance House. Were I you, I'd find better uses for your time, before I see fit to send you both there now."

With that, she wheeled away from them, made her way past Iko, and continued down the hallway toward the staircase.

Aron remained motionless, hammered by Marilia's threat.

Endurance House . . .

And then Lord Baldric would be informed, and then—

The thought of it made him want to collapse where he stood, even if Galvin Herder laughed at him or beat him for his weakness.

Galvin seemed in no further mood for trouble himself, however. He gave Aron a final glance, neither smiling nor frowning, then walked away, heading in the direction of the other staircase, the one that led down toward the kitchen on the lower level.

Aron turned to go back to his own room and found himself looking directly at Lord Baldric.

The sight of the man's bald head and narrow glare startled him so badly that he jumped, then flushed from embarrassment at the fright. Lord Baldric was standing only a body's length from him, and the Lord Provost's arms were folded, his hands concealed in the sleeves of his gray robes.

Was he holding daggers in both fists?

Aron's legs wobbled, but he kept himself upright.

"It's late," Lord Baldric said without moving the hands in his sleeves. His tone was firm, and he overpronounced both words.

Aron had to will his lips to form words. "Yes, sir."

Lord Baldric waited for a few seconds, then sighed. "When it's late, people sleep."

"Yes, sir," Aron said, then took the man's meaning and started toward his own bedroom.

Lord Baldric relaxed his arms as Aron drew near. His finger slid from his sleeves, and Aron saw no weapons. He almost fainted from relief when the Lord Provost swept past him and headed off in the direction Galvin Herder had taken.

As soon as Lord Baldric was out of sight, Aron gathered his wits enough to limp straight to Iko and stop in front of the Sabor. "I thought you were here to protect me."

Iko shrugged one shoulder. "You were in no real danger."

Aron's mouth came open. He wanted to kick Iko's knee next, and might have, if his foot wasn't already hurting so badly. "So it won't trouble you if some older, bigger boy breaks my shoulder and toes— or if the Lord Provost executes me if he thinks I'm dangerous and breaking the rules he set?"

Iko gazed at him steadily, then said with that irritatingly calm voice, "It is not for me or anyone else to fight your battles. I will not interfere with your training or your life, but if I believe you need protection, I will offer it."

Aron pushed past Iko and limped back to his room without looking back at the Sabor, even when Iko added, "And you injured your own toes."

The door to Aron's bedchamber opened easily, and he managed to close it quietly instead of slamming it as hard as he wished and waking Zed along with everyone in the Den. The fire was burning lower, so Aron found the bucket of tender beside it and added some small branches before stripping off his tunic and breeches and returning to his own bed. The entire time he was moving, his aches and pains refused to ease.

After the fire grew to his satisfaction, Aron took off his clothes and sat on the edge of his bed and examined himself. A bruise was form-ing on his shoulder, and his foot was an unpleasant shade of purple just below his second toe.

He closed his eyes and let a few new tears spill down his cheeks before catching himself and speaking to himself in his own mind.

I'm too old to sob like a little boy.

The words came out in his father's voice, or maybe Seth's, and that only made the tears flow more freely.

I wish . . .

I wish my mother were here.

That desire made Aron flush with shame, then anger, and he could hear Stormbreaker now, speaking to him after he woke following the Shrine incident.

We're a guild, not a stable of wet nurses with infants to be tended.

Aron turned and slammed his fist into his feather-stuffed pillow.

Down belched from the cloth covering and floated past him, small gray shadows in the low light of the moons and fire.

He needed to sleep. Some part of him knew that, but how would he ever manage to close his eyes?

Aron punched the pillow again, and again. Then again.

He'd probably fail at whatever tasks Stormbreaker set for him on the morning. And Galvin Herder and the rest of the apprentices would be right there to see him, to see the runt make a fool of himself yet again. Perhaps Lord Baldric would decide he wasn't worth the trou-ble, and send him on for judgment after all.

Grinding his teeth to hold back a shout, Aron drove his knuckles into the ripping, tearing pillow so many times that goose down filled the air around his bed like a small, dark cloud.

Zed turned away from the noise and groaned. Then he pulled his blanket over his head and left Aron to throw himself on his own bed and lie awake, refusing to risk the closing of his eyes.

CHAPTER TWENTY-EIGHT

ARON

Aron clawed his way out of bloody nightmares about killing the Brailing Guard to find Zed already dressed and shaking him by the foot. The room smelled of dampness and the smoke of a dying fire. Faint gray light slanted in through the bedchamber's arched windows. Not enough light, by Aron's dim reckoning. Either it was too early, or raining, or both. Either way, Aron wanted nothing more than to sink back to his pillow and sleep again, this time without his violent dreams.

Zed gave Aron's foot another shake. "Hurry. We'll be late, and you never, ever want to be late for training days."

Aron ignored him.

"Have it your way." Zed seized both of Aron's ankles.

Before Aron could even get off a kick to defend himself, Zed flipped him to his side and turned him loose. Aron tumbled sideways out of the bed, blankets and all, and struck the stone floor hard with both elbows and his hip.

The crack-shock of the pain made his eyes fly open.

His vision cleared along with his mind. He rolled to his feet, intending to ignore the throb in his arms and leg and pound Zed for pitching him out of bed, but a knock at the bedchamber door brought him up short. Instead of swinging at the ready, waiting Zed, Aron dove for his trunk to get out a clean tunic and some breeches, just in case it was Dari who had come calling.

Moments later, Stormbreaker swept into the room. Aron's heart lurched at the sight of his guild master, and he wondered what he should feel—relief at his return? Happiness? Fear? As it was, fatigue from poor sleep edged out all other possibilities, but Aron did experience a stab of curiosity about how Stormbreaker and Dari had fared in their search for Kate.

Stormbreaker bypassed Zed with only a cursory nod, and Zed immediately busied himself with cleaning out the fire grate. Stormbreaker came straight to Aron, who was tying the laces of his leather boots, and knelt beside him.

"I was concerned about you," Stormbreaker said when Aron finished with the laces. "I did not like leaving you alone on your first night at Triune."

"I'm no risk for running away." Irritation chased a bit of Aron's tiredness away. He frowned as he straightened himself and looked Stormbreaker in the eye. "I had Zed and Iko, too. This is a guild, not a stable of wet nurses, correct?"

Stormbreaker offered him what might have been a smile, were it not for the obvious exhaustion weighting his features. Aron noticed the traces of dirt about the man's face and the dust still clinging to his gray robes. "It was my responsibility to see to your needs, to make the transition to your new life easier, but I couldn't honor both that duty and our promise to Dari. I hope you understand."

"I do understand," Aron said, surprised to realize he meant it with the same force he spoke it. "I would have gone last night, if you had allowed it."

Stormbreaker rose, but kept his gaze firmly locked on Aron's face. "I have no doubt you would have done well, but guild training is dangerous enough with a full night's rest and no other concerns. I won't put your life at needless risk by taxing you with night hunts that may or may not ever bear fruit. Last night certainly did not."

An odd sort of sadness rattled Aron because he knew Dari must be so disappointed over the failure, and his gut clenched along with his fists. A second later, he had an absurd urge to belt Stormbreaker in the nose, for leaving him behind and for not finding Kate to make Dari happy. He might have done it, too, if his better sense hadn't informed him that he'd have to climb on his bed to reach that high.

"It's that important to you to help Dari," Stormbreaker murmured, as if realizing this for the first time. He placed a hand on Aron's shoulder. "A matter of honor? Of love?"

Aron said nothing, but he knew his face must be turning very, very red.

"Very well. This evening, you'll assist us with the maps and plans. If we receive solid information about Kate's location, if a raiding party is required, you have my word that you won't be left behind."

The tension inside Aron eased enough that he managed to look at Stormbreaker again without hitting him. He would at least have a chance to give Dari what her heart most desired, to see Kate delivered into her waiting arms. For now, that chance was enough, and he would take it.

"Remember your lessons from yesterday, Aron," Stormbreaker was saying. "You'll begin learning from others today in the same fashion I taught you. Your teachers will repeat nothing without penalty, and few concessions will be made for your lack of experience. It's important that you stay alert, that you listen, watch, smell, taste, and touch, that you gain every piece of information you can possibly gain, in every situation." He took his hand from Aron's shoulder, but not before giving it a gentle squeeze. "A Stone Brother's mind is his most formidable weapon. By the end of each day, you'll know your own thoughts better, and you'll be that much closer to being useful to the guild."

"And if you get into trouble," Zed added, grinning as he finished with his own boots, "if you're late to anything, you'll spend the day stuck in Endurance House."

Aron couldn't help a shiver. He glanced at Zed, wondering if Zed had ever suffered that punishment. What *did* happen to apprentices sent to that shadowy, awful little building? Endurance House, the Shrine of the Mother—both felt intricately wrapped into the violent nightmares that had left him bone-weary this morning. And on the other side of all of it, every threat and punishment and bad dream, Lord Baldric and judgment waited.

"We shouldn't be late, then," Aron mumbled, moving out of the bedchamber ahead of Stormbreaker and Zed, even though he had no idea where to go. From the corner of his eye, Aron saw Iko leave his post at the bedchamber door and follow quietly, keeping a distance from all of them as they hurried across the stone floor.

Zed caught Aron in a few strides and directed him down the main stairway to the front of the courtyard surrounding the High Master's Den. Stormbreaker followed them at a distance, like a tall gray ghost sweeping down the castle steps. The Den's wooden front doors stood slightly ajar, as if awaiting their arrival, and Aron could see the harsh rainfall outside.

He slowed.

Zed reached the front doors, grabbed the edge of one, and looked back at Aron. "First thing every morning at Triune, we dance the *fael'feis*. If you learned a celebration of the air from your family, you can stand in the back and use it—lots of people do their own celebrations. If you don't have a family version, just follow me and learn Stone's."

Aron had seen the *fael'feis* performed in the village nearest his farm, and learned a few beginning steps from his father. Soldiers in the Guard did it every day to prepare for the day's labors, as well as noble families and rectors at the Temple of the Brother, but Aron had never really learned a full celebration of the air.

"It's raining," he said. "How can you dance the *fael'feis* in the rain?"

"Weather comes and weather goes," Stormbreaker said as he reached the doors himself. "We train in all conditions because we must hunt and survive in all conditions."

He moved past them and headed into the wet cold of the morning without even raising his cowl over his head, taking himself to the far side of the courtyard. Aron gazed past Zed, through the separation in the doors, noting shapes in the rain that were probably Stone's other High Masters. On the side of the courtyard closest to him, a few more shapes waited in three small lines, some taller than him, some similar in size.

The other apprentices, already gathered, staring toward them as if they were slowing down the day already.

He wanted to groan.

From the darkened landing a few paces away, Iko sniffed like he might share that sentiment, and Aron decided he liked the Sabor boy a bit better.

"Let's go." Zed tugged Aron's arm as he dove into the storm, and Aron followed. As soon as Iko came through, Aron closed the doors behind him as the heavens and skies drenched him for his efforts. By the time he joined Zed behind the rest of the apprentices, he was so soaked and chilled that his teeth were chattering. Once more, Iko moved off to a short distance away, watching as the dance began.

Each step and stretch felt like frozen, clumsy torture to Aron. He squinted at Zed, trying to mimic each lift of the arms, each extension of the legs. It didn't feel strenuous at first, but as the moments passed, the muscles along Aron's back and neck began to ache. He ground his teeth, forcing himself onward through the celebration of air as rain splattered into his mouth and eyes.

"You'll get used to it," Zed murmured as they shifted again, to face north instead of south. "Try to let your mind fade into the movements, join with them, flow with them."

Aron drew a slow breath, reached forward in mimicry of Zed's reach—and someone slapped against the back of his head. He pitched forward, going knees and palms first onto the courtyard's smooth, wet stones.

A few of the other apprentices laughed as he fought to regain his footing on the slick rocks, most of all Galvin, who had the position right behind him in the formation.

"You should take more care," Galvin said as Aron finally made it back to Zed's side and lifted his left arm as Zed's was lifted. "You might injure yourself, and that would be a shame."

Aron managed the rush of rage through his limbs, then welcomed the warming anger and used it to move better and faster. He kept his eyes on Zed and Zed alone, ignoring Galvin, and directing his mind away from Endurance House and the possibility of being confined there, now or ever.

Galvin struck the back of his head again, a harder blow, enough to make lights flash in Aron's eyes, but he managed not to fall. Zed fluidly swapped positions with him. Wet breech cuffs slapped against stone as the boys behind them shifted position, too. Aron had no doubt Galvin was behind him once more.

Aron leaned into the next stretch, only to hit stone and puddles again when Galvin jammed his foot into the back of Aron's knee.

"Have a care, boy." Galvin's tone was even and calm, but when Aron looked at him, the tall boy's eyes seemed bright at the sight of Aron's discomfort. "One day you'll be facing the likes of Canus the Bandit. You'll need much better balance and skill to survive a combat like that."

Anyone not looking directly into Galvin's eyes might take his words for teaching. An older brother working with a younger brother to be certain lessons were learned.

Aron knew better. He struggled to erase all trace of emotion and reaction from his own expression. He didn't need to give Galvin any sign of weakness or indication of pain. Pain seemed to feed this boy in ways Aron didn't even want to consider.

Galvin went back to the morning dance, and so did Aron.

If he got into some spat with this boy, he might be sent to Endurance House, but really, that was the least of his worries. Nothing Galvin could do was worth the risk of Lord Baldric and judgment.

If he was to stay alive, Aron knew he would have to learn to suffer the likes of Galvin Herder without response—and likely, much, much worse.

• • •

Aron passed Lord Baldric at least three separate times on his morning's travels. He had no doubt that the Lord Provost didn't usually trouble himself with the day-to-day training of apprentices, and that Lord Baldric probably didn't make a habit of traipsing around the grounds. The man was making good on his promise—his threat—to watch Aron closely.

Not knowing what else to do, Aron gave the Lord Provost a wide berth each time he noticed him, and wondered how many times he *hadn't* noticed his watcher. He also tried to ignore Iko, who was standing a few paces away as Aron seethed and stewed about Galvin and his nightmares and Endurance House and the rain and everything else. He tapped on Dari's door, but wanted to bang on it with his fists instead. Going through the Veil was the last thing Aron wanted to do after last night's urges and his horrible dreams, but he supposed he had no choice in the matter.

Worse yet, he was still dripping like a toddler just fished from a lake, in part from morning celebration and in part from his journey to and from the forge. His new gray *cheville* felt cold and heavy against his ankle, and he had to work not to remember the crack and crumble his Brailing *cheville* made when the stone masons broke it apart. He had no time for soft sentiments. He didn't even have time to change his wet

breeches and tunic. Only an hour for those with legacies to go to training, while those who were Quiet spent their time in meditation.

Even if Aron could have spared a moment to throw on dry clothes,
there would have been little point. From Zed, Aron knew that as soon as
he finished his session with Dari, he had to be at the archery and knife
ranges, ready to humiliate himself with the infernal throwing daggers he
had failed to master during their ride to Triune. After that, he and Zed
would head for the stables and talon barns for mounted practice, the
forge for weapons construction, the general armory and mock battlefield
for practice fighting in groups, then back to the grazing fields, lake, and
woods to gain experience marking trails and tracking prey.

Aron didn't want to admit it, not fully at least, but he was grateful
Stormbreaker had left him out of last night's search. His few hours of
dream-filled sleep were better than nothing. He had no idea how any
person could stand up to the training schedule Stone demanded, and
even envied Dari her right to remain in chambers, maybe catch up on
her rest, before she had to attend to her own duties, whatever they
might be past his training.

Dari opened her bedchamber door and gazed at him, from his wet
hair to the soiled knees of his breeches. Her dark hair was pulled tight
against her head and fastened at her neck, and she wore a simple green
robe belted at the waist. Aron noted that her ankle remained bare, and
he wondered if she would be going to the forge today, as he had done.

What would happen when the stone workers tried to band a
Stregan?

Could such a thing even be done without the rock exploding?

But Aron supposed Stormbreaker and Dari had a plan for such
things, so he kept his questions to himself. Besides, Dari looked completely worn-out, and in no mood for chatter. Her eyes were blood-
shot, and her frown seemed to be etched into her very essence as she
stepped away from the entrance without even greeting him.

He followed her inside, noting Blath's silent presence near the chamber's arched window. The older woman didn't glance at him, though her eyes did travel to Iko, who remained visible in the hallway until the chamber door swung closed behind Aron.

Dari gestured to a bare spot in front of her fireplace, and Aron settled himself on the floor, feeling guilt at the way his wet, dirty clothes dribbled muck and mud on the edges of the hide rug nearest his knees. Dari sat down on the rug, closed her eyes, and took a breath.

Aron recognized her posture for going through the Veil, and quickly assumed his own.

There would be no time wasted today, not anywhere, it seemed.

"Be quick," Blath said in a low voice as she stared outward, into the seemingly endless rain. "A Stone messenger approaches. He bears a summons to the retirement quarters near the Temple of the Brother."

"A death," Dari said with her eyes still closed, even as Aron wondered about the extent of Sabor mind-talents, and how the woman knew such a thing just by looking at the messenger. "And no doubt they believe I have the Ross legacy. I'll be expected to dispatch the dead if guild members are otherwise occupied."

Aron tried to relax his arms, but he was still shivering from the cold and rain. He peeked at Dari again, then at Blath.

"You'll have no peace, Dari," Blath cautioned, staring even more intently into the weather outside the window. "What with training the boy and seeing to duties as a Ross. Such will be your life here, unless you choose to return to Dyn Ross, or better yet, I could take you to—"

"I'm not leaving Eyrie without my sister." Dari's face relaxed into a mask of near-sleep, despite the sharpness of her tone. "My peace and rest will be forfeit, if that's the price."

Aron slammed his eyes closed, determined to go through the Veil as quickly as he could, and do whatever Dari instructed him to do. The envy he had felt when he knocked on her door was long gone now, and he was determined that training him, at least, would be as small a burden as possible.

Thank you for that. Dari's sweet voice enveloped him as his mind awakened to the details of her beauty, the green threads of her gown, and each nook and cranny and shadow in the bedchamber. *You're no burden to me, Aron. Many times, you're the brightest moment in my days.*

Aron wondered if she sensed the rush of warmth that claimed his essence at those words. Everywhere else, with everyone else, he felt so little, so much of numb and nothing mingled with irritation or anger, but with her—with her, he still knew compassion. Perhaps even kindness. He was glad for that, and more than glad for her, and for a moment, he couldn't remember all the things that frightened him or made him furious.

We'll find Kate, Dari, he said, letting the thought be audible on the other side of the Veil. *I'll find her. I will. You'll see.*

Her perfect image nodded to him, as if believing or wanting to believe every word. Then she beckoned for him to follow her farther through the Veil.

Now twice as determined to keep his promises, Aron turned his own essence loose, letting it flow toward her as she moved. He had so much to learn, and he knew he needed to learn it fast and well.

I'll do it, he said over and over again, keeping the words inside his own mind and heart, private and silent, until he couldn't sort them from instinct or the whisperings of legacy itself. *One day, I'll be the one to find your sister.*

CHAPTER TWENTY-NINE

ARON

Aron's first week, then his first two weeks and first cycle at the Stone Guild stronghold in Triune passed in what felt like flurries and spinning blurs. His days took on an exhausting pattern of avoiding Galvin Herder and Lord Baldric whenever possible, *fael'feis* and *graal* training, then what felt like endless work with weapons, weapon-making, fighting and tracking skills, and training for strength during the day. Iko stood vigil during all of these activities, neither contributing nor intruding. After dinner, the Sabor took his leave for a time, and Stormbreaker and the other High Masters schooled the apprentices in language, mathematics, history, philosophy, etiquette, and protocol. Then, every third evening, Aron would watch as Dari and Stormbreaker resumed the hunt for Kate.

Especially on those later nights, Aron would reach his bed, convinced he would sleep soundly—but he was rarely so fortunate. Images of the Brailing Guard woke him and sent him pacing through the Den hallways with Iko a few lengths behind him, trying to resist his own murderous urges and ignore the whispers of vengeance that wanted to settle deeper and deeper into his essence.

So it went, as more cycles passed and the air grew colder, sunlight grew shorter, and time crimped inward and twisted, running too fast at some times, and too slow at others. Too slow, especially during weapons practice during the fourth cycle of the next year, after Aron's fifteenth birthday.

"Lift your arm higher," Stormbreaker instructed at the archery and knife ranges, kneeling beside Aron and helping him to line up his dagger with the target.

From his vantage point under a nearby evergreen, Iko looked bored and disinterested—though a casual observer would not have been able to note any expression on his blue face at all. Aron's breath issued in an icy fog, and he had to purse his chafed lips to keep his teeth from chattering. His shoulder was already aching from throwing and throwing, but he hadn't hit the target enough for Stormbreaker to move it more than a few body lengths away from him. He hurled the last dagger with as much force as he could muster, but it struck the straw bale hilt-first and bounced to the side.

"Again," Stormbreaker commanded, and Aron had to swallow a groan. As he collected the four practice daggers and returned to his stance, Stormbreaker said, "You were brilliant at archery and short swords this morning, and I see you carrying water buckets and heavy baskets for hours each day to increase your strength. Training master Wilson told me yesterday that you surpass even the older and more seasoned apprentices at tracking on all terrains and at making trails through thick brush."

Aron glanced at the daggers at his feet and the single blade in his hand. "Thank you" was the best he could manage as he tried to keep his arm relaxed and take the respite Stormbreaker's conversation offered. He couldn't help thinking of how he had hunted the Scry with his father and brothers, how all that practice had prepared him to be at Stone in ways he couldn't have imagined. An image of his father's pleased expression pierced Aron's heart like the tip of a blade, and he couldn't stop his quick, deep frown.

He rubbed his chest with his free hand as Stormbreaker studied him, and Aron wondered if the hurt from his losses would forever be so sharp. Many moons seemed to be passing and yet would he ever be able to turn loose his past, his history?

Stormbreaker remained in his kneeling position, beside Aron, as he so often did when they spoke or worked together. "The pain of loss, of remembering what has passed beyond your grip—it doesn't heal, as we discussed when you first arrived. But if you shift your focus to this day, this time, to the sound of my voice, you can lessen its sting."

Aron nodded and set his jaw, determined not to lose any of the ground he had gained in putting aside the agony related to the deaths of his family. He stopped rubbing his chest and listened intently as Stormbreaker continued with, "Training master Wilson is particularly impressed with your ability to remain still for long stretches, yet keep your alertness and wits about you. That will serve you best of all when you draw stones on the Judged who choose flight."

Stormbreaker's strange, bright eyes fixed on Aron's face, filling Aron with a strange sense of pride and worry, all at the same time. "Often it's the louder, bolder fighters who win accolades in training, but in true hunts and single combats, it's patience, caution, and intelligent choices that will save your life and bring down your Judged."

Aron stood a bit straighter and tightened his grip on the hilt of the dagger. Other apprentices and masters began to pass by, but he ignored them and turned his own mind back to the target in front of him. He stared at the mark on the bale of hay until he could see it, sense it, even feel it in the center of his mind. After a slow, even breath, Aron raised his arm.

This time, when he released the dagger, the blade flew true—and struck the mark hilt-first, bouncing off again.

Stormbreaker patted his shoulder as Galvin Herder watched from nearby, standing alone, his hands clenched on his own throwing daggers. Aron had an urge to keep Stormbreaker between himself and the other boy, lest one of Galvin's daggers go astray and find its mark in Aron's shoulder or thigh.

"You hit the bale at the center," Stormbreaker told Aron. "Striking the target consistently is progress—and quite possibly, it would be enough to gain you time in a battle. Not everyone will attain the same skill with every fighting method." Aron glanced from Galvin to Zed, who was approaching with Windblown, then stood and dusted off his robes. Loudly enough for Galvin to hear, Stormbreaker said, "Aron, I am needed in the chambers of the Lord Provost to go over the latest messages and news of the war. Would you take the rest of this training block to assist Zed with his talon skills? Your abilities with the animals are unmatched by most of our apprentices, and many of our masters as well."

Aron went still with surprise. "Alone, Master Stormbreaker?"

Very few apprentices, even in later years, were allowed to ride talons unsupervised.

Stormbreaker favored him with a smile. "I believe you have earned that privilege, yes."

The awarding of this freedom drew a frown from Windblown, a grin from Zed, and brought an abrupt halt to Galvin Herder's casual observation. The tall boy pivoted back toward his targets and drove his daggers home with swift, sure throws.

Aron couldn't quite believe his good fortune, but he motioned to Zed, picked up the two buckets of rocks he carried with him everywhere to build his arm strength, and the two of them headed off toward the talon barn with Iko following close behind.

Aron and Zed barely spoke as they moved, but Aron could feel Zed's pride and excitement, as well as his nervousness at approaching the big, scaled lizards that had caused him trouble in the past.

When they crossed through the barrier separating horses and talons and neared the barn, they could hear Tek whistling the moment she scented Aron's approach.

The sound of the little talon's greeting gave Aron a pang in his chest; then his heart seemed to open wide. As if chasing after the bits

of sun showing through the gray, wintery clouds, Aron pushed past
Zed, left Iko behind as well, and ran down the last bit of the path
between the stable barrier wall and the talon barn. He put down his
rock buckets, shoved his way through one of the ten entrances, ran the
considerable length of the straw-covered dirt floor, carefully opened
the thick, large doors separating the male and female sections, and
slipped into the secondary hall. Familiar odors of grain and manure
and rank goat meat met his nose, and dust swirled around him with
each step he took. The talon barn was warmer than outdoors, because
the Stone Guild kept their talons like noble families did, with fires
burning in hearths spaced along the barn wall. He found Tek where he
knew she would be, in front of one of those heated grates, in the last
stall in the female section. She was squeaking and whistling and stamp-
ing around, even waving her withered foreclaws to express her absolute
joy at his presence.

"Sweet girl," he muttered as she butted against the reinforced
wooden stall door. For a few beautiful moments, Aron imagined he was
back home in his father's barn, outside the stone stall they constructed
just for Tek after she was rescued. If he closed his eyes, he might see the
gardens, the crops, the house—might even hear the music of his sisters
laughing, or his mother calling out to Seth and his brothers to gather
the little ones for dinner. He pulled open the stall door to hug her, but
she butted him right in the gut. Aron grunted from the blow and stumbled backward, and Tek shrilled all over again, excited, but also tense at
Zed and Iko's approach.

Aron gathered her lead halter from a peg beside the stall, slipped it
over her head, and whispered comforts to her as Zed edged up beside
him. Iko seemed to fade into the woodwork, as if aware that the addition of his unfamiliar—and perhaps predatory—scent might make
Tek too nervous to accept Zed's presence.

Tek stared at Zed, her round eyes wide and her hinged jaws open
just enough to show rows of jagged white teeth stained with blood

from her afternoon meal. She smelled of gore and scale oil, but Aron didn't care. He pressed his face and arms against her broad side and tried not to cough at the stench.

"She's still smaller than the rest, but I think she's growing." Zed leaned away from Tek as she went to sniff him, and Aron realized Zed was skittish around her. Maybe around all talons.

"If you relax with them, they'll relax with you." Aron straightened himself enough to rub his fingers across Tek's slick, glassy head scales. When he pushed against the tips of her relaxed neck ring, the sharpness made him catch his breath. "You can't be afraid of talons. They'll bite and kick—throw you off and stomp you into the dirt, just like horses, only it's farther to the ground."

"Yeah." Zed put his hand on his left side and rubbed, as if remembering fierce pain. "Regular apprentices don't train much with talons, but we had to learn the basics of care, tending, and riding. Will I be safe to take out a bull if you're on Tek?"

Aron tugged Tek toward the barn wall so he could tie her and saddle her. "She's still cycles from her first mating season. See her neck ring, here?"

Zed nodded as Aron stroked the deadly pointed scales again.

"These scales flush like Mab's rubies when females near their breeding time," Aron said. "It's only once a year in spring—but you won't be able to miss how the scales look, or how the females behave. Like deranged rock cats with the scent of blood."

Zed pointed to the neck ring. "I hate it when the scales come up. That never means anything good. I—I guess High Masters usually choose bulls for riding because they don't want to be down for the cycles of breeding and laying and sitting?"

Aron shrugged as he left the tied talon and headed into the tack room. "It takes only about two cycles, three at the most, and hatchlings do well without their mothers for hours at a time. Bulls have more even temperament, and they take to training better." He located Tek's saddle on its wall peg and pulled it down. When he emerged, Zed was still standing quietly, as if eager to learn everything Aron knew about talons. "Females tend to bond with one rider and one rider only, and they can be vicious with anyone else who tries to handle them."

"Trainers told us that last year." Zed moved away from Tek as Aron approached her with blanket and saddle, but not before she splattered him with a big, snotty sniff. "Just not in such simple words. The way you say it, it's easier to remember. I'll go back to the front of the barn and saddle one of the bulls."

As Zed shied away from Tek, then hurried away to get his own mount, Aron felt a passing pleasure that he could help Zed with his talon riding. Zed had been very helpful to him since he was taken, after all.

Or am I just glad to finally be better than Zed at something? Anything? The questions made him frown, especially when he couldn't give himself honest answers. His mother would have told him to pray to the Brother and ask forgiveness for such jealous and unkind intentions, but Aron couldn't imagine doing that.

"If the gods even bother with the likes of us." Heat burned in his cheeks all during the time it took to finish saddling Tek and swap her halter for a riding bridle. Then he used a bench to climb into Tek's saddle. It felt good to be with her, yet even the freedom of riding unsupervised or the opportunity to help Zed improve at his talon skills didn't ease the anger that seemed to stalk Aron and come back to him with the smallest of thoughts. After all these days, it was beginning to make him weary inside.

He rode through the opening separating male from female sections too quickly, then had to rein Tek hard to lean back and push the doors closed behind him. To his credit, Zed had already managed to pick out a talon, and he had done a fair job of rigging the saddle and bridle. Aron pointed at the center cinch, to the loose buckle at the middle. "Tighten it there or you'll slip off, saddle and all, if he leaps."

Zed complied without comment, then wrestled the bull to a bench and mounted.

Aron led the way outside, barely looking back at his companion, even though he knew Zed was nervous. When the talon barn door thumped into place behind them, the riding field seemed to stretch endlessly in all directions, beckoning with frosty brown grass. Newly emerged sunlight touched Aron's face, warm in the otherwise cold breeze, and the air smelled so much fresher, like chilled mud and winter forests. Like the Watchline. Like home.

Aron urged Tek forward, giving the talon her head and letting her find her own speed. The chilly breeze became a steady stream of cold wind, and Aron found the rhythm of the talon's loping gait easily. It *was* like home, like running down the byway near their farm, dodging toward the trees that separated the Watchline from the Scry.

For a moment, Aron did let himself close his eyes and pretend. He could see every detail of the place that had been his home, his heart, right down to the worn wood of their barn and the pegs he and his father had hammered the day before Harvest.

The day before everything had changed.

"Aron?" Zed called from behind them, but his voice seemed small and distant, and for the moment, unimportant. He would catch up soon enough on a bull. The bigger talon could double Tek's stride, or better.

"Aron!" Zed yelled again, and this time Aron wanted to wheel Tek around, fly back to the other boy, and punch him like he might have punched Seth for interrupting such a good ride. Instead, he let Tek romp down the barrier wall separating horse pastures from talon grounds. The frigid fall air braced him, soothed him, seemed to drive back the uncomfortable fire of the rage he couldn't seem to release.

The barrier gate swung open, but Aron didn't worry about the breach, because he was still many lengths away. Whoever had come through would fasten the gate back long before he drew close enough for Tek to make a bolt toward the horses. He let her run another few paces—then sucked back an icy breath and blinked in the blaze of afternoon sunlight.

The gate—

It was still open.

"Close the gate!" he shouted, but the tall figure in the gray tunic who had come through walked slowly down the wall in the other direction, leaving the barrier wide-open. "Hey! Secure the barrier!"

Tek yanked against him, turning her formidable strength straight toward the scent of fresh meat.

"Hold!" Aron jerked back on the rein and threw his body weight as far back in the saddle as he dared. "Tek, hold!"

From behind him came Zed's frantic, incoherent shouts and the doom thunder of charging bull talon clawfeet on the frozen ground.

Blood surged through Aron's chest and his throat pinched until he couldn't speak another word to control Tek. All he could do was saw the bit back and forth in her mouth and pray to the heavens he got her attention. Not likely, with fresh horse meat only a few dozen loping strides through the open barrier gate.

The bull talon stormed past them a few paces from the breach in the barrier, and Aron saw Zed clinging to the bull's neck with one arm, fighting the reins with the other.

From the other side of the barrier, horses began to squeal in terror.

Aron prayed the horses would stampede back to their own stables, attracting as much attention and aid as possible. He saw the tall figure in the gray tunic standing some distance away. Galvin Herder was watching with eerie calmness as Tek blasted through the open gate. Her battle ring flipped up at the sight of horses, blocking Aron's view as Zed's bull talon threw Zed aside like a straw dummy. The big bull leaped into the air and aimed his clawfeet at a running, bleating mare.

The awful crunch of bone and the final screech of the mare filled the afternoon. The bull talon let out a spine-rattling battle screech, and Tek answered with one of her own.

Aron let out his own cry of frustration. Dread and terror hammered through his veins. Tek would try to challenge the bull for his kill, and the riderless bull would slay the little female just as fast as he killed the horse.

"No!" Aron bunched the reins in his fist and leaned so far back in the saddle he felt himself slipping toward the talon's rough, scaly rump. The thrust of her stride threw her hips against the back of his head so hard that his vision swam.

No, no, no! Panic burned him like wildfire. *Stop. Stop!* He was thinking it, screaming it as he fell and slammed into the grassy pasture.

Pain fractured his thoughts, crushed away his breath, and left him wordless and gasping on the icy dirt, staring into blue-white sunlight and shifting gray clouds. His ears roared as he wheezed, and he couldn't hear anything but his own struggling breath. He dug at the hard ground with his fingers, trying to get up, trying to get himself to Tek before she died, but he knew he was failing. She would be gone in seconds. He was losing her, and there was nothing he could do to stop it.

CHAPTER THIRTY

ARON

Tek.

Tek!

Aron got enough breath to yell, but still no words came. Just a wail like a wounded rock cat daring some predator to approach it.

Something streaked past him, shoving him sideways; then voices seemed to come from everywhere at once.

Still fighting for every taste of air, Aron managed to push himself upright. He saw Zed first, up but coughing and staggering in a circle. Zed was holding his ribs and his mouth was bleeding. From the horse stables, six Stone Brothers were coming on the run. Between Zed and the onrushing guildsmen, the bull feasted on its kill, slowing only to let out sharp bleats of satisfaction.

Aron gripped his own ribs and sucked down breath after breath despite the pain in his head and sides. Where was Tek? Why wasn't she at the meat, or dead at the bull's feet?

He turned to search the field—and he saw Tek standing to his left, head down against tight reins.

Iko had her.

The Sabor was standing completely still, facing Aron, steadying Tek's reins in one big blue fist.

The aches in Aron's body seemed to fade into so much nothing as he stared at the little talon. She wasn't bleeding anywhere, and no part of her seemed crooked, not a scale ruffled or out of place. She blew a film of snot across Iko's shoulder and head, then snorted again and pulled her head back toward the bull and the meat.

Iko held the reins with no difficulty.

Aron had an urge to run to Iko and throw his arms around the Sabor's neck, but a movement to his right caught his attention.

Galvin Herder had come through the breach, closed the gate behind him, and reached Zed. The older boy was mopping blood from Zed's mouth with the sleeve of his tunic.

Fresh, hot fury bubbled through Aron, and he was walking, then running toward Galvin before he even formed another thought.

Galvin didn't see his approach. All the better.

People were shouting at Aron, calling his name, but Aron ignored them all. He was only a few feet from Galvin now, fist doubled, feet churning through the brittle grass. His breath whistled through his clenched teeth as he threw himself at the older boy.

Galvin shifted sideways, and it was Zed who caught Aron in mid-flight, tumbling to the ground with him. Zed rolled with him twice, then three times, refusing to let go of Aron's tunic even when Aron started hitting him to get loose.

"You know what he did!" Aron's mind buzzed with the force of his rage, and he shouted so loudly the words seemed to tear his throat. "Why are you helping him?"

"Let him go," Galvin called to Zed, his tone even and calm.

From his vantage point flat on his back, pinned beneath Zed's chin, Aron could see the older boy's long legs striding toward them.

Zed slammed Aron's shoulder hard into the wet ground to get his attention. "We're all Stone, Aron. No matter what Galvin does, it doesn't give us an excuse to act the same way."

Aron glared into Zed's brown eyes and blood-streaked face. He stopped beating his fists against the other boy's back, but only because he was wearing himself out and accomplishing nothing. "That stream of mocker piss got that mare killed. He almost got you and Tek killed, too."

Zed kept his grip firm and used his bodyweight to control Aron completely. "And how will hurting him change any of that? That's what Stormbreaker'll ask you."

"It would—it would—" Aron fished for something apart from, *It would make me feel better*. He came up with, "It would teach him a lesson."

"Only if he wants to learn." Zed shifted his weight enough to let Aron breathe. "I've been at Stone long enough to learn that bad eggs rot without any help from me." He pushed himself up on both hands, giving Aron enough room to wiggle. "You don't want to end up at Endurance House, do you?"

A frigid rush of reality chilled Aron into stillness just as Galvin reached them. "Let Aron go, Zed."

The command was definite. Calm. And to Aron, the words sounded deadly. Blood pulsed steadily in his temples and he made himself lie still, increasingly horrified by what had happened—and what he had almost done in response. Lord Baldric wouldn't tolerate assault with fists and feet any more than he would tolerate attacking someone with *graal*, no matter what the provocation.

"Let him face me," Galvin said to Zed, matter-of-fact, like a teacher might instruct a student.

"There'll be no facing anyone here today," said a man's stern voice, and Aron recognized Windblown's tone and cadence immediately. Other Stone Brothers joined him, tips of their gray robes dusting the brown grass Aron could see from where he lay.

Seconds later, he and Zed were on their feet before the men. Windblown's face was red, as it always seemed to be when he was angry. He was breathing hard, and his thinning brown hair looked slick and limp against his rounded face. The silver medallion on his chest with its braided silver chain and the single spiral carved into the metal gleamed as sun broke through clouds once more. Beside Windblown, the Stone Brothers unfamiliar to Aron, all with Quiet eyes and hair, alternated between studying Aron and gazing over at Iko and Tek. Their expressions reflected mild curiosity.

"Explanations," Windblown demanded, directing his gaze to Galvin.

The older boy's expression remained flat, but his voice took on a ring of importance as he responded, "Aron and Zed were careless with the talons."

His words made Aron's jaw clench, but Zed grabbed his wrist and squeezed. The shock of the discomfort captured Aron's awareness before he spoke out against the lie.

Windblown stared at the tall boy, but Galvin didn't react to the scrutiny. Aron waited for Windblown to turn on him and Zed, to start lecturing them and handing out punishments, but instead Windblown said, "From where I stood, Galvin, you had your share in that carelessness. Why did you leave the gate open for the talons to run through?"

Galvin kept his relaxed stance, but Aron noticed a slight flush spreading across the older boy's cheeks. It took him a few moments to compose his response, and when he spoke, his words came out too slowly. "Aron ran his female too fast, and he left an inexperienced rider behind him on a full-grown bull. He needed a lesson."

"You have no business giving lessons to other apprentices without my leave." Windblown's sharp tone made even Aron flinch. He stood still beside Zed, surprised, then saw the weight of the words sink across Galvin's shoulders until the older boy stooped. As if to be certain the blow landed in the center of Galvin's essence, Windblown added, "Since you are still an apprentice yourself."

A bitter wave of shame and anger flowed across Aron's awareness, but he knew immediately that the emotions weren't his own. His *graal* was giving him a taste of Galvin's feelings at the continual denial of his final trial and graduation from the ranks of apprentices. Aron wished he could peel the sensation away from him and throw it to the ground.

"Endurance House," Windblown said, his voice calmer now as Galvin Herder was offering no defiance or argument. "Three days. I'm sorry, boy, but you and I must be clear on who is master between us. For now, at least, it isn't you."

Without so much as another glance at Windblown or a look in Aron's and Zed's direction, Galvin Herder walked away. His breath trailed in a silvery plume behind him as he headed north and east out of the frozen grazing fields, and Aron knew he was complying with Windblown's instruction. A strange mixture of relief and pity formed in Aron's belly, and he couldn't help thinking of his older brothers, and how they often accepted punishment from their father with an attempt to maintain their own pride and dignity.

But Galvin was nothing like any of his brothers. He never needed to think of Galvin that way, because Galvin had ice around his heart. No doubt, he would avenge himself on them.

The Stone Brothers around Windblown were dispersing to take control of the Bull and clean the remains of the mare from the pasture. Windblown appraised Zed next, cleaned the boy's face with his robes, and asked Zed if he was injured.

"No, High Master Windblown," Zed said, a touch of pride in his words as he used his master's title. "Just some bruises and scratches."

"Good." Windblown patted Zed on the head. "We have much work to do on your talon skills. I'm sorry Aron wasn't more help to you today."

Aron looked up sharply at the rebuke, then thought about what Galvin said before Windblown devastated him with those pointed reminders. About the talons, and Aron's behavior, and the "lesson."

Aron swallowed back a surge of disgust with himself.

He *had* been careless with Tek, letting her run like that in unfamiliar territory, in such an open space where he could lose control— as he had done. And, Aron realized with an expanding sensation of misery, he had left Zed behind him, even though he knew Zed needed his help with the bull.

This is a guild, not a stable of wet nurses. The memory of Stormbreaker's admonishment worsened the discomfort building deep inside him, followed fast by Zed's argument when he wouldn't let Aron attack Galvin.

We're all Stone.

And though Aron had no choices on some levels, on other levels, and in day-to-day activities, he had dozens to make.

This one, he had made poorly.

Zed had given him a promise of fealty, of service and assistance, and shown him nothing but kindness in all the days he had been at Stone. And how had Aron repaid that? By running off with Tek and leaving Zed to struggle on his own.

If he truly was nothing but the sum of his own choices, Aron figured his worth had just dropped, and appreciably. He wished he could apologize on the spot, but figured it would be better to wait until they were both back in the Den tonight.

Windblown didn't kneel to talk to Zed, as Stormbreaker usually did when he spoke to Aron, but his voice did seem much gentler and kinder now. "If you had let Aron face his battle with Galvin in the hallways of the Den the night he arrived, this might have been avoided."

He paused, letting the meaning settle in for Zed, then glanced at Aron, who could only stand with his mouth open and fists starting to double all over again.

"Galvin would have faced penalty for the fight, but the consequence would have been less. And in turn, he would have had less to prove, to you and Aron, and to me." Windblown looked back to Zed. "Endurance House, for one day, and I want you to think about what favors you do, protecting Aron instead of letting him gain his own strength."

Horror struck Aron like a physical blow, and it was all he could do not to bend forward at the waist to absorb the shock. "But Master Windblown, it was my fault. Zed was only being kind. He was helping me."

"If you stand on your own feet, Aron Weylyn, then others will not be forced to carry your weight." Windblown put emphasis on the name Stormbreaker had given Aron following their *dav'ha* ceremony, and Aron couldn't tell if the man was shaming him, poking fun at such an honorific, or simply making a point that Aron needed to live up to the name he had claimed.

Gravity seemed to grip Aron's head and pull it down, until he was staring at his own grass-stained tunic and breeches.

"It's okay," Zed muttered to Aron, where only Aron could hear. Aron could tell Zed was trying to sound brave, trying to make him feel better, but it didn't work at all. Zed gave Windblown a quick bow and jogged away, following the same path taken by Galvin Herder.

Aron shivered as he watched Zed leave. Then his insides roiled as he waited for Windblown to pronounce his own penalty. By all rights, it should be worse than Zed's. Maybe even as bad as Galvin Herder's.

Perhaps this was it, come so soon. The moment when he would once again face Lord Baldric and go to his own judgment.

Windblown studied him for a long time, long enough to make him feel so sick he wanted to shout or spit, or do anything to break the tension. Images of Endurance House flashed through his mind, followed quickly by the frightening figures he had seen several times now, at the Shrine of the Mother. His fear of both was surpassed only by the horror of how it would feel to march into the Judgment Arena with other condemned criminals, and face down a fully vested Stone Brother in combat.

"Stable your talon; then take your Sabor companion back to the

Den." Windblown gestured north. "High Master Stormbreaker will deal with you when he finishes his meeting with Lord Baldric."

Aron almost protested, almost demanded an immediate penalty, rather than suffering through the anxiety of waiting. All of a sudden, Endurance House seemed easier than facing Stormbreaker, but Windblown was already walking away, returning to whatever business he had been torn from when the chaos began.

In time, Aron managed to get himself to move, and he headed over to Iko and took Tek's reins in his cold, aching fingers.

"Thank you," he murmured to the Sabor as he pressed himself into Tek's chilly scales, grateful to feel the life coursing through her armored body. Even if he didn't survive, he was fiercely glad Tek would, and he hoped if he did have to go to judgment, Iko would see to the little talon. Though he had no reason to assume it, Aron's instincts told him Iko would do that, for the talon, if not for Aron himself.

Iko gave no response other than a grunt, though he did walk beside Aron as Aron led Tek back to the barrier, through it, and toward her stall in the talon barn. When he reached one of the barn's doors, Iko stopped and turned, obviously planning not to go inside with him.

Aron paused and considered his next question carefully, fingers inching up and down Tek's reins as if to search out just the right inquiry. "So . . . you won't interfere in my training or my life, but you'll save Tek if she's threatened?"

"Yes," Iko said, gazing out across the talon fields, his dark eyes focused on some point in the distance Aron couldn't see. "I will help Tek if I can."

Aron let the reins run through his fingers again and again. "Why?"

This time, he got no response.

After a moment, Aron decided he didn't much care what Iko's reasons might be. For now, Iko's answer—and his actions back in the grazing fields—were enough. And whatever penalty Stormbreaker dealt him, Aron knew he would accept it without protest or rancor, even if it meant a showdown with Lord Baldric. He didn't intend to let Zed down again, or Dari, or his guild master, or himself.

As he led Tek into the talon barn, Aron had a knifelike flash of his new life continuing to unfold before him. His *graal* showed him rapid glimpses of longer and longer hours at training, the pain of conditioning his body and his mind, the hardship of overcoming his weaknesses and learning to fight, and more important, learning over and over again what it meant to be part of a guild. He saw yet more nights lying awake, plagued by nightmares of what he wished to do to the Brailing Guard, and equally bad dreams about Endurance House and the strange, dangerous beings at the Shrine of the Mother.

So it has gone, a voice told him—not his own, yet young like him, and somehow familiar, with a touch of both kindness and sadness. *And so it will go. I still hold you to your oath. Don't forget it. Don't forget me.*

But Aron had no idea who was speaking in his mind, or how, or why, or what oath was at issue. He tore his awareness away from the sound—and came face-to-face with the vision of a man wrapped head to toe in dark robes, covered completely, in the style of travelers who crossed the deserts of Dyn Altar. The man had a sword, and scarred hands, and murder and violence rose off his shoulders like shimmering curtains of darkness.

Bandit, Aron's own thoughts whispered, and he remembered Lord Baldric mentioning such a villain, then hearing about him many more times, from Stone Brothers and apprentices alike. *Canus the Bandit. The outlaw who has been murdering guardsmen and villagers alike.*

Aron tried to jerk himself out of his vision, but he remained fixed in place, staring at what had to be a vision of the agent of his own death. He felt a blazing sureness that the man was real, and deadly, and that the man was searching for him as diligently as a Stone Brother who had drawn a stone on one of the Judged.

The man's eyes snapped open, and his hand dropped to the hilt of his sword.

Aron cried out and stumbled backward, and the image vanished like sand blown by the wind. Slowly, the dull wood and stone of the barn pushed its way into Aron's reality, as did the stench of goat blood, heated grain, and scale oil.

Tek butted Aron in the shoulder, and he grabbed her neck and held on tight, hating the mind-talent that showed him these pieces of his coming days, and the legacy that told him the vision was the absolute truth.

How could he ever hope to survive the escalation of Stone's rigorous training and avoid Lord Baldric's wrath? And how could he ever grow strong enough to face down the criminal his mind had shown him? The man was no better than Lord Brailing, running about the countryside, lawless and killing without mercy or reason, and Aron was coming to hate the mention of the bandit almost as much as the name of his former dynast lord.

"Why did I see him?" Aron's words came out a whisper against Tek's oily scales, and she answered him with a mucky, loud snort.

Aron wanted to cry, but the day was too much with him, life was too much with him, and he could do nothing but hold his talon and try to breathe.

That, in itself, was hard enough.

CHAPTER THIRTY-ONE

NIC

Nic knew he was falling.

He grabbed at air, tried to catch some stone or branch, anything that might save him from smashing into the ground.

Brother save me! I need to fly!

Fire ignited across his neck and shoulders as blood hammered in his ears. Spit filled his mouth as he tried to will himself to sprout wings and soar away from his doom—but all he could do was fall.

Nic opened his mouth to scream, but no sound left his throat.

"Who is he?" Tia Snakekiller's voice drifted through Nic's stupor, tapping his mind like a gentle finger.

Who is he?

The falling sensation eased.

Who is . . . who?

Nic grew aware of his breathing, of the knifelike pain and stiffness in his legs and arms, and the rough blanket beneath him. When he opened his eyes, he saw darkness and stars and the moons, and a thin canopy of icy *dantha* leaves hanging far above him.

A fire crackled and popped, and as Nic pushed himself into a sitting position, he thought he could smell rabbit cooking on the spit. Despite the warmth of the fire and a pile of blankets, cold air chewed into his ears, his elbows, his toes. He didn't mind the sting of the cold, because it helped his head clear more quickly. Moments later, he worked through the fact that his surroundings seemed familiar, and he realized they were in the same clearing he remembered from several days earlier—still somewhere on the vast and seemingly endless grasslands of Dyn Cobb.

"I'm sorry I make our traveling so slow," he mumbled to Snakekiller, his tongue still feeling too thick to form words in any proper fashion. He managed to turn his stiff, throbbing neck enough to see her, to watch as she worked a rabbit hide with her dagger. She wore nothing but her gray robes and a pair of boots, no extra coats or blankets, yet the cold never seemed to bother her. Her dark skin and light hair seemed even more exotic in the firelight, and her hands moved with the same fluidity and grace that marked her words.

"Who is he, Nic?" she asked again. "This boy you speak to when the fits and fevers come?"

Nic's heart stuttered with horror at her question, and its meaning. He managed to glance around the rest of the campsite, and he saw that Hasty, the other Stone Brother traveling with them, and Hasty's apprentice Terrick, were absent. He figured they must have headed out to find a village to barter for more supplies, if any were to be had so deep and late into winter.

"I don't know who the boy is," Nic admitted. "Or why I go to him. I—I didn't even know I was still speaking to him. You asked me not to go through the Veil until we reached Triune and I received training, and I wouldn't cross your wishes on purpose."

"Of course not." Snakekiller kept up her work with the rabbit skin, fashioning it into what looked like part of a lining for boots. She had been teaching Nic her pelt skills whenever he was lucid and able to use his hands with some coordination. "You're not in your right mind when these things happen. I know that. But with the little training I've been able to give you, have you gained any sense if this boy you're drawn to is a friend or a foe?"

Nic squeezed his fingers open and closed, testing his strength, but his hands were still trembling from the weakness that seized him after a long fit or fever. "A friend. Or so it seems."

Somewhere in the back of his mind, Nic thought the boy might have saved his life once, but he couldn't be sure of that. He had only an image of the boy standing before him, shining with a blinding blue-white light as he ordered Nic's essence back into his body. The scene had the same shimmering, fuzzy consistency of Nic's memory of flying away from the castle where he once lived, in the trees above Can Rowan.

Fancy. Just a dream.

But why did his mind keep returning to the boy when he wasn't conscious enough to control the direction his thoughts chose to take?

Nic rubbed his jaws and tried to soothe them into relaxing, so his head wouldn't hurt so very much.

Snakekiller put down her dagger and laid aside her pelt. "Do you need a sip of nightshade wine?"

"No, thank you." He had been trying to keep himself off the pain-relief mixture, for fear he was beginning to like it overmuch. "I think this discomfort will ease of its own accord."

"Perhaps." Snakekiller's hand lowered to the skin at her belt, the one that held the elixir she kept ready for him, for those moments when he felt as though his spine might tear from its moorings, or his skull might crush inward on his brain until he died. "Nic, you may not be able to live without nightshade. Your injuries were grave—I'm surprised you've healed as well as you have."

Heal. Heal yourself!

The words struck Nic like a command issued from his father at the peak of anger. It came in the boy's voice, as a memory, coated in blazing blue light. He knew, somehow, that he had indeed been commanded to heal, and that he couldn't refuse the order. Not then, and not now.

The boy *did* have some power, and he had used it on Nic.

Against me? For me?

Or maybe something in between.

A round of shivers claimed him. He shook all over, rattling blankets from his legs. Snakekiller stood, grabbed up her dagger, and brought the wineskin to him, this time accepting no refusal as she tilted the sweet-tasting mixture against his lips.

Nic drank without protest, watching moonlight play off the dagger in Snakekiller's fighting hand. He knew she meant him no menace. She simply never moved a few steps without being armed, weapon at the ready. He had come to understand this across their many days of journeying.

As his throat accepted the nightshade, then his belly, relief sank through him, pushing back his agony and the chill that was trying to cut to his very center. Snakekiller restrung her wineskin and sat on one of his blankets. She gazed at him for long, quiet moments, saying nothing, but obviously thinking about a great number of knotty problems.

"We'll finish the winter in Dyn Cobb," she announced at last. "You're too weak to keep traveling through this weather. Three days ago, I sent Hasty and Terrick to find a village agreeable to receiving us, or the Mother willing, a guild house."

Guilt trickled through Nic almost as fast as the effects of the nightshade wine. "You're a High Master with business at Stone. You should leave me behind and make your way to Triune."

Snakekiller frowned at him, keeping her dagger tight in her fist. "My business is with you, until I say otherwise. I would be remiss in my duty to Stone to abandon you—and my duty to all of Eyrie."

Nic startled at her choice of words and quickly studied her face. The knowing look she gave him left little room for misinterpretation of her meaning, and his heart started to beat slow, then fast, slow, then fast, as he reached for denials, misdirections—anything that might put Snakekiller off from the truth of his life, of him.

In the end, he could only lower his head to escape the cold fire in her snowy blue eyes and murmur, "I was almost sure before that you knew I was . . . someone. You know the full truth of who I am. You've known since the day I woke in your wagon."

Snakekiller seemed to relax a fraction, as if glad the truth had been bared between them. "I knew the day I scooped you from that alley in Can Rowan, though Hasty and Terrick did not, and do not. I didn't want whoever had tried to kill you to have a second go at succeeding."

Nic tensed, but tried not to bring on another round of tremors, or worse yet, a fresh fit or length of fever. "I think . . . I think it might have been rectors. The rectors at the castle."

As he spoke, he closed his eyes and waited for her to scoff at him or grow angry at such a disrespectful suggestion.

Instead, she let out a snort of anger. "Raise your head, boy. No treachery from Thorn or those trained by Thorn, no matter how great the magnitude, would make me so much as lift a brow in shock."

Nic stared at her openly then. He had never heard anyone speak of Thorn with such a tone of disgust. He had thought perhaps he wouldn't be believed when he shared his impressions of the day he almost died, but clearly, Snakekiller was ready to accept any dark comment he made about the Thorn Guild.

"Centuries ago," she said, looking more into the dark night than at Nic, and speaking as if she had an audience of unseen sympathizers, "Thorn was as honorable as Stone, and as committed to its duties. Healing, medicines, spices and crops, tending the orphans of Eyrie no matter their station or legacy—they were the perfect balance to Stone and worked in harmony with Triune, the land, and Eyrie itself. These last generations, much has changed within the walls of Eidolon." She thrust her dagger into the dirt beside her knee. "Many have paid the price for Thorn's dereliction of duty and their shortsighted meddling in affairs beyond their guild walls."

As she finished her diatribe and glared at her dagger, Nic knew without question that Tia Snakekiller was one of the people who had paid for Thorn's straying from their sanctioned path, though he couldn't say why or how. Thorn had wronged this Stone Sister, and she did not appear willing to forget the slight, or forgive it.

He found comfort in her anger, and a steadying of his belief that she would never turn him over to Thorn or to any rectors. Still, he wasn't certain where she stood on her earlier promises and bargains. "You said I could go to Stone, that I could take vows at Stone, should I choose to do so."

"I will guard your secrets, if that's what you desire—though in time, I hope you will choose differently, for yourself and for Eyrie." Snakekiller kept her strange blue eyes locked on his. She leaned forward, as if she might be hoping he would suddenly think differently, believe differently about his new life and his new opportunities.

He didn't know what to say, so he said nothing, but found himself shaking his head as if to deny her wishes in some gentler fashion than outright refusal.

Snakekiller settled back on the blanket and sighed. "I will keep you safe, as I was once kept safe. Stone will protect you as they protected me, and as they protected my brother, despite his own stubborn risk taking."

"Thank you again," Nic said quietly, but this time it was Snakekiller who shook her head.

The dark night and orange light of the fire seemed to color her unusual hair as it moved, and when she spoke, her voice was firm and direct. "My brother and I are not nobles, Nic. We have no destiny that mixes with the throne of Eyrie."

Nic stared up at the moons winking through the frosty *dantha* leaves and almost laughed. "My destiny doesn't lie in Mab. Not anymore. I was . . . cast out."

"By an act of attempted murder, not the force of law." Snakekiller dismissed his argument with a wave of her hand—the one not holding the dagger she had pulled back out of the dirt. "Eyrie has gone to war because goodfolk and nobles alike believe that Mab has no heir, and this does not feel like a normal war to me. My mind, my heart tells me—well, never mind that. But, Nic, the time may come when you have to step out of your fear and pain and claim what rightfully belongs to you."

She stared at him again, and the strident tone in her words faded into something softer, maybe even desperate. "The time may come when you have to give yourself up to save us all."

Nic tried to catch his breath, but he was having trouble keeping his chest from caving inward. "I don't have that kind of power. And who would follow me? I'm the hobbledehoy, remember?" He gathered some steam and volume as the words spilled out, words he knew Snakekiller didn't want to hear—but she needed to hear them and remember the truth of who and what he was before somebody pitched him out of Can Rowan's castle. "Goodfolk and dynast nobles laughed at the hobprince when I was fat and soft in the body, and now I'm crippled and soft in the head. I barely have a hint of legacy—"

Snakekiller's bark of laughter cut him off. "You cannot be serious. A hint of legacy? Is that what you believe?"

She turned on the blanket to face him completely, her legs only a few hand widths from his own knees. "Nic, in the older days before the mixing disasters, those with the Mab legacy often came to their mind-talents much later in life than those from other dynasts."

Nic couldn't see how anything from the past applied to him. He pressed his fingers into the stack of blankets covering his own legs. "I know how it was, but the Mab legacy has long been cycling back to nothing, just like all the other legacies."

Snakekiller leaned forward again, this time bringing her marked face very close to Nic. Even in the firelit darkness, he could see her *benedets*, and how the spirals seemed to move of their own accord. "These fits you've been having, I believe they're from the injuries to your head. But the fevers—that's the Wasting. Though it's one of the strangest presentations I've ever seen."

Nic gaped at her, not even bothering to pull back from her scrutiny. "It can't be the Wasting. Mab rarely gets the sickness, and besides, I've had too many bouts. I should be dead."

"Yes, I don't argue. You should be dead from it, but you're not, and that's a mystery we'll both have to unravel." Snakekiller eased back of her own accord, then stood and stretched her arms out to both sides, as if to get the blood flowing. "The Wasting isn't killing you, and it doesn't seem to be taking your mind away, either. As for why you got the sickness, I think it's the strength of your legacy, and whatever it's mixed with."

Nic kept shaking his head, not believing, or not wanting to believe. "I think our long days on the road have made you tired."

Snakekiller laughed, then gazed upward at the moons. "You have the Mab legacy, and I believe you have it in full measure. It's blended with something I don't quite understand, but once you're trained, you'll be able to track and sense the future. I believe you'll even be able to project yourself into possibilities, lay paths to outcomes, and literally call the future to you, as you choose it." When she looked back at him, a fervent certainty seemed to have claimed her beautiful face. "Who can stand against a mind-talent like that, Nic?"

Once more, Nic said nothing, this time, because there was nothing he could say. Nothing at all.

"That's why Mab has always ruled. That's why Mab *should* rule." Snakekiller sheathed her dagger and held out both hands, beseeching him to see the logic of her belief. "It's not just the gifts of the sea and the bounty of hardwood that your dynast commands. It's your legacy. Used with kindness and forethought, the Mab mind-talent has always shown the Fae the path to survival."

Nic kept his silence, but he couldn't quite shove away everything he was hearing. He nodded because he agreed with what she said about the Mab legacy, even if he had no trust at all that he possessed such a mind-talent.

Snakekiller kept her arms outstretched. "It was the Mab legacy that led us from our first world to this one, before we were wiped away by the greed and power mongering of humans who cared nothing for the old ways and old peoples. It was the Mab legacy that saw us through the Great Migration, and the making of the dynasts, and the forging of our life in this world."

Nic's mind reeled back to Can Rowan, and the castle, and the reality of the Mab left on Eyrie's throne. "But if my mother has the legacy, it may be the Mab mind-talent that brings us all to a bitter finish."

Snakekiller lowered her arms and dropped to her knees in front of him. The action was so swift and forceful that he leaned away from her as she spoke. "Then you must restore your own strength, gain the training you need, and stop her, Nic."

"I can't," he whispered, wishing he were strong enough to scramble to his feet and flee into the frigid night.

Snakekiller's intense expression didn't shift, and Nic could feel the heat of her breath on his face. "Who else could do it, if not you?"

He tried to swallow but coughed instead. His mind reeled crazily from one excuse to the next, from one *truth* to the next, but his lips and teeth and tongue wouldn't speak them aloud. He stammered until Snakekiller brought her finger to her lips to silence him, stood, and drew her swords. She turned to face the southern section of the darkened woods surrounding them.

Nic's blood roared in his chest and ears, making him dizzy with fear and confusion. He tried to make himself get up, but his limbs felt like weak twigs, and he couldn't even make it to a kneeling position. How was he supposed to save Snakekiller and all of Eyrie when he couldn't even sit up?

But Snakekiller was already lowering her blades, and a smile had replaced her fierce look of conviction.

Seconds later, Hasty and Terrick pushed their way past a *dantha* trunk and some undergrowth. They were both so tall they had to duck to get past the last branch and into the clearing. Terrick's gray tunic and breeches were soiled from their long hours on the road, and his brown hair looked as scraggly and mussed as Hasty's, but both looked well and hardy, and happy, as well.

"We're in luck," Hasty announced in his booming bass. "Finmont, on the edge of the Scry and near the border of Ross, will give us shelter until we wish to move on to Triune. It's two days' ride with the wagons. Terrick and I have already secured lodging at the little inn."

"They have no patrons, with the war in such motion and the treachery of Canus the Bandit on the roads." Terrick grinned despite his grim words. "Good fortune for us, at least."

"Is the Bandit active in this area now?" Snakekiller had been sheathing her swords, but Nic saw her hesitate.

"We heard he struck a soldiers' encampment near the Ross border four days ago." Terrick's grin didn't wane. "A raiding party of Brailing Guard, come to steal winter stores—but ten of them won't be going home."

"No great loss." Snakekiller finished sliding her blades into their leather scabbards. "And the war? What did you hear?"

At this, Terrick's jovial expression finally faded, and Hasty frowned. "Thorn is stirring to the east. They've sent emissaries to Stone guild-houses near their borders and laid claim to orphans and the sick."

This brought Snakekiller's head up fast. "Why? Thorn hasn't troubled themselves with the needs of Eyrie in decades—the needs of the poor, I mean."

Hasty's frown remained fixed on his usually friendly face. "Strange times, strange measures, perhaps."

Snakekiller let out a snort of disgust. "I'd sooner believe they have some hidden purpose."

Neither Hasty nor Terrick argued with her, and Nic wondered if they shared her poor regard of Thorn. It surprised him that so many people harbored dark sentiments about the guild most revered by the nobles of Eyrie, and he wondered just how protected he had been inside the walls of Can Rowan's castle, even with all the personal tragedy he had faced.

"Brailing and Altar forces have claimed the westernmost section of Mab," Hasty added as he put down his pack. "And Lord Cobb isn't acting to expel the Brailing raiding parties from his borders."

"Mother bless us, is he wavering in his neutrality?" Snakekiller shook her head. "No. No, I won't believe that, not of Lord Cobb. He and Lord Ross would never make themselves a part of this madness." She turned her gaze to Nic and stared at him until he had to look away from her. "Goddess willing, the greater dynasts save for Mab will never stir, and this will end before it becomes an exercise in endurance and corpse counting. Before the damage done to our land and people grows too great."

If he could have pressed his hands to his ears to block out her words, Nic would have done so. The spineless urge shamed him almost immediately, and he forced himself to raise his head enough to see her again.

"We'll send word to Stone when the season breaks," Snakekiller was saying, her attention back on Hasty and Terrick. "You and Terrick might return when it's warmer."

Terrick flopped to the ground near the fire and his bedroll, while Hasty settled himself near the flames in a more dignified fashion. "Nic might be able to travel more steadily and safely by then."

Snakekiller shrugged as she sat down, and Nic could tell she was giving effort to appearing offhand and casual. "Perhaps." Her blue eyes shifted back to Nic, and this time they gripped him like two unrelenting fists. "For now, we'll lodge in Finmont. Later—well, later, we'll all make our choices about where life will take us."

CHAPTER THIRTY-TWO

ARON

Stormbreaker stood in front of the fireplace in Aron's bedchamber, his arms folded and his pale, marked face grim with anger and disappointment.

Aron held his position beside his bed, one palm resting on the soft blanket. The room smelled of lingering smoke and sweat from Zed's dirty robes on the other bed, but Aron was too miserable to be embarrassed over their poor housekeeping. His heart kept up a dull pounding, as it had since he had stabled Tek and returned to his room to await Stormbreaker's arrival and the consequences he would face for the incident with Tek, Zed, the bull talon, and Galvin.

Stormbreaker had required him to recite his version of events, but the man hadn't spoken a word since. His silence made Aron's tired muscles ache. Sweat coated the back of Aron's neck, and he had to struggle not to beg Stormbreaker to forgive him. He would have rather faced a whip or fist or even Lord Baldric's temper than this.

Stormbreaker's unusual eyes remained fixed on Aron's, and Aron couldn't look away. He couldn't even form a proper prayer to the Brother, to ask to be spared from judgment so soon. He wasn't even sure he deserved to be spared. He had improved in his basic strength and sword skills, but certainly not enough to survive a combat.

"Is it or is it not your intention to be my apprentice?" Stormbreaker's question was clipped and sharp. "Do you plan to complete your training at Stone and become useful to this guild?"

Aron's pulsing emotions flared in a hot rush. "Yes!" He clenched the spread in his fist, then made himself relax, lest Stormbreaker take offense at his upset. "Yes," he said again, this time with a bit more control.

Even as he made the declaration, Aron had a hurtful memory of his father's voice, whispering to him that he would always be Wolf Brailing's son. Stone and Stormbreaker had made no effort to erase Aron's history or to ask him to forget his origins. They asked only that Aron understand who he was now, and who he would be tomorrow. He was a Stone. He *was*. Why had he allowed himself to behave with such disregard for Tek and Zed's safety?

Stormbreaker let his arms fall to his sides, and his gaze softened just enough to allow Aron to breathe. "If you wish to serve Stone, then you must make peace with your Brothers and Sisters even when that peace comes at great price to you. You have enemies enough in the world outside these walls. You cannot afford to make adversaries within them."

Aron waited until he was certain he could speak without being disrespectful, then shared his truth with Stormbreaker, as his master had so often encouraged him to do. "Galvin Herder's heart is cold like a winter's night. He's—I think he's cruel."

Stormbreaker's stiff posture eased, and he raised a hand to rub his chin, as he often did when making a decision. "I don't argue that point, Aron. Perhaps it would help you to know that Galvin's family surrendered him to Stone when they couldn't control his aggression, then died in the fevers that swept through Graal Valley the following year. He, too, has lost the people most dear to him. Without the proper care and support, such a devastation could make anyone cold inside. Wouldn't you agree?"

Aron's mouth came open, and he lowered himself to sit on the corner of his bed. Scenes from his bloody dreams about the Brailing

Guard tried to batter down his self-control, and his cheeks burned from a fresh rush of emotion. He didn't know whether to feel sympathy or humiliation.

Was he, Aron, like Galvin already?

Did those dreams mean he was destined to grow ice around his soul, too?

"Galvin has nothing but Stone," Stormbreaker continued. "He has no one but Stone. We—you—are his family now. Be a brother to him."

The cover of Aron's bed felt silky beneath his fingertips as he stroked it, taking what little comfort the softness offered. "How can I be a brother to Galvin? He won't allow it."

"Try to convince him." Stormbreaker came to stand directly in front of Aron, gazing down with the kind expression Aron associated with Stormbreaker's teaching and encouragement. His tone shifted to sad, then worried as he spoke. "The time may come when you must trust Galvin Herder to slay a murderer at your back. I know of no better way to seal your loyalties to each other than to force you to fight together."

Aron gazed at Stormbreaker, confused. Was he speaking of sparring? Aron could best Galvin with his bow, and perhaps with the short sword, but at daggers and broadsword, the older boy would cut him to pieces. In a contest of strength, Galvin probably could pound Aron down to a fine pile of teeth and toenails. How would fighting each other lead to greater loyalties?

"If you mean for us to train together, I'm not sure that would be helpful, High Master."

Stormbreaker agreed to this too quickly, and Aron's anxiety rose. "I don't intend for you to fight each other," Stormbreaker said. "I mean for you to fight with each other. Depend on each other for your safety. I believe the best course of action is to send both of you to the one place in Eyrie that knows no loyalty, no fairness, no right, and no wrong. Perhaps there, you will forge an accord."

Aron went still, certain Stormbreaker would order him to the Shrine of the Mother, or to Endurance House, or maybe even to Lord Baldric's chambers after all. He never imagined that Stormbreaker's decision would be much worse than any of those options.

Stormbreaker gestured toward the southern aspects of Triune, as if they were clearly visible through the thick stone walls of the High Masters' Den. "Once every cycle, we check supplies and weaponry in the Ruined Keep. Normally, the High Masters see to this duty due to the risk, but when Galvin returns from Endurance House, you will go with him to complete this task."

To this, Aron could offer no reply, especially not the shout of disbelief that tried to tear out of his tight throat. All too well, he remembered Stormbreaker's response to Lord Cobb's inquiry about how bad the Ruined Keep could be, after all the rumors and folly he had heard.

It would be difficult to form lies worse than the truth about that place.

"You will go during the light of day," Stormbreaker said, though Aron scarcely heard the words over the mounting noise in his own mind. "And you'll be going as a pair. That will make the journey safer than your guild trial, and perhaps it will prove good preparation as well."

Aron still couldn't begin to speak. He had heard stories already, of how many had died at the Ruined Keep. Of how many never even made it to the crumbling stone walls. The soft cover of Aron's bed suddenly felt absurd to his touch, and he drew his fingers away as if the cloth had wounded him. He fixed his eyes on Zed's bed, and wouldn't look up at Stormbreaker.

This was worse than a judgment with no reading of charges.

How could Stormbreaker do this to him? Combat or even Lord Baldric's Mercy might have been kinder. Aron tried to swallow, but his throat was too dry, and he coughed.

"You're already stronger than you were when you arrived, and you're excellent with bow and arrow, and with your short swords." Stormbreaker sank to one knee, forcing eye contact with Aron. "Galvin performs well with daggers and the broadsword. You will do well, if you work together."

Aron tried to look away, but Stormbreaker caught his chin. "When you and Galvin return, you will understand each other better, and he will be less of a risk to you and your future."

"If I survive," Aron said as he pulled free of Stormbreaker's grip and returned his gaze to Zed's bed.

"That will depend on you," came Stormbreaker's quiet response. "And on Galvin."

Stormbreaker waited in silence for a few moments, then said, "Eat double portions until Galvin returns from Endurance House. Work on your stronger fighting skills, but not enough to weary your muscles— and see to your rest."

Aron said nothing.

What good would those precautions do? It wasn't like he could gain enough mass or skill in three days to affect the outcome of this suicide march into the worst areas of Eyrie.

Stormbreaker placed a hand on Aron's head, and Aron used the entire force of his will not to knock the man's hand away from him. In time, Stormbreaker withdrew from the contact, then left the chamber, abandoning Aron to silence and his own dark thoughts.

The door closed behind Stormbreaker with a soft thump of wood on rock.

Aron found that all he could do was sit on his ridiculously soft cover. He was trembling too much to stand, and he knew if he succeeded in getting to his feet, he might run—though he had nowhere to go.

Like Galvin.

A bitter taste rose in Aron's mouth.

He would *not* dwell on any sense of kinship to the older boy. Aron had no doubt that Galvin would sacrifice Aron or anyone else to survive, if the situation demanded it or gave sufficient excuse. This excursion would not bond them. The journey to the Ruined Keep would serve only to prove to Galvin that Aron was weak and as yet poorly trained. That Aron didn't deserve to be at Stone, or to be in line for Stormbreaker's duties some far day in the future. Lord Baldric and Windblown would probably be pleased when Galvin brought Aron's body back through the gates of Triune.

Aron realized his death would make everything much simpler for Stone. No more risk to anyone from his *graal*. No more concern about what Lord Brailing and his allies might do if Aron's presence at Triune was revealed to them.

Was that what Stormbreaker had in mind?

A tear slipped from Aron's eye and forged a hot path down his cheek. He bit his bottom lip and hated himself for wanting to cry, for needing the release, and for doubting Stormbreaker. He trusted the man, even though he was a trained killer, well capable of treachery. The *dav'ha* mark on his arm smarted as if to remind him of all that had passed between them since Stormbreaker Harvested him from his family.

"Don't start thinking about the past," he instructed himself, then rubbed the *dav'ha* mark, trying not to think about the sign of Cayn, of death itself, burned into his skin. It seemed too prophetic.

Sometime later in the evening, Dari knocked, probably to determine why Aron had missed his *graal* training, but Aron didn't open the door. He didn't think he could bear having to explain his earlier actions to her, or knowing that she sensed both his shame and his fear. He ignored Stormbreaker's suggestions about double portions and avoided dinner as well, and gave little thought to what consequences he might face for missing evening studies. He didn't even build a fire against the night's cold, but he did borrow Zed's blanket since his chamber mate was spending the night in Endurance House.

Wrapped in his own sheets and blanket and Zed's, too, Aron stared out of his chamber window as moonslight claimed the castle grounds and gleamed silver-white off the thick stone walls protecting Triune. He couldn't see the southern or eastern reaches of the compound, beyond which lay the pointed tip of Eyrie that extended into Barrens, Outlands, and Deadfall—but he knew it would be misty terrain, covered in brambles and rocks. The path to the Ruined Keep would be hunting grounds for mockers, manes, rock cats, and other horrors Aron couldn't bring himself to imagine.

Aron's teeth chattered, and his breath came in chilly white puffs.

He was tempted to pray to the Mother, and even as he thought this, as he opened himself to the possibility, he heard her voice. A voice. *The* voice, the one he had grappled with the first night he dreamed of killing the Brailing Guard. It came to him with the same sweet brutality, an almost melodic deadliness he never could have described, not even to Dari when they worked mind to mind.

I will be with you, the voice said, and Aron's teeth chattered all the harder.

He pulled his blankets tight around his shoulders, then went back to his bed and curled himself into a tight knot, not at all sure if he was comforted by that promise.

CHAPTER THIRTY-THREE

ARON

The next three days were among the longest Aron had ever experienced. He made excuses to avoid Dari and his lessons with her, he ate double portions, and he worked twice as hard at his training with long swords and daggers. He scarcely managed to sleep—and to refrain from striking Windblown in the gut each time the man cast a satisfied smile in his direction. Stormbreaker wouldn't discuss the upcoming punishment, but when he was present, he drilled Aron hard and fast on his blade work.

When Zed returned from Endurance House, he vowed that he would take the journey with Aron and Galvin, but Aron ignored this blustering. He knew Stormbreaker would never allow such assistance. As for Iko, the Sabor remained near, but mute on the subject of whether he would insist on accompanying Aron.

At the end of the third day, Galvin Herder returned from Endurance House and discovered their fate in a brief meeting with Windblown, Stormbreaker, and Aron. The older boy did nothing but nod and retreat to the kitchens for a meal, and Aron didn't see him again until the *fael'feis* the morning they were to leave. When they danced their greeting to the dawn and the new day, Galvin kept his gaze straight forward and his hands to himself, and seemed completely focused on each dip and bow, each stretch and sway.

Aron tried to maintain the same level of concentration, but his heart stuttered each time he allowed himself to wonder if this would be his last celebration. The thick, mossy walls of Triune gleamed in the white-blue sunlight. What lay on the other side of those walls, Aron didn't want to contemplate, even in the glare of breaking day.

Dari had joined them this morning, and Aron felt her intense stare more than once. He didn't want to talk to her or explain what was about to happen, or even look at her too long, for fear he'd cry like a stupid little fool. Maybe Iko had told Blath and Blath had shared the news. But when the *fael-feis* ended and Lord Baldric made his approach, Aron realized Dari had not been informed of his upcoming punishment.

As Stormbreaker took Aron aside in the courtyard and checked the buckle on Aron's weapons belt, Dari approached them without Blath, her posture stiff and her movements hurried. "What is happening here? Why did Windblown take Zed away—and what is Lord Baldric doing at the Den so early?"

Aron's heart gave quick double beats as he took in Dari's beauty and her obvious anger.

Stormbreaker removed Aron's short sword from its scabbard and tested its sharpness on his thumb. "Aron and Galvin Herder will be making this month's inspection of the Ruined Keep. When Galvin has retrieved his weapons from his room, Lord Baldric and I will escort them to the side gate and direct them to the Lost Path."

The other Den apprentices caught sight of Lord Baldric striding through the courtyard gates, and they scurried off in different directions, heading to weapons practice or studies, depending upon their schedules.

Dari ignored the commotion of the other apprentices as her eyes went wide. "This—you—no." Her dark hair glistened like fine metal in the morning light, and her black eyes flashed like Stormbreaker's did just before thunderstorms exploded from clear skies. "You cannot be serious. This is what—a punishment? For a fight between two boys?"

Stormbreaker continued his deft inspection of Aron's weapons. "They aren't boys, *Cha*. They're nearer to men, and they must learn to be brothers in their guild tasks, if nothing else."

"That's a death march," Dari snarled.

Lord Baldric was barely out of earshot and coming toward them even more quickly now. Aron's stomach clenched, and he wished Dari would have a care about what she said in front of the Lord Provost. What if Lord Baldric turned on her, too? If he cast Dari out of Triune, Aron might never see her again.

"If Aron and Galvin fail to cooperate with each other, they might be killed, yes." Stormbreaker sheathed Aron's last dagger and patted him on the shoulder without looking at him. "But I have faith in Aron's ability to win Galvin's respect."

Dari seemed about to launch into a more forceful argument, one that might involve fangs and claws.

"Thank you," Aron said before she could become any angrier. "But this is something I need to do."

As he spoke the words, he felt the truth of his statement resonate in his mind, like a bell striking one clean, pure note. The sensation sent a ripple of gooseflesh up his spine and made him shake his head to clear his senses.

Was that what it felt like to hear from his own *graal* unbidden?

He hadn't been certain of his statement—had really said it only to keep Dari from bringing trouble on herself by standing up for him in a matter in which Lord Baldric and Stone would give her no say. Now, though, he was more sure he was correct.

He managed to keep his eyes on Dari, who didn't relax even a fraction. Her eyes still flashed like she was ready to kill, but she said nothing as Lord Baldric came to stand beside them.

"We await Galvin's return, and then we're ready," Stormbreaker said, keeping his hand on Aron's shoulder.

Lord Baldric eyed Dari, as if daring her to say anything, but Dari was not so foolish. When his gaze shifted to Aron, Aron was surprised to see that Lord Baldric wasn't regarding him with his usual suspicion or irritation. The Lord Provost's expression was difficult to read, but Aron thought the man might actually be impressed that Aron was facing such a dangerous task with no begging or sniveling.

Stormbreaker seemed to notice the direction of Aron's gaze and the shift in Aron's expression, and he spoke in low tones, where only Aron could hear him. "I believe that if you complete this journey with your own skills and wits, without using your legacy, it will go far in proving to Lord Baldric that you belong here. Perhaps it will earn you some reprieve from needing to be without fault in his eyes."

When Aron looked into Stormbreaker's pale face, he saw unguarded worry and affection, and the fact that Stormbreaker didn't want to send him on this dangerous journey.

"I understand," he told Stormbreaker, keeping his voice quiet and as calm as he could manage. "And I believe this is the right choice. A chance—perhaps my only chance—to make it to my trial without being sent to judgment."

Stormbreaker seemed both relieved and pained, and Aron experienced a rush of warmth. This was a man who had death in his eyes and *graal*, even in the ferocity of his smile. Aron knew Stormbreaker would kill him if duty and righteousness demanded such an action, and Aron knew that he loved the man like the father he would never again get to embrace.

When Stormbreaker pulled Aron to him, Aron returned the force of his embrace. Fate willing, and should he survive to return to Triune this night, Aron would do all that was within his power to live up to the grave responsibility of being an assassin's apprentice.

When Stormbreaker turned Aron loose, Aron gave his master a

quick bow, straightened himself, and checked the daggers and short sword on his weapons belt himself, finding them all ready and satisfactory.

Dari stood silent beside him, arms folded, refusing to glance in Stormbreaker's direction. Blath was no longer at her side, and Aron assumed she had retired to the Den. Windblown and Zed hadn't returned, and Aron assumed Windblown was making certain Zed didn't make a rash attempt to slip out of the castle to give aide to Aron.

Iko—Aron glanced in all directions.

Iko was absent.

There was no trace or sense of him, and Aron realized he hadn't seen the Sabor boy since the night before. Aron's heart sank with a disappointment he couldn't explain. He would have at least liked to bid Iko farewell, in case . . .

In case he didn't make it back.

His breath caught hard in his throat.

Galvin Herder came through the front doors of the Den, wearing two swords on his belt, as well as a host of sharp, glittering daggers. He didn't spare a look or comment for Aron, but bowed to Stormbreaker and Lord Baldric before setting off, out of the courtyard and down the path that ran along the western wall of Triune.

Aron followed him, trying to force his thoughts to the sound of their feet on grass and dirt and gravel, on the light chill of the air, and the sound of robes rustling against the legs of Stormbreaker, Lord Baldric, and Dari as they offered a small escort party to the gates that led to the Lost Path. The time had come for silence, both within his mind and without. He had to concentrate now, and he could not let his terror overtake his judgment or fighting skills.

Aron kept his chin forward and his eyes wide as he strode behind Galvin, to the gates, and through them.

The rustle of robes against legs stopped abruptly, and Aron knew their escort party had remained within the safety of the castle walls.

He felt the separation from Dari and Stormbreaker like a cut to his very essence, but he didn't cry, and he didn't look back, not even when the massive gates thundered as they slammed to a close.

A blast of Stormbreaker's *graal* lightning crackled overhead, giving Aron a surge of courage as mist struck him in the face. The unnatural gray fog of the Deadfall immediately obscured his vision, and it smelled of old graves and bones left to mildew in caves. Aron decided to breathe through his mouth, at least until he grew accustomed to the odor. His eyes watered in the wet air, but he kept his gaze on the gray folds of Galvin's tunic.

Whispering met his ears, not human, not intelligible, and somewhere nearby, a rock cat howled. Something moaned, setting Aron's teeth on edge.

Something screamed. Up ahead. Not far away at all.

A sly, grinding sound came from behind Aron, like creatures sidling and slithering across the same rocky ground he had just crunched beneath his boots.

"I'm an assassin's apprentice," he said to himself to drive down the rolling gallop of his heart. He closed one hand on the hilt of his short sword and the other on the metal grip of a dagger.

From in front of him, Galvin Herder grunted, and Aron saw the mist swirl as the older boy drew his long sword and held it at the ready.

"I'm an assassin's apprentice!" Aron yelled, taking strength from the words as he drew his own blades.

He could only hope the creatures flying, crawling, creeping, and charging to meet them would know him for what he was, and fear him as much as he feared them.

S R VAUGHT is the author of *Stormwitch, Trigger, My Big Fat Manifesto,* and *Exposed.* She is a neuropsychologist for adolescents and lives in rural Tennessee.

J B REDMOND has been a lifelong reader and fan of fantasy fiction and has overcome complications from cerebral palsy to record his portions of this novel. Mr. Redmond also lives in Tennessee.